DESIRE

Stacey tried to despise Wade Savagge. She told herself he was an unscrupulous gambler, a callous user of many women, a man who mocked every law. She desperately clung to her love for Ben Clayton, whom she already had come so far to find again, and who still remained a thousand miles of wilderness away.

But Stacey could not pretend she did not feel the response in her body when Wade Savagge kissed her so deeply, so tenderly. She could not ignore the effect of his expert, exquisite caresses. And even as she fought him off, she could not close her ears to his mocking voice: "Before this wagon trip is over, Stacey, you'll be begging for what I have to give you."

Stacey was not falling in love with this handsome, hard and ruthless man. She was falling into a far more dangerous trap—the bottomless pit of flaming desire. . . .

RETURN TO YESTERDAY

Fabulous Fiction from SIGNET

RETURN TO YESTERDAY

June Lund Shiplett

A SIGNET BOOK

NEW AMERICAN LIBRARY

TIMES MIRROR

PUBLISHER'S NOTE

This novel is a work of fiction. Names, characters, places, and incidents are either the product of the author's imagination or are used fictitiously, and any resemblance to actual persons, living or dead, events, or locales is entirely coincidental.

SIGNET TRADEMARK REG. U.S. PAT. OFF. AND FOREIGN COUNTRIES
REGISTERED TRADEMARK—MARCA REGISTRADA
HECHO EN CHICAGO, U.S.A.

SIGNET, SIGNET CLASSICS, MENTOR, PLUME, MERIDIAN AND NAL BOOKS are published by The New American Library, Inc., 1633 Broadway, New York, New York 10019

First Printing, March, 1983

1 2 3 4 5 6 7 8 9

PRINTED IN THE UNITED STATES OF AMERICA

This book is dedicated to Barbara Keenan from "Affaire de Coeur," Fremont, California; Barbra Wren from "Barbra's Critiques Ltd.," Independence, Missouri; and all the fabulous bookstore owners and fans across this great country who had faith in Stacey Gordon's first journey into the past. Your help and support have made all this possible. God bless you. I love you all!

PROLOGUE

On May 26, 1975, Stacey Gordon dived into the swimming pool at her sister's home and disappeared. She had been transported one hundred and ten years back in time to May 26, 1865. At first the shock had overwhelmed her, but when she met Ben Clayton, a tall, good-looking widower, life took on meaning again. As she accompanied him and his two teenage daughters on a wagon train west, she found herself falling in love with him. For a long time she tried to make herself believe she wasn't in love, but she was. And finally, throwing all caution to the wind, she married him.

As the wagon train threaded its way across the western territory, Stacey gave up any thoughts of ever returning to her husband and daughters in her former life and settled comfortably into her new world. Then, late one afternoon, there was an Indian attack and Stacey once more disappeared.

On September 19, 1975, when her body floated to the surface of her sister's swimming pool, dressed in old-fashioned clothes with an arrow protruding from her back, the news media were agog to hear the story of a woman who claimed to have gone back in time. There were those who believed and those who didn't.

On the night before her release from the hospital, Ben Clayton's great-great-great-grandson, Jason Walker, appeared in her room and handed her the diary she had kept while living in 1865. It was musty and crumbling with age, but the words were still clear enough to read. Walker had also brought tintypes of herself with Ben and his two daughters that had brought tears to her eyes. Tears she had tried, but been unable to hide, even from her husband, Drew. But the diary and the pictures had proven to the world she really had traveled back in time. That was last night. Now, she was going home. . . .

CHAPTER 1

Slow, steady rain turned the parking lot below her hospital window into a series of small rivers. Stacey Gordon pushed a strand of deep red hair back from her face and stared absent-mindedly at the gushing water, remembering another day when she stood on the banks of the swollen Loup River. That was weeks ago. She bit her lip. No, not weeks. Years! One hundred and ten years, to be exact.

Stacey brought her knuckles against her teeth, trying to keep the tears in check. So much had happened. Now here she was back in 1975 again, trying to pick up the pieces of her former life. Was she going to be able to take up where she'd left off four months ago without any repercussions?

She pulled a handkerchief from the pocket of her dark green suede jacket and blew her nose, admitting to herself reluctantly that it wasn't going to be as easy as she'd thought. Last night, sitting on the bed beside her husband, Drew, she had been so sure everything would be all right. But now she wondered.

She turned to the small white bundle that lay on the table next to her bed. Tears still glistened in her bright blue eyes. Wrapped in that small bundle was the diary she'd kept when she had lived in another time. It was a part of her, a part of her no one knew except Ben Clayton. He had given life to the woman who wrote in that diary when she thought her life was over.

She reached up and gently touched her left shoulder. The doctor had taken the arrow out of it, and the wound was still healing. She sighed, closing her eyes. Ben had been so close, his arms reaching out to catch her. A split second in time, one tiny second between now and then. Why couldn't God have let Ben's hands reach her? With her eyes closed Ben's face rose before her and she remembered his shock when he realized she was slipping away from his grasp into the deep water some fifty feet below. She had seen his face in her dreams so many times since then.

That was the hard part, trying to forget. She had promised that

3

she'd put away her memories of Ben, but it wasn't that easy. She loved Drew, but was it the all-consuming love she had always imagined it to be? How many times since her return had she been afraid to really ask herself that question for fear of the answer.

She opened her eyes and checked once more to make sure she hadn't forgotten anything. She was waiting for Drew to take her home to Gates Mills, to the beautiful house by the river that he had designed and built for her. He was sure that she would finally be able to accept her present life again. At least that's what he'd said last night. But had he seen the fear and uncertainty in her eyes when he'd kissed her good night?

Once more staring at the diary, she took a deep breath, and clenched her jaw with determination. It would be all right. It had to be. She was with Drew again and she was going to make her marriage work. Hadn't she loved him before? Perhaps she wouldn't have the complete love she'd found with Ben, but it would be enough.

She exhaled wearily and picked up the small bundle that held the diary. She had realized last night, after reading some of it, that to keep reading it would only make matters worse. Not only did it hurt to relive those days, it only made her more discontent. If her marriage was to work, she had to pretend the diary didn't even exist so she shoved it into the bottom of her suitcase beneath the white peignoir set her daughters, Renee and Chris, had bought for her.

She managed a half-smile as she remembered her daughters' reactions to her return. Thirteen-year-old Renee had been ecstatic, enjoying the notoriety her mother was getting and never doubting for a moment that things would be the same again. But Chris knew. She was almost seventeen, just old enough to recognize the uneasy looks passing between her parents. Old enough to know that Leslie Kyle, the photographer her father had been dating during her mother's absence, had been more than merely a friend.

Stacey frowned. Drew never talked about Leslie. At first Stacey thought maybe it was to shield her, but more and more she wondered if he was also shielding himself.

John Morris said Leslie was beautiful, blond, about twenty-eight, with green eyes and a good figure. How well had Drew known her? Well, there was nothing to worry about. Leslie had left for New York City the day Stacey came home.

Home! Once she had wanted to come home so badly. Now it just wasn't the same. She turned abruptly as the door opened and Drew stepped in.

His tawny hair was damp from rain and his London Fog raincoat was dripping.

"Damn, it's wet out there," he said cheerfully, the soft dimples in his tanned face meeting the crinkles at the corners of his eyes.

She watched him curiously. He was terribly good-looking. "Did you bring my raincoat?" she asked.

He tossed a bundle at her and she caught it unfolding a tan raincoat. Settling it on her shoulders, she closed the suitcase and took one last look about the room.

"Except for the flowers and plants, I guess that's it," she said.

He grabbed the suitcase, then hefted one of the plants off the nightstand, maneuvering it into the crook of his elbow. "Put the other one in my hand," he said quickly. Stacey gave him the plant and they left the room, heading toward the elevator.

When they reached the car, after running the gauntlet of reporters and TV news cameramen waiting at the emergency entrance, Stacey furtively watched Drew as he helped her into the seat. He seemed a little nervous, although he was trying to hide it with a warm smile.

"All set?" he asked as he sat next to her.

"All set," she affirmed.

He put the keys in the ignition of his pale blue, Olds convertible. It was strange to be here again in the car with him. The rain had begun to let up and she watched the wipers clear it off the windshield. Such a simple thing, yet without them . . . she remembered the covered wagon with its patched canvas top and jolting, rough ride. It was weird. And the traffic light . . . so many things taken for granted.

They lived only a short distance from the hospital and she frowned apprehensively when they pulled off the River Road and moved up their long drive. She could see the house starkly molded against the hillside in the bleak afternoon. Even the trees, with their soggy red and gold leaves, looked woebegone.

Glancing surreptitiously at Drew again, she realized that the dreary weather hadn't affected him. He was humming a tune, smiling as he shut off the ignition.

He glanced over at her. "You're home, lady love," he said softly.

"I know."

He touched her face tenderly, his eyes filled with desire. "It's been so long."

"I know."

He frowned. "Is that all you can say?"

"Drew, give me time. I feel so strange."

His frown deepened momentarily, then faded as he sighed and opened the car door. The rain had stopped, but there was a chill in the air that made Stacey shiver as they headed for the house.

"I'm scared, Drew," she whispered softly as she stood ready to open the back door.

"Of what?"

"I don't know. Just me. It was so different then."

His eyes became suddenly wary. "So different that you're a stranger now?"

"No, it's not that. It's, well . . . oh . . ." She shrugged. "I'm being foolish," and she turned the knob, swinging the door open, her eyes surveying the kitchen where she had once felt so at home.

It hadn't changed. Everything was just as she'd left it in May. She let her eyes caress the furniture. It wasn't a huge kitchen, but she had designed it herself and she'd loved it. Yet, it seemed strange as she gazed at the modern appliances.

She walked over and gingerly touched the knobs on the dishwasher, then glanced down over the wrought-iron railing on the stairs leading to the recreation room below.

"I never did ask, who's been doing the cooking?"

"Mrs. Garret's been coming in about ten in the morning and leaving about seven."

Mrs. Garret was Stacey's cleaning woman. She usually came once a week to help with the heavy housework.

"I didn't know she could cook too," she mused.

"Well, she's not really that great, but we survived."

She started toward the dining room.

"Here, I'll take your coat first, honey," he said.

She started to wriggle from it, her back to him, then tensed slightly as his hands pulled her against him. She heard his quick intake of breath, then he released her and she stepped forward, her knees trembling slightly. He tossed her coat over the back of a kitchen chair, placed his own beside it, and followed her into the living room with its overhead beams, huge fireplace, and floor-to-ceiling window that overlooked the river.

Drew watched her move from one piece of furniture to another, touching, smoothing, as if she wasn't sure it was real, then he walked over and turned on the stereo, filling the room with the soft strains of music.

Slowly he moved behind her and encircled her with his arms, bending his head to nuzzle her neck affectionately.

"It's so good to have you home, honey," he whispered, his lips caressing her ear.

She leaned back against him, closing her eyes. His arms felt reassuring, his muscular body reminding her of what they'd once had together. But the haunting melody of her favorite song, "The Way We Were," invaded her thoughts with memories of another time when she'd played it on the piano for Ben. The lyrics had so much meaning for her, both then and now. Memories! They were frightening. She remembered praying to return to Drew, longing to be in his arms. Yet, she remembered too the way the memory of him had slowly faded, to be replaced by Ben's dark compelling eyes and unnerving smile set in a face so arresting that even now the thought of it made her shiver.

She bit her lip, wishing the music would end, yet loving the soft strains that soothed the hurt inside her. Reaching up, she took Drew's hand, entwining her fingers with his as his lips sought the warm flesh of her neck, sending tingles down her spine. In spite of her love for Ben, Drew still had the power to arouse her, and she turned to him now, knowing that the only way to forget was to lose herself in the present. She lifted her face to Drew, letting his lips find hers hungrily.

The kiss deepened as his hands moved up to cradle her head, and then he drew back, gazing into her brilliant blue eyes.

"I want you now, Stacey," he whispered softly. "The girls are in school . . . we have the house to ourselves . . ."

She stared at him breathlessly. Yes, that was Drew. When he wanted her it was always just a simple request, without a big buildup or flirting and coaxing. She stared at him uneasily. She wanted him too, at least her body did, but something in her challenged him.

"What if someone comes?"

"They won't."

"You're sure?"

"I'm sure."

She stared into his hazel eyes, her own darkly passionate. Forcing herself to relax inside, she shifted against him.

"Come," she whispered softly, and took his hand from her face, leading him from the room. Her heart was pounding by the time they reached their bedroom, and when she saw the familiar print bedspread, the pounding was suddenly replaced by a strong sense of urgency that gripped every nerve in her body.

Why was her face so flushed and her breathing so labored? She was with her beloved Drew. They had shared years together, moments of love and ecstasy. And yet she felt almost shy with him.

She turned to him, her expression hesitant. "Be patient with me, Drew," she whispered, "but love me. Please love me."

He stared at her, wanting her more now than he'd ever wanted her before. "That's all I ever wanted, to love you," he said slowly and began unbuttoning her suit jacket.

His eyes held hers captive as he undressed her gently, then led her to the bed. With his own clothes removed, he stood watching her, remembering all the years before and the wonderful moments when her body had surrendered to him, then slowly, he dropped down beside her, his hand touching her lightly, caressing her breast, running down her naked body. His eyes followed his hand, devouring her sensuous curves, then suddenly, reluctantly, it was as if he was watching another hand tracing the hills and valleys he knew so well.

His jaw clenched tightly as he pushed the thought of the other man to the back of his mind. He'd sworn he'd forget that she had willingly given herself to someone else. That she had married this other man. He had rationalized it over and over again since this whole thing began. She thought she'd never see him again, never be with him like this. He had to keep remembering that the same thing could have happened to him, that she loved him as much as she had loved this . . . this Ben Clayton. The man's name ripped into his thoughts, making him even more determined, and with sheer intent, his eyes caught Stacey's passionately, and he softly whispered words of love to her, pushing the hurt from his heart, letting only his need for her possess him.

Stacey yielded to his lovemaking. His hands caressed her, his lips devouring her, and when he finally moved over her, thrusting into her, there was only the remembrance of what once had been and Stacey gave herself to him gladly. She climaxed breathlessly, her hands kneading Drew's bare shoulders, her body tingling with sensations long remembered.

Drew shook spasmodically, the force of his release possessing him completely, and covered her lips in a long, lingering kiss.

"Now you're really home, love," he whispered softly, and she flushed self-consciously. "What is it?" he asked, still spread over her. But she only shook her head.

"Nothing," she said. How could she tell him when she didn't even know herself? It was the same as it always was with Drew. The fire and heat of their coming together. The explosive charge that ignited them and satiated their bodies. Then the sudden end to all the fury and passion when it was over. Stacey stared up into his hazel eyes and unexpectedly felt a strange prickling at the base of her neck, an empty feeling gripping her insides. She knew now what was the matter: Suddenly she knew exactly what Drew was going to do next. He'd kiss her lightly, slide off her, and head for the refrigerator, as hungry for food now as he had been for her only moments before. And while he nibbled on anything handy, he'd smile at her with his eyes as well as his mouth, telling her without words that he was content. This was Drew. It was his way, and suddenly she wanted to cry out to him, to stop him, to tell him to keep on making love to her as Ben always had because the fire within her had not been quenched yet. It still raged, and as she watched him do exactly what she knew he'd do, she wanted to scream, and only his lighthearted banter as he slipped into his clothes, saved her from revealing the loss she felt inside.

She tried to imitate his casual manner, hiding from him and trying to hide from herself what she knew was missing by relaxing as she rose and slipped on a pair of black silk lounging pajamas. And yet deep in her heart she knew what was the matter. It was plain and simple. Drew wasn't Ben.

Ben had given her a love that far eclipsed what she'd had with Drew. She loved Drew, yes, but it was a comfortable love after the heat of passion was released. With Ben, the fire had not only filled her, but consumed her, and even after their initial coupling the flames still warmed her, so that merely a touch or a look could once more trigger the urgent tingling in her loins. She'd been content with Drew all these years because she'd never known the difference, but that was no longer true. Yes, Ben was what was the matter, and she knew it, and Ben was dead.

Her jaw tightened bitterly as she tried to concentrate on what Drew was saying, telling herself she was lucky to have him to fill the void the loss of Ben had made.

Stacey sighed and followed Drew into the kitchen, where he slowly devoured a Swiss-cheese-and-salami sandwich. Since it was lunchtime already, he tried to get her to eat too, but she just wasn't hungry. The aftermath of their lovemaking had left a tight feeling in her stomach.

Stacey sat across from him at the table and sipped at her coffee, then looked out the window and Drew glanced over, studying her. He swallowed hard as he watched her gazing out at the sun trying to dry up the wet morning. God, she was beautiful. How many times had he sat here wondering if she were dead or alive? And now here she was with him again.

His eyes caressed her auburn hair, watching the way the sun

made it look like it was on fire. She had firmly chiseled, high
cheekbones, and the hollows in her cheeks were a little deeper
than normal because of the weight she'd lost while in the hospital. Was it any wonder he loved her.

He frowned as he saw her full mouth tighten provocatively.
Whenever there was something wrong the corners of her mouth
always tilted crazily like this. He looked at her eyes. They held a
troubled, faraway look, and as suddenly as the happiness of
being with her again had thrilled him, a feeling of dread now
swept over him.

"Stacey?"

She turned to him abruptly. "Yes?"

"What is it?" he asked.

She looked down. "I wish I knew."

His jaw tightened as resentment began to goad him on. "You
keep saying you don't know. I think you do. It's him, isn't it?"

"No."

"Oh, for Christ's sake, Stacey, I'm not stupid," he said, his
quick temper taking the upper hand. "I saw last night when you
looked at those pictures of him. Do you think I don't know
what's been going through your head? I've been married to you
for almost eighteen years, Stacey. I know when you're upset and
when you're pushing, and you pushed yourself in there just now,
didn't you, honey? You didn't want to make love to me, you
wanted to make love to him, didn't you?"

"Drew stop it!"

"Why? So you won't have any reason for feeling guilty?" He
stared at her across the table. "I thought I could do it, Stacey. I
thought I could forget that you'd loved someone else, but I guess
it's not going to be that easy, for either of us. I needed you
today, Stacey. I haven't had a woman since you left and I guess
that's why I could forget for a few minutes, but I didn't forget,
not really, and I don't know if I ever will because I don't think
you ever will either," he said fiercely.

Tears welled up in her eyes and she grabbed his hands holding
them tightly. "Drew, please," she begged tremulously. "You
have to forget, we both do. We can have what we had before. I
know we can. It'll just take time."

He felt her hands on his, soft yet cold. "Maybe it's time we
don't have honey. Did you ever think of that?"

She stared at him, confused. "What do you mean?"

"I mean the world and the girls think everything's hunky-dory
with us. They know nothing of you and this other man. So what
do we do, put on a good show for them?"

"Drew you're acting crazy. I love you, remember?" She let the tears fall. "I couldn't have given myself to you today if I didn't love you, you must believe that. It's going to be hard, I know, but today, Drew, today was a start. Don't turn from me, I need you now more than anything. I lived in another time, Drew, in a world people today can only imagine, and now I have to live again in this one. I can't do it without your love, Drew. Please help me . . . help me to forget, to be myself again."

His eyes bored into hers, watching the tears making them sparkle like star sapphires, and he saw the misery he was causing. He was jealous of a man who'd been dead for one hundred and ten years. Suddenly he felt stupid. If he couldn't compete with a dead man, then he might as well give up. He took a deep breath, his fingers twining about hers.

"You know I can't help loving you, don't you," he said softly. "But I won't play second fiddle to a memory, Stacey."

She swallowed hard, her eyes still misty. "That's something I'll never ask you to do," she said. "I promise." As he leaned forward to kiss her hard on the mouth, sealing the bargain between them, she hoped to God she could keep her promise.

The rest of the day went as smoothly as possible under the circumstances. Chris and Renee came home from school, anxious to see Stacey and excited at the prospect of having her home again. Drew made arrangements for Mrs. Garret to come over every day and give Stacey a hand until she was completely well again, and it wasn't until evening that the full impact of Stacey's strange journey began to take its toll again.

Chris was curled up in an armchair, a book in her lap. Her long copper hair was hanging loose about her shoulders, and her gold turtleneck framed her small heart-shaped face. She wore no makeup and the freckles on her nose made her eyes seem even paler blue than they were. With tight jeans over her slight figure she seemed almost lost in the big chair.

Renee was sprawled out in front of the TV with her homework, bare feet in evidence as she lay on her stomach kicking her legs up, trying to concentrate on both her homework and the television at the same time.

Stacey sat on the sofa beside Drew, wishing the day would end so she could lose herself in blessed sleep.

She glanced at the girls, then moved closer to Drew, basking in the reassurance of his arm around her shoulder. Closing her eyes contentedly, she began to lose track of what was going on around her and sleep started to overtake her. Suddenly her heart lurched and she gasped, as the image on the TV screen abruptly changed from a harmless commercial to a western, complete with covered wagons, gunfire, and whooping Indians.

Stacey bolted upright, her forehead beaded with perspiration. "Shut it off!" she shrieked helplessly, staring wide eyed at the screen. "My God! Shut it off!"

Renee jumped, scared, and turned off the TV, while Drew tried to calm Stacey.

"Stacey, come on, it's only the TV," he said sternly, trying to break her sudden hysteria. "It's only make-believe." But she buried her head in her hands, her ears still ringing from the bloodcurdling Indian screams. "Come on," he said, more tenderly this time, and pulled her to her feet, walking her to their bedroom.

Stacey sat down on the bed, shaking her head. "I'm all right now, Drew," she said, trying to convince him. "It was silly of me. I feel like such a fool. But I was tired and half-asleep. I didn't mean to yell at Renee."

"I know, but I still think maybe you'd better turn in. It's been a long day."

She glanced at him. He was really concerned and she thanked him for that. "Are you coming too?" she asked.

"If you like."

By the time he told the girls to lock up, undressed, and climbed in beside her, Stacey moved into his arms readily.

"I'm sorry, Drew," she whispered, her lips against his neck. "Please be patient with me."

"That's the second time you've asked me today," he said huskily, and she sighed.

"I know, but I'm having a very hard time. Darling, it's easy to say forget, but just today so many things made me remember. Please help me forget, Drew," she whispered. "I know you can if you want to. Please, Drew, help me," and when Drew kissed her, kindling memories of what once had been, Stacey hoped and prayed that this wasn't the end, but the beginning for them both.

The next few days were hectic. The phone rang constantly, as reporters swamped Stacey with requests for exclusive interviews. She refused them all.

"I just want to forget," she told John Morris the afternoon she went to his office for her checkup after she'd been home a week.

She had taken her sister Shelley along with her for moral support because since realizing Drew had been right all these years, and his best friend was in love with her, Stacey had suddenly become more aware of John as a man rather than a friend and her doctor. Their parting when she'd left the hospital had been a little more intimate than she had wanted to admit.

He was as tall as Ben, with the same dark compelling eyes, but his black hair was frosted at the temples rather than curling about the ears as Ben's had been, and he didn't have Ben's deep dimpled smile. Maybe it was his resemblance to Ben that caused her such unease, she wasn't quite sure. But John was ruggedly handsome with a charming bedside manner that wasn't easy to ignore, and she felt safer today having Shelley along.

Shelley didn't know Stacey had married Ben. Stacey had wanted to tell her, but Drew had forbidden her to, even though Stacey was certain Shelley suspected something. So she'd never told her the truth, nor anyone else for that matter. Only John and Drew knew about her relationship with Ben.

"I told you they wouldn't let you forget," John said as he rebandaged her shoulder, then helped her on with her black blouse, watching her fumble self-consciously with the buttons as she fastened the front. "You've done something that's never been done before, Stacey. You're still a celebrity, whether you like it or not." He put the tape back in the drawer, then turned to Shelley Russell, who was a year older than Stacey.

The two sisters looked nothing alike, except about the mouth. Where Stacey's hair was deep auburn, thick, and luxurious, Shelley's was wispy and short, the color of pale copper. And although both had blue eyes, Stacey's were startlingly brilliant, while Shelley's were pale like chicory blossoms faded in the summer sun. But their mouths had the same fullness, the same provocative way of moving.

In a way, John wished Stacey hadn't brought Shelley along, but then again, it was probably for the best. "Has she been behaving herself, Shelley?" he asked casually.

Shelley studied Stacey thoughtfully. "It all depends."

"Oh?" His eyebrows raised.

"She thinks I've got a case of nerves," Stacey explained.

John frowned. "Have you?"

"No."

Shelley exhaled irritably. "No? I suppose you don't call it nerves when you jump out of your skin every time the kids turn on the TV or Drew goes near the stereo?"

"I have my reasons."

"Ask her what they are, John," said Shelley.

"Well, Stacey?"

"I don't jump, she's exaggerating," she explained softly. "But Renee and Chris love westerns, even the reruns. Don't you see, John. They're all reminders. Every time I see one, I watch for things I know, and it's all brought back to me even more vividly. And as far as the stereo goes, Drew knows my favorite song's always been 'The Way We Were,' but I never had the heart to tell him I played the song back then once and it has special meaning for me now. So he plays it and plays it until I want to go out of my mind with remembering."

John looked worried. "Maybe you'd better tell him you don't like it anymore."

"What reason do I give?"

"I don't know, but you'll have to do something. You can't go on like this."

She laughed bitterly. "I could break the stereo!"

"See what I mean, John?" Shelley said. "At this rate she's going to be nothing but a bundle of nerves in no time."

John sighed, doubting if anything would help. "Maybe you should just tell the girls and Drew how you really feel, Stacey."

"And make their lives revolve around me like some sort of queen?" she asked, surprised. "I can't make the girls give up their favorite shows just because I haven't learned to cope with this."

She walked to the window and looked out toward the hospital across the street. "And I can't hurt Drew," she said quietly, staring at its familiar lines showing stark and clear in the crisp, sunny autumn afternoon. "I've already hurt Drew enough." She turned once more to face John, feeling sure that even though Shelley didn't understand, he would. "He thinks he's helping, John. How can I tell him the truth when the mere mention of what happened upsets him so terribly." She fidgeted with the waistline of her skirt. "I'll manage, John. Shelley's naturally concerned, but I'm a big girl now. All I need is time to make Drew believe in me again, and time to start believing again in myself."

John saw a strength in Stacey he'd seen only once before, shortly after she'd been operated on. Shelley was judging Stacey by her own standards, and the two sisters were far from carbon copies of each other. Stacey had survived a journey to another century. It took a strong woman to endure, and seeing the vivid determination in her eyes now, he was sure Stacey would see this through.

"If I can help, let me know," he said softly.

"You mean you're not going to give her something for her nerves?" Shelley asked.

John continued looking into Stacey's eyes. "She won't need anything," he said. "Except to be left alone."

Shelley wasn't quite so sure, and let Stacey know it when they left, remarking too on the strange way John and Stacey had communicated during the visit. She glanced over at Stacey as they headed for the car, watching her tighten the belt on her coat. "I have a feeling you're finally taking Drew's suspicions about John seriously," Shelley said as they reached the car.

Stacey stared across the top of her small white MG at her sister, then unlocked the door and slid in, scooting across the seat to unlock the door for her. "Are you asking if I've finally admitted John's in love with me?" she asked as Shelley slid into the seat beside her.

"I guess you could say that."

"I wish Drew hadn't been right, Shelley," Stacey said as she started the car. "You know, the more I see John, the more I realize how much like Ben he is," she said sadly. "Isn't that ridiculous?"

Shelley stared at her dumbfounded. "Oh, no, Stacey," she whispered. "Don't complicate things any more than they already are, please."

Stacey's eyes sharpened. "I don't know what you mean."

"Don't you? You can't kid me, sis," she said. "I know this Ben Clayton meant more to you than you've been telling everyone. You're asking for trouble if you don't steer clear of John."

"Don't be silly, Shelley." Stacey looked behind them as she backed out. "I don't intend to do anything foolish," she said. "I said he's a great deal like Ben, not that he is Ben. But it doesn't help matters, does it?" She maneuvered her MG out onto the main road. Shelley watched her sister out of the corner of her eye, hoping she wasn't headed for more heartache.

CHAPTER 2

The next few weeks seemed to go by quickly as Stacey's life fell into more of a pattern. The week before Halloween Drew announced that he'd made plans for them to attend the costume party at the country club. At first Stacey was angry because he hadn't consulted her first; then she'd become apprehensive. The prospect of being the center of attention again made her uneasy. But she let him talk her into it, and as Halloween drew closer, she threw herself into the preparations with an enthusiasm she hadn't expressed since her return.

Drew was pleased to see her taking an interest in something again. Stacey had always been an effervescent person. When she wasn't working at the hospital as a surgical nurse, she was golfing, riding, swimming, or sewing. There was always something. Now as she worked on their costumes, her old self was reflected more and more in her attitude toward everything.

She didn't even mind the westerns the girls watched on TV anymore. In fact, she even began to join them, often remarking about the lack of authenticity and laughing at the mistakes. Sometimes, the way she enjoyed the programs bothered Drew, but then he'd castigate himself thoroughly and smile wistfully as he watched her, the lazy dimples in his cheeks deepening.

Halloween night rolled around quickly. They had decided to go as Robin Hood and Maid Marian. Renee was staying all night at her girlfriend's, and Chris was going on a hayride. Her boyfriend, Roger, John Morris' son, was back at Ohio State for the school year, so she had agreed to go with a quarterback from the football team.

Both girls were already gone, and Stacey was half-dressed when Drew came out of the shower toweling his thick head of tawny brown hair, another towel wrapped around his middle. He stopped motionless across the room, his eyes intent on Stacey. She was standing in front of the vanity finishing her makeup and looking delightfully seductive in a one-piece creamy satin undergarment. He watched her shapely legs pose artfully as she leaned

16

forward for a better look, then held his breath, feeling himself harden.

"Stacey?" he whispered huskily, and she looked into the mirror to where he stood behind her. Her heart sank because she knew exactly what he was going to say. "How about it before we go, honey?" he asked lightly.

She stared at him, her eyes traveling from the towel around his middle to his face, then she turned.

"Now?" she asked hesitantly. She tried to find the words. "Drew, I'm all ready . . ."

She watched his eyes flicker over her. "So am I," he whispered, tossing the towel over his shoulder and taking her in his arms.

She felt him hard against her and her insides tightened rebelliously. Not now . . . not now! Not when she was so worried about the party and who might be there and all the questions they'd ask. How did he expect her to want it now?

He kissed her lightly. "The kids are gone. We have the house to ourselves."

"Drew, I'd have to get dressed all over again."

"You don't want it?"

"Not now."

His eyes darkened. "You never refused me before," he suddenly said, and his arms dropped, releasing her.

"You never asked when I was almost ready to go out."

"That's the only reason?"

"You know that's the only reason."

"Do I?"

"Drew, please!"

"Please what? Please forget it, Drew? Don't touch me, Drew? You're not in the mood, is that it? Did you ever refuse him, Stacey?" he asked.

"Drew!"

"Well, did you?"

The suddenness of his question shocked her speechless.

He glared at her for a long, heated moment, then, "That's what I thought," he said angrily, and stalked to the other side of the room. "Don't worry, I won't force myself on you again," he said as he began putting on his clothes. "I'm afraid you'll have to forgive me, I thought I had a right."

"Had a right to what?" she asked. "Is that what you call making love to me, your right? I thought it was something done from the heart, by mutual consent. I didn't know you considered it my duty to give myself to you."

"Don't be ridiculous."

"You're the one who's being ridiculous. I only said I didn't want it now. I didn't say I never wanted it. I didn't say you couldn't touch me. I just don't want to get all cleaned up again."

"Too much bother?" he interrupted sarcastically.

Her jaw clenched. He could be so stubborn if his pride was hurt. She stared at him as he angrily fastened the belt about his leather tunic. His olive-green tights emphasized his well-shaped, muscular legs, and she watched him for a half-minute more, then picked up her own costume, and slipped the simple blue dress over her shoulders.

She hadn't acknowledged his sarcastic remark and while she finished getting ready, he moved about the bedroom briskly, finding a dozen things to do just to annoy her. First he moved to her side of the bed to throw something in the wastebasket, then went over to the other side to get something out of the nightstand forcing her to move aside. When she moved to the vanity to recomb her hair, he found it necessary to open one of the drawers, pretending he didn't know she was in the way.

She put up with his silence just so long, then decided to use other tactics. She put on her beaded velvet hat with its filmy veil, then took her cloak from the bed.

"Are you ready to leave?" she asked calmly.

He stopped abruptly, staring at her. "What are you trying to pull?" he asked.

She sighed. "Look, Drew. I know things aren't all that great with us. I know you resent my relationship with Ben and that you think I had some ulterior motive for not wanting it just now. I can't help that, but we did promise to go tonight and it wouldn't look too good if we walked in there not speaking to each other. If you want everyone to know we're having problems, that's up to you. But I don't think it's a good idea."

His hazel eyes glared at her. "Then you admit we're having problems?"

"I'm not having them," she said. "But you seem to be."

"The only problem I have is you," he confessed softly. His voice was husky with emotion. "You've changed, Stacey," he went on. "Somehow you're different. It's something I feel in here," and he touched his chest. "I need all of you, like I had before, not just the little you care to give. Every time I ask you lately, you're reluctant. I know I haven't changed, honey, so my only conclusion is that you've changed."

Stacey felt sick inside. "Don't be silly. I haven't changed."

"Haven't you?" His eyes held hers. "Stacey, I've known you too many years not to see the difference," he said. "Not once since you came back have you taken the initiative . . . not once have you snuggled up to me affectionately, letting me know you want it. A man likes to feel wanted too, you know. It's not a one-way street."

"I didn't say it was."

"Well, you sure as hell act like it."

Tears threatened the corners of her eyes. "I can't help it!"

"Can't you?" Their eyes clashed; then he glanced at his watch. "Well, we don't have time to argue the point," he said, trying to ignore the hurt in her eyes. "Are you ready?"

She swallowed hard. "Yes."

"I guess I can honor a truce long enough to make everyone think we're still happily married," he said sarcastically, and gestured for her to leave the room first, then grabbed the cloak he was to wear and followed.

Stacey stifled her hateful words. What good would it do to keep the anger alive? She lifted her head proudly as they walked to the car.

It was a beautiful night for October, with the smell of dry leaves in the air. He reached down to open the door for her, then suddenly stopped. "Stacey?" he whispered close to her ear.

She looked up at him, the huge harvest moon tinting her blue eyes a golden green.

"I love you," he said hesitantly, his heart twisting inside him. "I guess that's why I get so angry with you, because I do love you."

He was apologizing. It was his way, and she felt a warm glow spread through her. For tonight it'd be all right again.

"I love you too, Drew," she murmured softly, and she melted into his arms as his kiss reached deep down inside her.

By the time they reached the club, almost everyone else had arrived. Stacey was hesitant as they stood in the hall outside the main dining room, the thought of creating a stir when they stepped inside bringing butterflies to her stomach. She shifted nervously, then looked up into Drew's handsome face.

"I'm ready," she said, and he smiled, his eyes crinkling as if he was amused.

"Then by all means," he said, and they stepped into the main dining room, where the party was being held.

Crisp cornstalks were in every corner of the room while

orange and black crepe paper streamers twirled from the ceiling, holding up black cats, pumpkins, and witches covered with glitter, and at each table was a centerpiece of fall flowers. Even the orchestra was in costume. People were everywhere, seated at tables or dancing, overflowing out onto the terrace where jack-o'-lanterns hung. It was a riot of color and deafening noise.

At first Stacey thought maybe their presence would go unnoticed, but suddenly her name echoed across the room and a pregnant hush fell over the crowd as all eyes began to center on her. She blushed crimson, and held tightly to Drew's arm, trying to look calm, as she surveyed the room until she saw a pair of comforting eyes looking at her from beneath a black mask.

She stared at John, oblivious of his wife, Beth, sitting beside him, her eyes blazing furiously beneath her silver mask. Drew flushed slightly until he too saw his old friend John rise and walk over to greet them.

"Join us," John suggested. "I saved a place at our table."

Drew nodded, and as they worked their way across the room, the furtive whispers once more rose in volume until they were lost in the jumble of noise.

Even though the talking had resumed, Stacey could feel everyone's eyes on her as she and Drew sat down. She tried to ignore it, but bits and pieces of the conversations at the other tables drifted her way. She clenched her jaw stubbornly, hoping no one could tell she was disturbed.

"How've you been?" she asked Beth casually. "I was hoping you'd drop by."

Beth Morris' masked eyes perused the woman beside her. She had always disliked Stacey. This slim, attractive woman was everything Beth had always wanted to be. "I haven't really had time," she answered. "The kids have been keeping me busier than I'd planned this fall."

Stacey considered Beth's hostile look and frowned, then suddenly gasped inaudibly, her composure shaken as she realized the significance of the costume John's wife had on.

Beth's normally frosted short blond hair was hidden beneath a red wig in an old-fashioned hairstyle and her makeup was done just so, adding fullness to her mouth. Her blouse, white and lacey, was all too familiar, and Beth didn't have to stand up for Stacey to know that she also wore a dark green floor-length skirt with some of the decorative beading missing. Stacey had come to the party as Maid Marian, Drew as Robin Hood, John as a gambler à la Maverick, but Beth had come as Stacey Gordon. Not the Stacey Gordon of 1975, but the Stacey Gordon of 1865.

She was wearing the same clothes Stacey had had on when she reappeared in her sister's swimming pool. A strange feeling gripped Stacey. What was Beth trying to prove? She glanced quickly at John, and for a brief moment, his look tried to reassure her, then he turned to Beth.

"Don't you think it's time you asked your wife to dance, darling?" Beth suddenly asked him, and her mouth twisted slightly. "Or maybe you'd rather order me another drink."

John frowned. "I think I'd rather dance."

Drew watched John usher Beth onto the dance floor. He started to look away, then stared at Beth, puzzled. There was something . . . Suddenly it dawned on him what Beth had done. He looked at Stacey in disbelief. "She's wearing the clothes you had on when they brought you to the hospital," he said, astounded.

"I know." She took a sip of her grasshopper, trying to keep her hand from shaking. "What I'd like to know is, why?" she asked, her voice unsteady.

"Come on, Stacey," Drew said. "We both know why she'd pull a stunt like that."

"Do we?" she asked, pondering Drew's words. She hadn't told Drew that his suspicions were true, that John had declared his love for her before she'd left the hospital. If she had, the friendship between the two men would definitely have been over. She turned to Drew, sitting close at her elbow. "I was hoping Beth would have outgrown her aversion to me by now," she said thoughtfully. "I should have realized she hadn't when she didn't bother to get in touch."

"You really expected her to call you?" asked Drew.

"It wouldn't have hurt. After all, John's your best friend."

"And he's in love with you."

"Oh, for heaven's sake, Drew," she whispered irritably. "You sound like a broken record. John's not in love with me, and even if he were, it wouldn't matter, because I don't happen to be in love with him."

"Tell his wife that."

"Would it do any good?"

"It might."

Stacey's eyes darkened passionately as she stared once more at the couple on the dance floor, watching John's tall, muscular body move to the music. She was glad the Halloween mask hid her expression, because the more she watched John, the more he reminded her of Ben, and it hurt. She tried to hide the hurt with indifference.

"Well, I'm not going to let it bother me. I intend to have a good time in spite of Beth."

"I hope you can," Drew said, leaning close to her ear. "Why not start by letting me have the first dance."

She looked into Drew's hazel eyes, half hidden behind his green mask and for the first time in a long time the thought of having Drew's arms about her, even while dancing, made her anxious. She wanted him, needed his strength if only he'd give it. As he led her to the dance floor, she let him hold her close while she tried to ignore the whispering around her.

It was an hour after midnight. The unmasking was over and all the prizes were handed out. Realizing John was worried about the amount of liquor Beth was consuming, Drew had asked her to dance, then minutes later, Stacey accepted the same invitation from John. But with the crowd on the floor dancing shoulder to shoulder, John maneuvered her out to the shadowed lawn where they ended up alone.

"It's cooler here," he said as they danced slowly past a huge evergreen.

Stacey took a deep breath of fresh air. "Thank God," she sighed. "It was so stuffy in there."

John stopped dancing and stared down at her. "All right, Stacey, what's the matter?" he asked.

She stared at him. "The matter?"

"I know something's wrong. I just hope it's not what Beth did tonight. I had those things at the house and I had no idea what she was up to until she got dressed. By then it was too late to warn you."

She shook her head. "It's not just that, John."

"Big problems?" he asked.

She gazed into his dark eyes. "Are you asking as my doctor or as a friend?"

"Both."

"I don't know exactly how to tell you." She avoided his eyes. "It isn't easy to talk about some things."

He cupped her chin in his hand and forced her to look directly into his eyes. "Stacey?"

"It's Drew," she said softly. He dropped his hand. "Well, not really Drew. Maybe it's me, I don't know. But something's dreadfully wrong."

"Like what?"

"Like . . ." She hesitated, but looking up at him, it suddenly seemed easier. Her voice lowered to almost a whisper. "John, every time Drew says 'how about it tonight, honey,' I just want to scream."

He frowned. "Has Drew always approached you like that?" He seemed surprised.

"Almost always. Oh, once in a while he'll give me a kiss first, but usually . . ." She shrugged lightly. "It's his way."

"And it never bothered you before?"

"No."

"How about in bed?"

She flushed. "That's just it. By the time we get into bed, everything turns out fine. It's just that . . ." Her eyes flashed angrily. "It's just that I guess I resent him being so casual. I could be in the middle of frying eggs and he'd expect me to drop what I was doing and be eager just because he suggested it. Like tonight. I was almost ready to leave, and making love was the farthest thing from my mind. He got furious because I said no, and he accused me of being cold toward him. He says I've changed."

"Have you?"

She was close to tears. "I don't know, John, maybe I have . . . but I do know that I never felt that way with Ben."

John watched the way the light from the jack-o'-lanterns played about her face. She was so lovely. It made it hard to be impartial.

"Maybe that's your clue," he said. "How did Ben approach you?"

Her eyes suddenly softened, and a passionate warmth transformed her face. "Ben never asked," she replied breathlessly. "He never had to."

John looked at her skeptically. "Then how did you know he wanted it?"

"By what he did. John, he never said 'do you want it, honey,' but by the time we finally managed to be alone, I always wanted him so badly he never had to ask."

John smiled knowingly. "Stacey, I think you just found your answer."

"What do you mean?"

He reached up, gently stroking a stray hair from her face, then let his hand drop, touching her ear lobe lightly. "Evidently Ben Clayton knew the art of seduction," he said softly. "Remember the conversation we had in the hospital, when I told you men make love differently?"

She nodded, unable to answer because suddenly her whole body began to tingle deep inside as John's hand lowered and he caressed the nape of her neck. His eyes embraced hers, holding them like a magnet.

"A woman likes to be touched, Stacey," he whispered huskily. "She likes to be made aware of her sensuality." His hand traced her jawline while he drew her against him, molding her body to his. "Right now, Stacey, you've begun to come alive. A word, a gentle caress, a tender gesture . . . if I were to keep this up, I could have you in bed so easily. Am I right?"

"John . . . you can't!"

He tensed. "I know . . ." He looked deep into her eyes. "But it's true, isn't it?"

Her heart was pounding against his chest.

"Isn't that what Ben did to you, Stacey?" he asked.

"Oh, God, yes," she cried helplessly. He flinched at the pain in her voice. "I never knew, John . . . Drew was the only man who'd ever touched me. What am I going to do?"

"Do you want me to speak to Drew?"

"Lord, no. He'd never forgive me for telling you."

John's arm eased on her waist. "You'll have to do something, Stacey. Sex is a funny thing. It's one of the few areas in life where pretense is hard to achieve. A person can try, but it doesn't work too well. I know firsthand."

"John . . . I'm sorry," she said softly. He smiled wistfully, moving with her again in a pretense of dancing.

"I know you are," he said affectionately. "But let's get back to your problem. Is there any way you could make him understand how you feel?"

"You have to be kidding. I can't even so much as start to criticize his lovemaking."

"He's that touchy?"

"He's that touchy." She shook her head. "I'll think of something, John, don't worry."

He rested his chin on her hair as they danced a bit longer. Suddenly he stopped and gazed down at her. "Maybe I can find an answer for you," he said thoughtfully.

She frowned. "How?"

"Drew and I are still close. Maybe I can feel him out, get him to confide in me, and throw a few suggestions his way."

"But why can't he think of them himself? Why can't he just let it happen instead of treating it like a production? Why doesn't he just start kissing me and . . . well, you know . . ."

He stared at her hungrily. "Because some men have no idea what a woman needs," he said reluctantly. "Stacey?"

"Yes?"

"You said it was all right once you were in bed. Are you sure?"

She flushed an even deeper crimsom. She had never talked about her love life before with anyone, and it almost seemed like a betrayal, yet . . . "It is, and it isn't," she said hesitantly. "While he's making love to me it's . . . it's all right, but when it's over, well, it's always the same."

"Good or bad?"

"Oh, John!" She sighed. "I hate to say it, but I feel so empty inside when it's over. I never used to care when Drew just kissed me and went right to sleep. Now . . . something's missing."

"Ben?"

"John, how can I tell you?" She took a deep breath. "When Ben made love to me, it was never over. He knew I still needed him as much after the first encounter as I did before. He never turned away from me, and usually we'd make love again before the night was over. I've been married to Drew all these years, John, and he never realized that I needed more. I want things to be right with us, John," she said helplessly. "I love Drew. We've had a lot of good years together, and if I can just lick this thing, we can have a lot more." Suddenly, "John," she asked hesitantly. "Do you think maybe, if I asked Drew without letting him know why, that I could change him?"

"You mean make him aware without actually telling him?"

She nodded. "The next time I could maybe ask him to hold me longer, or touch me or something."

"You could give it a try. And if I get the chance, I'll throw in a few subtle hints. I want you to be happy, Stacey."

She sighed. "I know."

They were back on the terrace now, and the music had stopped. She looked up at him, relief in her eyes. It had been good to talk to someone and John smiled with her, but as they walked back into the main dining room, Stacey's heart sank while Beth's brash voice rang out for all to hear. "Well, well, well, and did you and my husband have a cozy time outside alone in the dark?"

It was two in the morning when Drew and Stacey finally got home from the party. Stacey was still upset about what had happened at the club, and all the way home her anger had been simmering. Now she stopped in the middle of the living room and threw her cloak on the couch.

"The way Beth cut into me, I didn't have much chance to defend myself, did I?" she said bitterly.

"She was drunk," Drew reminded her.

"When isn't she?"

"Stacey!"

"Well, it's true, Drew," she said. "The least little thing sends her running for the bottle. She's lucky John even stays with her. Most men wouldn't put up with it."

"Maybe if John paid more attention to her and less to you, she wouldn't need the bottle."

"For God's sake, Drew," she cried. "John and I only danced together. It was hot and we needed some fresh air. There was no call for her to rake me over the coals in front of all those people." Pain filled her eyes. "You don't know what it's like to be treated like something that crawled out from under a rock. I do. I used to think I put up with a lot from the women around here, but it was nothing compared to the hell I put up with on that wagon train from vindictive people like Beth. I was accused of adultery, witchcraft, you name it. . . . I won't stand for it again, Drew. I've done nothing to deserve it. I didn't answer Beth tonight. I let her carry on like a banshee because I felt sorry for John. But, by God, if it ever happens again I won't hold my tongue and Beth Morris is liable to wish she'd never brought up the subject of her husband's fidelity!"

Drew stared at her, puzzled. "What do you mean by that?"

"Nothing . . . I . . ." She stammered, flustered. Suddenly tears welled up in her eyes and she moved close to him, pleading. "I don't need any more pain, Drew," she whispered passionately. "I've had enough to last a lifetime. All I want is to be with you and be left alone."

He put his arms around her and she melted against him, feeling the strength of him becoming a part of her. This was what she needed, what she craved. Her arms circled his neck and she gazed into his hazel eyes.

"Drew, I meant what I said earlier tonight. I need you more than you could ever know." She pressed her body against his, feeling his arousal. "Make love to me, Drew," she whispered desperately. "Make me feel whole again. Please, darling, please!"

He was surprised for a moment at her passionate outburst, but his lips came down on hers and she kissed him back fiercely, then he lifted her up into his arms and headed for the bedroom where he made love to her, kissing and caressing her until she could stand no more, bringing her to a peak of pleasure that left her breathless. Yet she couldn't let go. Half-laughing and half-weeping with joy, she pressed against him desperately. Drew hadn't come yet, and as he thrust in and out, she moaned with pleasure.

He kissed her lips, her neck, and her breasts as he moved slowly, rhythmically, then suddenly she let out a soft cry as another wave of bliss swept over her. She clung to him greedily, feeling him tremble with the first surge of his release. He gasped and shuddered, then lay still with his broad chest resting against her full breasts.

He exhaled. "Mmm . . . that was worth waiting for," he whispered huskily.

"Drew?"

"Yes?"

"Kiss me," she begged softly. Her body was still throbbing.

As his lips met hers, she felt another wave of desire sweeping through her, and opened her mouth slightly, hoping to receive the same deep kiss that had ignited their desire. Instead, Drew only touched her lips softly, then slid off, nestling close to her.

God, no! He was going to fall asleep. She listened helplessly as his breathing became slow and steady. "Drew?"

"Mmmhmmm . . . ?"

"Honey, will you touch me?"

"Touch you?" He put his hand on her rib cage and cuddled closer. "How's that?" he said.

His hand lay motionless, and she wanted to scream. Her breasts were throbbing, her whole body still primed. Holding her breath, she lifted his hand to her breast so there was no mistaking what she wanted.

As he smiled lazily and caressed her breast slowly, Stacey moaned with pleasure. Then suddenly Drew squeezed her breast affectionately and let his hand wander to her side. "It was nice, honey . . . so nice," he murmured contentedly. "But hadn't we better get to sleep?"

She couldn't answer. Her words were choked by a silent sob.

She didn't want to go to sleep. But she couldn't force his love. It had to come naturally, the way it had with Ben. Ben! She closed her eyes, trying to still the ache inside.

"It is late, isn't it," she whispered softly.

He tightened his arm momentarily as he whispered, "Good night, honey."

"Good night, Drew."

For a long time she lay in the darkened room, feeling his arm like a deadweight across her. Then suddenly the tears she'd been holding back came like a flood, washing down her face and she cried herself to sleep.

CHAPTER 3

The weekend went quickly. Saturday Drew stayed home and raked leaves while Stacey went shopping with Chris and Renee and ran into Craig Paxton when they stopped for lunch at a restaurant at Eastgate. Craig was a local politician who was always running for office but never quite making it. He was distinguished-looking, with slate-gray eyes and the suave charm of a con man.

"Well, my God, Stacey," he said, dumbfounded as he almost knocked her down outside the restaurant. "Where the devil have you been keeping yourself since you got out of the hospital?"

Stacey smiled. "At home."

He straightened, trying to look important. "At home? We could use you down at campaign headquarters. Presidential elections are next year, you know, and we're already working on a campaign. And we could have used you for the local elections, but it's too late now."

"I know," she said. "Voting's Tuesday. I'm sorry, Craig, but I really didn't feel up to it."

He smiled solicitously. "I understand. But it sure isn't the same down there without you." He asked Chris if she was going to the party his daughter Nancy was having that night, and smiled cheerfully when Chris nodded.

"Good!" he said. "Nancy was disappointed because she missed the Halloween hayride last night. We didn't get in from Philadelphia until late. Had to go see Muriel's parents, her mother's been ill, you know. Even missed the party at the club. First Halloween we've missed for ages. Imagine it was the usual dull affair."

Stacey stared at him, surprised. So he hadn't heard yet. Well, maybe by the time he got home someone would have called Muriel. She knew it wasn't going to take long for Beth's outburst to make the rounds.

They talked a little longer while the girls squirmed impatiently, then Craig left and they went on into the restaurant.

That evening they all attended a charity football game at the local high school, then Chris went on to Nancy's party with her football player, and they headed for home. The next day they all stayed around the house enjoying the crisp November day, and by Monday morning Stacey was almost glad to see Drew leave for work and the girls catch the bus for school.

She sat at the kitchen table watching Drew's car disappear down the drive toward the main road, enjoying her coffee. Mrs. Garret was only going to come on Fridays now, and for the first time since her return Stacey had the house all to herself.

She sighed, finishing her coffee slowly, then rinsed the dishes, put them in the dishwasher, and walked leisurely through the house. It was so quiet. The only sound was the faint hum of the refrigerator and the steady ticking of various clocks. It was somewhat frightening. She tightened the sash on her robe, then walked more briskly to the bedrooms.

She checked the girls' rooms. They'd made their beds, but she had to push in a tuck here and there, nodding her approval as she left each room, then she went on to the master bedroom.

The huge empty bed overwhelmed her as she entered, and she stood for a long time, frowning as she stared at it. It had been so easy to say things would be all right. And she wanted them to be so badly. Why couldn't she be content again? Damn the whole thing anyway!

She marched to the bed, determined that she wasn't going to give in to self-pity. After hurriedly making it, she showered, threw on a pair of jeans and a turquoise velour pullover, and ran a comb through her hair. There, she was all set.

She stared into the mirror, perplexed. For what? What was she going to do? She looked around the bedroom. Everything was still in place, and it was the same as she went back through the rest of the house. She stood in the kitchen pondering. Maybe she could run the vacuum again. For the next half-hour that kept her busy, even though the carpets looked no cleaner after than they had before, and it was only nine-thirty. My God! She had the whole rest of the day. This was ridiculous. On the wagon train there had been more than enough to do. But she wasn't on the wagon train anymore.

She had another cup of coffee, then headed for her sewing room in the basement, where she kept herself engrossed in cutting out a pattern for the next several hours.

At noon she set the dress aside and went up to the kitchen, where she opened a can of tuna and threw it in a dish with some lettuce, onion, and mayonnaise. While she ate, she glanced up at the wall phone. It hadn't rung once all day. But then, why should it? Drew had had the old number changed, and no one knew the new one except Shelley, who was out of town. The phone had rung so much before, it had almost driven her crazy. Now she'd give anything to hear from someone. Anything to break the monotony.

Lunch over, she cleared away her mess, then stood staring at the railing that heralded the basement stairs. She shrugged. It was the sewing room or go crazy, so she slowly descended into the basement again.

It was a little after two o'clock when she finally set the dress aside, rubbed her back trying to get out the kinks, then went over to the window. The sun was shining, and it looked so inviting. She glanced toward the door that led outside to the terrace and backyard. What the hell! Grabbing an old leather jacket off a hook beside it, she stepped outside, taking a big gulp of fresh air. The terrace was full of leaves that had fallen since Drew had raked them, and the unmistakable smell of the river was strong in the afternoon sun.

Stacey shoved her hands in her pockets and kicked the leaves haphazardly as she left the terrace and walked slowly past their empty swimming pool. She eyed it warily, then glanced back toward where the river wound its way across the property.

Slowly she made her way toward it, then ambled hesitantly along its banks. The air was cool, a few leaves still falling and the goldenrod had turned brown along with the rest of the weeds that were dried and lifeless, waiting impatiently for the snows of winter so no one could see them looking so unattractive. It was a strange time of year. A lull between fall and winter, a time of waiting. There were no crickets, or tree frogs, and only the shrill cry of the blue jays broke the silence.

Far overhead somewhere a jet passed and its faint hum filtered down through the tree branches. Stacey sighed, remembering the shocked look on Ben's face when she'd told him about airplanes. But he had believed her. Dear, sweet, wonderful Ben had believed her. She hugged herself, shivering momentarily from the memory. She wished she didn't have to forget. She was trying, but was she really trying as hard as she should, or was she subconsciously holding on?

She moved farther along the riverbank. A squirrel ran ahead of her, hiding somewhere on the ground, and a chickadee chattered at her invasion of his privacy. When she came to a slight bend in the river, she stopped to savor the smell of the outdoors, then looked down at the sparkling waters. It hadn't rained for over a week and the water was clear as it cascaded over a small rapid and splashed into a deeper pool. She sat on an old half-rotted log. It was so peaceful out here, so unexpectedly comforting.

She sat for a long time, letting her mind wander.

Suddenly she turned as she heard Renee calling frantically. She glanced at her watch and inhaled sharply. My God, it was three-thirty. She'd been sitting here for over an hour. She stood up quickly, waving, then cupped her hands and yelled for Renee, as she started back.

Renee was winded from running by the time she reached Stacey. "Oh, Mom, why didn't you leave a note! I hunted all over the house." Her voice was breaking. "I thought you'd disappeared again!"

Stacey stared at her guiltily. Oh, Lord! She hadn't thought. She reached out pulling Renee into her arms. "Oh, you poor baby," she exclaimed, stroking her auburn hair. "I'm sorry. I didn't expect to be out this long. It's all right, honey," she said, trying to reassure her. "I'm right here. Nothing's happened."

There were tears on Renee's cheeks. "I thought . . . I thought . . ."

"I know," said Stacey. "But don't worry. I only came for a walk." She wiped Renee's tears away. "Now, come on, perk up and we'll walk back to the house together."

"Golly, mom, don't scare me like that again," Renee said, relieved, and arm in arm they headed back toward the house.

Stacey was overjoyed to have Renee home. It was someone to talk to, and she bubbled over with enthusiasm as they started dinner.

A short while later when Chris joined them, it was like old times again, with all three up to their elbows in flour, sugar, and shortening.

Stacey relished working with the girls again, and now her melancholy mood from earlier disappeared and she decided to do things up special.

When Drew came home, he was ushered into the dining room, where the table was set with good china, silver, and flowers. Dinner was a complete success, and later, in bed, Drew let the mood of the evening influence his lovemaking, teasing Stacey affectionately, forgetting momentarily the discord that had often accompanied his feelings. He kissed her playfully, pretending to wrestle her into submission, and when his kisses deepened, Stacey gave herself to him with abandon, hoping that this time the fire within her would be quenched. But once more, as he rolled from her and settled down to sleep, she lay in the darkness, her body still throbbing, and felt empty inside.

The next morning Stacey once more sat alone in the kitchen watching Drew's car disappear down the drive. Her thoughts wandered back to last night. She stared, not really looking at anything, just staring. She was being foolish and shouldn't let it bother her like this. So Drew wasn't a perfect lover. A lot of men weren't, but that was no reason to wreck a marriage. After all, sex wasn't everything.

She clenched her teeth stubbornly, taking her empty coffee cup to the dishwasher. Instead of feeling sorry for herself, she was going to have to start being thankful for what she had, even if it killed her. She slammed the dishwasher shut and went upstairs and dressed. Then, once more, she stood gazing around at the neat room.

Well, she still had her sewing to finish. She spent the next hour in the sewing room putting in the last stitches, then she looked around, wondering what to do next. Her eyes fell on some gray houndstooth material and she shook her head. She wasn't about to sew another stitch.

She began to wander about the room. The first thing she spotted was her tennis racket. She stared at it for a minute, then took it down, letting the feel of it get to her fingers again. Maybe she could play tennis? She swung the racket, then winced, feeling the pull across her left shoulder. That settled that notion. She slipped the racket back into its case, then sauntered over to where her golf clubs were leaning in the corner collecting dust and took out a club. But when she started to swing, a soft cry escaped her lips as pain shot through her left shoulder. Well, so much for that, too. She put the club back and left the basement wearily. There had to be something to do. She'd go crazy wandering around the house all day.

She glanced at the kitchen clock. Ten o'clock. She wandered into the living room and stared out the back window. Suddenly a thought struck her and she went to the telephone and dialed a number. She listened to the rings, then frowned slightly as a woman answered.

"Dr. Morris' office. Ruth speaking. May I help you?"

"Ruth?" She bit her lip. "This is Stacey Gordon, is Dr. Morris busy?"

"Why, no, Mrs. Gordon. You caught him between patients," she said. "Just a minute."

The receptionist caught John heading for one of the examining rooms. "Mrs. Gordon's on line two, Doctor. Can you catch it?" she asked.

John stopped abruptly, surprised, then nodded. "I'll take it in my office."

Stacey heard a click as John took over the line. "Stacey?"

"You don't mind me calling, do you, John?"

The receptionist was staring at John curiously, and he shut the office door.

"I told you to call anytime," he said. "Besides, I was going to call you anyway."

"Oh?"

"First you. Having more problems?" he asked.

"All I want to know, John, is can I go horseback riding? I thought maybe a little exercise wouldn't hurt me, but then I thought I'd better check with you first."

He sighed, moving over to the window, staring out. "Where were you going?"

"Out on SOM Center Road, where Drew and I usually go."

"When?"

"Now. As soon as I get changed. Then it's all right? I won't pull any muscles in the shoulder?"

"You shouldn't." He hesitated. "Stacey, how would you like some company?"

She took a deep breath. She hadn't expected this.

"Look," he explained hurriedly, "I don't like the thought of you riding alone . . . and besides, I have to talk to you privately. I only have one more patient this morning. Please, Stacey, it's important."

"What can I say?" Her stomach tightened nervously. "Should I meet you there?"

"About ten-forty-five. Will that give you time?"

"More than enough."

"If I'm late, wait."

"I will." She hung up, wondering what that was all about.

Forty-five minutes later she pulled her little MG into the parking lot at the stables, maneuvering it next to John's big gray Lincoln Continental, then smiled as he opened the door for her.

"You beat me," she said, sliding from the driver's seat. "Drew called just as I was getting ready to go out the door."

"You told him where you were going?"

"And I also told him I had your permission."

He shut her car door, his dark eyes catching hers briskly. "But you didn't mention I was going along, I hope."

She half-laughed. "Don't be crazy. Beth is enough of a

problem without adding Drew to our worries. Now, let's go find some horses."

The fresh air did wonders for Stacey's morale, and John thought she had never looked lovelier. She was wearing western boots, jeans, a navy turtleneck sweater, and her red hair looked deep auburn under the gray overcast sky. It was so nice just being able to look at her without worrying about what people would say.

Traffic wasn't too heavy this hour of the day and they crossed the road carefully, then moved onto the bridle path. Stacey glanced over at John as the woods began to close about them. She thought he'd be wearing a suit and look out of place, but he was dressed casually in black slacks, suede jacket, and a sweater.

They rode along for a while, getting the feel of the horses, keeping the conversation impersonal. Finally Stacey turned to John. "All right, John, what is it?" she asked. "You haven't been with it since we left the stables."

He looked at her helplessly. "Can we stop?"

They were in the middle of the woods, and she pulled her horse over to the edge of the trail.

"Well?" she asked after he'd helped her dismount.

He took a long breath, looking deep into her eyes. "Leslie Kyle's back," he said softly.

Stacey froze. "You're sure?"

"She came to see me at the hospital yesterday afternoon."

"Why?"

"Because she knows I'm Drew's best friend, and because she knows I'm your doctor."

"What did she say?"

"She's been assigned to do a follow-up story on your return."

A sudden wave of nausea swept over Stacey and she trembled. "What do I do, John?" she asked softly.

He frowned. "What do you want to do?"

"I don't want to lose Drew!" she cried. "John, if she comes back into our lives now . . . I love Drew, maybe not as much as I should, I don't know, it's hard. But I can't lose him."

"You won't."

"You said she was beautiful, John. She's young, and Drew liked her once."

"But he made her leave."

"What is she really like, John?" she asked hesitantly.

His eyes softened. "Not half as lovely as you," he whispered.

"Oh, John, you're incorrigible."

"I know." His hand brushed a stray curl from her face. "You really want to know what she's like?"

"Yes."

"She's sophisticated in a way and seems rather nice. I only met her a few times."

"When did he meet her?"

"On the Fourth of July. It was rather sticky at first. She was sent here on the Q.T. to get an exclusive story. When he found out, he was mad as all hell. I don't know everything that happened between them, but in spite of everything, he kept seeing her. Her story was released the week before you came back."

"Did Drew ever talk about her?"

"Nope. He was always closemouthed when it came to Leslie. But I'll be honest with you, Stacey. I think Drew was beginning to care for her more than he wanted to admit."

"I was afraid of that."

"I could be wrong."

She shook her head. "No, you're not wrong, John. I know Drew too well. If he didn't care, he wouldn't avoid talking about her."

"I'm sorry, Stacey," he said, watching the worried look on her face. "But I thought it'd be less of a shock coming from me."

"I'm glad you told me," she said, trying to keep her voice steady. "Thank you, John."

He looked down into her blue eyes, watching the curve of her mouth, his insides in a turmoil. He loved her so damned much. "I told you before, I'm always here for whatever . . ." He helped her mount again, and as they rode back to the stables, he checked his watch. "By the time we get back in with the horses, it'll be lunchtime," he said. "My treat?"

"Do you think it's wise?"

"No, but right now I don't much give a damn," he said. "You're hurting and I can't stand to see you hurt, Stacey. Let me help." He caught her eyes. "It's only lunch."

She stared back at John, suddenly very aware of the love in his eyes. It made her feel warm deep down inside. So often she had to fight the strange effect he had on her. "All right," she answered softly.

He smiled, relieved.

CHAPTER 4

Drew sat in his office at his drafting table, humming a slow tune as he worked on a set of blueprints. He was still feeling the effects of the night before. Stacey had been in such a frivolous mood. He frowned for a second as he measured and calculated; then he stopped for a minute, staring at his work as his mind continued to wander.

Stacey used to be like that all the time. Laughing and happy, enthusiastic about everything. It was good to see her like that again. His frown deepened. But that was last night. He stood up and walked to the window, shoving his hands in his pockets and stared down at the street below. This morning she was restless and irritable again. What was he doing wrong? He'd tried to keep a level head about the whole thing, but, God, sometimes his stomach churned at the thought of her in another man's arms. Maybe that was it. Maybe he didn't measure up. But their lovemaking last night had been better than usual, and she had finally given herself to him without reservations. But, damn, something was wrong.

He turned abruptly as the buzzer on his desk went off. He walked over and hit the button. "What is it, Hazel?" he asked.

"There's a lady out here who wants to talk to you, Mr. Gordon," she answered lightly, pretending innocence. "Miss Leslie Kyle."

Drew froze, staring at the intercom, then sat down on the edge of the desk because for a second his knees felt like they'd turned to jelly. Leslie Kyle—my God! Of all people!

"Send her in," he said, trying to keep his voice steady, and his breath caught as Leslie walked in, closing the door slowly behind her.

She was stunning in a suit of burgundy velvet, with her blond hair falling in waves to her shoulders and as her green eyes met Drew's, a shock ran through him.

Hoping this ridiculous reaction to her would pass, he tried to

37

be casual. "I thought you weren't coming back," he said as he stood up.

Her jaw tightened. "That was your idea."

He stared at her, remembering all that had happened between them. "Well?"

"I have a new assignment," she said, staring at him steadily. "A follow-up story on the return of Stacey Gordon."

"The hell you have!"

"Drew, please!"

He walked to the window, turning his back on her.

"They have no idea there was ever anything between us, Drew," she went on helplessly. "What could I tell them?"

"You could have told them no."

"I couldn't," she whispered, and he whirled to face her.

"Couldn't or wouldn't?"

"Both!"

She watched him warily. He was mad, but there was something besides anger in his eyes. She had seen it the moment she walked through the door.

"Are you happy, Drew?" she asked unexpectedly.

He froze. "I was."

"You mean me?"

"You promised."

"I know I promised. But, Drew, I can't forget."

He stared at her and suddenly as their eyes met, he felt as if he couldn't breathe. It was the same giddy feeling he'd experienced the first time he'd seen her, and he fought it hard, inhaling sharply. "Leslie, this is crazy," he said, his voice deepening. "In the first place, Stacey will never give you the story. And in the second place, I don't want her to."

"Why not?"

"I have my reasons."

She studied him for a few minutes. When she had first been assigned to get an exclusive interview from him, she never dreamed things would turn out the way they did. She had been so sure she was immune to love. Now, as her eyes caressed his broad shoulders and she remembered the way he'd kissed her good-bye, she wanted to cry. She had missed him so terribly.

"I intend to ask her, Drew," she said stubbornly. "And I'll do the story with or without your permission."

"For God's sake, Leslie," he said angrily. "You can't just ask her. She knows all about you."

"All about me?"

He flushed. "As much as she needs to know."

As she moved closer, the sweet scent of her perfume filled the air around him, and he wanted to back away, but his feet were rooted to the floor. Sweat began to bead on his neck, and his throat constricted.

"Drew?" she whispered softly.

He tried to avoid her eyes, but couldn't.

"You owe me something, Drew."

"I owe you nothing. You knew what you were doing."

"Did I?" Her fingers traced his lips and she felt him tremble. "If I'd known what you were really like, Drew, I'd have run like hell the other way." Her hand dropped, but her eyes still held his. "No woman ever knows what she's doing when she falls in love," she said, and he inhaled sharply.

"Don't talk like that."

"Why not? What am I supposed to do, act like I don't care? Can you?"

"Yes."

"Liar!" Her breath was erratic. "You haven't forgotten. You know damn well that if I kissed you now, you'd kiss me right back."

"Don't be so sure."

"Do I have to prove it?" Her arms started to move up around his neck, but he stopped her.

"It won't work, Leslie," he said. "It's over between us."

"Is it?" She stared at him stubbornly. "Then why do I have the distinct feeling you and your wife aren't getting along?"

"Wishful thinking."

"No. I see it in your eyes." She let her hands rest on the front of his shirt, fingering his muscular chest. "I love you, Drew. I don't want you hurt," she said softly. "I left because you insisted. But if something's wrong . . . if it isn't working out . . ."

"Dammit, Leslie," he said huskily, "why'd you have to come back? I could cope with it, at least I had a chance . . . why do you want to complicate things?"

"Is that what I am? A complication?"

He stared into her emerald-green eyes. She seemed to look right into his soul and touch it with her sensuality. He could love her so easily. No, she wasn't just a complication, she was a dangerous one, especially now, so soon after Stacey's return when things were so unsettled.

"You know very well what you are," he said passionately. "I want Stacey to stay my wife. With you here . . . it would be too tempting to run to you when things go wrong." He lifted her hands from the front of his shirt and held them. "I don't think I can take that kind of pressure, Leslie. I don't want to have to try.''

She squeezed his hands, then walked over and leaned on the edge of the desk. "Then let me get my story and get out. I mean it, Drew, I'll leave again if you really want me to. But not until I get my story. The article about you was a winner, you know that. I got an exclusive. With this story I can make it big, and I need to. Writing's my career. Next to you it's the only thing I care about. Talk Stacey into doing this story, and I promise I'll get out of your life for good.'' She was trying to look calm, but her eyes held pain.

He didn't want to hurt her more. He walked over and stood looking down at her. "I'll try, but I don't think she'll do it," he finally said. "She's never told the whole story to anyone except me and Dr. Morris. In fact, I really don't suppose I've even heard it all. I imagine there's a lot she hasn't told anyone . . . we try not to talk about it too much.''

She touched his arm. "I'm sorry, Drew. I didn't mean to make you angry," she said.

He smiled, hoping to make her feel better. "I'm not mad. I guess I'm just a little scared. Whenever I look at you, I can't help remembering things . . .'' He flushed. "I don't like memories getting in the way.''

"I'll try not to let them. It'll be strictly business, Drew, I promise," she said. "Unless you want it otherwise. It'll be up to you. I only want a story, Drew. Will you try?''

"I'll try." He watched her stand up and smooth her skirt. "Where are you staying?" he asked.

"For now, in Lyndhurst with my sister and her family. You should still have her phone number.''

He nodded. "I'll call when I get some kind of answer.''

"Make her understand how important it is, Drew," she pleaded anxiously. "I've waited so long for a story like this . . .''

He smiled at her, more relaxed this time.

"You're a doll," she whispered affectionately. "No wonder I love you," and before he had a chance to back away, she kissed him soundly on the mouth, and walked out, closing the door firmly behind her.

He stood for a long time, his heart pounding, then exhaled, swallowing hard. He touched his lips reverently, trying to stop the tingling sensation, then swore softly. What had he let himself in for? Damn!

*   *   *

Stacey was in the kitchen tearing up lettuce for a salad when she saw Drew pull in the drive. She glanced at the clock, surprised to see him home already, then remembered he was going to stop and vote, and since the polls closed at six he had to leave the office early. She watched him start up the back walk and saw that something was bothering him. Usually he walked with a casual grace, his body fluid and easy. But now he was walking as if he was on his way to a bullfight, muscles tense and alert. She leaned forward a little and watched him hesitate on the back porch, taking a deep breath before coming in, then she straightened, tensing for the explosion.

Drew forced a smile as he stepped in and sniffed, smelling supper cooking in the oven. "Smells good," he said.

He walked over, kissed her lightly on the cheek, then took a Coke out of the refrigerator. "How'd the riding go?" he asked lightly.

She glanced at him apprehensively. "Fine," she said. "It felt good to get back on a horse again."

He sipped at the Coke, his eyes bristling. "Where are the kids?"

"Chris stayed after school to try out for a play, and Renee's outside somewhere painting a picture for tomorrow's art class."

He eyed her steadily. "How was lunch today?"

Her fingers stopped abruptly, then slowly continued tearing the lettuce. Her insides were fluttering wildly. "Any special reason you're so concerned about my lunch?" she asked casually.

His eyes snapped as he slammed the Coke down. "You're damned right there is," he said, finally exploding. "I heard who you had lunch with today! Everybody down at the polls was talking about it, and they made damn sure I knew. Was it your idea or his?"

She let the rest of the lettuce drop in the bowl. "It wasn't like that at all. I called John to ask him if I could go riding."

"And he asked you out to lunch?"

"Well, not exactly."

"You asked him?"

"No . . . it . . ." She might as well tell him the whole of it. "He went riding with me," she said quickly.

"He went riding with you!" He laughed cynically. "Oh, fine. After everything Beth threw at you Friday night, you go riding with him!"

"He didn't want me riding alone."

"Oh, I'll bet he didn't."

Her eyes flashed "Don't make it into something it isn't, Drew," she said. "We didn't do anything wrong."

"Tell the people in the village that."

"It's none of their business."

"They make it their business." His face was livid. "For Christ's sake, Stacey, the whole town's talking. My wife and my best friend!"

"Drew, we went riding, then went to Howard Johnson's and had lunch. That's all!"

"That's enough. It's just what everyone's been waiting for. For God's sake, Stacey, even if you didn't do a damn thing, don't you have any more brains than that?"

"Even if I didn't . . . ?" Her eyes were glistening with indignation. "I'm telling you I didn't, you can believe it or not, I don't give a damn. And I don't care what the people in town think either. Not anymore. I care about me, Drew, me! I'm sick and tired of always having to defend myself. And I don't like you accusing me of having a clandestine meeting with John. If you must know, he had a legitimate reason for seeing me. He wanted to tell me that your precious little journalist from New York is in town," she said heatedly. "But I imagine you already know that, don't you?"

She felt triumphant as she saw his shocked look. "What's wrong, Drew?" she asked. "Didn't you think I'd find out?"

He inhaled sharply. "How did John find out?"

"It seems the lovely lady went to see him yesterday. How long has she been here, Drew? Or don't you want me to know?"

"Don't be ridiculous," he said. "I just found out she was here today. She came to see me at the office this afternoon."

"To your office? You mean you were there alone? Just the two of you? My, how cozy. Now who's having clandestine meetings?"

"It wasn't a clandestine meeting."

"Prove it," she said angrily. "Prove to me that you didn't kiss her or make love to her!"

He flushed crimson, remembering Leslie's good-bye kiss.

Stacey gasped. "You can't, can you?" she said breathlessly, and he flinched. "In fact, you look guilty as hell!"

Drew straightened, his eyes clashing with hers. "I can't prove it, any more than you can prove nothing happened between you and John," he exclaimed.

She thrust her chin up stubbornly. "Good. Then we're even."

He stared at her for a long time, his insides in a turmoil. "Stacey, this is ridiculous," he finally said.

"But you started it," she reminded him bitterly.

"Well, how was I supposed to feel? I stop by the polls and the first person I run into is Craig's wife, Muriel, who very snidely lets me know that she saw you and John having an intimate lunch together. Then, not two minutes later, I'm confronted by another of our so-called friends who informs me that you and John were holding hands over lunch. You said you'd gone horseback riding alone. I felt like a damn fool, Stacey. If you'd only told me John was going with you I could have had an answer for them. Instead I probably looked like the poor unsuspecting husband, and that's just how I felt."

"You poor thing," she said sarcastically. "And what do you think everyone's going to be saying about me when they discover your girlfriend's back?"

"She wasn't my girlfriend."

"Oh, come on, Drew, you can at least be honest about it," she demanded. "Maybe you didn't sleep with her, but I bet you sure came close, so don't pretend there's no reason for me to be upset. I have just as much right to accuse as you do."

She opened the refrigerator door and grabbed a bottle of salad dressing, then walked back to the table and began tossing the salad lightly.

"Well, what does she want?" she finally asked.

Drew frowned, surprised. "She wants an exclusive story," he said cautiously.

She stopped, her mouth rigid. "What did you tell her?"

"That I'd ask you."

"Why?"

"Because I owe her something. You're right, honey, it's time I was honest with you and with her. I didn't sleep with her, no . . . but that doesn't mean I didn't want to, and I guess I can only blame myself for letting her fall in love with me, so I feel obligated. You were gone and . . . This story means a great deal to her. It could make her career. It's the least I can do for her."

She stared at him, panicking. The truth hurt. She didn't want to hear about Leslie Kyle, not from Drew. It was bad enough just knowing she existed, but to hear Drew confess that he cared . . .

"You really want me to tell her the whole story?" she asked, her hands trembling.

"Not about your relationship with Ben Clayton, no," he said somberly. "But the rest . . . When I was on the way home I got to thinking. Maybe that's what you'll have to do before people will leave you alone. Everyone's still curious. Maybe if you give Leslie this exclusive, it'll settle the matter.''

She stared into his eyes. "You really want this, Drew?" she asked.

He sighed. "Yes."

She walked over and pretended to check the food in the oven, but her eyes didn't even focus on it, then she shut the door and stood in front of the stove, going over everything that had happened since Drew came home. Did this young woman mean more to him than his marriage? She bit her lip stubbornly, and turned to face Drew. She wasn't going to lose him. No she'd fight for him any way she could.

"All right," she finally said. "I'll give her the story, but on my terms."

"And your terms?" he asked curiously.

"The interviews are conducted here at the house, during the day, and not when the girls are home."

"Or when I'm home?"

"That's right. I'm not that stupid, Drew," she said, her eyes flashing.

"I'll tell her."

"When?"

"Now."

He reached for the wall phone while she went back to fixing dinner. She watched him furtively as he dialed a number, realizing regretfully that he knew it by heart and wondered, had she made the right decision? Just how deep were his feelings for this young woman? She listened to his conversation, dying a little inside when his voice lowered huskily. His conversation was innocent and quick enough, but it was still disconcerting.

After hanging up, Drew watched Stacey setting the table. She was still upset, and knowing Stacey, it was going to take some coaxing to make things right again. Her back was to him and his eyes wandered down her figure, admiring the curves, aware of the effect she always had on him. He was still jealous of her afternoon with John, but was willing to accept it for what it was.

"She'll be here tomorrow afternoon about one," he said softly.

She shut the silverware drawer and turned to face him. "Then that's settled, isn't it," she said abruptly, starting to brush past him, but he took her arm.

"Stacey?"

"What?"

"You're still angry?"

"Shouldn't I be?"

He cupped her head in his hand, looking deep into her blue eyes. "Will it help if I say I'm sorry?"

"That's just the trouble, Drew, you're always sorry," she said. "Until the next time."

"There won't be a next time."

"Won't there? I have an appointment with John again next week, Drew," she said deliberately. "Will you believe I'm just going to have my shoulder checked?"

"Don't be foolish."

"I'm not," she said tearfully. "I'm supposed to trust you, but you can't trust me. I want a promise from you, Drew. No more accusations, no more tearing into me before I get a chance to explain, and no more throwing Ben up to me. If I can bend enough to tell my story to your little paramour, then you can start understanding about Ben."

The way his eyes glistened, she thought he was going to buck her, but then they softened with unmistakable tenderness, and a warm tingling sensation swept through her. His lips touched hers sensuously.

"Agreed," he whispered.

"Promise?" she asked softly.

"Promise," he said passionately and at that moment Renee burst in the back door, ready for dinner.

The next morning Stacey once more stood in the kitchen and watched Drew's car disappear down the drive. They had made love again last night, but there had been no joy in it for her because she couldn't put the coming encounter with Leslie Kyle out of her thoughts.

She spent the whole morning nervously straightening up the house. If anything, she didn't want Leslie Kyle to think she was a lousy housekeeper. By twelve-thirty she was standing in front of the big double closet trying to decide what to wear. She kept shoving clothes aside, until her hand stopped on the deep green velvet slacks Drew had bought her last Christmas. They had a matching top trimmed with fluffy green angora. Just the thing. Casual, yet elegant. And she'd wear a pair of green suede spikes. That should prove to Miss Kyle that she wasn't a dowdy little housewife.

After dressing, she put on a little makeup, quickly fixed her riotous hair with a dab of perfume behind each ear, then headed for the living room to wait, checking her fingernails on the way.

My God, she was nervous. She glanced out the front window

toward the road, wondering what kind of car Leslie would be driving, then wondering if she'd come to the front door or back. After all, Leslie Kyle had been here before. It wasn't like she was a stranger to the place.

This was ridiculous. She was acting like an ant on a hot stove. She sat down in the armchair near the picture window in front to wait. It was a beautiful day. Sunny, but crisp.

Suddenly she felt a hollow feeling in the pit of her stomach as she saw a blue Gremlin slow down and turn in the drive. She was here. Oh God!

Stacey stood up and straightened her clothes, trying to keep her heart from pounding, then exhaled loudly, trying to relax. What was the matter with her anyway? This was her house, and Drew was her husband. Leslie Kyle was the intruder, the one who should be apprehensive. She took a deep breath as the front doorbell echoed through the house.

She stepped out to the entrance hall, not knowing quite what to expect, then opened the door and stood quietly poised as she faced a beautiful young woman whose classic features were enhanced by emerald-green eyes, and champagne-blond hair that fell to her shoulders. She was dressed all in black, and as Stacey looked into Leslie's disturbingly lovely face, she was suddenly conscious of every one of her own wrinkles. Leslie Kyle was young, fresh, everything she no longer could be.

"Miss Kyle?" she said with a forced calm. "Come in."

Leslie stepped in hefting her camera and briefcase as she watched Stacey out of the corner of her eye, avoiding direct contact momentarily. A tingling sensation swept over her at the sight of the familiar house. She watched Stacey Gordon shut the door, then turn, and her heart sank. Stacey was gorgeous! Her deep red hair was like a halo about her sensuous face, and she was so self-assured. Leslie felt like a bumbling schoolgirl in her presence.

"I hope you don't mind my coming in the afternoon," she said, apologizing. "But I had to get some supplies this morning."

Stacey tried to look relaxed. "Just so you're gone before Renee gets home at three-thirty."

"I'll be gone by then," she assured her.

"Maybe you'd better set your things down," Stacey suggested as they moved into the living room.

Leslie sat down and took out a notebook and small tape recorder. "You don't mind, do you?" she said warmly. "I find that it's best to compare my notes with a tape recorder. It makes for more accuracy."

Stacey smiled as best she could. "No, that's all right. Shall we begin?"

"Before we do," said Leslie, her green eyes studying Stacey boldly, "there's something I have to get out in the open. First, I want to thank you for doing this for me. Under the circumstances, I wouldn't have blamed you if you had refused. And . . ." Her face flushed slightly. "Just because we happen to love the same man doesn't mean we have to be mortal enemies. I'll try not to do anything to make you feel uneasy. But I must say that I'm very glad you do still love him, Stacey, because if you didn't, I might not feel as cooperative about keeping my distance as I do. You see, I want him to be happy, so I'll get my story and get out. Agreed?"

"Agreed."

"Good. Now we can begin," she said firmly and Stacey, who had marveled at Leslie's frankness, suddenly felt like she was the intruder.

For the rest of the afternoon Stacey told her story once more, but there wasn't time for everything the first day, or the second, and much to her dismay, Stacey soon realized that Leslie was going to have to come back again and again.

For the next few weeks, Leslie indeed came almost every day, and she probed into all the little things, asking for endless details about Stacey's everyday life and surroundings, and it was this probing that finally forced Stacey to turn to her diary.

It was the week before Thanksgiving. Stacey was already dressed for Leslie's visit, even though she wasn't due for a few hours. As she combed her hair, Stacey's thoughts turned to the questions Leslie had asked the day before. Strange, there were some things it was hard to remember. Like the day they had those tintypes taken. Who was the photographer? And what was playing the night they went to the theater? Her eyes moved to the bottom drawer of the dresser.

She hesitated, then opened the drawer and gingerly took out the small white bundle that held her diary. She hadn't touched it since she had come home. But now, with Leslie urging her on, there was no way she could put Ben out of her thoughts. She held the bundle close as she walked to the bed and sat down spreading the things out beside her.

With trembling hands she picked up one of the tintypes and gazed into Ben's face. A weak feeling spread through her and she felt tears welling up in her eyes. Lord, how she missed him. Just looking at his picture brought an ache inside her that hurt, and she wiped the tears away, then laid the tintype down and picked up the diary. She carefully opened it to the first page and once more read the caption.

> May 27, 1865. My name is Stacey Gordon. How I got here, I cannot explain. The only thing I know is that last night, May 26, 1975, I dove into my sister's swimming pool and when I came up out of the water I was in a small lake, in a pasture on the farm of Joshua and Emma Miller and it is no longer 1975, but 1865.

For the next two hours Stacey read the diary, reliving all the intimate details of her other life. Once more Ben lived and by the time Leslie arrived, Stacey was in a melancholy mood, her body throbbing with longing for him, and for the first time since the interviews began, Leslie sensed a restlessness in Stacey that puzzled her.

From that day on, every morning, as soon as Drew and the girls were gone, Stacey showered, dressed, then took the diary from the bottom drawer and let the past become a part of her life again. Without knowing its cause, Drew saw a change in Stacey, and once more the interplay between them became strained.

CHAPTER 5

Stacey, Drew, and the girls were spending Thanksgiving at Shelley's and Cliff's. Cliff's brother and sister and their families were also spending the holidays with them. Stacey was a little nervous about going to Shelley's and seeing the swimming pool again, especially after reading the diary so much lately. Just the day before, she had found an entry that had shocked her to tears. She had been reading about the journey along the North Platte River and had come to the last entry, made the evening the Indians attacked. As she sat now watching everyone enjoying an after-dinner swim in the indoor pool, her thoughts turned to the previous afternoon.

After reading the last entry, she had casually flipped the pages, not expecting to see anything, when suddenly, two pages farther on, her heart had frozen. There was writing, and she had read the words through tears of joy and sorrow.

> September 22, 1865, Fort Laramie.
> My darling Stacey,
> How do I begin this, my darling? There's only one way, I guess, by telling you how much I love you and always will. I know that someday you will read this, the same way I know deep down inside that your worst fears have become a reality. A reality we both knew might come someday, yet prayed would not. I know now that somehow, some way, you have been snatched back to your other life. The life you told me about the night I made you my wife. How cruel fate is to us, my darling. To love so very much, yet have to lose that love. But I will not lose you, not altogether. When we rode away from the campsite and I saw no cross to mark your grave, somehow I knew where you were, although it has not eased the pain. Why God decided to take you from me, I will never know or understand, but in spite of the distance that now dwells

between us, my love for you will never die. And each day, if you read on, I will tell you of all the wonders of my journey, and we can still be together. My life, my love, my own, I miss you so, and my heart cries out for what we had together. Stacey, I don't know how many years will pass before you find this, but I don't think it will be long after your return. I have read your diary thus far, my love, and I can only say I wish you had confided in me sooner so that we could have had more wonderful days together. I admit it would have been hard to believe, as it was that night you told me. But I did believe, both then and now.

I am writing now so that you can know that I am all right. We made it to the fort and are camped inside the walls. Everyone is settling down for the night and it is quiet and lonely without you. These past two nights have been the worst, and I wonder if I will ever get used to the empty bed again. Doc Farraday and two of the Manganos' children were killed in the attack, along with George and Hattie Webster, but you do not have to worry about Ethan. He has joined our wagon and will stay with us through to Oregon. Tomorrow morning we start out again. There are only eleven wagons left, darling, and families have had to double up, but I pray the worst is over.

The words went on, telling her everything that had happened since she'd been gone. She savored every word and cried softly to herself when he closed the day's writing:

That is about all for now, my love. It is late and my candle is almost gone. But I know that when you read this it will bring us close once more. I only hope you have been able to bear our loss better than I. I will never love again, my darling, for I will never stop loving you. I hope that when you read this you will remember the love we once shared. Good night, my darling.

Yours forever,
Ben

Sitting now at the side of the pool, Stacey yearned to go back to Ben and leave all this mess behind. Tears came to her eyes as she watched Drew cavorting with the girls in the water. She was so torn inside. She watched Drew teasing Renee and Chris, and her heart went out to him.

Love was such a strange thing. You couldn't touch it, hold it, or see it, yet without it life could be so empty. Some loves were quiet, or rewarding, or unselfish, while others destroyed and were demanding. Her love for Drew was comfortable, a refuge in a world that had made her prey to all men's eyes. But the love she had shared with Ben was explosive. It was so strong that even the years that separated them didn't make a difference.

She watched Chris dive from Drew's shoulders and suddenly felt guilty. She had thought so little about the girls lately, and had actually been irritable with them, almost resenting them because they made her feel guilty for wanting to go back. Chris practically had a life of her own now. She was always at play practice or school or out on a date and sometimes Stacey felt that Chris wouldn't even miss her if she were gone.

She continued to watch the water as Renee swam to Drew, climbed onto his back, and hugged him, teasing him by splashing water in his face until he threw her off. There was such a change in Renee lately. She was getting so grown up. Her body had begun to develop and she was taller than Chris already. But the two girls had always been such opposites, even in their temperaments.

Lately Renee had taken an inordinate liking to her father. They had always been close, but this was different. Lately, whenever Stacey and Drew were at odds about something, Renee would subtly take her father's side. She never openly joined in the disagreements, but afterward she would console Drew. Of course Stacey couldn't blame her because lately Stacey seemed to be finding fault with everything Renee did. She didn't really mean to. They had always been so close. But Renee was growing up and cutting the apron strings, and there were times when Stacey felt shut out of her daughter's life. Under other circumstances, she would have welcomed Renee's independence, but with things as they were, Stacey felt she had only disrupted her children's lives by coming back. During her absence they had undoubtedly enjoyed more freedom and responsibility. Now they were thrust back into what they probably considered unimportant roles.

Stacey remembered a chance remark Leslie had made one afternoon about Renee. It had come out so naturally that Leslie hadn't even realized it, but it had warned Stacey that this woman had already wormed her way into the girl's affections.

But why should that bother her? She was the one who was

dissatisfied, who wished she could be with Ben. She was so mixed up. She wanted Drew, needed him in a way she couldn't really explain. Yet, if she went back, she'd glory in Ben's arms, but since she couldn't, she'd hold on to what was hers for dear life.

She dipped her feet in the water, enjoying its warmth on her calves. She hadn't been in yet. A tight feeling in her stomach always overwhelmed her every time she stared into the depths of the pool. She swallowed hard, trying to get the courage to slip off the side into the deep water, and was concentrating so hard that Drew startled her by suddenly dropping down beside her. She gasped.

"What's the matter?" he asked cautiously.

"I can't go in," she whispered.

"Still afraid?"

She nodded.

He glanced at her eyes and saw a faraway look in their depths. Jealous twinges surged through him. She was thinking of Ben Clayton. She had been staring with such an intensity, she must have been with him in her thoughts. The pool had been a reminder, and he cursed his stupidity for bringing her here.

Realizing she was drawing away from him, he attacked her bitterly. "You were thinking of him, weren't you?" he said.

She flinched. "You promised."

"That's when I thought there was a reason." He lowered his voice so only she could hear. "How long do I have to play second fiddle to your memories, Stacey?" he asked. "He doesn't even exist anymore, except in your mind!"

"You're wrong!" she whispered. "He does exist."

"He's dead!"

"I can't believe that, Drew."

"Stacey, for God's sake! You'd better believe it," he said furiously, "because there's no way in hell you'll ever see him again." She stared at him long and hard, incensed because she knew he was right and hating him for forcing her to accept the truth.

"Oh, won't I?" she cried heatedly. Suddenly she stood up, stuffed the bathing cap on her head and walked to the diving board, stepping out to the end, then just before plunging into the blue-green water, her wild eyes caught Drew's and he felt a cold chill run through him.

Her body knifed into the water, making only the slightest splash and his eyes stayed glued on her, his heart in his throat. When she rose to the surface, her eyes opened hesitantly. She saw Drew and her eyes hardened again. She used long smooth strokes to reach the side, and pulled herself up out of the water, ingoring shouts from Chris and Renee. Rage driving her on, she was intent on only one thing.

Once more she went to the diving board and plunged in, as Drew watched with trepidation. Again she knifed the water, diving so deep she thought her lungs would burst. When she finally surfaced, she was still met by music, laughter, and Drew's accusing eyes.

Twice more she climbed to the diving board and plunged in, trying to go deeper with each dive, her eyes sparring with his each time before leaving the end of the diving board. Drew stood motionless, fear gripping his insides. The fourth time, as he watched her body glide beneath the surface, he dived off the side of the pool after her.

Stacey broke the surface and opened her eyes, knowing what she'd find. It hadn't worked. There was no going back. Drew was right and she'd never see Ben again. She wiped the water from her eyes and inhaled sharply.

Drew was right beside her. "Are you through?" he asked bluntly.

Her eyes filled with tears. "You knew?" she asked.

"I guessed." His eyes flashed as he asked simply, "Why?"

"I don't know." She felt bruised and beaten. "I don't know why I do anything anymore. Yesterday, today, tomorrow . . . Drew, I don't know where to go from here. I don't want to lose you!" Her tears mingled with the chlorine water on her face. "I love you, Drew! I need you!"

It was the last thing he'd expected her to say after the performace she'd just put on. "Then why did you just do all that?"

"I told you . . . I don't know, except . . . I guess I thought if I wasn't here anymore, life would be easier for all of us."

"We never thought it would be easy."

"But does it have to be this hard?"

"It doesn't have to be, Stacey."

"I'm sorry, Drew," she said penitently. "It's just that talking to Leslie every day, going back over everything that's happened, has been too much." She couldn't tell him about the diary. If he knew Ben had written to her in it, he might make her throw it away. "And it hasn't helped to know that she's in love with you," she went on, her eyes darkening sadly. "You're so worried about Ben, Drew. How do you think I feel about Leslie? Ben's dead, as you so aptly reminded me, but she's alive."

He studied her thoughtfully for a few minutes. "I wonder why we always do this to each other," he said.

She shrugged. "Your temper and my stubbornness, I guess."

He looked at her sheepishly. "It wasn't just Ben you were thinking about, was it?" he asked.

She shook her head. "No, it was everything, but mostly fear. I was so afraid it would happen again."

"But it didn't, did it?"

She stared at him hesitantly. She had challenged the pool and defeated it, and suddenly she felt relieved. "Oh, Drew, can you forgive me?" she whispered softly.

He moved toward her in the water. "I'm the one who needs to ask forgiveness," he said, pulling her into his arms.

She looked hard at him, knowing this was the only way. She was back to stay, and Drew was her reason for staying. It was impossible to rationalize her feelings, so she wouldn't even try and she flung her arms about his neck hugging him warmly.

"I love you, Drew," she whispered in his ear, and he hugged her back, neither of them aware that Chris and Renee were at the shallow end of the pool watching them curiously.

It was the Friday before Christmas. Drew sat at his drawing board, working on a set of blueprints he wanted to get out of the way before the holidays. Leaning closer, he put in the last few lines carefully, then sighed. At last! He set the pencil down slowly and started to raise his head. His neck was stiff and he stretched his broad shoulders, trying to relieve the tension as he studied the print for a minute longer. Satisfied, he reached into his shirt pocket, pulled out a cigarette lit it, then checked the clock. It was five-forty-five and dark already. He hated it when it got dark so early, but then, it was that time of year. Frowning, he took a drag off his cigarette and stood up, surveying the room.

At the moment Hazel had managed to disrupt the tranquility of his office with silver and white bells hanging from every fixture, evergreen boughs loaded with tinsel and small shiney ornaments wherever she could find room. It was like this every Christmas, and had been for the past six years she'd been working for him, but he didn't really mind, and his frown faded slightly as he noticed a new fancy ornament on his desk.

He put out his cigarette, then walked to the window, staring out at the lights below on Euclid Avenue, heavy with early evening traffic. A Santa Claus was hunched near the corner, ringing his bell, trying to keep warm, his face etched in the glow from the street light, and a Salvation Army band strolled by playing carols. His thoughts began to wander.

He'd been having a hard time getting into a holiday mood this year. Usually he loved the holidays. He got a big kick out of taking the girls out into the country to cut down their own tree, and then decorating it when they got home. And he enjoyed buying special gifts for everyone, and going to all the parties, where everyone seemed friendlier because it was Christmas. But for some reason, this year, he just couldn't seem to get excited.

They were putting the tree up tomorrow, only it wasn't real this year. They hadn't taken time to go to the country because Chris and Renee were too busy and Stacey said there wasn't much point in them going alone. Instead, she'd bought an artifical tree, and then both girls had begged off helping to decorate. It was going to be just him and Stacey. It didn't seem right. Things were changing too fast and he didn't like the change.

Chris would be seventeen in the spring and was already talking about going away to college and Renee was turning into a lovely young lady.

At times like this, he felt far older than his thirty-nine years. Only it wasn't getting old he minded so much, it was the change. He had liked things before, when they were simple and uncomplicated. Now . . .

If he could only figure Stacey out. His hazel eyes brooded. Sometimes she would be her old self again, laughing and carefree, then suddenly she'd become moody and withdraw, talking little, her mind miles away. She was holding back part of herself. The part he so desperately needed. Was it because of Leslie?

His thoughts turned to the last time he'd seen Leslie. God, she was beautiful. He remembered her soft green eyes, like fiery emeralds, and the sensuous way her mouth moved when she spoke his name.

Leslie again. He had to forget everything that had happened between them. He had Stacey now. He had to remember how things used to be and how they could be again.

He was still staring out the window and saw that it had started snowing. Just a few flurries, yet he wondered if maybe they'd have a white Christmas after all. At least that might help.

He was jolted abruptly out of his daydreaming when the private phone on his desk suddenly rang. He turned, staring at it for a minute as if it didn't have a right to interrupt him, then he straightened to his full six feet, and walked over, picking up the receiver. It was probably Stacey wanting him to stop at a store on the way home for something she'd forgotten.

He took a deep breath. "Hello?"

He felt a warm thrill run through him as Leslie Kyle softly asked, "Drew?"

"Leslie?"

"Don't hang up, please, Drew," she begged breathlessly.

He swallowed hard. "What is it?"

"I have to see you, Drew," she said softly. "It's important. It's not for myself. It's about Stacey."

"What about her?"

"I can't tell you over the phone. Not like this. Where can I see you?"

He didn't know what to say. He knew he was vulnerable as all hell when she was around, yet . . . "We can't take a chance on being seen together," he said hesitantly.

"I know."

"Can you come up here? Hazel leaves in about five minutes."

"I'm sorry to put you on the spot like this, Drew," she said reluctantly. "But there's no other way."

"You know what Hazel looks like. When you see her leave, come up. I'll watch for you."

"Drew, I *am* sorry."

"It's okay," he said discreetly. "I'll see you in a few minutes."

She hung up without saying anything more. Staring at the phone, he cursed himself for not being stronger, and yet he wondered what could be so important.

CHAPTER 6

Hazel stuck her graying head in to say good night, and noticed that Drew wasn't ready to leave yet. "You staying over?" she asked curiously.

He walked back to the drawing board and sat down as if he still had work to do. "Thought I'd get the finishing touches done," he answered. "But you go ahead, Hazel. You probably have shopping to do . . ."

"Boy, have I," she said wearily, buttoning her storm coat. She had already changed into a pair of shoe boots. "It's snowing and the radio said to expect two inches by morning."

"Well, be careful, and Merry Christmas," he called as she waved and left the outer office, shutting the door behind her.

He left the high stool he'd been sitting on and moved into the outer office, opening the hall door barely a slit and watched as she got on the elevator, then he closed the door, lit a cigarette and sat down on her desk nervously watching the clock. At ten after six, the door slowly opened and Leslie walked in.

"Lock it behind you," he said grimly.

She reached down and turned the lock.

The stark white coat and beret she wore was softened by the blond hair, that fell to her shoulders in waves, and although her green eyes were lightly made up, there was only a natural blush of color to her cheeks and lips. She pulled off her gloves, then looked into his eyes as he stood up. "Hi," she said.

"Hi, yourself."

They both felt awkward. He swallowed hard and ushered her into the inner office.

"Let me take your coat," he offered.

He hung it on the rack in the corner where his own coat hung, then hesitated for a second. Chiding himself for being foolish, he turned to face her.

She looked exactly as he knew she would. She wore deep blue slacks, and a matching V-neck sweater with a single gold chain about her throat, and her face was young and fresh, still pink from the cold. It made her look less sophisticated than usual. Drew stared at her for a moment, remembering too much and wishing he could forget. "Sit down," he said abruptly motioning toward his desk.

"Drew, please," she said. "Do we have to be so formal? Can't we at least try to be friends?" She glanced around the room. "Let's sit on the sofa. At opposite ends, if you insist on keeping your distance." She tossed her hat aside, slipped off her shoe boots, and curled up on one end of the sofa waiting for him.

Drew hesitated briefly, walked over, lowering himself on the opposite end, and spoke abruptly. "You said you wanted to talk."

"Uh-huh. Only I just have to look at you for a minute first. I hope you don't mind, Drew. But I don't get to see you that often." Her voice lowered seductively. "And you do look so damn good."

He could feel himself turning crimson. She had the strangest way of making him feel like a tongue-tied kid again.

She looked directly into his eyes for a long moment, then turned away abruptly. "God, I'd better not do that too often," she said, shaking her head as if to get out the cobwebs, then turned to him again, but he was still staring back at her, and this time she was the one who turned crimson.

"I guess I deserve that, don't I?" she said curtly.

"What's it all about?" he asked.

She pulled her legs up farther beneath her, curling into more of a ball on the comfortable sofa. "Drew," she began hesitantly. "Oh, damn, . . . how do I tell you?"

"Tell me what?"

"That your wife's . . . Drew, how much do you know about what went on between Stacey and this guy named Ben?"

Drew's eyes narrowed, but he didn't answer. It was the last thing he'd expected her to ask him and he stared at her dumbfounded.

She frowned, searching his face, then suddenly it dawned on her what was wrong. "You know, don't you?" she cried helplessly, watching the angry, hurt look in his eyes. "My God, Drew, you've known all along that your wife's in love with another man, haven't you? How can you stay with her?"

"You . . . you don't understand . . ." he said. His eyes hardened. "Who told you?"

"Told me? Nobody had to tell me. Good heavens, Drew, just talking to her . . . I've sat for days and listened, yet I didn't want to believe it. But lately . . . Drew, what happened between them?'' she asked.

He stiffened. ''I don't really think it's any of your business, do you?''

''Drew, I have to know!''

''For yourself, or your story?''

''For myself,'' she said softly.

He was hesitant, the pain in his eyes intensifying. ''No one else must ever know, Les,'' he cautioned her.

''Drew, I promise,'' she said tenderly, ''I'd never do anything to hurt you, you know that.'' She moved closer. ''What happened, Drew?''

His jaw tensed. ''Stacey married him three weeks before she came back,'' he said slowly, and saw the stricken look on Leslie's face.

''Oh no! How could she do that to you?''

''I knew you wouldn't understand,'' he said angrily.

''Understand?'' Her eyes widened. ''Do you?''

''I'm trying to.''

''Oh, Drew, my poor darling.'' Her hand touched his cheek.

A shock ran through him at her touch and he grabbed her hand. ''Don't!'' he gasped, catching his breath. ''That doesn't help.'' He was still holding her hand, but instead of letting it go, he caressed it affectionately. He just couldn't let go.

''She thought she was never going to see me again,'' he began hesitantly. ''She was frightened and alone.'' His fingers tightened on her hand. ''She's my wife, Les, and what happened doesn't change that. I'm still in love with her.''

''How can you be, knowing how she feels?'' she asked boldly.

''That doesn't mean she doesn't love me. Don't you see,'' he said. ''We had something good once, and I know we can have it again.''

''And in the meantime?''

''In the meantime I'm trying to be patient. I have to, Les. When I first learned about Ben, I wanted to kill her.'' He drew her hand close, touching it gently against his cheek refusing to fight the warm sensations that flooded through him. ''But then I thought about you, Les. About the way you always make me feel . . . I remembered the way you have of turning me inside out with just a look. Like you're doing now.''

She was still on her knees beside him, and he pulled her close. Her nearness made his head reel.

''Why do you always do this to me, Les?'' he whispered huskily. ''I look at you and . . . oh, my God!'' he groaned softly as he leaned toward her slowly, like a moth being sucked into a flame. His lips touched hers, hesitantly at first and then with a passion he felt deep in his loins. His hands slipped beneath her sweater and her flesh set his fingertips on fire.

Leslie felt the tip of his tongue touch her lips and she trembled at its insistence. Her arms circled his neck and she slowly eased her mouth open, letting him explore and tease until she was burning with desire. She had wanted this for so long, and now that it was happening, she was in heaven, her body responding passionately as she surrendered completely.

Drew crushed her to him, feeling her surrender, and as the heat of his passion rose, pulling him toward the brink of no return, a sudden danger signal went off somewhere in his subconscious and with an extreme effort he began to pull himself back to reality. His hands trembled, slowing their caresses, and with a moan he pulled away from her.

"Les," he whispered hoarsely, "I'm sorry. Can you forgive me?"

"Forgive you for loving me?" she asked breathlessly.

"That's just it," he said. "Do I love you? Or am I just turning to you at the first sign of trouble?"

She caressed the back of his neck, her fingers warm, affectionate, her eyes still lingering on his. "Don't apologize, Drew," she said passionately. "I loved every minute."

He frowned. "That's the trouble," he said angry with himself for losing control. "It wasn't supposed to happen." He pushed her away gently and stood up, taking out a cigarette, lit it, then walked over to the window. It was still snowing, harder than before, but he didn't notice. All he was conscious of were her eyes boring a hole in his back. His jaw clenched angrily. He shouldn't have let her come. Damn! The worst part of it was that he'd enjoyed it as much as she had.

He took his time finishing the cigarette, then strolled back to the couch.

"I suppose now you hate yourself," she said.

"Shouldn't I?"

"I'm sorry, Drew. For your sake, I wish it hadn't happened," she said, then her eyes grew misty. "But for my sake, I'm so glad it did."

He knew she was hurting, and he pulled her to her feet. "What do I do now, Les?" he asked softly. "How can I face Stacey knowing what I've done?" He reached up, toying with her hair. "I can't help loving her, Les," he said huskily. "She's been my whole life, and now suddenly I don't know what's happening. A year ago something like this would never have happened.''

"A year ago you had your wife's undivided love. You expected her to come back and be the same person she was before all this happened, and she's not.''

"I don't want to lose her, Les,'' he whispered. "And I'm not going to work things out with her by making love to you.'' His arms dropped and he walked back to the window.

This time he saw the snow that had been piling up and thought of the long ride home. He'd called Stacey and told her he'd be late, not telling her why. Now he'd be later yet. He closed his eyes and thought of her as she'd been that morning when he'd left the house, all warm and seductive in a plush robe, her hair helter skelter making her seem young and vulnerable. He had turned to Leslie too easily tonight. Just as he had thought about her too much over the past few months. In fact, every time he and Stacey argued, he'd think of Leslie, and it would soothe him over the rough spots. More and more lately he questioned his feelings for her.

But nothing justified what he'd done tonight. He turned to Leslie. "I'm going to try to forget about tonight.'' He paused briefly. "And I'm having second thoughts about the story, too.''

"Drew, no!'' she cried. "Please, not that! Don't ask me to give it up.'' She was really upset. "I can't . . .''

"But it's been worse ever since the interviewing started. It makes her relive it all again, and I thought maybe if you eased up, it might help. Please, Les, take a breather. At least until after the holidays. Let her get things sorted out.''

"You think she's going to forget Ben Clayton?'' she asked.

His eyes hardened. "I'll make her forget.''

"Good luck.'' Leslie walked over and slipped into her boots, took her coat from the rack, and started to put it on. "When I came here, Drew, I thought I was going to tell you something you didn't know,'' she said. "And I thought maybe, just maybe, when you learned about it, it might jolt you out of the dream world you've been living in the past few weeks. Wishful thinking I'm afraid. I guess in a way I'm glad for her sake, Drew. You see, as much as I'd like to hate her, I can't. I feel sorry for her because she honestly needs you. Mind you, I didn't say she loves you, Drew. You're her security blanket, a substitute for a man she can't have anymore. She's used to you so she'll hang on to you for dear life. You call it love. Maybe it is, but it's not the kind you deserve. It's the kind that hurts, and I don't like seeing you hurt.''

"What do you expect me to do, Les?" he asked, his voice heavy with emotion. "Leave her?"

"I wish I could say yes, Drew," she said curtly. He saw tears spring to her eyes. "Unfortunately, I'm not that heartless. I love you so much I die inside everytime I look at you, and I'll be here to pick up the pieces when she's through with you, but I'll never tell you to leave her. That's your decision and yours alone." Her chin tilted and a tear ran down her cheek. "But I'll do as you ask, I'll leave you alone until after the holidays. Only I don't think it's going to work. I think you and Stacey are both trying to hold on to something that died months ago. You're in love with a memory, Drew," she said bitterly. "And if you ever decide to let go, I'll be around."

She turned to leave, and he finally found his voice. "I'll never leave her, Les," he said huskily.

She stopped, her hand on the door. He was so sure, so very sure. She tensed, a lump in her throat and her voice was low when she spoke. "Never's a long time, Drew," she said softly. "A long, long time," and she left, without saying good-bye.

He stood in the quiet office, listening to his own breathing and the hum of the clock on the wall and he felt so empty inside. Jesus! If only he had the answers! He breathed deeply, noticing the faint smell of Leslie's fragrance that still clung to the air.

Damn her anyway! She was wrong, dead wrong, and he'd prove it. His feelings for Leslie weren't going to interfere with his love for Stacey, and suddenly he knew what he had to do. He'd been going about everything all wrong. He'd been trying to pick up with Stacey where they'd left off. But that wasn't the answer. He was going to have to go back. What was it Stacey had said one time about being friends as well as lovers? That's what was missing. They hadn't even been close since she'd returned, not really close, not like it used to be.

His jaw set stubbornly and he walked over to the coat rack, pulled on his boots, then slipped into his coat. He had to focus all his attention on Stacey, and stop thinking of himself. He'd been so wrapped up in his own feelings . . . well, that was going to change. He flicked off the lights, and locked the office.

As he left the building and stepped out onto the sidewalk, the noise of the traffic mingling with the Salvation Army Band and the Santa Clause's bell began to ignite a spark of the old Christmas spirit in him and he smiled, the hint of dimples in his cheeks tilting his mouth lazily. He gazed up, squinting into the bombardment of snow, and a sudden warmth went through him.

He walked around the corner to the parking lot, cleaned off his car and got in, and a few minutes later as he pulled out of the parking lot making his way to the freeway, he noticed that even the downtown area was decorated for Christmas. His spirits rose even more, and by the time he pulled onto the off ramp, twisting down off Route 271 onto Mayfield Road, heading toward Gates Mills, he had everything all worked out in his mind.

Drew found Stacey in the basement, sorting through the box of old Christmas ornaments. She was both surprised and pleased when he came downstairs, still in his coat. His hazel eyes were sparkling with feeling, and the sight of their warmth took her breath away. Together they went upstairs and ate a light supper, while Drew talked about his plans for the next day.

"We aren't putting up any old artificial tree, Stacey," Drew informed her enthusiastically. "We'll save that for our old age. And if the girls don't want to get a real tree with us, that's fine. We'll go without them."

She started to protest, but he wouldn't let her.

"No," he said forcefully. "I've made up my mind." He reached across the table and squeezed her hand affectionately as he talked. "We're going to pick out a tree, and on the way back we're going to have lunch, just the two of us. Then we're going to come home, decorate the tree, and to hell with the kids." His voice lowered passionately. "And tonight, Stacey Gordon, I'm going to make love to you like you've never been made love to before."

After eating, they finished sorting the ornaments in the basement and Drew paid rapt attention to Stacey, kissing and caressing her every chance he had, so that by bedtime she was eager to melt into his arms and that night Drew took Stacey to heights of rapture she hadn't experienced for a long time. Afterward, Stacey once again braced for the disappointment that came when he rolled over and went to sleep. But instead of rolling off her, Drew began kissing her again, his lips sipping at her mouth.

"I love you, Stacey," he whispered softly. "God, how I love you," and his mouth moved from her lips to her breast, his hands caressing her body, drawing her even closer against him, and much to even his own surprise, he grew hard again. This was wild, sensuous, and a warm glow spread through him. He couldn't remember ever being aroused again so quickly.

He'd never dreamed anything like this could happen. His body was on fire as he felt her warm, velvety skin against his.

He kissed the valley between her breasts, the sweet scent of her mixing with her musky, womanly scent until he wanted to crawl inside her, and then his eyes locked with hers and faint, ecstatic sighs escaped her lips as he began to move in and out again. Stacey, who had been prepared to spend another night with her body aching to be fulfilled, instead clung to him, her body not only fulfilled, but satiated. By the time Drew finally did roll off her, putting his arms around her, holding her close, she cuddled next to him, contented for the first time in months.

Only now it was Drew's turn to lie awake. His body trembled as his eyes traveled from her long lashes, resting on flushed cheeks, to the classic, tapered lines of her nose and the sensuous curve of her lips. Her features were exquisite even in sleep. His eyes moved across her bare shoulders and down to the flaccid, rosy tips of her breasts. The sight of them was erotic in a pleasurable way and he licked his lips slowly, remembering the way they had hardened beneath his mouth.

Her body had always awed him, but suddenly a sense of profound guilt overwhelmed him and he went cold inside. It wasn't just the memory of his encounter earlier with Leslie that fired the guilt inside him, it was the shameful fact that while he was making love to Stacey, while her breast had been at his lips, he'd been thinking of Leslie. Not intentionally, but suddenly thoughts of Leslie had been there and there was no way he could deny it.

"Damn!" he whispered, his arms tightening about Stacey. He couldn't hurt her, not for Leslie or anyone else. He would prove Leslie was wrong, and he had started proving it tonight.

Yet, as Stacey settled down into a deep sleep, he still lay awake for a long time, praying that it wasn't too late.

CHAPTER 7

When Stacey and Drew woke Saturday morning, the sun was shining brightly and three inches of new white snow covered the ground.

Renee's girlfriend's parents were picking her up around noon and Chris was going out about one with her boyfriend, Roger, who was home from Ohio State for the holidays.

"Well, we won't be back by then," Drew said as they all finished breakfast. "And since you'll both be out until late tonight, your mother and I'll leave a note if we decide to go anywhere after we trim the tree."

"When are you putting it up?" asked Chris.

"When we get it home," he said lightly. "Didn't I tell you? We're not putting up that artificial tree. Your mother and I are going after a real tree by ourselves." He downed the last of his coffee, as both girls watched him curiously. They were surprised to see him in such a carefree mood.

And he stayed like that all day. Stacey was dumbfounded. She and Drew always used to have fun together, and now suddenly it was like old times again. She cuddled close and they talked and sang in the car all the way out to the country, then laughed through the sleigh ride at the Christmas Tree Farm, taking over an hour to pick out just the right tree.

By the time they got the tree home and set up in the living room it was pitch dark outside, and Drew made a game of putting the lights on, making sure all the green, blue, or red ones weren't together in one spot. When the tree was finished, Stacey and Drew sat on the sofa and cuddled close in front of the fire letting the glow from the lights bring the holiday season to life, and Drew almost cried. The day had been so perfect.

"Happy?" he asked softly against Stacey's ear.

"It's going to be a nice Christmas, isn't it, Drew?" she said anxiously.

"The best ever," he whispered against her hair, and once more she was in his arms. That night Drew made love to her with a fervor that was almost frightening, and again when it was over, she lay weak and contented in his arms.

The next few days were like a dream to Stacey. Drew was a different person. He showered her with attention, taking her Christmas shopping, helping her wrap presents, and taking her out for evenings of dinner and dancing. And the nights were heaven. They made love or just lay close, savoring each other's nearness. Leslie had called and postponed their interviews until after New Years and there wasn't even time for Stacey to read the diary. At first, she missed it. But on Christmas Eve, as she sat with Drew in the living room watching Roger and Chris holding hands and Renee anxiously waiting to open her presents, and felt Drew's eyes devouring her, she was glad she hadn't let Ben's messages interfere.

Ben was gone and she couldn't have him anymore, but she could have Drew, and she wasn't going to let anything spoil it. Not now.

They opened their presents Christmas Eve and spent Christmas Day with Shelley and Cliff, and once more Stacey challenged the pool. Only this time there was no anger in her, no wanting to hurt. The afternoon was lazy, with snow drifting outside and the warmth of love inside as they lounged around the pool. Renee and Chris were with them for a change and Roger was with Chris, and the day was beautiful.

It wasn't until New Year's Eve that the glow dimmed and Stacey's dream shattered into little pieces. Every year the Craig Paxtons had a New Year's Eve party. After the fiasco at the country club on Halloween, Stacey thought they might not be invited this year, but the gold-embossed invitation arrived as usual.

The Paxton party was a formal affair and Drew dragged out his midnight-blue tux and bought a pale blue silk shirt to wear with it. Stacey wore a dress she had designed herself, and as she slipped it on the night of the party, she suddenly realized that it was very much the style worn in 1865. It started to bring back memories, but she refused to let them take full form and let Drew rescue her.

"Well, how do I look?" she asked hopefully.

Drew's eyes sifted over her, taking in her full form. The dress was a deep burgundy velveteen, with a close-fitting bodice and a neckline scalloped with velveteen cording. A small replica of a bustle lay in folds across the skirt and ended in a floor-length train. On Stacey it looked lovely, and Drew's eyes revealed more than just appreciation.

"You look ravishing," he whispered softly. He pulled her into his arms and his lips captured her warm, sensuous mouth.

This was the way it was meant to be, he told himself as he held her close, then a few minutes later, he sighed with longing as he watched her putting on her small ruby-and-diamond drop earrings and her ruby-and-diamond necklace as he pulled on his suit coat.

Stacey watched him in the mirror as she adjusted her earrings. He looked so handsome. Things were going so well she was almost afraid to go tonight. She wondered if John and Beth were going to be there, yet knew they undoubtedly would be. Maybe that's why she was so apprehensive.

Craig and Muriel Paxton lived in a sumptuous home, with stables and a ballroom. Drew had gifted Stacey with a fur coat for Christmas and Muriel smiled enviously when she met them in the entrance hall. Not that Muriel didn't have her own minks, but she knew that no matter how expensive her clothes were, she'd never look as elegant as Stacey. Stacey had a way of wearing clothes that made other women envious, and Muriel was no exception.

Muriel's hair was dyed black to cover the gray, and its severity emphasized her prominent chin and sharp features. Tonight she was dressed in a bright red nylon chiffon that fluttered haphazardly as she walked. In a way, Stacey felt sorry for Muriel. With all her money, Muriel could have been a fashion plate, but unfortunately, she had her own ideas about fashion and they left much to be desired.

Craig was as overpowering as usual in his slate-gray tuxedo that complimented his gray eyes and silvering hair, and by the exuberant way he was receiving everyone this evening, Stacey knew he'd started drinking early.

After a quick hello with their hosts, Stacey and Drew wandered into the ballroom, where people were milling about the buffet table and dancing. The huge room was dimly lit and decorated with multicolored balloons and crepe-paper streamers and Stacey easily picked John out of the crowd. He was taller than any other man in the room. He caught her eye, and after admiring her briefly, he nodded to Drew.

John had left Beth with friends at the buffet table some ten minutes before, and he was pleased to see Drew and Stacey arrive. He hadn't seen either of them for weeks. He didn't like it, but the less he saw of the Gordons, the less Beth drank. In fact, he almost hadn't come tonight because he knew Stacey and Drew would be here, but Beth had been especially elated about the prospect of the party. Even when he warned her that the Gordons would probably show up, she surprised him by pretending to be glad. Beth's peculiar change of heart was still worrying John as he made his way through the crowd to where Drew and Stacey were standing.

Drew smiled as he shook John's hand affectionately. "Where have you been keeping yourself, John?"

"The hospital, where else?" He turned to Stacey, and as she kissed him lightly, he felt the bottom drop out of his stomach.

As John turned to Drew and began talking with him about some remodeling they were planning at the hospital, Stacey stared at him curiously, trying to gauge her strange reaction to him. Despite her happiness with Drew the past two weeks, the sight of John unnerved her, and now, watching him closely, she suddenly realized why.

John was dressed in a tux, with a fancy shirt that had ruffles down the front, and a black silk bow tie, and as he turned in the dim light of the ballroom, it was, for a brief moment, like seeing Ben again, and all the old fears began creeping back. Stacey felt like dying inside.

She wouldn't let it happen. The past two weeks had been like being reborn, and she wouldn't give that up. She turned away from John and gazed about the room, but suddenly she felt a weird prickling at the nape of her neck. At the same moment, John's eyes fastened on someone behind Drew. Something was wrong.

Drew saw it too, and he turned. Suddenly he felt a cold sensation sweep over him. Leslie Kyle was standing just inside the ballroom door, holding on to the arm of Dr. Nick Rigotti, Muriel Paxton's thirty-year-old brother. Drew stared at Leslie. Her pale hair was drawn back casually into a neat chignon, and her dress was deep green satin clinging to her seductively. Its low neckline ended close to her waist, revealing her youthful breasts and the string of seed pearls resting in the valley between them.

Suddenly Drew felt Stacey's eyes on him.

"What's she doing here?" Stacey asked abruptly.

Drew continued staring at Leslie, anger kindling inside him. "I don't know," he answered. "But it looks like she's Nick Rigotti's date for the evening."

Stacey frowned. "I didn't know she knew Nick."

"She knew him in New York before his divorce."

"Oh." Stacey saw the fire in Drew's eyes. "Well, looks like an interesting evening ahead, doesn't it?" she said unsteadily.

Drew pulled his troubled eyes away from Leslie and looked down at his wife. "We don't have to stay," he said defensively.

"Oh, but we do," she said, getting her courage back. "If I run now, Drew, I'm through in this town. They'll make a laughingstock out of me. I won't give them the satisfaction. I was so sure that after Halloween we wouldn't even be invited this year. Now I know why we were. It was a setup, Drew. Muriel knew all along what she was doing. Every one of them met Leslie when you were dating her, didn't they?"

He didn't want to answer.

"Didn't they?"

"Yes."

She tilted her head stubbornly as a sickening dread swept over her. "All right, if that's the way they're going to play the game." Realizing John was still standing by them, Stacey turned to him. "And I bet Beth knows all about it too, doesn't she?" she asked.

Anger smoldered deep inside John as he realized why Beth had been so eager to come. She wanted to see Stacey squirm. "I had no idea when we came tonight, Stacey," he said. "But now, looking back over Beth's actions, I'd say yes. I think she knew all about it."

"Well, then, I guess I've got my evening cut out for me, haven't I." She turned to Drew. "I thought it was over, Drew. These past two weeks I felt like I'd really, finally come home, but I guess I was wrong."

"Stacey!"

"No, don't, Drew. I'm getting used to it." she said. "They hate me. I saw it in their faces on Halloween and I can see it now. But I won't let them know I even care. I'm going to stay tonight and see the new year in, and I'm going to have a good time." She couldn't let Drew know she was afraid of Leslie. She had seen the look on his face when he had first set eyes on Leslie, and it had frightened her. He had been looking at Leslie in a way she'd never seen him look at a woman before, except herself. He cared, and she knew he cared, and she didn't like it, but she was ready to fight for what she felt was hers and hers alone.

Drew looked deeply into her eyes, remembering the past few weeks, and remembering Leslie's taunting words. "I love you, Stacey," he said firmly.

"Then bring them on," she said confidently as she took his arm, and John, watching her curiously, had a strange feeling that her nightmare was only beginning. He wished to hell he was wrong, but a sudden voice at his elbow confirmed his fear.

"Stacey, Drew!" It was Beth. She had a drink in her hand and a satisfied look in her eyes. Her frosted hair was swept back from her face, and she wore a black chiffon dress that was highlighted with delicate black lace across the high-necked bodice. Stacey thought she looked lovelier tonight than she had in a long time, but the effect was spoiled every time she opened her mouth. "How delightful," Beth cooed cynically as she took a quick sip of her drink.

John cursed himself for not keeping a closer eye on her, for foolishly believing her promise to stay sober.

"How are you?" Stacey asked cordially.

Beth licked her lips and smiled. "I'm fine, Stacey. And you?"

"Never better."

"And you, Drew?" Beth asked, her eyes studying Drew over the top of her glass as she took another sip.

"Fine," he said uncomfortably, wishing she'd quit playing cat and mouse.

"My, you're really talkative, aren't you?" she said, then smiled again, her mouth twisting crookedly. "But I guess I can't really blame you. After all, it must be embarrassing for you to have your wife and girlfriend at the same party. Anybody'd feel awkward under the circumstances."

"Beth! Will you stop this nonsense," John demanded, staring at her furiously. "You know damn well that all that's over now."

"You've got to be kidding, darling," she said, ignoring his admonishment. "Once in love, always in love, or so the saying goes. Hadn't you heard?" She turned to Stacey. "I think it's absolutely marvelous you have the courage to stay tonight, Stacey, dear," she went on. "But then, how were you to know? I only hope it won't spoil your evening."

"It won't," Stacey said, looking more poised than she felt.

"Well, you'll soon find out for sure, dear," she said triumphantly, as her eyes lingered on a spot behind Stacey. "Here come Leslie and Nick now."

For a brief moment John actually hated Beth, but he tried to ease the tension by greeting the approaching couple. "Nick, Leslie, didn't know you were both coming tonight," he said a little louder than was probably necessary.

Nick smiled sheepishly, his macho Italian charm lost somewhere in the shuffle. "Well, hello everyone," he said, looking

directly at Stacey. Suddenly he understood that she knew that
bringing Leslie had been strictly his sister's idea.

"I didn't know you two knew each other," Stacey said as she
studied Leslie's face.

"We knew each other in New York, then met again this year
during the summer," Leslie replied, trying to be pleasant. "Did
you all have a nice holiday?" she asked as her eyes surveyed the
group, unconsciously coming to rest on Drew. She saw him
flush as her eyes held his captive, but she wasn't about to let
go. "How about you, Drew? Was the holiday everything you
expected?" she asked.

Catching Leslie's innuendo, Drew set his jaw. "It was like a
dream come true," he answered, knowing she'd get his unspoken message. But it was an unusual answer, and Stacey glanced
up at him for a brief moment, then quickly looked at Leslie,
realizing they were communicating with their eyes as well as
their words, but she gave no outward sign of the turmoil it was
causing her.

"How nice," Leslie said, picking her words carefully. "It
isn't everyone who gets to live a dream. Most people merely live
in a dream world, which makes it all the harder when they
suddenly wake up to reality."

Drew's eyes narrowed shrewdly. "Being with Stacey again this
Christmas was better than dreaming," he said softly. "No present could have been greater than having her back."

Leslie wavered. She'd gotten the message, but she wasn't
quite sure she believed it. She tried to smile casually and looked
at Stacey. "I'm pleased the holidays have been so good to you,
Stacey," she said. "But I hope you don't mind starting our
interviews again on Monday. It's been a nice break, but I do
have my work. Shall we say the same time as usual?"

Stacey straightened, Drew's nearness giving her moral support. "Monday will be fine."

Beth frowned. She had been watching the exchange curiously.
"What interviews?" she asked, bewildered.

"Why, Leslie's doing a story about my journey into the
past," Stacey said confidently. "We've been going over the
story for some weeks now."

"She's been going to your house?" Beth asked, shocked at
this new revelation.

"Don't tell me you didn't know?" Stacey said, imitating
Beth's cutting tone. "Why, I'd thought the way gossip travels,
everyone would know by now," she said. She could feel the
tension as Beth's self-satisfaction faded into disbelief.

Beth and Muriel had been so sure that by arranging to have Nick bring Leslie here tonight, they could get even with Stacey for all the heartache she had caused over the years. They had never dreamed the two women had actually met face to face before.

"I hope the revelation hasn't spoiled your evening, Beth," Stacey continued as she watched Beth's consternation. "It'd be a terrible shame to have your new year start out on the wrong foot." For a few moments Stacey felt an exhilaration at the thought of besting Beth, but she knew the evening wasn't over yet.

Beth's mouth was drawn and white. She lifted her glass, only to discover it was empty. She studied it thoughtfully, then turned to John, her eyes misty with frustration.

"I can't have this dear, can I," she said, trying to hold back the tears as she spoke. "My God! What would people think if they saw Beth Morris with an empty glass in her hand!" She straightened, trying to look unaffected and self-assured. "Are you coming, John?" she asked hopefully as she headed toward the bar.

John watched her hesitantly, then turned to the two couples, trying to conceal his humiliation. "Sorry, folks, but I guess I better tag along. You know how it is . . ." He hurried after her, hoping he could talk her out of filling her glass again. Stacey had her doubts. By midnight Beth would probably be passed out somewhere oblivious to the world.

Leslie watched John following after Beth and her eyes were solemn. "A shame, isn't it," she said, then turned to Nick. "You did say we were going to dance, didn't you, Dr. Rigotti?" she asked lightheartedly. "After all, it's New Year's Eve and I did come here to have a good time."

Excusing the two of them, Nick put an arm around Leslie's waist and led her to the dance floor.

Drew was staring absentmindedly after Nick and Leslie when Stacey turned to him with an unsteady voice.

"Drew?"

He wrenched himself away from some unwelcome memories and looked down at Stacey. "Would you like to dance, honey?" he asked.

"I'd love to," she whispered, a reassuring feeling of warm intimacy enveloping her, and Drew sighed, pulling her close as they made their way onto the dance floor.

As the evening wore on, Stacey had to admit she was having a hard time accepting Leslie's presence. Drew stuck close most of the evening, but sometimes it just wasn't convenient and they were obliged to dance with mutual friends. Shortly before midnight, Stacey, who had just finished dancing with one of the doctors from the hospital, left Drew with Craig and some other men and headed for the powder room.

In order to reach it, she had to go down a dimly lit hall, past the library and music room, and use a staircase up to the second floor. She wasn't gone long, but when she returned Drew was nowhere in sight.

She looked for him casually at first until she spotted Nick Rigotti dancing with Muriel. Then suddenly she realized she hadn't seen Leslie either.

She bit her lip, and spotting John, standing near one of the windows, staring out, she quickly made her way to him. She hated to interrupt his thoughts because she knew Beth had passed out in Muriel's bedroom an hour ago, but she needed him.

"John?"

He turned abruptly, his eyes troubled.

"Have you seen Drew?" she asked hurriedly.

"No. Do you want me to help find him?"

She nodded, and they searched the crowd again. If anyone could spot Drew, John could, but he came up with nothing.

"Maybe he went to the men's room," he suggested. Stacey felt like a fool. "I hadn't thought of that."

He escorted her into the empty, dimly lit hall. No one else seemed to be around. "We'll just wait out here," he said, and they moved away from the ballroom entrance, closer to the library door.

John pulled out a cigarette and lit it, then suddenly froze as he saw Stacey tense. He hadn't noticed before. The door to the library was open a crack. He started to ask her what was wrong, but stopped abruptly when she held a finger to her lips and motioned for him to come closer, and they stood near the crack in the door listening to the conversation in the next room.

Drew had wanted to talk to Leslie all evening, but it had been impossible to see her privately. Her appearance tonight had really thrown him. He knew she wasn't a saint, but he never dreamed she'd go along with something like this, and the more he thought about it, the angrier he got. So when he saw her leave the ballroom by herself, undoubtedly on her way to the powder room, he slipped out after her. He caught up with her just outside the library, and his first words made it clear he was furious.

"I don't want to talk about it, Drew," Leslie had said stubbornly. "Not here."

But he wouldn't take no for an answer. He pulled her into the library, and now he stood facing her with blazing eyes. "Why, Les?" he asked again, staring at her vague shadow in the darkened room. "I know you said Nick asked, but you could have said no. You knew we'd be here."

Her eyes smoldered as she stared at him. "Why not?" she said defensively. "I said I'd lay off the interviews over the holidays, but I never promised not to see you."

"You said you wouldn't interfere."

"And I haven't."

"What do you call it?"

"You've had almost two weeks without so much as a hint that I'm alive," she said angrily. "How do you call that interfering?"

"And tonight?"

"Good Lord, Drew, surely one night isn't going to make any difference . . . unless . . . ?"

"Unless what?"

"Unless it isn't working." Her eyes grew apprehensive, yet anxious. "That's it, isn't it?" she said breathlessly.

But he protested. "Don't be ridiculous. Things couldn't be better."

"You mean you can honestly say you haven't thought of me once these past two weeks?"

Thought of her? Drew hesitated. God yes he'd thought of her. But he wasn't about to let her know. Leslie stepped out of the shadows into the moonlight, and he caught the seductive warmth in her deep green eyes.

"Was I supposed to?" he countered, fighting the effect she had on him.

She sighed. "Oh, Drew, for heaven's sake, why do you keep fighting it so? When I walked in here tonight, your eyes told me you cared."

"That's not true."

"Isn't it?" Her voice softened. "Then why are you looking at me like that?"

"I'm trying to understand you. I know you're not purposely cruel, Les, but what you've done by coming here tonight . . . you knew what it'd do to her . . . what it could do to me . . . ."

"Oh, Drew, please don't. Don't blame me too much. I just had to come. I've put in a terrible two weeks. I had to do something to shake you up. Drew, I love you, I always will, and I want you so badly I hurt inside. Do you know what that's like?

You said I wasn't cruel, but right now I hate myself, because I'm not thinking of her, I'm thinking of you and me and what we had together before she came back. I don't want to lose you, Drew."

"You never had me to lose, Les," he replied.

She laughed softly. "Oh yes I did." Her voice was low, sultry. "You can deny it all you want, but I know better, Drew. If Stacey hadn't come back when she did . . ."

"But she did!"

"That doesn't change the facts, Drew," she said. "I knew that two weeks ago, that night in your office. No man kisses a woman the way you kissed me unless he wants her. No, you can kid yourself, but you can't kid me. Your feelings for me haven't changed. . . ."

As Leslie continued to talk, Stacey strained her head against the doorjamb, trying to shut out the words. Two weeks ago? His office? The whole thing sank in. My God! Drew had been seeing her all along. . . .

Stacey stared up at John, her heart pounding, tears in her eyes, as Leslie went on.

"I know I said I'd never ask you to leave her," Leslie was saying. "But God, it's so hard. I need you, Drew, as much as she does. Please, don't be angry because of tonight. I'm not a saint, darling, I'm a woman."

"I wouldn't be in this mess if you weren't," he answered huskily.

"You have to look at it that way, don't you?" she said. "I'm just a complication." She stopped momentarily and took a deep breath. "All right, I concede. What I did tonight was wrong, I shouldn't have come, but I'm glad I did it, because just seeing you again has been worth it." She moved closer to him, putting her hand on the lapel of his tuxedo. "For the first time in my life, I don't care if I've caused hurt, Drew, because she's hurt me too, just by coming back. All I wanted tonight was to see you. Is that asking too much?"

"Les, I . . ."

"Drew, it's almost midnight," she whispered. "Please, Drew . . . one kiss . . . kiss me like the last time. Please, I need you as much as she does . . . I love you . . ."

There was silence from inside the room and Stacey held her breath, waiting. She had expected to hear Drew decline, but all she heard was her own heart pounding. There was no answer from behind the open door. No audible answer at least, and suddenly she realized why. After all, how could he talk if he was kissing her.

She let the realization sink in, and it was more than she could bear. Suddenly she bolted from the doorway and began to hurry down the hall, toward the main part of the house, unaware that John was right on her heels. He reached her in seconds and pulled her into his arms.

"Stacey, Stacey," he said soothingly, his lips against the top of her head. "Please, you don't know what's happening in there. You can't be sure."

"What else, John?" she said tearfully. "Why else couldn't he answer unless he was kissing her?"

John gazed down into her face. She looked so defeated. "Stacey, I wish I could help," he said.

She blinked the tears from her eyes and tilted her head up stubbornly. "Did you know, John?" she asked deliberately. "Did you know he's been seeing her?"

"No," he answered. "But then, we don't know that he has. Not for sure."

"Don't we?" She glanced back toward the library door. "You heard her . . . just before Christmas. John, the past two weeks it's been like old times for us. He's been so different. Now I know why. He's been trying to salve his guilty conscience."

"Don't be silly, honey."

"Oh, John, you heard them. It was all arranged and she promised not to interfere. She couldn't interfere unless he cared, now, could she? I've been such a fool!"

"Love has a nasty way of making fools of us all, Stacey," he said passionately, and she caught her breath at the meaning of his words.

For a few brief moments she had let herself forget that John was in love with her. Now, suddenly, seeing the desire in his eyes, Stacey felt a shiver run through her.

"John, what am I to do?" she said softly. "I need Drew."

"Do you really need Drew, Stacey?" he asked. "Or do you just need someone to love you?"

She stared at him, trying to think of an answer. Her thoughts were in a turmoil. John could soothe the hurt inside her. She knew he could, because he was so like Ben.

She grabbed his hand and held it between her own. She had felt so lost and alone. Now just his sensuous touch filled her with a warm intimacy that took away her horrible feeling of despair. Call it friendship, love, compassion, sympathy—whatever it was, she needed it desperately.

Tears clung to the corners of her blue eyes. "Whatever I need, John, I need it now," she whispered. "I need something to hang on to, something to stop the world from tumbling down so fast around me."

"I'm always here, Stacey," he said softly. "Hang on as long as you want."

"Oh, John, no," she answered. "It isn't fair to you—"

"Hey." He put a finger to her mouth, closing her lips, then held her head so she couldn't avoid his eyes. "Have I ever complained?" he asked huskily.

She bit her lip. She was still holding his other hand and now she brought it to her breast, basking in the strength it gave her. "Thank you for being you, John," she whispered softly. At that moment, an uproar exploded from the ballroom. People began shouting and blowing noisemakers as the orchestra struck up "Auld Lang Syne."

John felt the warmth of her bosom against the back of his hand and the softness of her skin and silkiness of her hair against the fingers of his other hand. Beth was upstairs dead drunk and Drew was in the library with another woman, and he wondered, would Stacey be willing to accept what he wanted so badly to give? He leaned toward her.

"It's midnight," he whispered eagerly. "A new year, Stacey."

She stared at him, mesmerized, her heart overflowing for this man who asked nothing but to love her, and then her lips parted warm and inviting. "Happy New Year, John," she whispered tenderly, and suddenly he knew.

His lips descended slowly, and she didn't back away. The touch was light at first, and much to Stacey's surprise, she felt a warm thrill tingle through her. She hadn't closed her eyes and John's dark eyes were open too, looking deep into hers. The sensation was unnerving, the love in his eyes overwhelming, and suddenly Stacey felt his lips move against her hers in a surge of passion that made her tremble.

Her eyes closed, her head tilted back, and she accepted him, kissing him back with an urgency driven by need, while inside the library Drew had finally answered Leslie after long minutes of silent soul-searching.

"I can't kiss you, Les," he said roughly. "I can't do that to Stacey or myself. Not again. I felt guilty as hell the last time I gave in to my baser instincts." He looked away quickly as a confusion of noise, bells and yelling, accompanied by the strains of "Auld Lang Syne" filtered in through the crack in the door.

"Drew, it's midnight," she said.

But he wouldn't look at her, instead he stared toward the intruding noise.

"I have to find Stacey," he said urgently.

She grabbed his arm as he started for the door. "Drew, not yet, please."

"It's no good, Les," he said with finality. "I told you before, it was over when Stacey came back."

Feeling her fingers begin to ease on his arm, he wished he could bite back the words. Yet he knew he had no choice. "I'm sorry, Les," he said gently. "But it has to be this way."

"I know," she said through her tears. "Only I don't have to like it."

He turned abruptly, opened the door, and stepped into the hallway. For a brief second he hesitated, his eyes adjusting to the dim light, then suddenly he went rigid, his eyes glued on the couple only a few feet away who were deep in an embrace.

His stomach constricted and a savage anger shot through him. It was Stacey. Stacey and John! He stood motionless as Leslie's voice came from behind him, fueling the flame of hatred that was already building inside him. "Well, well, well, and she told me he reminded her of Ben Clayton," and Drew suddenly came to life like an avenging angel, lunging toward the couple still lost in their passionate embrace.

CHAPTER 8

Stacey's heart was in confusion. John's lips caressed hers, her body molding to his, and for a brief few moments while he held her, she forgot the hurt and anger she had felt while listening outside the library door. For a few minutes it felt good to be loved and held and comforted by this big strong man who reminded her so often of Ben.

But before she had a chance to even begin to sort out the confusion inside her, she was violently ripped from John's arms as Drew attacked and took a swing at John's chin. Startled, John threw up his arms to defend himself.

"Dammit, Drew!" he yelled as he hit the wall. "What the hell's the matter with you?"

"The matter with me?" cried Drew. "I find you making love to my wife and you ask what's the matter with me?" He took another swing, but John caught his arms, holding him off. "I'll kill you, you bastard," Drew shouted.

John braced himself, tightening his grip on Drew's arms, and suddenly realized people were filtering in from the ballroom and the three of them were the center of attention.

"Drew, for Christ's sake cut it out!" John panted as he held him at bay. "You've got it all wrong. It's New Year's Eve, remember. We're friends. I was just wishing her a Happy New Year."

"The hell you were," snarled Drew. "That was no friendly New Year's kiss."

Drew's eyes were vicious, and the veins in his neck were like taut cords. His face was livid, and John saw he was beyond all reason. Yet, he knew he had to stop Drew.

John glanced past Stacey, and caught sight of Leslie near the open library door. Her face was ashen, eyes centered on Drew.

"All right," John gasped breathlessly, his dark eyes narrowing shrewdly. "I concede, I got a little carried away. But what about you, Drew," he whispered brutally, so that only Drew could hear. "What about you and Leslie in the library? Why do you think your wife was so willing to fall into my arms? You should take better care in shutting doors, Drew. Stacey and I heard every word the two of you said.''

Drew froze, staring at John, and suddenly, he felt helpless, his jealous fury subsiding. Wrenching his arms from John's, he straightened, took a deep breath, then became conscious of the murmuring voices of the crowd around him.

He reddened, his jaw tightening as he stared at the man he had always called his friend. He smoothed his clothes and turned to Stacey, aware of the anguish in her face.

''Don't ever go near him again,'' he demanded caustically. She inhaled sharply, stifling her own angry words. She couldn't respond, not in front of all these people. She had enough to live down as it was. She looked quickly at John, but he motioned for her to go with Drew.

''Don't worry, it'll be all right,'' he said firmly.

She turned to Drew, her eyes smoldering.

''I think it's time we left,'' Drew said angrily, but Craig's booming voice interrupted him.

''Drew, did I hear you say you're leaving?'' he asked incredulously. He was waving a noisemaker and carrying a drink in his other hand. ''Hey, you can't leave. It's barely midnight. What way is that to celebrate the new year?'' He glanced around. ''And what the hell's been going on anyway?'' he asked, suddenly aware of the tension permeating the hall.

''Let John explain,'' Drew said belligerently. ''He's always so good at explanations. Now, if you don't mind, Craig,'' he took Stacey's arm. ''Stacey and I've had a marvelous time, the party was grand, but it's over now. At least for us. The new year's in and I'm tired . . .''

Craig started to protest but Muriel stopped him, discreetly explaining the scandal everyone would be talking about for months to come, while in the foyer, Drew helped Stacey on with her coat, then ushered her out to the car.

It was bitter cold and the snow was crisp beneath their feet. As she slid into the passenger seat, Stacey fought the tears that threatened her eyes. She could see her breath in the air and huddled deeper into the warmth of the mink. She wasn't going to give in, not this time. Drew slid into the seat beside her, started the car, and they headed down the long drive. She waited for Drew to break the deadlock, but he only concentrated on his driving and said nothing.

Anger was simmering in every nerve of Drew's body. If he'd been capable of murder, he would have strangled John on the spot, but then he remembered the words John had whispered in his ear. Stacey had heard everything!

He glanced at her surreptitiously. Still, that was no excuse for kissing John like that. Suddenly he winced as a pang of guilt gripped him, and he remembered the way he had kissed Leslie that night in his office. But the memory of that kiss only made matters worse. He had kissed Leslie because he had wanted her so badly and now he was certain that Stacey had kissed John for the same reason. He knew his reasoning didn't make sense, but he was too angry to care.

They had stopped for the light at the bottom of the hill and Drew tensed, sensing Stacey was about to say something. "Don't you dare say you're sorry," he snarled, stopping her.

She glanced at him in surprise. "Me? Sorry?" she snapped back. "Don't worry, I don't intend to say I'm sorry. I wouldn't give you the satisfaction even if I were, but I'm not!"

"I didn't think so."

Her eyes were blazing. "Well, why should I be sorry? I don't hear you begging for any forgiveness, and you're the one who started it, not me!"

She saw his quick intake of breath; then the light changed. He started to ram his foot down on the accelerator, but caught the brief glimpse of a police car just in time. It was backed into a spot along the riverbank, across the highway. He exhaled and eased up on the accelerator, and instead of roaring across the highway, the car slowly glided past the police car at the speed limit.

Stacey knew it was killing Drew not to be able to vent his temper on something, even the car. Her own knuckles were white as she clutched her velvet evening bag.

"What's the matter, Drew?" she retorted as they left the intersection behind. "No accusations? Don't tell me you're not going to lecture me about how scandalous and unfaithful I've been. It couldn't be that you're going to let me have the floor for a change?"

He watched a few snowflakes begin to fall, his eyes brooding. "All right, just what did you hear outside the library door?" he asked belligerently.

She fumed. "Enough!"

"That's not an answer."

She turned toward him to watch his reaction as well as she could in the dark. "All right . . . how long have you been seeing her?" she asked deliberately. "Since that first day when you came home so eager to have me do her story? Or maybe before that? Did she kiss you and tell you that I'd never suspect a thing?''

"That's not the way it was."

"Then how was it? And make it good, Drew, because I don't like being played for a fool!''

"I saw her the first day she came back, then not again until the Friday before Christmas, when she came to the office to tell me she suspected something had gone on between you and Ben.''

"Only twice?"

His hands were cold as they tightened on the wheel. "I told her about you and Ben and then I told her that what happened between us was a mistake.''

"Was that before or after you kissed her?"

"For Christ's sake, Stacey," he yelled. "Will you stop it! This won't get us anywhere.''

"Won't it?" She tilted her head up stubbornly. "Well, I'll tell you, Drew. It's going to get me the truth for a change,'' she said. "You're always accusing me, but the shoe's on the other foot now. Yes, I kissed John. I kissed him because I was hurt. Because I'd just heard a woman ask my husband to kiss her and I sure as hell didn't hear him say no. Tell me, Drew, why was it all right for you to kiss Leslie in the library, but not for me to kiss John in the hall?''

"I didn't kiss Leslie," he said firmly.

Stacey laughed. "You didn't . . . You don't expect me to believe that, do you?''

"It's the truth."

"Come on, Drew. If you didn't kiss her, then why didn't I hear any refusal when she so eloquently asked?''

"Maybe because you didn't stay around long enough," he said flatly.

She stared at him confused. It was hard to see in the dark, but dammit, Drew looked like he was telling the truth. She hesitated, remembering the long silence in the library. "I don't believe you,'' she said slowly. "I listened outside that door too long.''

"But I didn't kiss her . . . not tonight."

"Drew, I heard!"

"You heard what you wanted to hear," he replied angrily. "Maybe because it makes your own guilt a little easier to take.''

"My guilt?" She stared at him incredulously. "Oh yes," she said complacently, as he pulled off the main road, heading up the drive. "I did kiss John, didn't I? Of course it's all right for you to kiss Leslie anytime you want, as long as you don't get caught, right? I guess that's what I did wrong. I wasn't discreet enough. Well, I promise, the next time I'll be more careful.''

"There won't be a next time!"

"Is that a threat?"

"Dammit, I don't care what you call it!" He stopped in front of the garage doors, hit the button to open them, then drove inside. "I'm not going to have my wife making a fool of me in front of the whole town." He slammed on the brakes and shoved the car into park, hit the door button again, then shut off the motor. "My kissing Leslie has nothing to do with you and John," he retorted. "I didn't want to kiss her that night, but I couldn't help myself."

"Don't give me that," Stacey cried furiously. "You kissed her because you wanted to! Well, I kissed John because I wanted to, because it was New Year's Eve and my husband was kissing another woman. So who's guilty of what?"

They stared at each other hard, both their eyes flashing. Moonlight coming in the garage window filtered into the car and fell across Stacey's face, and without warning, Drew's heart turned over at the sight. Her eyes were wide, and the contours of her face were shadowed sensuously in the moonlight. He swallowed hard, and took a deep breath as he felt a tingling sensation creep through him. "Stacey, for God's sake, do you know what I went through when I saw you in John's arms?" Drew asked breathlessly.

"The same thing I went through when I heard what was going on between you and Leslie," she answered helplessly.

He touched her face. "There's nothing going on between us," he insisted softly. "Please, honey, believe me, I've told you. There was a time, when you weren't here, that she became a part of my life. But it's over between us. You have to believe that."

"Is it over between you? No, Drew," she said reluctantly. "I don't think it is. Ben's dead, Leslie's not. I can't cope with that. I don't know how to compete."

"There's no reason for you to compete."

"Yes there is. Every time I see her I'm reminded of how much younger she is and I feel inadequate. I know you still care about her, Drew. As she said in the library, you can deny it all you want, but it shows in your eyes whenever you look at her. Until tonight I'd never seen the two of you together, but now I know. Well, I'm through living in a dream world, Drew. I'm through pretending I'm the only woman in your life and that everything's just like it used to be."

He saw the tears in her eyes. "Stacey, honey, I didn't know

. . . I don't like what I feel for Leslie, I can't even understand it, but I know it hasn't changed how I feel about you. Please don't let her come between us.''

"She's already done it, Drew," she said flatly. "Can't you see that? What we have together just isn't the same. We tried to recapture it the past few days, but it won't last. It can't be any other way simply because she exists."

"No! It won't ever end for us, honey," he whispered desperately. "I won't let it. You're my whole life and I'll make it up to you. I promise, I'll do anything."

"All I want is your love, Drew," Stacey said. "Nothing more. But I can't share it. I'm no good at that sort of thing."

"Neither am I," he said. "That's why I got so mad tonight, honey. I could no more share you with John than I could ask you to share my love."

"Do you really have any control over it, Drew?" she asked. "I didn't ask to fall in love with Ben or even you for that matter. People can't always control their emotions. So how are you going to tell yourself not to care about Leslie?"

He knew she was right, but he couldn't admit it. The last few days had been too good. He pulled her close and bent his lips to her neck, but she stiffened beneath his hands. "Stacey, please," he whispered softly, his breath warm against her flesh. "Don't turn from me. I blew up like a madman, but when I saw you and John . . . I didn't know you were hurting too. I don't want to hurt you."

His hands slid inside her coat as his lips traveled up her neck, searching for her mouth.

Stacey tried to be indifferent to his lovemaking, but their years of intimacy overpowered her anger. A giddy warmth spread through her, sliding down her back and exploding in her loins. However deep the pain of Drew's betrayal, to turn from him was impossible.

The kiss was deep, sensuous and demanding, and she answered him passionately, hoping to still the ache that made her feel empty and lost deep inside.

After long moments, Drew released her lips. "When we drove up I noticed the lights were out," he whispered urgently. "That means Renee and Chris aren't home yet. We have the whole house to ourselves, darling. We can bring in the new year the right way."

Her eyes grew distant and she stared at him, bewildered. "Do you really mean what you just said?" she asked incredulously.

He looked puzzled. "Why not? What's to stop us?"

"Do you honestly think we can just forget everything that's happened tonight and make love?"

"Don't you?"

She shook her head hesitantly. "I don't know." She looked away, feeling the cold that was beginning to penetrate the car now with the heater shut off. "Drew, I don't know if I'm ready," she said helplessly. "I can't just shut off the hurt as if it were controlled by a switch."

"Can't we try?" he asked. "If I can understand about John, can't you understand how I feel in all this?"

"But it isn't the same," she said reflectively. "I kissed John, yes, but I'm not in love with him. Can you say the same about Leslie Kyle?"

He studied the anguish in Stacey's face, and suddenly her question took on a significance he had never dreamed he would ever have to face. How could he rationalize what he felt for Leslie? He had to admit that seeing her with Nick Rigotti had been surprisingly hard to take.

His eyes bored into Stacey's. What could he say? How should he answer? He couldn't hurt her . . . and yet. Did he dare lie and say he didn't care at all?

"I'll be honest with you, honey," he finally said, a rough edge to his voice. "I don't know how to answer because I can't analyze what I feel for Leslie. But I do know how I feel about you. I love you, Stacey, and nothing else matters. Nothing!"

But Stacey couldn't agree. He was lying to himself, and she knew it. She stared at him, wishing the world could change. If she could only go back to what they had before, or go back to Ben. Anything but face what she was forced to face here. But it wouldn't change. They could never be the same again. And yet she needed Drew to erase the empty feeling that gripped her. "I'm willing to try," she whispered softly. "But first, you have to know that I can't go through with the interviews anymore. Oh, don't worry, she'll still get her story. I'll use my tape recorder and send her the rest. But I won't have her in my house again. I can't."

"If that's the way you want it, honey. I want you to be happy." He kissed her lightly. "Now, can we try to salvage some of tonight?" he asked. "Or are we going to stay at each other's throats over something that neither of us can change?"

"It *will* be a Happy New Year, won't it, Drew?" she asked anxiously.

"The happiest," he said huskily. He smiled, forcing himself

to accept that they were both at fault and knowing the forgiving had to begin somewhere.

Later, after their lovemaking, Stacey lay in Drew's arms and the tears came freely. They were tears of pain and hurt, and tears she wasn't certain wouldn't come again, because although Drew swore he loved her more than life itself, she also knew Leslie had managed to knock a chink in the armor that surrounded that love and she couldn't forget it. Even while Drew kissed her and took her, she was tormented by the knowledge that his love was no longer hers alone. And because of her doubts and fears, it hadn't been the same, and she wondered if it would ever be the same again.

New Year's morning, Stacey stretched in bed, and squinted against the bright sunlight streaming through the window. For a few minutes the night before seemed like a nightmare overwhelming her, and she had to fight the despair that tried to grip her. She glanced at the empty bed next to her. Drew rarely got up this early, especially when they had been out late the night before. She frowned, ready to throw back the covers and climb out when he waltzed into the room carrying a large bed tray.

"Hey, where do you think you're going?" he asked playfully. "Stay in there. You're going to start the new year with breakfast in bed."

"But the bed'll get full of crumbs," she protested, pulling herself into a sitting position. "Really, Drew. What about you and the girls?"

"Renee is still in bed, and Chris is on the phone with Roger. She ate half an hour ago. I guess they're going tobogganing today."

"And you?"

"I'm going to climb in and join you."

Stacey saw the familiar crinkle to his eyes and her heart constricted. He was trying so hard to make it right again. He set the tray in front of her, then moved over to his own side of the bed, climbing in.

"What better way to enjoy a meal," he said tenderly as he moved close to her. "We can make love between bites. Now, let's forget about last night and really make it a new year," and he lifted the lid off a steaming dish of scrambled eggs and ham.

They had finished their breakfast and were talking and laughing quietly when Chris suddenly appeared in the doorway staring at them. Her face was drained of color and her pale blue eyes were rimmed with red as if she'd been crying.

"What is it, Chris?" asked Stacey, concerned.

"You had to do it, didn't you, Mother?" she accused, gulping back sobs. "You just had to spoil it, didn't you!"

Stacey's mouth gaped open. "What on earth . . . what are you talking about?" she asked bewildered.

Chris's eyes sifted over her mother, and for the first time in her life she saw what others saw when they looked at Stacey Gordon. This wasn't her mother, this was a beautiful, sensuous woman capable of seducing any man with just a look from her brilliantly blue eyes. She was a gorgeous woman, but to Chris the idea of her mother as a sex object was appalling.

Chris swallowed hard, hating what her mother suddenly represented. "I was just talking to Roger," she said, trying to control her tears. "He called to say he couldn't go tobogganing with me. He said his mother has forbidden him to see me again . . . he isn't even allowed to talk to me on the phone anymore, and all because of something that happened last night." She was crying hard now. "He said Dad caught you and his father making love and there was a fight and . . . he said everyone's talking about it, and I'll never be able to see Roger again . . . and I'm so ashamed!" Her hands flew to her face and she covered it, sobbing into them. "So ashamed . . ."

"Chris, it was all a mistake, honey," Stacey began, but Chris cut her off.

"No! Don't try to tell me that," she cried furiously. "Don't try to pretend everyone else is wrong and you're right, because it won't work." She straightened rigidly, her petite body stiffening in anger. "I love Roger, Mother, we . . . we've even talked about getting married someday, but now his parents will never consent . . . and all because of you . . . because you can't stay away from men! I hate you!" she screamed hysterically, running from the room and they heard her bedroom door slam shut with a fury.

Drew cursed and started to go after her, but Stacey stopped him. "It won't help, Drew, please," she pleaded as she held his arm. "Let her cry it out. Right now she hates me, and I can't blame her. There's no way she's going to understand. All she knows is that her heart's been broken. Let her hate me for awhile if it'll make the hurt any easier to bear."

Drew looked at the tears rimming Stacey's eyes. "She had no right to talk to you like that," he said grimly.

"I know," she agreed. "But right now I don't much care who has what rights. Right now I just feel numb." She paused. "Do you think we could call Beth and try to explain?"

"You've got to be kidding. By now everybody in town probably knows all the sordid details whether they were there or not, and you know how Muriel likes to gloss things up." Stacey flinched and Drew's eyes softened. "Don't worry, honey. We can live it down," he said as he pulled her into his arms.

But Stacey wasn't so sure, and the next few days proved her right. Whenever she had occasion to go into the village, backs were turned to her, and conversations were short and curt. Even Chris remained cool toward her, although she apologized for her outburst. When Stacey tried to explain she knew Chris didn't believe her and wondered if maybe she should have told Chris about Drew's part in the evening's events. But how could she tell her daughter that her mother kissed another man because her father was kissing another woman? You didn't spring things like that on innocent young girls who were just learning about life and love.

The tension was relieved some, but then John's daughter Sheila made sure Renee heard about it when they ran into each other over the weekend, and by that time the story was that Stacey and John had been surprised in bed together in one of the Paxton's guestrooms.

By Monday morning, however, Stacey and Drew had managed to convince both girls that the whole thing had been magnified way out of proportion, although Stacey wasn't sure they had managed to convince Chris enough to really ease her mind. But Roger had seen Chris on the sly in order to say good-bye before leaving for college, and she was somewhat appeased.

Over the weekend, Stacey canceled her interviews with Leslie, then spent the next week making tapes and sent them off. After that, she was left again with a lot of spare time on her hands, and by the end of the following week was so bored she wanted to scream. She had picked up the guitar again, but the melancholy music only depressed her, and she had even called several charitable organizations to volunteer her time, but no one was interested. It seemed strange they all seemed to have plenty of help this year. She couldn't even get on the committee to save the seals, and finally gave up trying.

She knew she was being systematically snubbed. Well, who the hell cared! It was Friday morning. Stacey sat at the kitchen table with a cup of coffee, listening to Mrs. Garret vacuuming in another part of the house. She had made up her mind barely ten minutes ago, and now it was just a matter of carrying out her decision.

She finished her coffee and picked up the phone. After several rings, a voice answered.

"Dr. Morris here."

"John?" Her voice was so weak she barely recognized it. "John, it's me. Stacey."

He inhaled sharply. "Stacey? Are you all right? You sound so strange and far away."

"I'm all right." She straightened. "How've you been?"

"Fine . . . at least I think I have."

"John, may I come see you?" she asked anxiously.

He hesitated. "Across the street?"

"No, there at your office at the hospital."

"When?"

"Today, this morning, this afternoon . . . please, John, it's important. I'll duck in quietly so no one will see me, but I have to talk to you. Is it all right?"

"You know better than to ask that." He glanced at the clock on the wall. "Can you come right now? I have to go up on the floor to see a few patients, but I should be down again by ten-fifteen."

"I'll make it. And, thanks, John."

She hung up reluctantly. It had been good to hear his voice again. There was something calm and soothing about him, yet . . . but she wouldn't think of that now. It wasn't the time. She dressed quickly, told Mrs. Garret she was going shopping, and drove to the hospital.

When she arrived at his office, John greeted her warmly. "Take your coat?" he asked.

She hugged her arms. "If you don't mind, I'm still cold."

"Then come over by the heater," he offered, and they walked over to the window where the wall heaters were and Stacey held her hands out to warm herself.

"Now that the formalities are out of the way, what's it all about?" he asked, glancing at her curiously.

"John, I want to come back to work," she said and saw a startled look come into his already troubled eyes. "Please, John, listen to me first before you give a flat no. I've been trying . . . I can do just so much sewing, and Mrs. Garret does the cleaning, and . . . It's for my sanity, John," she said abruptly.

He stared at her, his eyes darkening. "Is it that bad?"

"I suppose it could be worse. But I think if the house were burning down they wouldn't even send out the fire department.

No one talks to me. Then there are all the organizations I used to belong to. Funny how they suddenly don't need any help. No, it's not bad, John. It's terrible. It's disgusting what they're doing.''

"Stacey!" he said, reaching for her.

"No," she cried, pulling away. "I didn't come here for that."

He stared at her thoughtfully. "Does Drew know what you're planning?" he asked.

"No," she said. "But I'll tell him tonight."

"Oh joy."

"I know, but I have to do this, John. I can't just sit at home and stagnate. They've stopped me every other way, but here you're the boss. You can't afford to turn down a good surgical nurse. I know you can't. Please, John."

"And if Drew blows a gasket?"

"Let me handle Drew. Just say you'll do it."

"If I do . . . you know what they're going to say, Stacey."

"I know, but they're saying it anyway, so what's the difference?"

He studied her for a long time until a flush began to creep into her face and he realized she was becoming uneasy. "You're not really happy, are you?" he asked thoughtfully.

She sighed. "I will be as soon as you say I can come back to work," she whispered lightly. "Please, John?"

He relaxed a little, his big frame slumping in resignation. "All right," he conceded. "You knew I wouldn't say no, didn't you?"

"I was hoping."

"You can start Monday morning if it's all right with Drew."

"Thanks, John. Oh, thank you so much," she said. "You just saved my life."

"Don't bet on it too heavily, Stacey," he said unsmiling. "The day may come when you'll wish I'd said no."

"Never, John." She rose to leave, then paused for a minute. "Oh, by the way, you don't agree with Beth about the kids, do you?" she asked.

"You know better than that."

"I just had to be sure. You see, Roger's writing to Chris and I know Beth doesn't know it, but if anything ever comes of the two of them, I'd sure like to know that you're on their side."

"You can count on it."

"Thanks again," she said affectionately. "And don't look so serious. I'll see you Monday morning."

"My first surgery's at nine, a gallbladder. You just want to watch the first day, or get your feet wet?"

"I'll be here bright and early to pick instruments for you, Doctor," she said congenially. "Now I'd better go home and try to figure out how to break the news to Drew."

"I don't envy you."

"I don't blame you. But it'll be all right. It has to be, because I don't intend to go crazy staying at home." She paused again at the door. "Good-bye, John, and thanks again for everything."

"My pleasure," he said huskily, watching her leave, and he hoped he hadn't made a mistake.

CHAPTER 9

Drew sat at the kitchen table, the food on his plate growing cold. "You what!" he shouted heatedly.

Stacey forced herself not to cringe, but Renee and Chris both jumped and stared at her warily. "I said I've decided to go back to work at the hospital," she replied calmly.

"Why?"

"Because I can't stand sitting here day after day doing nothing, Drew. I have to have a purpose, you know that."

"What happened to all your charities? All those luncheons and meetings you used to go to?"

"What happened? New Year's Eve happened, that's what," she said. "Suddenly this town's swarming with volunteers for everything from school projects to sit-ins and protests. I probably couldn't even join the YWCA if I wanted to."

"Then why don't you just stay home where you belong?"

"Where I belong? Since when have you been a chauvinist?"

"Don't be ridiculous. I'm just wondering why you have to work. Why don't you just go skiing or skating, or go back to your sculpturing or your music? There are a dozen things you can do besides working."

"And do all of them by myself. How nice. Don't you see, Drew," she pleaded. "I'm tired of being by myself. I want to be around people. I can do that at the hospital."

"And you can see Dr. John Morris at the hospital too, can't you?" he said viciously.

"Drew, I thought we had that all settled."

"I guess it wasn't as settled as you thought. And there's another thing. What do you think he's going to tell Beth? That you're just a cozy little twosome working side by side again?"

"Oh, for heaven's sake, Drew! Do you have to do this in front of the girls?" she pleaded anxiously.

"I'd rather they heard it from us, instead of the gossips in town! Listen, Stacey, I've gone along with you on a lot of things, but don't ask me to do this! I gave up Leslie, you can give up John."

"Give up John? You haven't heard a word I've said, have you? All I want to do is get out of this house where I can meet people, Drew. No one will let me do anything. The clerk at the post office won't even talk to me when I buy stamps."

"What makes you think it's going to be any different at the hospital?"

"Because I won't have to work with the patients on the floor. I'll be doing surgery, and the doctors know that a person's reputation has nothing to do with her abilities in O.R. Drew, it's a godsend for me, and John said I can start work Monday morning if I want."

"You've already talked to John?"

She eyed him sheepishly. "I went to see him today. He said it's okay, if you'll agree. Please, Drew," she pleaded. "I need this. I'll go crazy if I have to stay home every day trying to find things to do."

He stared at her hard. It was the same old argument all over again. Throw her in with John, listen to the gossip and watch Beth getting worse every day. The scars of New Year's Eve had been dug too deep and his heart constricted jealously as he tried to come to some decision. If he said no, she'd probably do it anyway. Then what? Well, he was going to find out, because he'd be damned if he'd say yes. There were other things she could do.

He stood up, his face pale, hazel eyes grim. "I'm sorry, Stacey," he said sternly. "I can't sanction it."

"And if I go anyway?"

"You go without my consent."

"Then I guess that's the way it'll have to be," she said stubbornly.

He glared at her, his eyes narrowing. He had to get out of there and quick, before he said something he'd really regret, because at the moment he hated her stubborn independence more than he ever dreamed he would. He pushed back his chair, then walked to the closet and pulled out his boots, shoving his feet in forcefully, his back to her, while Chris and Renee watched out of the corner of their eyes. Then he grabbed his sheepskin lined coat and put it on, heading toward the kitchen door.

"Where are you going?" she asked.

His eyes shimmered, challenging her with their intensity. "Out!" he shouted resentfully. "Just out! And I don't know when the hell I'll be back either."

Stacey winced as the door slammed shut, and sat motionless for a few minutes, her lips pursed. Then slowly, she reached up, pulling the curtain aside and peeked out in time to see Drew's car swing out of the garage and head down the drive.

"What happens now, Mom?" asked Chris uneasily.

"Why, nothing," Stacey said, frowning hopefully. "Your father will probably cool down and I'll start work at the hospital Monday morning and everything will be all right, you'll see."

"I sure hope so, Mom," Chris said. "But I don't know . . . I don't think I've ever seen Dad that mad before."

Chris was right. He'd never been so angry before. But then, Stacey had never crossed him so badly either. But she couldn't compromise this time. If she did, she'd never respect herself again. Anyway, Drew would give in, she was sure of it. She let Chris and Renee finish clearing the dishes away, then brushed her misgivings aside and went to her bedroom.

She looked around, feeling a little lost and alone for a few minutes, and then her eyes fell on the bottom drawer of the dresser and without realizing it a warm sensation swept through her. The diary. With Drew's angry words still ringing in her ears, she was tempted to find solace in those pages.

She started toward the dresser, then changed her mind. No, not tonight. If she was ever going to forgive Drew's angry words, consoling herself with Ben's love wasn't the way. She turned quickly and left the room.

Drew drove around for almost an hour. He wasn't going anywhere special, and he went through the motions of driving automatically. When he found himself out in Chardon, he went around the square once, then headed back toward Mayfield Road and Gates Mills. But the closer he got to the village, the more he realized that he couldn't go home yet. He was still too angry.

A few minutes later he found himself pulling up in front of a small ranch-style home in Lyndhurst. No one seemed to be home, and he was glad, because he really had no right to be here. He stared at the house for a long time, wondering if maybe . . . Why the hell had he come here anyway? Dammit, he knew why! Stacey had just shoved him out again. She'd hurt him again, only this time the hurt had been deeper than anything she'd ever done before, because she had done it deliberately. It was the same as saying she didn't care what he thought. Well, dammit all, he cared . . . he loved her and he cared, and he didn't like being shut out of her life!

He clenched his jaw and was about to shove the car into drive when he glanced out the window. A small blue Gremlin was pulling up alongside his Olds. Leslie rolled down her window and smiled broadly. "I knew right away it was your car," she said affectionately.

Drew felt uneasy. He wasn't sure he wanted her to know he was here.

But she didn't seem to notice his discomfiture. "In fact," she said hurriedly, the cold air turning her breath to steamy crystals, "I was planning to call you Monday morning."

"Call me?"

"Drew, we have to talk. It's about the story. How about now? Can you come in for coffee?"

"I don't know."

"Oh, for God's sake, Drew, you'd better come in. You look like you could use a friend, and I'm sure you're not sitting here simply because you like looking at my sister's house."

"You know me pretty well, don't you?" he said, trying to smile.

Her eyes caught his and held. "Better than you think," she said. "Now, follow me in. You can park behind my car."

He pulled in the drive behind her little Gremlin, got out, then helped her with some of her packages.

"Don't worry, no one'll know you're here," she assured him as she opened the door and they set the packages down on the boot bench in the small foyer. She took off her shoe boots and stood in her stocking feet. "My sister, her husband and the kids left this afternoon," she informed him. "It's his folks wedding anniversary tomorrow, and they won't be home until Sunday."

He stared at her uncomfortably, frowning at the effect her words had on him. They were alone in the house and he suddenly realized how lovely she looked. Her cheeks were red from the cold, and her lips void of lipstick, her only makeup a little mascara and eyeshadow. He watched her readjust her burgundy hairband and casually arrange her long blond hair in waves across her shoulders. It was fascinating.

"What are you staring at?" she asked curiously as she hung her coat in the closet.

He frowned. "You."

"Oh." She blushed. "Take off your boots, hang up your coat and I'll get some coffee started," she said, and flipped a switch, flooding the house with light as she headed for the kitchen.

Drew watched her walk away. Her slacks and sweater were burgundy too, and she'd been wearing the same white coat and hat she'd had on that night she'd come to his office. He was tempted to forget the whole thing and walk out, but a defiant streak made him hesitate. Without letting himself think about it, he took off his coat and boots, then followed her into the kitchen.

"Now, what were you doing out front?" she asked matter-of-factly.

He stood in the doorway, staring at her. "Do I have to answer that now?"

"Well, for a man who said there was nothing between us, it seems a strange thing to do."

"Stacey and I had a fight."

"And I'm to console the loser?"

He shook his head. "I don't know what I'm doing here," he said abruptly.

"I'm sorry, Drew," she said. "I didn't mean it like it sounded."

"I know you didn't, it's just that . . . I feel empty and confused and . . . dammit, Leslie, I've been trying so hard."

She moved close to him and fingered the front of his shirt. "What did she do?"

"She said she's going back to work at the hospital."

"The one where Dr. Morris works?"

"Yeah."

"So you said no."

"But she will anyway," he said angrily. "And there's not a damn thing I can do to stop her, short of leaving her."

"And it's not worth it?"

"I can't leave her, Les."

She gazed up at him, wondering how he could love someone who tormented him so much. "What do you want me to do, Drew?" she asked abruptly.

"I don't know." Suddenly he was very aware of her nearness and the faint smell of her perfume. Slowly he reached out, taking her face between his hands and looked deeper into her eyes. A flood of warmth filled him, and his empty despair was replaced by a throbbing urgency. He bent down and reverently touched her lips with his. Seconds later, he drew back, still mesmerized by the fervent love in her eyes. "Why do you always make me feel so good, so alive," he whispered breathlessly.

"Because I love you so much," she said.

He took a deep breath and his large frame trembled at the pleasurable sensations that were wreaking havoc on his loins. God, what would it be like to hold her in his arms and forget everything but the feel of her.

His hands dropped from her face, and he pulled her close, his body molding to hers. "If I could take you to my heart and fill you with all the longing I possess, what would it be like?" he asked, surprising her, and she didn't know what to say. "If I could fill the emptiness inside me with what you have to give, would it make everything all right? Or would I hate myself and you when it was over and never be able to face the world complete again? Ah, Leslie, if I only knew what waited for me in your arms."

Leslie stared up at him, amazed at the passionate yearning in his words. It was a side of Drew she'd never seen before, and it fascinated her.

"Do you know what I'm asking, Les?" he said, and she swallowed hard.

"Yes," she whispered breathlessly. "I know."

"Yet, I can't decide," he groaned helplessly. "I want to be a man again. To love, to feel, but not on her terms, on mine. I want to give myself completely, not to soothe or appease, but simply because I'm me and love is love. But if I do . . . what happens to me then?"

Her eyes filled with tears.

"I shouldn't have come tonight," he whispered passionately. "I don't know how to say what I'm feeling. I'm only confusing you."

"No," she said softly. "I know what you mean, Drew. You're wondering, if you make love to me, will you hate yourself for it afterward. Isn't that it?"

"I guess that's it."

"Do you think you would?"

He shook his head. "I don't know. Once I'd have said yes, but tonight : . . I don't know what I feel, Les. Right now I want you so badly I ache inside, but will going home and making love to Stacey make the ache go away? She used to soothe me, but now she only gives me pain because I can't help wondering if she really loves me, or if she just needs me. I don't want to be just needed, Les. I want to be loved and wanted. Les, help me find an answer," he begged helplessly, but she shook her head.

"I can't tell you what to do, Drew. I begged you once. I won't again." She pulled away and went to the cupboard for the coffee cups.

He watched her reach up and take them down, realizing that it wasn't just her body he wanted to possess, but her thoughts and everything about her. For the first time since Stacey's return he admitted to himself that he had missed Leslie terribly. The long walks with her, the fun they'd had taking pictures together for her stories, and laughing like kids at times. And there were moments spent alone, just the two of them, without the need of words to bring contentment, when it took all the strength he had to keep from making love to her. God, how he wanted her. But he hesitated, wondering if he just felt this way because of Stacey. Damn! He watched absentmindedly as Leslie set the cups on the table and poured the coffee, then suddenly he cursed softly to himself. What a fool he'd been. Had it bothered Stacey to give herself to Ben Clayton? Had it bothered her to rush into John's arms? She felt no guilt for her betrayal. Why should he?

He watched Leslie's face as she held the cup of steaming coffee out for him to take. His eyes were unwavering as he slowly took the cup from her and set it back down on the table, then he raised her hand and kissed the palm. It felt soft against his lips.

"Where's the bedroom?" he whispered huskily.

She held her breath, then motioned toward the other part of the house with her head. "In there."

"Lead me," he commanded softly.

"You're sure?" she asked.

He nodded. "I'm sure."

She twined her fingers about his hand and led him to the master bedroom.

"It's their bedroom," she said tremulously.

He squeezed her hand. "This'll do fine." He stared at the bed and felt the surge of passion building up within him.

"Leslie!" he whispered passionately.

She moved toward him, and he grabbed her hungrily, pressing her head against his chest, love for her filling every fiber of his being.

He caught her head and lifted it until her mouth was beneath his. "I love you, Les," he whispered roughly, and their lips touched.

The kiss was deep, sensuous. His hands traveled down her body and he kneaded the skin across her back, slipping his hands inside her slacks, smoothing her well-rounded contours. Her body moved beneath his hands, exciting him beyond reason, and with one quick motion he swung her up and sprawled with her haphazardly onto the bed.

She ended up beneath him, and he laughed gently, burying his lips in the warmth of her neck. "I hope we didn't break the springs," he said amused.

She laughed lightheartedly. "We didn't."

Suddenly Drew grew serious as his hand moved up beneath her bra, pushing it aside until the mound of flesh beneath it filled his hand, then his fingertips stroked her nipples until they hardened. Her body yielded, and the rest was easy. He undressed her as if performing a ritual, then stripped himself and stretched out beside her.

She felt so soft and warm. His mouth caught hers hungrily as the fire of passion burned through him. His hand moved down her body, pulling her even closer in his arms, and he thought nothing of Stacey, only of this woman beside him whose flesh was filling him with a rapture that made him whole again. He kissed her and caressed her, his body tantalizing her until she wanted to crawl inside him. Her legs were long and supple, and she lifted them, arching her body up when he moved over her, and with a groan wrenched from deep inside, he entered, thrusting hard, and felt a pulsing throb begin to swell, filling him until he was consumed by it.

Leslie wrapped her slim legs about him like a vise, holding him inside her, then moved with the rhythm of his thrusts until she exploded in a peak of pleasure that made her cry out. Half-choking with delight, she sighed as she felt Drew shudder above her, and plunge deeply into her flesh one last time, then lay still.

Slowly, his lips moved to her neck, searching for her mouth. His kiss was long and seemed to suck the life from her, leaving her spent. He drew his mouth from hers and let his head drop into her blond hair spread across the pillow, his lips barely touching her ear.

"My God!" he whispered, panting breathlessly. "I feel drained."

She sighed. "Me too."

He kissed her earlobe. "Was it what you expected?"

"More!"

He was still inside her, and much to her surprise he was still hard. He shifted lazily and began to move slowly in and out again.

"Ah, Les, what love you give. It's like the nectar of the gods," he whispered.

She wanted to cry. She'd waited so long, but now all she could do was revel in the wonder of it. She sank her hands into his tawny hair and sighed in ecstasy as she felt desire building again between them, and once more Drew brought them soaring to a climax that sapped their strength.

When it was over again and his body finally felt satiated, he slipped off her and gathered her close in his arms. She lay quietly, the touch of his flesh soothing her, and together they melted into sleep.

But Drew didn't sleep long, and a short time later, when Leslie opened her eyes she realized uneasily that he was already awake and staring at her in the semidarkness.

"What's wrong?" she asked him hesitantly.

He exhaled. "I could use a cigarette."

"I suppose they're in your shirt pocket."

"Uh-huh."

"Then I guess you'd better get one."

He extricated himself from her reluctantly and sat up on the side of the bed, searching on the floor for his shirt. He pulled out a pack of cigarettes, but instead of dropping the shirt back on the floor, he left it lying across his lap, half hiding his nakedness.

Leslie watched him light a cigarette, inhaling deeply, and instinctively she knew something was wrong. He was staring out the door toward the living room where a light reflected down the hall.

"What is it?" she asked apprehensively.

He shook his head. "Nothing."

She raised up on one elbow. "So now the guilt starts, right?" she said, her voice breaking.

"I'm sorry, Les . . . I guess I'm just not cut out for this."

"And I am?"

He squeezed her hand. "You know better than that."

"Drew?" She sat up, moving close to him, so her head rested on his shoulder. "Drew, you have to know," she said quietly. "I know you can't help being a little old-fashioned. The fact that I'm not a virgin, Drew . . . it isn't what you think."

"It's all right," he said, interrupting her.

"No, it's not all right. Not until you know. I don't just sleep around, Drew. I was engaged once five years ago. That started it. I thought I was in love, but it went sour. I won't say there's been no one else since, because I'm human. But each time, something happened, and I knew it was a mistake. Then I met you. I've never felt like this before . . . ever."

He kissed her softly. "I'm not a virgin either, Les, remember?"

She kissed his shoulder and rested her cheek on it again. "You can't forget her, can you?" she said unhappily.

"I don't like hurting her."

"Then don't. Don't tell her, Drew. Not yet," she said hurriedly. "She doesn't have to know. . . . I don't mind. I'd rather have part of you like this, darling, than none of you at all."

He frowned, but she went on. "It's really very simple. I know damn well you'll never leave her, you've been quite insistent about that. For some reason you still think you can hang onto your dream world. Well fine, go ahead if that's what you want, but I'll be here for you whenever . . ."

"Les, you can't—"

"I can." Her hand caressed his neck. "I don't mind being the other woman, really, as long as I can be near you." She paused. "There's usually an ashtray on the stand," she said quickly, and rummaged in the dark, then held it out to him.

He crushed out his cigarette, then sat for a long time staring at the ashtray in his hand. "I should leave," he said softly.

"Not just yet. Please," she begged.

He sighed. "That's right, you said you wanted to talk."

"I forgot, too," she admitted, lifting her head. "I wanted to ask you if you thought Stacey'd change her mind, because the tapes aren't working out too well. But never mind. I couldn't do another interview now even if she consented."

He sighed. "I really have to go."

"Not like this," she whispered.

"How else?"

"Tell me you'll be back."

"I think you know that without me telling you."

She took the ashtray from his hand and stood up, setting it back on the night stand. "You haven't had your coffee yet," she said.

His eyes darkened passionately as they sifted over her still-naked body in the half light and he felt himself harden again. "Come here," he whispered roughly.

She hesitated momentarily, then walked slowly to him. He reached out, running his hand up the side of her thigh, then let it curl about her waist, pulling her against him, burying his face in her breasts, smelling the warm, fragrant scent of her.

"Forget the coffee," he murmured huskily against her flesh, and slowly he fell back onto the bed, pulling her over with him. His body took hers, and once more there was only Leslie to love and Stacey ceased to exist.

Stacey was still awake. She had told herself she wasn't waiting up for Drew, but the book she was reading was dull. It was two-thirty when she heard Drew's car pull in the drive. She smoothed the covers across her stomach and stared into her book, waiting nervously for Drew to come into the bedroom.

By the time Drew came home, he was in the full bloom of guilt. After leaving Leslie, he'd ridden around for almost half an hour, prolonging his meeting with Stacey. He knew she'd be up. For one thing it wasn't like Stacey to settle down for the night after an argument without making up, and then too, he'd never remembered staying away so long before to cool off.

When he finally came into the bedroom and saw her propped up in bed, wearing a sexy black nightgown, he froze in the doorway. His eyes dropped before her apprehensive gaze, and he flushed self-consciously. Without saying anything, he walked over to the dresser, and began taking the things from his pockets, wondering if Stacey could see the guilt written in his eyes.

"Are you still mad?" Stacey finally managed to ask, her voice unsteady.

He shook his head. "I guess not."

"Where have you been?"

"Around."

"I was worried."

"No reason. The roads are clear and all I've had is coffee."

She stared at him curiously. There was something about him . . . "Drew, are you all right?" she asked.

"I'm fine," he said abruptly, and headed for the bathroom to change into his pajamas.

He stalled as long as he could, trying to collect his thoughts, then surveyed himself in the mirror. My God! He looked as guilty as hell! He felt embarrassed and ashamed, and yet there was no denying that he had enjoyed every minute with Leslie. When he'd held her in his arms, he'd justified it by telling himself that Stacey had betrayed him in Ben's arms first, but that part of it didn't seem important now. The only thing that mattered at the moment was the fact that he had to go out there to face Stacey and pretend that nothing was wrong.

When he finally came back into the bedroom, he avoided Stacey's eyes. He climbed into bed and lay quietly, the covers folded across his chest, all too aware of Stacey stretched out beside him.

"You are still mad, aren't you?" Stacey said, looking over at him.

He was staring at the ceiling, breathing deeper than usual. "No, Stacey, I said I'm not. I told you it was all right," he insisted.

"You mean I can go to the hospital Monday morning and you won't be angry?" she asked.

"That's what I said."

"Oh, Drew." She raised up on one elbow, looking down into his face. "Thank you," she whispered lovingly. "Thank you."

This time he couldn't avoid her eyes. They were glistening and misty, full of love. She bent down impulsively and kissed him, making the kiss long and deep. "I'm sorry," she said remorsefully, running a finger across his lips. "I'm sorry I made you so mad."

A pang of guilt seized him and he suddenly wanted to die. She looked so penitent, and he felt so ashamed. Yet he knew that tonight with Leslie was only the beginning, and he hated himself for it because he knew that in spite of everything, he still had feelings for Stacey he couldn't explain. He reached up, cupping her head in his hand. "Forget it, honey," he said huskily, staring into her eyes. "It's over. I got a little carried away, that's all. It was dumb of me. If you think it'll work out . . ."

"It will, Drew," she whispered passionately. "You'll see, I know it will."

He tried to smile. "I hope so." There was a faraway look in his eyes. "Only I'm so afraid your decision today was the worst mistake you've made in your life."

She frowned, puzzled by his strange words.

"Now, it's late, honey," he said softly. "Suppose we forget the whole thing and get some sleep."

She stared at him for a minute longer as he released her head, then she turned off the light and cuddled close to him. "I love you, Drew," she said softly, her voice filled with emotion.

"I love you too," he whispered, and he wasn't lying. In spite of everything, he still cared. But as he pulled her close against him, he knew it was too late. He'd shattered their chances, and there was no going back.

Bright and early Monday morning, Stacey arrived at the hospital ready to take on the world. Although some eyebrows raised when she came in, no one seemed unduly bothered by her presence, and she was relieved.

John's first operation was at nine o'clock. Stacey felt good to get back into the familiar green scrub dress again, and the routine of the work came back to her like an old friend. John was equally pleased to have Stacey working with him again, and he smiled to himself as he watched her leave his office to set up the instruments for him, wearing the shapeless scrub dress, her beautiful red hair hidden beneath the unglamorous headgear. His only regret was that he hadn't had the courage to tell Beth about it over the weekend. Now, of course, it was too late, but he decided to go home and confront Beth at lunchtime, so he left his office and went to scrub up for surgery, unaware that Beth had already learned of Stacey's return.

Since Nick Rigotti was one of the first people to see Stacey at the hospital, it was no surprise that by eight-thirty his sister Muriel had already heard the news, and by eight-forty-five, Muriel was on the phone with Beth. New Year's Eve had been hard enough for Beth, but Stacey's return to the hospital was more than she could bear. She washed her breakfast down with two glasses of brandy and by midmorning she had consumed more than enough liquor to bolster her courage.

After making a hurried, irrational decision, she dressed quickly, grabbed her coat and headed for her car, determined to tackle the problem at its source.

It was close to noon. John and Stacey were back in the operating room, performing exploratory surgery with Nick Rigotti standing by, helping when needed. When the commotion first started, no one paid much attention, but it wasn't long before the operating team couldn't help but be diverted. Then abruptly, the door flew open, and Beth came bursting in, verbally abusing the man who was trying to restrain her.

Stacey glanced quickly at John as all eyes centered on his wife, who had suddenly stopped yelling, and stared at them, as if in shock. The realization that John wasn't making love to Stacey in the operating room was almost enough to sober Beth, but she'd had too much to drink to think rationally, and after the first initial shock of recognition was over, she came to life again, and the accusations flew from her mouth.

"Get her out of here!" John yelled furiously at the orderly who'd tried to keep her out in the first place.

"How can I take her out when I couldn't even keep her out," the man replied, holding Beth as securely as he could.

John's face reddened and he turned to Nick Rigotti. "Take over," he said grimly. "I'll get her out of here," and he left the operating table, forcing Beth to leave by picking her up bodily. She screamed pathetically, then collapsed in his arms, crying and asking his forgiveness. John headed for an empty room somewhere, hoping the hospital board wouldn't get wind of the ugly affair and call him on the carpet for it, and praying that Beth's interference hadn't done any irreparable damage to the patient.

By the time the afternoon was over, the whole hospital was buzzing about the incident. Stacey tried to keep out of everyone's way and waited for John to call and set her fears to rest, but John had taken Beth home and no one had heard from him since. Finally, Stacey went home herself, only she didn't dare tell Drew. It was all he needed in order to tell her I told you so, and it was the last thing she wanted to hear.

She worried about Beth all night, but the next morning at

work John told her that after sleeping it off, Beth had remembered little of what she had done, and he assured Stacey that people would soon forget about the whole thing. The days that followed proved John right. Before long, the gossip quieted down and Stacey's work at the hospital fell into a daily routine. She enjoyed working with John. His warm charm was just what she needed to help her over the rough spots in her personal life.

And she was having problems. Ever since the night of their argument, there had been a change in Drew. It was hard to put her finger on it, but he just wasn't the same. The laughter was missing from his eyes, he seemed quieter than usual, and the warm intimacy they had shared during the holidays had vanished. He spent more and more time at the office, claiming he had gotten behind in his work over the holidays. But what bothered Stacey the most was that his appetite for her seemed to have disappeared, and when he did make love to her, it wasn't the same.

Never once in those first few weeks did Stacey suspect that Drew was being unfaithful. It wasn't until after the Valentine's Day dance at the hospital that Stacey began to guess at what was going on. Surprisingly, it was a chance remark of Dr. Nick Rigotti's that started her wondering. Unfortunately, Nick had brought Leslie Kyle to the dance. This in itself was a shock, because, with Leslie's article due to be released in March, Stacey had been certain that she was back in New York.

But the real shock had come when Stacey overheard Nick telling one of the doctors that this was his first date with Leslie in months, because someone else had been keeping her completely tied up.

For the rest of the evening, Stacey kept a furtive eye on Leslie and Drew, and more than once she was rewarded for her vigilance. Unhappily, she saw that there seemed to be a strange, silent communication going on between them. At first she didn't want to believe it, but there was too much evidence to ignore.

In the days that followed, Stacey kept her eyes open, but there wasn't anything more to see. If Drew said he was working late and she called, he always answered. If he left the office, he always let her know where he was going and why. But her doubts remained and became a nagging suspicion that was driving her crazy.

It was April 18, Easter Sunday. The weather had been cool and rainy, but the forsythia near the hospital entrance was in full bloom when Stacey passed it on the way inside. The lobby was practically deserted, but she had expected that. After all, it was almost eight-thirty in the evening. Visiting hours were over and even the receptionist looked tired.

They had been spending a quiet holiday at home when John had called. Drew had put up an argument when she had to leave, but she really had no choice. There had been an accident, and the patient needed immediate surgery. John was waiting for her by the time she reached the scrub room, and for the next two hours Stacey had all she could do to keep up with John. The patient had internal bleeding, a ruptured spleen, and enough other injuries to kill him, but John pulled him through.

It was ten-twenty when she and John finally sat down in his office to have a much-needed cup of coffee before leaving.

"Did you ever see so much rain?" John said as he took a drag off his cigarette, then gazed out the window.

"The perfect night for an accident," Stacey said softly, hugging her arms. Then she turned to the phone and added, "I think I'll see if Drew waited up."

John heard her talking to someone, but paid little attention until she hung up and made another call. She talked to Drew for a few minutes, then hung up again. John turned as she approached the window.

"Drew went down to the office," she said rather vaguely.

"Something the matter?" John asked.

"I don't know," she said, biting her lip.

He frowned. "Stacey, what is it?"

She took a deep breath. "John . . . I think Drew's having an affair with Leslie," she said hastily, and saw his eyes darken.

"You can't be serious. Drew loves you, Stacey. It doesn't make sense."

"Doesn't it? The late nights at the office, the change in his lovemaking. There's no warmth in Drew anymore, John," she said unhappily. "I've suspected something was going on for a while, but I've been unable to prove anything. At least, not until now."

"What do you mean?"

"Come with me, John, please," she pleaded suddenly. "He's at his office, said he'll be leaving for home in about an hour and a half. I have to know if he's there with Leslie, and I can't go alone. I don't want to go alone."

John stared at her with troubled eyes. "I'll have to call Beth and tell her I'll be delayed. She'll never believe it." He shrugged. "But then, she never does."

John made his call, then they put on their rain gear, shut off the light in his office, and left.

Forty minutes later, Stacey parked her MG in front of Drew's office building on Euclid Avenue. There was a steady downpour of rain and the streets were deserted. She sat behind the wheel for a minute, holding it tightly in her hands, then took a deep breath.

"Do you want me to go up with you?" John asked.

She shook her head. "No, I'd rather go by myself."

"No matter what you find up there, Stacey, I want you to remember I'm always here," John whispered.

Stacey looked at him, her heart pounding. "I know," she answered. "But I can't count on you. I have to have Drew, John, because without him this life is nothing to me. Pray for me," she said hurriedly as she left the car.

When she reached the fourth floor, Stacey hesitated, but she knew she had to have the truth. She went to Drew's office and unlocked the outer door with her key as quietly as she could, still the faint click made her wince as she looked around Hazel's empty office. She waited motionless, wondering if Drew had heard, then moved silently toward the door to the inner office.

If he was working, he certainly wasn't using much light, because from what she could see under the door, the only light on was the small one on his desk. She walked to the door and stopped, her heart racing. Well, this was it.

She pulled the door open with a quick movement and stepped inside, shattering all her illusions in one brief moment.

She had expected to be shocked, but the actual effect was terrifying. Drew was propped up on one end of the couch, shirt open, hair messed up, and Leslie was lying across his lap. Her feet were bare, her blouse was half-open, and they were in the middle of a passionate kiss.

When Stacey burst in, they both stared at her, dumfounded, then suddenly Drew came to life and extricated himself from Leslie's arms, his face reddening by the minute, but his eyes were both hostile and relieved. He stood and tucked in his shirt as Stacey watched in horror.

"So now you know," he said, his voice breaking. "I wanted to tell you, Stacey," he said huskily. "Oh, God, I wanted to tell you so many times, but I couldn't. I couldn't hurt you."

"Hurt me?" she gasped. "What do you call this?"

His eyes faltered momentarily and he glanced at Leslie, then looked back at Stacey.

"You'd been through so much," he said hurriedly. "And I couldn't just throw eighteen years down the drain."

She bit back the tears. "And I trusted you. I had to give up Ben, and what do I get in return? Why, Drew?"

"Because you *didn't* give up Ben," he yelled bitterly. "You didn't need me anymore, not to love. All you wanted was someone to fill the void that was left when you lost him. It didn't have to be me. I love Leslie, and I can't help loving her. Stacey, what we had together is over, it ended last May when you dove into your sister's swimming pool."

"No, Drew, please. That's not true!"

"Isn't it?" he asked angrily. "Well, it is for me. I tried, Stacey, but I just can't play second fiddle to a dead man. I never meant to hurt you, but I just can't cut it anymore!"

Stacey felt bitter bile in her mouth. She swallowed it down and wiped a hand across her face, smearing the tears. She couldn't take it, not anymore. Her whole world was falling into little pieces and she couldn't pick them up again.

She let out an agonized sob and turned abruptly, running out the door.

When John saw Stacey push open the lobby door and run out into the rain, he knew she had found her answer. The minute she closed the car door, he saw she was crying.

"They were there?" he asked quickly.

She nodded.

"Did he say anything?"

"They were on the couch in each other's arms," she cried hysterically. "And he doesn't love me . . . and I hate him . . . and I can't go on, not anymore!"

John reached over. "Stacey, honey, please, you can," he begged softly. "I'm here, you know that. I'm always here."

"And so is Beth, and she needs you . . . and I can't take you from her. Oh, God, John, I wanted Drew!"

She slammed her foot down on the accelerator, turning the key at the same time, shifting the car quickly into gear, and the little MG flew away from the curb. She was lucky there wasn't much traffic because she couldn't even see where she was going. John tried to calm her down, but she was crying hysterically, begging God to end the misery her life had become because she'd lost both Drew and Ben, and she was weaving all over the road, barely missing parked cars.

When John saw the flashing lights behind them, he tried again to slow her down, but she paid no heed. She was driving like a maniac, just barely in control of the wheel and she had no intention of slowing down for anything or anyone. When they reached the square, she slid recklessly around the corner onto Ontario and finally lost control of the car completely. John yelled, trying to startle her into rationality, but it was too late and the car came to an abrupt stop, wrapping itself around a telephone pole.

John, hitting his head on the windshield, was momentarily dazed, and before he had a chance to stop her, Stacey staggered out the door on her side that had been half ripped off and started stumbling along in the rain. She was running away from everything and everybody so she wouldn't have to know or think or feel anymore.

John cleared his head, then stumbled out after her as the police car slid around the corner and came to a halt behind them. The police leaped out, and went after them on foot in the rain, but it was getting harder to see by the minute. It was raining so hard now it was like a wall of water, and John had to wipe his face with both hands to see.

"We've got to catch her," he yelled back at the police frantically. "She's upset and there's no telling what might happen!"

The police moved up even with him and all three ran toward the figure about ten feet ahead, clearly visible now in the streetlight. Suddenly, as a wall of water enfolded Stacey, blocking her from view, John stopped, the hair at the nape of his neck standing on end. He couldn't move.

The police took a few steps past him and then they too stopped, staring puzzled, as two men carrying umbrellas emerged out of the rain where only seconds ago Stacey had been. The police halted both men, quickly wiping the rain from their eyes to get a better look at them.

"You see a lady run along here a few seconds ago?" they asked, panting, but both men stared at them bewildered.

"No one but us on the whole sidewalk," one of the men said.

John lifted his head. The rain was gradually beginning to let up now, and what was once a wall of water obstructing their vision was now only a light shower.

"She has to be here somewhere," said one of the policemen. But as they searched the dripping doorways, there was nothing, and a strange fear gripped John.

"Do you really think you're going to find her?" he asked helplessly.

"Who was she?" they asked simultaneously. "And who are you?"

"My name's Dr. John Morris and the woman we were chasing is Stacey Gordon," he said quietly. "She was upset and crying and she doesn't normally drive like that, but the rain and everything . . . I think we better keep looking."

They searched for over ten minutes, but found nothing, then the police informed John he'd have to go back to the precinct station with them and make out a statement, but first they stopped by the car and John gathered up Stacey's purse. He had a strange foreboding as he took it off the seat and stared off toward the square, then down Ontario, his eyes troubled.

They were about to go back to Drew's office and confront him with the news, when he and Leslie pulled up in Drew's car. They had both reached the lobby as her car pulled away from the curb, but had to take time to run around the corner to get Drew's car, now they accompanied John to the police station and waited while he made a statement, and then all three left together.

Before getting on the freeway, Drew cruised around the Public Square area a few more times, trying to spot Stacey. When he finally realized it was hopeless, he gave up and they headed for home.

It was well after one in the morning by the time Drew pulled into his drive. Drew was glad John had agreed to stop by the house, because he needed someone to talk to.

"I didn't want it like this," he said to John as they walked with Leslie toward the house. "But Stacey quit loving me the day Ben Clayton came into her life, and I couldn't fight it any longer. Try to understand what it was like for me, John."

John stared at Drew as they entered the kitchen. Love was a fickle thing, a strange emotion that ruled men's lives and ruined them at the same time. Yes, he could understand. They stood side by side staring at each other, then realized they weren't alone.

Chris and Renee were sitting at the table, not saying a word, and Renee held something in her hands. Their faces were pale, and both girl's eyes were red from crying.

"Where's Mom?" asked Chris anxiously.

"Why aren't you kids in bed?" Drew asked, avoiding her question. "You've both got school tomorrow."

But Chris wasn't about to be put off. "Where's Mom!"

"Your mother had an accident with the car . . ." said John, trying to explain.

"But she's not dead, is she?" Renee said as if she knew what the answer would be.

"No, she's alive. At least she was the last time I saw her."

"And that was?" asked Renee.

John was puzzled by the question. "About eleven-thirty or twelve. I was running after her in the rain, and she got a little too far ahead of me . . ."

"And she disappeared?" asked Renee.

John frowned. "That's right, she disappeared. But how did you know?"

"See, I told you!" said Renee, looking over at Chris. Tears welled up in her eyes again and her voice broke. "I showed you, but you said it couldn't be, you said it wasn't so."

"Hey, now, what's all this about?" Drew asked as he studied the girls.

"You didn't find Mom at all, did you?" Renee asked, sniffling.

"No, we didn't," he answered. "The police . . . everyone's looking for her."

Renee glared at her father, then glanced at Leslie. "Mother found out you're in love with Leslie, didn't she, Dad?" she said, and Drew didn't know what to say. "You don't have to answer," she added quickly. "I guessed it a long time ago. Chris and I both did, and we've only been waiting for you to tell her. And I know the answer to where mother is, too," she said.

"What are you talking about?" asked Drew. "What's she been up to, Chris?"

"Chris had nothing to do with it, Dad," Renee said as she lifted the object she had been keeping half-hidden with her hands. Drew felt a strange sensation sweep over him. She was holding Stacey's diary. "I've been wondering for a long time why you and Mom were having so many problems, and I thought maybe I could help. Tonight I decided to find out once and for all what Ben Clayton was like, so I went through her diary, Dad, and I found out she had married him. And I found messages he wrote to her because he knew where she was from and wanted her to read them someday, but I also found something else, something I don't think Mother ever found, because if she had, things might have been different." Tears were flooding her eyes and she set the ledger out and opened it to the right pages.

"She won't be back, Daddy, I know she won't," Renee cried passionately, and handed the diary to her father. "Here, read this, and you'll see."

Drew reluctantly took the crumbling ledger from Renee and moved closer to the light above the kitchen sink, his eyes glued to the page in front of him, and as he slowly began to read, a strange look came over his face, tears filling his eyes. "Renee's right,'' he said when he had finished, his voice breaking with emotion. ''She's right, John. Stacey will never have to worry about not loving me anymore. She's gone, and she'll never be back again.''

Chris and Renee watched tearfully as John turned away so they couldn't see his tears, realizing he'd been right, and Leslie stared knowingly at Drew, then walked slowly, deliberately into his arms and the silence in the kitchen was broken only by the soft patter of the rain that was once more falling outside.

CHAPTER 10

As Stacey staggered along in the rain, she felt empty and numb inside. Her whole world was over. All the things she cared about were beyond her reach. Ben was dead, Drew was lost to her, and she could never have John even if she had wanted him. Three men, yet she was alone. Even Renee and Chris were leaving her out of their lives more and more every day. What was the use?

She didn't care that there was a cut on her chin where it had hit the steering wheel, and the bruise on her knee didn't even hurt. She could hear John calling from behind her, but he sounded miles away instead of only a few feet. All she wanted was to get away, as far away from everything and everyone as possible.

It was raining harder now. She held her head up, and the rain filled her eyes and mouth, blinding her. It felt cold as it washed the tears away, but more tears came and she felt as if they'd never stop.

"Oh, Ben!" she screamed into the night. "Why did you leave me? I need you! I have to find you somewhere, Ben. Oh, God, please! I need him so!" Her voice was drowned out by a wall of water that choked her as she screamed her agony to the wind and rain. "Ben! Ben! Come back to me! Ben!"

She choked and sputtered as the water suddenly filled her nose and mouth, and for a minute she felt as if she were drowning, then she lowered her head, gagging with the sobs, and stopped suddenly as she felt something hard against her legs. She looked down, but was unable to see at first because of the rain. She felt for the object with her hands, realizing at the same time that she no longer heard John behind her.

She stood motionless and covered her eyes with her hand to shield them. As the rain gradually began to let up, she straightened and fingered the top of the pole or post she had run into. Her fingers slid over its wet surface, and a sudden chill ran through her.

A round knob? She frowned, sniffling. An iron ball with a large ring in it. Wiping the rain from her eyes, she stooped down to be on eye level with this strange object, forgetting for the moment that John, who had been right behind her, hadn't caught up with her yet. As her eyes adjusted more to the dark, wet night, Stacey stared at the object beneath her fingers, and a slow feeling of dread began to creep over her.

She glanced up to a sign that hung above a store window nearby. The sign read, "BAILEY'S DRY-GOODS STORE."

She felt the gooseflesh rise and her heart began to race. Oh, my God! Closing her eyes, she leaned against the hitching post she had run into and slumped to the cold, damp ground. God in heaven, it had happened again! Suddenly the trembling started and she shivered violently.

Hesitantly she sniffed back a sob and stared straight ahead, afraid to move. She hadn't been wrong. It wasn't a dream, she was seeing it. It was the same dry-goods store Jenny Brainard had brought her to when she had first gone back in time, the store where she'd bought the material to make her bras. Gradually she stilled her pounding heart and pulled herself up, using the hitching post for support. She was wet and bedraggled, but she wasn't feeling the cold anymore. She pushed her hair back from her face absentmindedly as she took in her surroundings.

Her eyes wandered to the sign again and then over to the buildings beside it. They were all the same; nothing had changed. She sighed, pulling the belt on her raincoat tighter. It made no difference because the coat was soaked, but she didn't notice.

Her eyes moved down Ontario Street and across to the park where budding branches stood stark and wet in the streetlights. Only they weren't streetlights, they were gaslights. Their flickering flames made shadows dance among the wet leaves and bushes where only a few moments before walks, benches, and the Soldiers and Sailors Monument had stood.

Tears once more rimmed her eyes until she could hardly see. She wiped them away and continued to look around. It was so dark, but there was no mistake.

She was back. Dear God! She had wanted Ben, prayed for him, and now miraculously she was back. Somehow, some way, she had traveled through time again. She raised her eyes to the sky, remembering the torment that had gripped her only moments ago. The terrible longing for Ben, to be near him and loved by him, and now she was here.

She wanted to sing and shout. None of the hysteria that had driven her from Drew's office remained. But as she stood on the sidewalk with her heart twisting inside her, a new fear suddenly seized her.

She was in Cleveland. Cleveland! She had left Ben on the trail to Oregon. . . . God no! Her heart pounded frantically as the questions came rushing at her. What year was it? Was it 1865 again, or was it before? What month? What day? If it were before 1865, Ben's wife, Ann, would still be alive. Would God be that cruel? No, he couldn't do that to her. Yet, if it was after 1865, Ben was gone.

Frantically she turned to the store window and searched among the clothes and shoes on display, looking for a calendar or anything that would give her a clue as to the date. Her head was pressed against the wet glass, but it was too dark to see anything. She began to feel the cold again, and shivered. Looking down, she realized her feet were soaked, her clothes dripping, and . . . her purse? She didn't even have her purse. She had left it in the car with John. Her eyes misted. Poor John, caught in the middle of everything. It would have been so easy to love him if Beth and Drew hadn't existed. But that was over. She was back again.

She left the store window and moved to the doorway, where no one could see her. But who would see her? The Cleveland she was gazing at now was far different from the Cleveland of 1976. It must be late, because she hadn't seen a carriage or anyone else passing by. Unconsciously she reached for her watch and pushed the tiny button on its side. It was eleven-fifty-three.

A sound made her perk up and she stepped deeper into the doorway. When she peeked out, she saw a carriage turning the corner farther up the street. The carriage was closed and only the driver was exposed to the weather. As the carriage came closer, she could see his collar turned up and his head bent down against the cold wind.

She watched the carriage pass, and sighed. Well, she couldn't stay here all night. She had to do something, find someone to help. The Brainards!

If anyone would help, the Brainards would. But what if they didn't know her? What if it was the wrong year? Lord! This whole thing was crazy, but she had to do something.

She hugged her arms against the cold and reluctantly moved away from the doorway of Bailey's Dry Goods Store. Directions. She had to remember the directions. She began walking slowly, then picked up her stride as the storm clouds dissipated and the stars began to fill the heavens. With the stars came a slight drop in temperature and she walked even faster to keep warm.

Suddenly she stopped, listening. Someone was whistling up ahead. Instinctively she moved closer to the storefronts, trying to blend in with the shadows. She strained to see in the dim gaslight. It was a policeman walking his beat, swinging his billy stick as he took long, casual strides.

She couldn't let him see her, not in these clothes. She moved behind a wooden rack in a doorway and crouched down, holding her breath as his footsteps neared, but he just strolled by.

So far, so good. Now to find her way. It had been almost a year, but she had to remember. She began walking again, more cautiously this time. In minutes she had left the square behind and made her way down Ontario, ducking into doorways every time a carriage passed. Once she went by a couple of drunks and they called out something obscene. She was glad they were too drunk to follow her without falling flat on their faces.

After some time, she came to a main street and glanced up at the sign, St. Clair. Aha, she was headed right. The next big intersection was Lake Street, and she stopped, not wanting to make a mistake. Let's see, they had turned left at Lake Street. Yes, that was it. She started out again.

It seemed like a terribly long walk, and being soaked to the skin made it worse. The sidewalks stopped just past Water Street, and she had to walk in the mud down Lighthouse Lane. There were no streetlights here, and it was quieter. Occasionally a dog would bark or a curious cat would come out to peer at her. Other than that, the street was deserted.

She crossed the railroad tracks carefully and began watching for Meadow Lane. The closer she got, the faster her heart raced. What was she going to tell them? The last time she had seen them she had been on her way west with Ben. Now she didn't even know what year it was. It had to be spring, because she had passed more than one forsythia bush in bloom. But what day was it? She'd have to play it by ear until she could find out.

She turned down Meadow Lane, watching on the left for the familiar barn and carriage livery next to the big weathered house. When she approached the empty field, her steps faltered. She tried to make out the vague shapes that were half-hidden in the darkness, hoping what she was looking at wasn't real. She stepped off the road and walked across the empty field.

Moving as if in a daze, she stumbled over a large board. The edges were burned and the white paint on it was blackened and blistered, but there was no mistake. It was the sign that used to hang on Matt Brainard's Livery Stable.

She let it fall to the ground and surveyed what had once been the Brainards' home and business. Now there were only charred ruins.

She stood for a long time staring at the soggy, blackened mess, wondering what to do next. The thought that the Brainards may have perished in the fire saddened her, but after a few minutes, she straightened, forcing her thoughts back to her own predicament. She was tired and wet. She stared toward the barn. Although the roof was gone, part of the stalls were still standing and she picked her way toward it in the dark. It wasn't much shelter, but it was better than nothing.

She sorted through the ruins until she found an old half-burned horse blanket which, much to her surprise, was dry. Pleased with her discovery, she sank down in a corner and pulled the blanket up around her, but sleep wouldn't come. After a while she gave up and just stared at the sky, watching the stars.

The thought of morning frightened her. What would people say when she emerged from her hiding place in a London Fog raincoat, slacks, and blouse?

By the time dawn arrived, she had decided on a course of action. While trying to get warm, she had shoved her hands in her pockets and discovered a couple of bills and some loose change.

The last time she had been here, she and Jenny Brainard had walked along Meadow Lane to Front Street and taken a horse-drawn trolley to the square. Now she stared at the pennies in her hand. Fare for the trolley had been only a few pennies. It shouldn't be too hard to get away with. The conductor would never look closely enough to see the date.

Stacey watched the sun come up and listened to the city awaken, but she didn't move. Not right away. She sat huddled in the blanket, postponing the rough day ahead. Finally, once the sun had warmed the air, she stood up and stretched out the kinks. Her coat was full of straw, muddy and wrinkled. She brushed it off and then realized her hair was damp and curling in straggly ringlets. People would surely stare, but she had no comb or brush.

She ran cold fingers through her hair to untangle it a bit, and looked around, hoping to find a fastener of some kind. Pushing things aside with her foot, she discovered a piece of leather cord. It was just long enough to fit around her hair. It wasn't much of an improvement, but at least her hair wasn't straggling around her face anymore.

Gathering her courage, she walked from the building. At first no one noticed her, but when she stepped onto the road she felt all eyes turn toward her. There weren't too many people out, only a milk wagon, an ice wagon, and some men on their way to work.

She glanced at her watch. If the times were the same, it was only six-thirty, and she wondered if the trolleys would be running yet. At first she had considered walking the distance, but she had decided she'd be less conspicuous sitting on a trolley. As she neared Front Street, she remembered it was a railroad depot as well as the trolley stop. The familiar crisscrossing of tracks, trains, buggies, and people made her stop and stare. There were so many memories.

She was still staring when she heard the clanging bell from the trolley and broke into a run. Before getting on the trolley, she hurried to the ticket office.

The man behind the wire cage dropped his spectacles when she walked up, as if he couldn't believe his eyes. "Can I help you?" he asked.

"I need to know the date," she said nervously. He was the first person she had spoken to, and her voice echoed back to her.

"The date?"

"That's right, the date."

He peered over the top of his glasses again. "How come you don't know the date?" he asked.

She looked disgusted. "Look, will you tell me or won't you?"

"It don't make no difference to me. It's Thursday, April 19."

"And the year, what year is it?"

"The year?" He frowned at her strangely. "Eighteen-sixty-six. Why?"

"Thanks," she said quickly, and ran off toward the trolley. She climbed on, taking some pennies from her pocket. "How many?" she asked hurriedly.

"Where you headin'?"

"To Superior at the Square."

The trolley conductor looked her over distastefully and told her the fare. She dropped the pennies in the coin box and hurried to the back of the car, where she hoped she would be less conspicuous. But everyone still gawked curiously as she went by. She slid into one of the seats and sat next to the window.

An amused smile curved her lips as she glanced back toward the coin box, wondering how long it would be before someone found her pennies dated in the 1900's. Someone was in for a real shocker with that one. She'd love to see their faces. She turned back to the window, and as she watched the familiar surroundings go by, a nostalgic sensation swept over her, and she realized that this time she wasn't afraid. A year ago, she had been petrified, not knowing what to do or where to turn. But this time it felt like coming home.

Last night, while lying huddled in the burned-out livery, she had wondered about Drew. Did he know? How could he, unless John realized what had happened. Her only regret was Renee and Chris. It would be so hard on them again, and she was going to miss them. Tears filled her eyes, but she knew she had to take the bitter with the sweet. The man at the ticket window had said it was April 19, 1866, and that meant that Ben was in Oregon. All those miles between them.

But she wasn't going to let it get to her. Somehow she'd find him. The trolley's clanging bell interrupted her thoughts and announced the Superior stop.

Again, people stared at her strange, dirty clothes, but she ignored them. Her only concern was that someone would think she was crazy and call a policeman. She elbowed past a bosomy young woman dressed in black and an older man whose stilted appraisal of her was unnerving, and stepped down onto the muddy road.

The horses gave a snort and the trolley started up again. Stacey headed for the sidewalk and started to walk east on Superior. Gradually the sidewalk narrowed and she left the stores behind until she was walking past beautiful homes with stately lawns and fine landscaping. After a while she reached a familiar iron fence and stopped. She fingered a spire on the fence and stood gazing at the big Gothic house. Daffodils bloomed along the inside of the fence and forsythia made a yellow camouflage around the big front porch, while the elms and maples made the long expanse of lawn look fresh and clean, especially after last night's rain.

This had been Ben's home, the house where she had first met him. Now strangers lived in it, but there was one person who should still be around. At least the people who had bought the house had said they were going to keep him on as handyman.

She hurried toward the carriage house in the back. He had to be around; it was her only hope.

Amos was feeding the horses when he heard the voice. His eyes weren't as good as they used to be and he squinted, wondering if maybe he'd made a mistake. He blinked and looked again at the figure standing just inside the carriage-house door. Nope, wasn't no mistake. Her hair was red like the roan horse in the next stall, but curly and kinda flying about. But it was her clothes that really made his eyes bug out. If he didn't know better, he'd swear he was looking at that young widow that went west with Ben Clayton a year ago come June. "You want me for somethin'?" he asked cautiously.

Stacey was nervous, her hands shaking. "Amos?" she said slowly.

"Well, by God!" he exclaimed, staring at her wide-eyed. "It is you, ain't it?"

Stacey tried to smile. "You remember me, Amos?" she asked.

The old man smiled back. "Lord, yes, I remember you. How could I forget anythin' so pretty? But what you doin' here? You was supposed to be with Mr. Ben in Oregon."

"I know, Amos," she said, shivering slightly as she looked at the old man's tired eyes. He was almost toothless, with gray hair that touched the collar of his worn coat and a face that was wrinkled like parchment. "It's a long story, Amos, too long to tell . . . but something went wrong and I need your help."

He eyed her skeptically. "What went wrong?"

"There was an accident and I was hurt," she lied. "Mr. Ben had to go on without me."

Amos shook his head. "No, ma'am. He wouldn't leave you to fend for yourself. He ain't that kind."

"Please, Amos," she begged. "I can't explain, but I need your help. Forget that I was supposed to go with Ben, just believe that I didn't. I'm here, and you're the only one who can help me."

He hesitated, eyeing her suspiciously. "What do you want me to do?"

"I haven't any money and I need some clothes."

"Where'd you get that there coat?" he asked. "Funny-lookin' thing for a woman to be wearin'."

"I had to put on some men's clothes," she lied again. "Do you know anyone who has an old dress or something I could use? Maybe the lady you work for?"

Amos didn't know what to think. He grabbed a bucket of oats and poured it into the roan mare's feed bin, frowning again as he gazed back at Stacey. "It sure don't seem right to me you bein' here," he said. "But I got to admit you ain't no ghost. You ain't, are you?"

"No, Amos, I'm no ghost," she assured him hopefully. "But I do need your help."

He chomped down on his toothless gums and squeezed his chin up, until his mouth was a firm line across his face. "Well, now, I'll tell you what," he said thoughtfully. "It ain't often I have pretty ladies askin' me to give 'em a hand, and I don't rightly know what's goin' on. But I can see you're in a bad way. Just might be I can get somethin' for you," he said agreeably. "And from the looks of you, I bet you ain't et for a while either, have you?"

"I'd forgotten all about eating," she said gratefully. "But now that you mention it, I am hungry."

"Thought so." He eyed her clothes again. "You want to go into the house with me, or do you think you'd rather stay out here?"

She blushed. "Will it be all right if I stay out here?"

"Don't want me to tell nobody you're here, do you?"

"Not just yet," she answered. He pulled out a box for her to sit on, and she did so with a sigh of relief. He excused himself and went into the house.

Half an hour later he was back with a couple slices of ham, some scrambled eggs, and a couple muffins.

"Hadn't had my breakfast yet," he explained. "Told the cook I was extra hungry and said I had some things to do in the harness room and I'd eat out here. She don't care, long as I take the dishes back in. I think she's glad to get me out of the kitchen. She's always complainin' my clothes're too dirty and I don't wash enough." He handed Stacey the plate of food and looked at his hands. "Frieda never used to complain," he said affectionately. Stacey agreed, remembering how thoughtful Ben's housekeeper had always been.

As they ate Amos' breakfast in silence, Stacey realized she had been hungrier than she thought. She was more than pleased when Amos said he wasn't really that hungry and ate only half his ham. Even so, she'd have been happier with another muffin, but she didn't say anything.

Amos finished first and checked one of the horses before coming back to sit with Stacey.

"I've been thinkin'," he said after a few minutes. "You said you needed some clothes. Well, now, the missus in there is about the same size as you, only I wouldn't dare ask her. But they's some clothes in the basement she's got ready to give to the poor box at the church. Don't know how good the stuff is, but could be we could find somethin' in there."

"That sounds great, Amos," Stacey said, setting the empty dish aside. "But I can't go in the house. I don't even want to go out in the yard dressed like this."

"I know that." He grinned. "But you see, I've been supposed to take that there box to the church for a week now, and I ain't taken the time. Just might be I can take it this mornin'."

Stacey grinned back at him. "Thank you, Amos."

"Now, you stay here. I may be in the house for a while, but I'll be back out for sure. Only, if you don't want no one to see you, stay back there in the harness room. Right now I got to hitch up the buggy for the mister. He works at the bank and should be leavin' soon."

In spite of his protests, she helped him hitch up the buggy before retiring to the harness room to wait. Amos took the buggy out of the carriage house and greeted his employer. She could faintly hear their voices as the man gave Amos some orders for the day, and much to her surprise, she heard him complain about Amos not having taken the box of clothing to the church yet. Amos promised he'd get to it this morning for sure, and they left.

Over an hour later, Stacey finally stood in front of Amos in an appropriate outfit. After taking the money from her coat pocket, just in case, she gave Amos her coat and slacks to burn. But she kept her own underclothes and blouse. To her russet blouse she had added a dark brown beaded skirt. Some of the beads were missing and the hem was worn, but with her permanent-press blouse it didn't look half-bad.

There was an old hat in the box, and she took some yellow and pink artificial flowers off it. She tied the flowers with a blue ribbon, and pulling up the V neck of her blouse, she fastened the flowers at the neckline with a safety pin she had found in a child's petticoat.

Amos had managed to sneak her a comb, and she got the tangles out of her hair and fastened it with a piece of blue grosgrain ribbon. It was still cool out and she was lucky to find a woman's black woolen coat. The edges of the sleeves were worn and the trim was ripped, but the lining wasn't too bad and it fit. Finally she tore a bunch of feathers off an old felt bonnet and tied it on her head.

"There," she said. "Do I look like a poor relative from the country?"

Amos' eyes twinkled. "You look fine, Mrs. Gordon, ma'am. Not quite as fancy as the first time I laid eyes on you, but danged nice."

"Thanks, Amos." She was pleased by his compliment. "Now I have to figure some way to get enough money to go to Oregon."

"Oregon?"

"I have to find Ben, Mr. Clayton. I just have to."

"Money's somethin' I just don't have, ma'am," he said sadly. "I wish I did, you could have it all."

"Oh, no, Amos," she said anxiously. "I'm not asking you for money. I was just wondering how I could make some. You know, get a job."

He rubbed his chin. "Hmmm . . . jobs is scarce. What can you do besides takin' care of young 'uns?"

"Oh, I can nurse or teach, or do any number of things. But the important thing is that I'm here." She took the old man's gnarled hands. "Oh, Amos, you don't know what it's been like. I'm so glad to be back again and have this chance to be with Ben."

The old man frowned, his wrinkled face puzzled. "Ma'am?"

Impulsively she hugged the old man while he blushed crimson. "Forgive me, Amos. I know you don't understand, but I'm so glad you were here to help."

Amos composed himself. "If you want, I can give you a lift to town," he said self-consciously.

Realizing she had rattled him, Stacey offered to help load the wagon with the box. He protested at first, but after he gave in, they were done in no time.

"What if they see me sitting on the wagon, Amos?" she asked as he maneuvered the wagon out of the carriage house.

"Don't reckon they will," he said. "They don't pay much attention to my comin's and goin's."

She was glad. The sun was warmer now, and as it filtered through the newly opened leaves, it made everything look fresh and green, and as they reached the end of the drive, the scent of daffodils filled the air.

Amos drove her as far as the square where she bid him good-bye affectionately, then reminded him to make sure he burned her old clothes. He assured her he would, and she was grateful he hadn't asked any more questions. But he had answered some.

On the way to town, Stacey had questioned him about the Brainards. He told her that the house had burned down over the Christmas holidays. The Christmas tree had caught fire and the flying sparks had reached the blacksmith shop and livery, but the Brainards had all escaped injury. As he last recalled, they had sold the land and headed for Texas. Amos also informed her that Ben Clayton's father-in-law, Mr. Tanner, had also left town, back in February. He and his daughter Paula Tanner had sold the house and everything else they could get their hands on and left town after an awful scandal about graft or some such. Stacey was just as glad. She never did like Ben's sister-in-law.

Now, as Stacey waved good-bye to Amos, the thought of Ben, with his wonderful deep dimpled smile and dark, compelling eyes, made her all the more determined.

The rest of the afternoon she made the rounds, from the Marine Hospital to the department stores and the newspaper offices, with no luck. She didn't know if it was because she was a woman, or because of her clothes, or because jobs were really that scarce, but she had a suspicion it was the clothes. They weren't exactly chic.

It was late afternoon when she left the Hower and Higbee store at 237 Superior Avenue. She stood on the sidewalk and stared across the broad dirt street, disillusioned again. She had thought her writing ability might have helped at the newspaper office, but it hadn't, and they didn't even want her here as a clerk. She looked down at the clothes. If only she had something a little less like Poverty Row.

She continued to gaze about absentmindedly until her eyes fell on something that made her frown. She lifted her hand and looked down at her rings. She hadn't eaten anything since morning and her stomach was growling. She couldn't impose on Amos, not again. She had to do something.

Her eyes lifted to the sign in front of the store in the Waddell House Hotel at the corner of Bank and Superior: "H. COWELL AND COMPANY." She made her way toward it.

The place was stuffy and smelled of old wood aging in the sun. It was very quiet with only the steady tickings of numerous clocks breaking the silence. She looked curiously at the display cases and then glanced up as a middle-aged man approached.

"Something I can do for you?" he asked politely, taking in her raggedy attire.

"I see you sell jewelry," she said firmly. "Do you by any chance buy it too?"

He looked at her skeptically. "If it's a good piece and worth it."

Reluctantly she took the wedding rings from her finger. She watched his expression as he looked at them. Drew had paid a little over twelve hundred dollars for them. She wondered what they'd be worth now.

The man studied them carefully, his manner brisk. "Do you mind?" he asked, motioning toward his jeweler's glass on a counter in the back.

"Not at all," she said, and followed him.

He put the glass to his eye and studied the rings carefully, humming as he did so.

"Well," she said after a few anxious minutes.

He dropped the glass from his eye and caught it expertly. "The most I can do for you is seventy-five dollars."

"Seventy-five dollars?"

"That's as high as I can go."

"But . . ."

"I'm sorry, ma'am," he said casually. "In the first place, the settings are strange. I've never seen anything quite like them before. Second, there's engraving on the inside, which means we have to change the settings. I'm giving you top dollar at seventy-five."

He saw the crestfallen look in her eyes. She was a beautiful woman and he felt a pang of sympathy for her. From the look of her clothes, she was probably parting with the rings as a last resort. So many people had fallen on hard times since the war.

"All right, look," he said quickly. "I know I shouldn't do this, but . . . well the diamonds are a good quality. I'll up it to an even hundred, but not one cent more."

She stared at him in disbelief. She had thought they would be worth at least five or six hundred. But then, prices and wages were both low, so the hundred-dollar offer was probably a good one.

"May I ask a rather strange question?" she said hesitantly.

"What's that, ma'am?"

"Will a hundred dollars be enough for a train ticket to Omaha, Nebraska?"

His eyebrows raised. "Nebraska? Ma'am, a hundred dollars will get you there twice. That where you're planning to go?"

"Yes," she said firmly. "And I'll take the hundred."

"I thought maybe you would," he said confidently. He set the rings down on a velvet cloth and wrote out a bill of sale. After she signed it, he turned to the cash drawer and counted out a hundred dollars in coin. She took the money, using both hands to hold it. This would never do.

"You don't happen to sell handbags, do you?" she asked as she stared at the money.

"Why, yes, we do," he said congenially. He walked over to the display window with notions in it and took out two handbags. She chose a brocade, paying him out of the money he'd given her, and left the store.

She stood outside and checked her watch. It was almost four-thirty. Most of the stores would close at five, so if she was going to accomplish anything, it would have to be quickly.

She hurried back to the department store, but this time a job was the farthest thing from her mind. Her first stop was the dress rack, where she picked out a dress of navy-blue grosgrain. The overskirt was trimmed with blue velvet ribbon and fringe and the high neckline had a white lace ruffle down the front. Next she found a small straw hat with navy ribbons and she topped it all off with a navy coat. The coat had a capelet that covered the shoulders and ended in a swallow tail that had wide fringe bands down the back. With the few minutes she had left, she bought a carpet bag and had the salesgirl put everything inside.

Back out on the street, she breathed a sigh of relief. Now, at least she had clothes, and she still had more than half her money left. It was amazing what you could get for so little. She hefted the carpet bag in her hands and headed back for the Waddell House Hotel. Ben had told her that Lincoln had spoken from the balcony there when he stopped in Cleveland on his way to his inaugural. If it was good enough for Lincoln, it was good enough for her.

The man at the desk wasn't quite as sure. He acted like he didn't want to give her a room, but in the end her money was good even though her clothes weren't fashionable. When she explained that there had been an accident and she'd been caught in the rain last night, he smiled apologetically. Five minutes later she was ushered into a room at the front of the hotel, and twenty minutes later she was lounging in a hot tub. It felt heavenly to sink into the hot water, and after washing her hair, she relaxed until the bath got cold. Then she dressed in her new clothes and went back down to the lobby. She asked the same desk clerk where she could eat, but he didn't recognize her.

"Excuse me, ma'am, are you the same Mrs. Clayton who registered a few minutes ago?" he asked, embarrassed.

"Yes, I am, and I'd also like to know if I can have my clothes cleaned, pressed, and repaired?"

"Certainly, Mrs. Clayton. I'm just sorry you were inconvenienced," he said. "Do you have any other luggage?"

She'd have to lie again. "My trunks have gone directly on to Omaha. I'm only staying for a day or so. If all goes well, I may even check out tomorrow."

He suggested she eat in the hotel dining room, and she was glad she didn't have to go out again. After being up almost all last night, she just wanted to fill her stomach and get to bed.

The sun was shining when she woke the next morning, and for a few minutes she had to take an inventory on where she was. She stirred lazily in the bed and pulled the covers up over her naked body. Don't tell me I'm coming down with a cold, she thought, and shuddered. That'd be just what she didn't need. She cuddled down in the blankets and quilts a bit longer, but she knew there was no use procrastinating. Throwing back the covers, she got up, dressed quickly, and left her room. She stopped by the desk to pay another day's lodging and left the hotel.

Breathing in the fresh morning air, she retraced her steps of the night before, walking to Water Street and bypassing Lighthouse Lane to go directly to Front Street. At the station, she was pleased when the ticket agent didn't recognize her. She bought a ticket for the train leaving the next morning, and then decided to take another quick look at what was left of the Brainards'. When she finally reached the square again, she was carrying her coat against a temperature that had risen considerably.

She still had quite a lot of money left, so she bought two plain calico dresses, one blue and one yellow. She also got some petticoats and bloomers, a pair of shoes, and a nightgown and wrapper. After taking them back to the hotel, she made one last stop to say good-bye to Amos, who was amazed at the transformation the navy-blue dress had made, and that night, as she climbed between the sheets once more, she was pleased with what she had accomplished. She had some clothes, a ticket to Omaha, and enough money left to get her there.

As she lay in the dark room and leaned from the edge of the bed, pulling back the curtain to look out at Superior Avenue, she wondered if everyone realized she wasn't coming back, and she hoped they understood. Strange how comfortable she felt looking down on the gaslights and watching the carriages going by. This was her time. She didn't belong to that other world, not really. She had never belonged. There had always been something missing.

"Please, Lord," she whispered softly, her eyes misting with tears. "Let them forgive me and make them understand. And most of all, God, let me find Ben and don't ever send me back again." With this prayer on her lips, she rolled over and closed her eyes, looking forward to the long ride tomorrow that would take her away from Cleveland and closer to Ben.

CHAPTER 11

Saturday morning Stacey got to the station early. The hotel maid had brought her old clothes back cleaned, mended, and pressed, and she had added them to her carpet bag. She had been too nervous to eat before leaving the hotel, and as her departure time approached, she grew even more nervous.

The last time, she had left with Ben and his family. This time she was traveling alone, and it was a little more frightening. She knew she'd have to change trains in Chicago, and she dreaded the long, stuffy ride and the haphazard eating at inadequate railroad lunch counters, where passengers sweated profusely while they gulped down their food. But they had left in June before, and now it was only April and the weather was cooler.

Still, by the time she found a seat on the train, she was perspiring enough to feel the dampness beneath her clothes. The train was crowded and an elderly man who smelled of tobacco and beer sat next to her. She hoped he wasn't going too far, because the smell was nauseating.

As luck would have it, he got off at the second stop, but the seat was promptly taken by another man who smelled like he'd fallen into a perfume bottle. The fragrance was a pleasant one, but after a while the strong smell got to her and she ended up with a headache that lasted through to Chicago, where they arrived in the early evening.

In Chicago she spent the night in a small hotel near the station that a policeman had recommended to her, then the next morning she boarded the Rock Island Line bound for Omaha.

Stacey was pleased to discover that the young woman sitting next to her was going all the way to Omaha. Her fiancé had been in Omaha for a year, and they were to be married the day after she arrived. Her name was Mary Ann.

Stacey tried to be friendly, but it was impossible to answer some of the personal questions the young woman asked, and after a while Mary Ann grew tired of prying and only made occasional comments about the scenery.

Stacey was sitting next to the window, and as she watched the cities and towns go by, she remembered with an aching heart the last time she had ridden through here. When they reached Rock Island in the late afternoon, she felt a tightening in her stomach as memories overwhelmed her. Stacey gazed at the island in the middle of the Mississippi for which the city was named. Ben had told her it had been a prison for Confederate soldiers during the war. She remembered that day so clearly.

They arrived in Des Moines, Iowa, close to midnight. To save money, both Stacey and Mary Ann slept in their seats, Stacey with her head against the window and Mary Ann with her head on Stacey's shoulder, then before the train pulled out again the next afternoon, they stretched their legs, grabbing a bite to eat in the Claridge House dining room, where she had stopped with Ben. If only the memories didn't make the longing so keen. By the time they left Des Moines, Stacey was almost in tears again.

It was early evening when the train finally arrived in Omaha, across the Missouri River from Council Bluffs, Iowa. As they slowly pulled into the station, Stacey's heart leaped inside her. The town looked much the same as it had before. When she had bought her ticket, Stacey had asked the ticket agent if the train went past Omaha yet, and he had laughed. "Ma'am," he had said, smiling. "If they ever get those tracks across Nebraska Territory, it'll be a miracle." Mary Ann had told her that the tracks weren't even fifty miles past the town yet. Mary Ann's fiancé worked at the railroad office, and he had informed her that the Casement brothers from Painesville, Ohio, had just taken over the job of laying the tracks and things were expected to really roll now. But until they did, Omaha was still the last town on the railroad frontier.

When Stacey and Mary Ann stepped from the train together, a crisply dressed young man with sandy hair came hurrying toward them, and without warning, swept Mary Ann into his arms, giving her a big bear hug while he laughed spontaneously.

Mary Ann's face was flushed when he finally set her down, and she introduced Stacey. Stacey felt like an intruder and was glad when the young woman finally bid her a polite good-bye, and a few minutes later, with a lump in her throat, Stacey watched the young lovers lose themselves in the crowd.

It was quite a distance to the Cromwell House, and, not having enough money for a carriage, Stacey picked up her carpet bag and started walking. She gawked about curiously at the changes here and there. The men were still wearing guns, but that was no surprise. There were a couple of new saloons and some buildings going up, but on the whole the town looked the same. Maybe a little bigger. As she gazed once more at the facaded buildings and bustling crowds, she wondered if it was wise to go back to the same hotel where she had stayed before, then shrugged it off. A year was a long time, and surely no one would remember someone who had only stayed there one day so long ago.

The desk clerk didn't remember, and by the time she reached her hotel room, which was furnished with a bed, dresser, armoire, and dry sink, she was exhausted. She dropped her carpet bag and slowly lowered herself onto the bed. Every weary bone in her body was aching. She fell back sighing, and stared at the ceiling, following a crack that ran from the window. It wasn't a big crack, but it reminded her of the fine line between the past and the future. What now? She had been so intent on reaching Omaha that she hadn't thought any further.

Tossing her hat on the bed, she sat up and took out what was left of her money. Not even twenty dollars. She had to find a job. The hotel was fifty cents a day, and between that and her food, it wouldn't be long before she was broke.

She dropped the money reluctantly back into the handbag and tossed it on the bed beside the hat, then stood up and went to the window, gazing down onto the street below. If she joined a wagon train going to Oregon, she'd need at least two, maybe three hundred dollars to pay for a wagon, a team, and supplies. Even then, it was doubtful anyone would accept a woman alone. She could take a stage. Mary Ann had told her that there were stage lines running to Salt Lake City, where she could connect with another stage to Oregon. She'd have to explore both possibilities. But the first thing she had to do was get a job of some kind. She sighed and lifted her eyes to the horizon, where the sun was dipping low. Another day gone. It was April 23, 1866, a Monday evening. She watched a buckboard pull away from the boardwalk, jostling some people aside. The street was anything but deserted, even at this hour of the night, and she wondered what so many people were doing here. They weren't all going west. Some of them would probably stay and build.

Shadows were filtering into the corners of the small room, and Stacey walked to the dresser and lit the lamp. She stared at the flame as she set the chimney over it. She was more tired than hungry, so she decided to forgo food for sleep. She undressed wearily, slipped her nightgown on, blew the kerosene lamp back out and climbed between the covers. She settled down comfortably, and before the saloon piano across the street had a chance to even begin to disturb her, she was fast asleep.

Stacey woke with a stomach growling for food. She checked her watch and saw that she had slept late. It was almost eight o'clock. The sun was filling the room with its warmth, and stretching lazily, she suddenly thought of Drew.

She had avoided thinking of him, but now her memories were too keen to ignore. She did love him in a way that was hard to define. He had a way of looking amused that showed all over his face. It must have been terribly hard for him to deceive her, to try to hang on while he was falling in love with someone else.

In spite of everything, it hurt to lose Drew. And poor John. What a delight he was. Never asking anything for himself, yet giving so openly. She could have loved him so easily if she had let herself. But Beth needed the love of a man like John, and Stacey hoped that now, with her gone, they would have a chance together. John deserved to be happy. He reminded her of Ben in so many ways.

She shivered at the thought of Ben. He didn't even know she was back. Her thoughts drifted to the diary, to the messages he had left for her. Aching inside for want of him, she pushed back the covers and forced her thoughts back to the present.

The water in the washbasin was cold, but she stripped bare and gave herself a sponge bath. After putting on her underwear, bra, and petticoats, she slipped into the blue calico dress that had a lace fringe about the scooped neckline. She began to come alive, anxious to discover what the town held for her.

That part of it didn't take long. By noon, she discovered no one was in need of any help. The hotels all had clerks and the restaurants all had cooks, waitresses, and dishwashers. About the only job for a woman was walking the streets.

Discouraged, Stacey was heading back to her hotel room when she suddenly realized she was standing in front of the telegraph office. The telegraph! Making a quick decision, she opened the door and walked in.

The telegrapher was sitting with his back to her, engrossed in sending a message. "Be right with you," he threw back over his shoulder. She stood by the counter to wait. After finishing, he turned around and stood up eagerly when he caught sight of her pretty face. "Well, what can I do for you?"

"Can you send telegrams to Oregon?" she asked.

"To Oregon and all points west, yes, ma'am."

"How much?"

"It all depends on how many words and how far it's goin'. What are you plannin' to say and who's it goin' to?"

"It's going to Mr. Ben Clayton in Portland, Oregon."

He handed her a pencil and some paper. "You write it on this and I'll tell you how much. How's that?" he asked. "You know how to write?"

She nodded, and put the things down in front of her on the counter. What was she going to say? She stared for a long time at the blank paper, searching for the right words. Finally she wrote:

> Dearest Ben,
>   I have come back through time to you. I am in Omaha. Come for me. I love you.
> > Yours forever,
> > Stacey

The telegrapher read the message over and frowned. "Is this the only address you have for him, ma'am?"

"Yes."

He looked skeptical. "Well, I don't rightly know. We can try." She paid him and gave her address in case of an answer, since he said it might take a few hours, then she left, feeling a little more confident.

But by late the next afternoon, having found neither work nor heard anything from the telegraph office, Stacy was in the grips of a gnawing fear. She decided to go by and check on her message.

"Have you had any word?" she asked the telegrapher eagerly.

"No, ma'am," he answered. "But then, the lines were down for a while yesterday. Indians again. We finally got through, but there's been no answer for you."

Pursing her lips nervously, she thanked him and left. Why hadn't Ben answered? She began to panic, but forced herself to think clearly. There could be any number of reasons. She didn't even have a house address for him, and Portland was probably a big city. With her money quickly running out, she'd have to concentrate on finding a job now.

Her mind on her troubles, she turned to walk away and bumped smack into a solid mass. "Oh, I'm sorry," she cried, extricating herself from the strong hands that were helping her keep her balance, and she looked up into a pair of slate-gray eyes that were appraising her from a rather good-looking face.

"Are you all right?" he asked solicitously. She straightened her straw bonnet and avoided his intense gaze. "Forgive me," she said quickly. "I guess my mind was elsewhere."

"Elsewhere?" He studied her even more closely. "An educated lady, I'd say. Am I right?"

Her eyes grew wary. "Excuse me?"

"Forgive my frankness," he apologized. "You see, although most of the women around these parts can read and write, their command of the English language leaves something to be desired. You sound like you've spent most of your time in drawing rooms."

What was this, some kind of new pickup line? She eyed him dubiously.

He was about Drew's height, and lean, but she could see muscles moving beneath his tailored clothes. His face was long and handsome beneath a head of dark, very curly hair that turned up softly about his ears. Instinctively, as she took in his pale blue brocade vest, gilded watch chain, ruffled shirt, and tight-fitting gray pants, she knew he wasn't just an ordinary working man. He looked too much like the gamblers she'd seen in western movies.

Her chin tilted up. "I'm afraid you're mistaken, Mr. . . . sir. . . ."

"Wade Savagge," he informed her politely. "With two g's."

"Mr. Savagge, I've spent little time in drawing rooms, I assure you. I'm a working woman just like anyone else. At least I will be when I can find a job."

His eyes lit up. "You're looking for a job?"

"It seems there are very few in this town, Mr. Savagge," she said. "But yes, I'm looking for a job."

"I don't suppose you can deal faro?"

She had guessed right. "I've never played the game in my life."

"Too bad." His gray eyes smiled. "You'd make one hell of a faro dealer."

"Oh?"

"Let's face it," he said, "the men wouldn't mind losing to someone who looks like you. Sure you don't know how to deal?"

"Positive."

"Well, if you can think of something you can do that would enhance the place and keep the men's minds off their money, I'm over at the Paradise across the street. Now, I must be going. Glad to have met you, Miss . . ."

"Mrs. Clayton," she said firmly. "Stacey Clayton."

"Mrs. Clayton. Ah, I might have known. The pretty ones are always married. Too bad you can't deal," he said thoughtfully. "A shame." He tipped his hat. "Well, I must be going. If you come up with anything, I'll be glad to listen."

She stared after him, frowning. It might work, it just might. It was her last resort.

"Mr. Savagge . . . Oh, Mr. Savagge!" she called, running after the man. Her face reddened as she approached. "I hope you don't mind. I have thought of something."

"Oh?"

"I don't deal cards, but I do sing, Mr. Savagge, and I can accompany myself with a guitar. If I had one, that is."

"You sing? Do you know how many women I have over there already who think they can sing?"

"Not the way I sing," she said, then added. "I'll tell you what. If you let me sing while I learn to deal faro, I'll deal for you."

"What if you don't catch on to it?"

"I will. I know how to play poker and black jack, so faro shouldn't be too difficult."

He rubbed his chin as he stared at her. She was a beautiful woman, with soft curling red hair and gorgeous blue eyes that had a way of looking right into a man's soul. Even in the plain little calico dress and straw bonnet, she was stunning. She'd be even better in silks and satins.

"You'll let me teach you?" he asked.

"Unless there's someone else who can."

"No . . . if you learn to deal, you'll learn my way, or not at all. You'll get paid by the night, plus a percentage of the table. So it's up to you. The more the house takes, the more you take." His eyes narrowed. "Are you sure you really want to do this?"

"I have to."

"Have to?"

She couldn't admit that she only planned to work long enough to get money to leave town. If she did, he'd never hire her. She needed this job. It was the only thing left for her, short of selling herself.

"Because I have to eat," she said softly.

"Don't we all," he said, pleased with her decision. "You come over to the Paradise tonight about six and I'll listen to you sing. If I like it, you've got a job."

"Thanks," she said gratefully. His smile broadened as he bid her good day.

Stacey stood on the boardwalk watching him leave, contemplating what she'd just done. Stacey Gordon . . . Stacey Clayton, saloon girl? It was almost funny. Wouldn't the gossips back home love that one. Suddenly a horrible thought occurred to her. What songs were they singing in 1866? She knew some that were all right for campfire singing, but to entertain in a saloon? Ah, Stacey, she thought, what on earth have you gotten yourself into this time?

On the way back to the hotel, she stopped at a store that sold tools and instruments of all kinds, including musical instruments. It took all but her last dollar, but as she told herself later while she was tuning the guitar, if worse came to worst she could at least earn money singing on the street corner with it. It was a used guitar, but it had a nice smooth quality.

It had been quite some time since she had played, and the calluses on her fingers had softened. She sat on the bed and propped the small songbook she'd also invested in up on a chair and ran her fingers through a few scales. She then proceeded to familiarize herself as best she could with some of the popular songs of the day.

After almost two hours of rehearsing, a new thought suddenly crossed her mind. Her fingers began picking at the strings in a slow, sensuous rhythm she had almost forgotten, and a new excitement filled her. There was no way she could sing any of the songs from 1976 that she knew, but there was nothing to stop her from singing her own creations. She had told Wade Savagge her singing was different. Now she'd prove it. For the next hour she tried to remember everything she had ever composed, and thankfully it all came back to her. By the time she left for the Paradise, she was determined to make good.

Wade Savagge stood in front of his office window on the second floor of the Paradise watching a figure leave the hotel farther down the street. The red hair and straw bonnet were unmistakable, and he smiled as he saw her guitar. She was an enigma. From the moment he had looked into those big blue eyes and heard her musically husky voice, he knew she wasn't what she purported to be.

Her appearance was that of a plain frontier woman, yet she walked with a grace and assurance that spoke of confidence. She had a sensual quality she couldn't hide. His eyes followed her through the crowds of people, and he wondered if, perhaps, Mrs. Clayton was widowed. Surely she wasn't divorced. Whatever, it didn't look like Mr. Clayton was in Omaha. That was one point in his favor, and seeing her disappear beneath the overhang of the building, he turned from the window and waited for her to come upstairs.

The brawny bartender named Ox ushered Stacey into Wade Savagge's office. It was just what she had expected. A touch of show with velvet drapes, heavy, ornate furniture, and crystal light fixtures that picked up reflections from the flames in the lamps and mirrored them about the room. At the moment, the setting sun reflected through them too, casting an orange light into the shadows.

"Well, I see you brought your own accompaniment," he said congenially. "Sit down, Mrs. Clayton," he said, motioning toward an overstuffed sofa.

She stood her ground. "You said you wanted to hear me sing."

"To be sure. But you do have to sit down to play that thing, don't you?"

"Not always." She unfastened her bonnet and set it down before swinging the guitar off her shoulder and sitting. "But it is easier to sing without this on, and I might as well sit down."

He walked over to his desk and sat in the big chair behind it. "Anytime you're ready, then."

She adjusted the guitar on her knee and ran her fingers up and down the strings a few times. They were sore as the devil, but she couldn't let him know that. Slowly she began to pick the strings, running right into the strains of a song she had titled "Sweet World." She began to sing.

> The memory of your smile is with me forever and ever,
> The longing here in my heart can't be stilled.
> The world was sweet, my love was new, I gave it all to
> be with you,
> And yet you're gone and I'm alone forever and ever.
> Give me back my heart, I'm lonely without it.
> Give me back my love, you've no right to keep it.
> Give me my world, make it sweet again, give me my
> life, let me live again,
> And the world will be a sweet world to me.

> The memory of your touch is with me forever and ever
> Your caress always made my heart sing.
> The world was sweet, my heart was true, I've cried a
> thousand tears for you,
> And yet you're gone and I'm alone forever and ever.
> Give me back my heart, I'm no good without it.

Give me back my love, you've no right to keep it,
Give me my world, make it sweet again, give me my
life, make it complete again,
And the world will be a sweet world to me.

Wade sat entranced, quietly listening. The melody was haunting and the woman singing was intriguing. "You do have a way
with it, don't you," he said after she finished. He sat up, forcing
himself back to the reality of why she was there. For a moment
he had almost felt she was singing just for him. "If you sing like
that for the men downstairs, there shouldn't be any problem. But
tell me, I don't think I've ever heard that song. Where'd you
find it?"

"I wrote it," she answered, and his eyebrows raised.

"You?"

"Why not? Is there some law that says a woman's not allowed
to write a song?"

He laughed. "Not at all. It's just that . . . the song's quite,
shall we say, touching. Quite good. How would you like to sing
it for the men tonight?"

"Tonight? I'd love to."

"Only I'm afraid you'll have to find something else to wear.
The men see enough women in calico and bonnets." He walked
to the door, opened it, and called out, "Ginger!"

A few minutes later a brunette with big brown eyes and
crimson lips sauntered into the room wearing a red-spangled
dress with black feathers. She leaned against the door frame and
gazed at Stacey curiously.

"Stacey, this is Ginger Dalton. Ginger, Stacey Clayton. I
want you to take Stacey to the back room and tell Lil to find her
something to wear tonight. Something that won't clash with her
hair and will keep the men's eyes on her. That greenish-blue
satin Lil ordered for Pearl should do."

"Pearl won't like it."

"To hell with what Pearl likes. Who's paying for it, me or
Pearl?"

"No skin off my nose," said Ginger, shrugging. "Comin'?"
she asked Stacey.

Wade walked over and Stacey let him help her up. "I won't
disappoint you," she said as she looked up at him.

"I have no fear of that, Stacey," he said huskily. "You don't
mind if I call you Stacey, do you? Mrs. Clayton's so formal."

"Stacey's fine," she said, pulling her hand from his. "And
thank you."

She followed Ginger down the stairs, turning right at a landing halfway down, then ascending the rest of the stairway into a hall. At the end of the hall they went through a door on the right and entered a large room filled with women in dresses exactly like Ginger's. In the dim light of Wade Savagge's office, Ginger's dress had looked flashy, extravagant, and sparkling, but in the brighter light that filled this room it and the other women's dresses were clearly shabby and worn.

The glamour of backstage, thought Stacey as she looked about the room at the other women whose faces were painted as garishly as Ginger's.

An older woman with graying black hair was fastening some feathers onto a dress, and Ginger called to her. "This is Stacey Clayton, Lil," she said so everyone could hear. "Wade said to fit her into that new dress he just bought for Pearl. Stacey, this is Lil, our mother hen." Stacey couldn't help but hear the gasp from the others at the mention of Pearl's dress.

Stacey smiled, fingering her guitar. "Hello, Lil."

"You play that thing?" Lil asked.

"Yes."

"Good at it?"

"Fairly."

"Well, take it off so I can get a look at your figure," Lil said, turning toward Stacey with her hands on her well-padded hips. With her generous bosom, Lil was anything but small in stature. Her eyes were a liquid blue with yellow flecks, and she had an acquiline nose and full lips. She may have been attractive in her younger days, but she hadn't aged gracefully. She had a gold eyetooth and her face was more wrinkled than most women's were at fifty. Stacey wondered how she happened to have a job like this, until she learned Lil was Wade's aunt.

After looking Stacey over, Lil opened up the armoire in the back of the room and brought out a gorgeous deep turquoise dress with shiny crystal beading all over the tight bodice. It had short puffed sleeves and a full, billowing skirt. Lil took Stacey behind a screen, and a few minutes later Stacey emerged looking like a vision. The dress molded to her figure as if it were made for her.

"We'll have to fix your hair, too," Lil said, pointing to a seat in front of a small dressing table and mirror.

Lil was adept with hairpins and a brush, and within minutes Stacey's hair was atop her head with jeweled combs adorning it. Lil then stared at Stacey's ears. She was still wearing the pair of small gold hoops she'd had on the night she had run into the rain.

"The gold won't do," Lil said purposefully. She moved across the room to a dresser and opened one of the drawers. The earrings she brought out were only imitation, but they sparkled like diamonds. In the lights on the stage, no one would notice they weren't real. She put them in Stacey's ears and started to reach for the rouge.

"No," said Stacey firmly. "That part I'll do myself, if you don't mind."

Lil shrugged. "It's your face."

Stacey used the rouge lightly and made up her eyes with the mascara, using it like eyeliner as she had so many times before. The result was far from the garishness of the other women. It enhanced her eyes so that even in the bright lights they looked inviting.

When she was through, Lil shook her head. "Not dark enough. They won't even see you got any on."

"That's the idea," said Stacey. "I don't intend to look like a painted doll."

"Who looks like painted dolls?" asked a sultry voice from the doorway. Stacey turned to find an attractive brunette with snapping hazel eyes. "And who told you you could put on my dress?" the woman asked.

"Pearl?" Stacey guessed hesitantly.

"You bet it is," Pearl answered, stalking up to Stacey. "And I asked you, what're you doing in my dress?"

"It's Wade's orders, Pearl," said Ginger.

"To hell it is!"

"He told me himself."

"He wouldn't do that to me."

"Wouldn't he?" Ginger stared at the other woman, who was poured into a frivolous concoction of coral silk and white satin. For a long time, Pearl had been the featured dancer in the show, the one who danced center stage and sang all the solos. She was a favorite with all the men, including Wade. Although Stacey had never met her before, the reason for her resentment was obvious.

"Well, we'll just see about that," said Pearl. She flicked her parasol curtly and headed up to Wade's rooms.

Wade was changing into a fancy gray frock coat when Pearl stormed in. She slammed the door, and he glanced away, knowing what was coming next.

"My dress!" she yelled furiously. "You've put that stupid redhead in my dress!"

"Your dress?" he asked. "Was your name on it?"

"Come on, Wade, you know better than that. You had Lil send for that dress special."

"That's right. I had Lil send for it," he said. "So I guess I have a right to say who wears it."

"Who is she, anyway?"

"She's going to sing for a while," he answered, straightening the cuffs of his coat. He walked over to the liquor cabinet and poured himself a drink. "Eventually she'll be working the faro table for me so I can circulate. She'll be a good draw."

"And what about me?" Pearl snapped.

"What about you?"

"You're impossible, Wade. You know very well what I mean. When we left New York last spring, you promised me the world on a silver platter. I'd be the toast of the frontier. Now, I finally have a chance to really look like something, and you have to ruin it. I don't like it."

"That's too bad. Because Stacey keeps the dress."

"She won't if I rip it off her!"

"You lay one hand on her and you're through," he said viciously.

"Why?" she asked, suddenly aware that he wasn't going to relent. Her voice lowered seductively. "What can she do that I can't do?"

His mouth curved into a half smile. "I haven't had a chance to find out yet, but I'll let you know when I do."

"You're not amusing," she said. Her expression softened as she lifted her hand to stroke his lapel. "Have I ever disappointed you, honey?" she asked. "We've been good for each other, you and I. Haven't I always been cooperative? You've never needed anyone else. Why all of a sudden this interest in someone else? Who is she, anyway?"

"I haven't the slightest idea," he answered. "All I know is her name's Stacey Clayton, she can sing like a dream, and I bumped into her outside the telegraph office."

"You don't know anything else about her?"

"Do I have to?"

"Evidently not," she said jealously. "But what am I to do now?"

"What do you mean?"

"Well, if she does the singing, what about me? I suppose you expect me to play second fiddle to some woman who's probably never even seen the inside of a theater. Wade, it isn't fair. You said we'd make it big with our own place, and I listened to you. Now you're cutting me out. I don't understand. Is it something I've done, or something I haven't done?''

He put an arm about her waist and pulled her against him. ''Neither,'' he said affectionately, remembering what it was like to make love to this fiery brunette. ''It's just that a pretty face is an asset in this business, and a pretty face who can sing is a double asset. Stacey Clayton has both, and on top of it, I'm going to teach her how to deal. Something you could never seem to catch on to. She's going to pack them in for us, Pearl,'' he said, kissing her below the ear. ''With you and the girls behind her, we're going to have the best damn show this side of the Mississippi and rake in more money at our tables than any of the other saloons in town. There's money out there, honey, and I aim to get every bit of it I can. With that redhead. . . . She's got class, Pearl, real class. I don't know where the hell she's from, and I don't much care, but right now, she's just what this place needs, and I don't want you scaring her away, understand? Besides,'' he said, his voice lowering sensuously, ''there's really no need, honey. You should know that.'' He kissed her lightly yet soundly on the mouth. ''Now, be a good girl, go downstairs and get into costume. You handle the girls like always and let me handle Stacey Clayton.''

''That's just the trouble. I don't like the way you use that word 'handle.' ''

''Jealous?'' he asked.

''What do you think?''

''That's what I like about you, honey. You never beat around the bush. Now, go down and behave yourself.''

She eyed him skeptically. ''I'll go, Wade,'' she said, an edge to her voice. ''But so help me, if you so much as look at her cross-eyed I'll . . .''

''You'll what?'' he asked.

But she didn't answer. She just snapped her parasol into her hand and left.

He leaned out the door and watched her sashay down the hall, skirts swinging. Women! Hard to live with them, impossible to live without them, and Pearl he couldn't live with at all. Thank God he'd never weakened and married her. She was hard enough to handle as it was, thinking she had an exclusive claim on him. To put a ring on her finger would have been sheer madness.

He walked back to his desk, admitting to himself that until he'd seen Stacey Clayton, Pearl had been woman enough to keep him from straying too far. He had always liked a pretty face and trim torso, but that delectable redhead was the most exciting thing he'd ever bumped into. Just thinking about her made him strain to keep himself in check. God, she was something. He tucked a couple of cheroots into his shirt pocket, then left his rooms.

Downstairs, men were filtering through the doors of the Paradise Saloon. The Paradise was still a new saloon, having been built the previous summer. But it was nothing like the other saloons in Omaha. Most of the others were just that, saloons. A place you could get a beer or a whiskey, a girl, and maybe a game of poker. When the Paradise opened late in the afternoon, they offered a few poker games and some beers. But after the sun went down, the tempo changed.

Wade Savagge had been brought up on the streets of New York and had learned his skill at cards from the men who frequented Aunt Lil's boardinghouse. At least, he thought it was just a boardinghouse until he was old enough to know better. But Aunt Lil was never what could be called a "madam." She sang in the theater when she could, but most of the time she lived off the rent from the women who used her rooms.

As soon as Wade was old enough to take over the purse strings, however, things changed. Aunt Lil's young women began to spend more time on the stage and less in their rooms, and by the time Wade was old enough to take advantage of their wares, Aunt Lil's bordello had become a semirespectable theatrical boardinghouse. Between card games, Wade found himself managing several of the ladies' careers, including Pearl's and those of the other four he'd brought west with him.

Two things precipitated his decision to leave New York: an extremely high-stakes poker game with some wealthy businessmen, friends of Tammany Hall, who were beginning to question his good fortune, and the fact that the ladies' show closed. For the first time in his colorful thirty-six years, Wade had enough money to do the things he'd always wanted to do, so he talked Aunt Lil into selling the house and moving west. His one ambition was to have a place of his own. Not just a place where a man could quench his thirst, but a high-class place where the women were special, the whiskey the best, and the gambling done with such finesse that the losers didn't mind parting with their money. A real gentlemen's saloon, with roulette wheels and a beautiful woman dealer. One who would decorate the faro table with such grace and charm that the men would fight to lose money to her.

He had his saloon. The Paradise was in the new section of town, sitting all by itself on a corner lot. Unlike its predecessors, it was not facaded. The main room downstairs ran the full width of the building and was equipped with a mahogany bar with mirrors, chandeliers hanging from the ceiling, and a small stage in the back. The stage had red velvet curtains and three scenery backdrops. To the left, beyond the main room, was the gambling room. Adjacent to and behind the stage was a door leading backstage to the dressing room. Another door at the back of the dressing room led into a long hall that gave Wade's ladies free access to the gambling room. The upstairs rooms, consisting of Wade's private office and bedroom and the girls' rooms, were reached by stairs that started beside the stage and forked at the landing. An outside balcony graced the overhang at the front of the saloon, and could be reached only from Wade's private office. Above the balcony hung the sign proclaiming "THE PARADISE."

It was the kind of place he'd always wanted, but it lacked one thing. Now, as he sauntered downstairs, Wade had a feeling all that was changing. As much as he and Pearl had gotten along over the past five years, he had never been able to teach her the fundamentals of faro. She wasn't dumb, but she just didn't have the class and her hands weren't nimble enough for the game. Of all the women he had gone through in New York, none had been able to match him at the game. But now, he had a gut feeling Stacey Clayton was going to be able to do the job. Along with her other obvious, and hidden talents, she was going to be the culmination of all his dreams.

Wade descended the last few steps and mingled with his patrons. Anticipation keyed him up as he surveyed his little kingdom.

Backstage, Stacey was nervous. It was one thing to sing for your family and friends, but this was different. Her stomach was in a state of shock. The thought of trying to keep so many men entertained was overwhelming. She watched the other women and wished she had their courage.

There were four young women besides Pearl. Ginger, who was outspoken in a way that tickled Stacey. Ellen, whom Wade affectionately called Ellie and treated like a kid sister. She was an amber blond with brown eyes and a voice that was a little too raspy to be really good. Next was Hazel, who was a little older than the others but still pretty, with chestnut hair and a thin, poignant face. She had a voice that still rang with the quality that had once graced the legitimate opera. And Mae, whose brown locks were turning prematurely gray. Lil usually hid it for her with dyes and hair colorings, but the men didn't seem to mind. She had a warm personality and her hazel eyes often gleamed with an impishness that was an open invitation to the customers. Last of all was Pearl. Pearl was different from the others. She had been brought up in the theater, the by-blow of an actress and one of her admirers. Although her voice wasn't all that grand, she could put over a song well enough to capture center stage. Too bad she had missed all the finer things in life. As Stacey watched her preen herself in front of the mirror, she felt a little sorry for her. Pearl was pretty and looked every bit a lady, until she began to talk and shattered the illusion.

Stacey picked up her guitar and strummed it lightly, testing her fingers. They were still so sore. She picked at the strings until Ginger informed everyone that it was time to circulate.

"That doesn't go for you," Ginger said when Stacey started to get up. "Wade said you don't mix until you've learned how to deal, so stay put until somebody gives you a holler. The show doesn't start for at least an hour yet."

"Thanks," said Stacey halfheartedly.

The next hour went fast. Stacey discovered that besides the bartender, affectionately called Ox, and the ladies, Wade had some men running roulette and dice tables. He also had several poker tables where men could enjoy a friendly game without a house dealer. Finally, there was the faro table, where Wade was king.

All this she learned from a short man named Rundy, who arrived a half-hour before show time. Introducing himself with a flourish, he informed her that he played piano for the show.

"I came all the way from New York with Wade," he said jauntily as he inspected his suit in the mirror. "Just bought this suit today. Hope it looks all right."

"It looks fine," Stacey assured him.

"A fella my size gotta make sure the legs ain't too long," he said hurriedly, then checked to see that his small mustache was properly twirled at the corners.

He was an energetic man, not nervous, but wiry, and would certainly look out of place walking down the dusty streets of Omaha. But he assured Stacey that he loved it here, just as he would like it anywhere his old friend Wade decided to drag him. His eyes lost their friendly sparkle only once, when Stacey told him she'd be accompanying herself with the guitar. Rundy seemed a strange friend for Wade Savagge to have, but when Stacey learned they had grown up together, it was understandable.

When the first show finally started, Stacey's insides started to churn. They had to like her. She touched the shimmering beads on her bodice as Pearl finished her last song and Wade made his way to center stage.

Stacey had requested that the curtains be closed and the stage cleared of everything save a chair. Rundy extinguished all the footlights except two directly in front of the chair, then Wade introduced her.

She inhaled nervously, saying a little prayer, then stepped out of the wings, and as she walked slowly into the golden light from the flickering footlights, a sudden hush fell over the crowd. Wade backed away, disappearing into the wings, and she was alone.

Forcing herself to ignore the faces staring up at her, Stacey slowly lowered herself to the chair, let the guitar rest comfortably on her lap and her fingers began to stroke the instrument in a slow, sensuous rhythm that within minutes had all eyes glued to the stage, the raucous noise and laughter of moments before, forgotten. And as she played, she relaxed more, the rhythm calming the frantic beating of her heart, then when she was sure the moment was right, the rhythm slowed, and she began to sing the haunting melody she had written, her voice lifting to the chandeliers, echoing through the room, and capturing every ear.

CHAPTER 12

When the last strains of her song died away, the silence was overpowering. Then the clapping began, slowly at first, but gradually increasing in volume until whoops and hollers filled the room. Stacey smiled, relieved. It was over. Her initiation into the life of a saloon singer was complete, and it looked like everything was going to be all right.

She began casually talking to the audience and once more silence reigned, as if each man felt he was the target of her voice. Before finally leaving the stage, she sang another of her own compositions as well as Stephen Foster's "Jeannie with the Light Brown Hair." The audience loved both songs, and their response overwhelmed her.

Later, dressed again in her blue calico, she stood in Wade's office and listened to the strains of Rundy's exuberant piano-playing floating up from downstairs. She was pleased. Who would have thought that Stacey Gordon, surgical nurse, could become Stacey Clayton, saloon singer? It gave her a strange sense of the unnatural. But it was real.

She gazed thoughtfully down to the street below. It was late and she watched as the patrons left, some shouting and singing, others silently mourning their losses at the gaming tables. There were also those who didn't leave, and she heard shuffling foot-steps out in the hall as the women went to their rooms with their men for the night. How could they do it? The thought of a strange man's bare skin against hers, claiming her, sickened Stacey. She could never do it. With a man she wanted, for love, yes, or even need, if she cared for a man, but not for pay.

She turned suddenly as Wade came in again. He had spent the last hour teaching her faro and had promised to walk her back to the hotel, as soon as he went downstairs to make sure Ox and Rundy would lock the front doors.

"Are you ready?" he asked, grabbing his broad-brimmed black hat.

She nodded and picked up her bonnet.

He watched her tie the ribbons beneath her chin and smiled. "You can't really hide it in those clothes, you know," he said.

"Hide what?"

"Whatever it is that makes you stand out in a crowd. I knew the minute I looked into your eyes that you weren't an ordinary woman. Who are you really, Stacey Clayton?" he asked. "And what the devil are you doing in this town?"

"I thought there was an unspoken law out here," she said graciously, "that a person's past was her own business, and only the present mattered."

He smiled. "Touché, my dear," he said, and gestured toward the door. "Shall we?"

As they left the saloon behind, Wade took the initiative. "I still think you'd be better off taking a room with one of the girls," he said.

She shook her head. "Not on your life. I'd rather not share my room with anyone, including your customers." She eyed him knowingly. "They give you a cut, I presume?"

"Why not? Why should I let them use the rooms for free? I spend enough on them as it is. They keep the biggest share, but I get paid back for my investment."

"And you don't feel guilty?"

"About what?"

"About being a glorified pimp."

He stopped abruptly and grabbed her arm. "I'm not a pimp, Stacey," he said deliberately. "Don't ever call me that. I don't make those girls sell themselves. They do it because they want to. If they never slept with another customer, I wouldn't give a damn. But, by God, if they're going to use my generosity to line their pockets, I think it's only fair I get a cut. You can call it anything else you want, but don't ever say I'm a pimp."

"You're serious, aren't you?" she asked curiously.

"Why shouldn't I be?"

"And it doesn't bother you, what they do?"

"Bother me? Certainly it bothers me, but they aren't about to stop just because I tell them to. You see, I can't afford to pay them the wages to which they think they should be accustomed. Only a millionaire could, so they'll keep right on selling themselves to pay for all their extra gewgaws and fancy clothes."

"It's as simple as that?"

"Nothing in this world is simple, Stacey. Life's one complicated mess after another. You should know that by now. Most people are born, grow up, get married, have families . . . then there are people like me, Aunt Lil, and the girls. I'll show you what I mean. Why was Ginger forced to sell herself for a loaf of bread when she was only twelve? Her father was dead, her mother a drunken prostitute. And little Ellie. As strict and wealthy as her parents were, they couldn't keep her brother's hands off her. He was three years older than she was, and she worshiped him. She was only fourteen when he introduced her to the pleasures of his body. That was all it took to get her started. And Hazel. Widowed at twenty by a husband who committed suicide because he couldn't stand the thought of going to prison for embezzlement. She lost everything. A fancy house, her reputation. Even her family ostracized her. She had no choice but to be nice to men. Now, Mae's something else entirely. I think Mae was born with a seductive smile on her lips. She'd sleep with the men for free if the other girls would let her. From the time she learned to swing her hips, she knew what they were for. So what else happens to a woman like that?''

"What about Pearl?"

He stared off down the street. "Ah, yes, Pearl. Now, she's different. The only time Pearl takes a customer upstairs is when she's mad at me."

"You're joking."

"Not at all. Pearl thinks her body is a weapon. An instrument for getting what she wants."

"You're in love with her?"

"Not really. I'm not even sure I know what love is. Let's just say Pearl's my security."

"Security?"

"Without Pearl, who knows what I might do when the urge moves me."

Her face reddened and she eyed him skeptically. They reached the hotel, and he opened the door for her.

"You look like you don't believe me," he said as he followed her into the lobby.

"Oh, I believe you," she said. "It just seems callous to use her like that."

"Use her? I've never used a woman in my life."

Stacey stopped in front of her door, and he glanced down at her. The dim hall light turned her hair into strands of deep red flame. Their eyes met, the gray in his stormy and turbulent.

"When I want a woman, Stacey Clayton, I want more than just a body to use," he said softly. "I want all of her, not to use, but to pleasure. And you, my dear lady, I could please quite easily."

"I doubt that."

"Ah, don't be too sure." He ran his finger from her temple to her lips, and she felt an unwanted but familiar quickening inside.

She brushed his finger aside and looked at him with cold eyes. "However did we manage to get on this subject, Mr. Savagge?" she asked curtly.

He smiled. "I have no idea. But it's fascinating."

"To you perhaps, but not to me." She took out the key to her room. "I want to thank you for walking me home, but now, if you don't mind, I do have to get my sleep."

"Not at all," he replied, ignoring the crispness in her voice. "Only I'd like you to come early tomorrow, about one or so, if you can. We can have a few faro lessons in the afternoon without being disturbed." He continued to gaze down at her. "You still don't want to tell me who you really are?"

Her eyes hardened. "Good night, Mr. Savagge."

"The name's Wade."

"If you insist. Good night, Wade," she said, and turned to open the door. Her fingers were closing around the knob when she suddenly felt strong hands on her shoulders and a voice close to her ear.

"Good night, Red," he whispered huskily, running his lips across her ear and nestling a kiss behind it, then as quickly the hands dropped from her shoulders.

She stood rooted to the spot as his footsteps echoed down the stairs. Her hand was gripping the doorknob so tightly her knuckles were white. What was it John had told her? The next time you meet a man who affects you like that, run like hell the other way. She should have known better. The chemistry was there and she should have recognized it the moment Wade looked into her eyes.

Dragging herself into the room, Stacey cursed herself for letting the man do this to her. She straightened, forcing herself to accept her body's feelings. She'd reacted the same way when Drew made love to her, even when John became affectionate. It was a natural response that had nothing to do with her love for Ben.

After all, wasn't that the way her love for Ben began? But all attraction didn't culminate in love. She knew the difference now between sexual desire and real love.

She lit the kerosene lamp and pulled out her nightgown. She couldn't let it throw her. Wade was good-looking and he had a charm that couldn't be denied, but he wasn't Ben. He was only a man. One who could satisfy her sexually, perhaps, but she wasn't about to find out. The fact that he could arouse her didn't mean a thing. She was in the same world with Ben again. He was out there someplace, and all the Wade Savagges in the world couldn't come between them. No matter how often her body betrayed her, she'd never let it win. By the time she blew out the lamp and climbed into bed, she had sorted out the whole incident in her mind, and she fell asleep remembering Ben and the last time she had stayed in Omaha.

The next morning Stacey slept late. When she finally did stir, she decided to use the advance on her wages that Wade had given her and, finally, take a bath. She hurried downstairs to the desk and ordered a tub to be brought up, and half an hour later she was luxuriating in the warm suds, her hair already washed and piled atop her head.

It felt good to be clean again, and afterward, dressed in her yellow calico, she knew exactly what she was going to do first. With the straw bonnet perched atop her shining curls, she headed for the telegraph office.

"Sorry, ma'am, he hasn't picked it up yet," the telegrapher told her. "And with no house address . . . The man up there never even heard of a Ben Clayton."

She walked out, her face mirroring her disappointment. Where could he be? If only she had kept reading the messages he'd left in the diary instead of putting it away. He might have mentioned where he'd gone, given some clue. But she had stupidly savored the messages, reading them day by day instead of rushing on ahead. It had seemed so nice to share each day with him. Now . . . But blaming herself wasn't helping. She'd just have to hope.

After a quick brunch at one of the home-style restaurants, Stacey made her way to the Paradise. The dressing room and gaming room were empty, so she climbed the stairs to the landing and surveyed the empty barroom. She took the digital watch from her handbag and checked the time. It was only one-thirty. The Paradise didn't open its doors until three.

She shoved the watch back in her handbag as Wade appeared at the top of the stairs. "Good morning, or should I say afternoon?" he said.

"I presume you haven't been up too long," she said.

"You presume right." He was wearing a quilted blue satin robe, and from what she could see, nothing else.

"I'll wait for you to change," she said as she followed him into the office.

"Nothing wrong with this outfit," he replied, taking a pair of glasses from the stand. "Brandy or wine?"

"Neither." She looked him over disdainfully. "And if you don't mind, I don't think I can learn faro from a man whose chest and legs are exposed."

His eyebrows raised and he looked amused. "Really?"

"Really," she said, her heart racing at the memory of last night. "Now, either you go put some clothes on, or I leave."

"You don't fight fair," he retorted.

"There's nothing to fight about," she reminded him. "I came here to play faro, not to fight your advances, Mr. Savagge. Now, if you don't want to teach me this unique card game of yours, there are a number of other things I can do before curtain time tonight."

"Mr. Clayton?" he questioned.

"Oh, you remembered there was one," she said, feigning surprise. "For a moment I thought you had forgotten."

"How could I forget?" he asked, heading for his bedroom. "It's just such a shame that he has you all to himself." His voice carried through the doorway as he changed inside the bedroom. "By the way, when does he get you all to himself? I presume he's not in Omaha."

"You presume right," she answered as she took off her bonnet. "As to when he gets me all to himself, as you put it, that's my business, don't you think?"

Wade appeared at the door, still buttoning his shirt. "As I told you last night, there are those who get married and have families, and then there are those like me and the girls, and perhaps you, Stacey Clayton?"

"Perhaps me," she half-whispered. "But that's my worry, Wade. The fact that Ben and I aren't together right now has nothing to do with the way we feel about each other. It's just something that happened."

"How long since you've seen him?"

"Eight or nine months. Somewhere in there."

"And he hasn't tried to reach you in all that time?"

"He thinks I'm dead."

"What happened?"

"Wade, please, I'd rather not talk about it. It's something I have to take care of in my own way. Don't make it harder for me, please."

"You make it rough for a fella, don't you? I can't promise you anything, Stacey Clayton. I've never met a woman quite like you. But I'll do one thing. I'll try hard."

She saw the desire in his eyes and fortified herself against it. "Just friends?"

"Dammit, you drive a hard bargain."

"I know, but it's either that or . . ."

"Or what? I thought you needed this job?"

"Not that bad. I'd rather rob a bank than be blackmailed into what you're suggesting."

"Is the prospect of making love with me that disgusting?"

"You're not a fool, Wade Savagge, you know better than that," she said. "But I'm not a fool either. There's only one man in this world I intend to share a bed with, and that's Ben Clayton. Nothing's going to keep me from him, including you. Now, do I learn to play faro or not?"

"You win. Pull up a chair and let's get at it."

Stacey wasn't certain if she had convinced him or not, but for the rest of the afternoon he was strictly business. By four-thirty Stacey had discovered the larcenous side of Mr. Wade Savagge. "But that's cheating!" she exclaimed as he showed her how to palm a card. "I thought you wanted me to deal, not cheat."

"Stacey, you're going to be up against men who really know the game. I don't expect you to cheat at faro, because the odds are in favor of the house in a faro game. But I want you to learn poker too, and all the men you play with won't be honest. There are times when you've got to play the game they're playing. If you know how to cheat, you'll know what to look for."

"Then you never cheat unless the other guy's cheating, right?"

"Not necessarily."

"I didn't think so."

"For God's sake, Stacey. I make a living at cards. There are times I can't afford to lose."

"So you cheat."

"Dammit, I play cards!"

"I won't cheat," she said softly.

He grabbed her hands and squeezed them. "All right, now I'll make a bargain with you," he said huskily. "I want you to learn all the tricks, Stacey. Everything, so you know how it's done. But the only time I'll expect you to cheat is if someone else starts it. But you've got to know. I've seen too many women who didn't make it at the tables because they didn't know when they were being taken. Please, Stacey. Your fingers are nimble enough. You're a natural, and I need you."

"Why can't you just let me sing and keep dealing yourself?"

He dropped her hands, walked to the window, and looked out for a few minutes. Then he turned and said, "Because ever since I was a grubby kid on the streets of New York I've had a dream, Stacey. Someday I was going to have a place of my own. A classy place with dancing girls, a roulette wheel, everything. And one thing my place was going to have was a beautiful woman to deal the cards. Someone special . . .'' He walked back to Stacey and captured her eyes. "You're the woman I want, Stacey. You've got everything it takes. Don't let misguided scruples ruin it. I'm not asking you to cheat unless it's necessary. Not to teach you would be like throwing you to the lions. Please, Red?" he whispered softly.

She wanted to say no, but she knew he was right. There were other gamblers as intense as he was about the game, and the fact that she was a woman wouldn't bother them one bit when it came to cheating.

"Can I use my own discretion?" she asked.

"It'll be up to you."

"All right, I'll learn your little tricks. But I doubt I'll ever use them."

He picked up the cards scattered on the table. "I hope you'll never have to, Stacey," he said. "But I'll wager the day will come when you will, and when it does, you'll be glad to know how, believe me." He walked over to the desk and put the cards away. "Now, that's taken care of . . ." He pulled the watch from his pocket and checked it. "It's almost five o'clock and neither of us has eaten yet. Do you think you could find it in your heart to join me for dinner, or are you afraid to be seen with a man who cheats at cards?"

"Don't push, Wade," she said. "I'm not used to this sort of thing."

"Neither am I," he retorted. "I never dreamed I'd ever run into an honest woman." He smiled. "Will you go?"

"Why not," and she watched him go back into the bedroom.

A few minutes later when he came out, he had added a small black tie over his white shirt, a gray satin vest, black frock coat and was carrying his broad brimmed black hat.

"Shall we?" he said as he ushered Stacey to the door.

She stepped into the hall and almost bumped into Pearl.

The girls had been around all afternoon, but Stacey hadn't seen Pearl yet. She was wearing a flimsy wrapper that barely covered the essentials. Seeing Stacey with Wade, her eyes suddenly became pained. "Going out?" she asked belligerently.

"We've been at the cards all afternoon," Wade explained. "So I thought we'd catch a bite to eat before the show."

"That's the only reason?" Pearl asked.

Stacey caught the implication and glanced over her left shoulder at Wade, then addressed Pearl. "What other reason could there be?"

"Just remember he's mine, honey." Pearl sneered viciously, then pursed her lips and stared directly into Wade's face for a long, hard minute before walking back to her room.

"Don't mind her," Wade said as he took Stacey's elbow. "Pearl thinks she has a claim on me. A misguided notion."

"Have you told her as much?"

"Dozens of times."

"But the lady doesn't believe you, right?"

"I know what you're thinking, Stacey," he admitted. "But it's not that way at all, and it hasn't been from the start. She knows that if it had been any different, I'd have had a ring on her finger years ago. Pearl's Pearl, that's all. What she imagines has nothing to do with reality, so don't let her little remarks bother you."

"You're a strange man, Mr. Wade Savagge," Stacey said thoughtfully. "And at this point I'm not sure whether I want to stay friends with you or not."

"The honesty showing again?"

"Maybe . . . maybe I feel sorry for Pearl. Love's a powerful emotion. I hate to see it taken lightly."

"So do I. That's why I've always been completely honest with Pearl about where she stands."

"And that makes it all right?"

"Why not? The lady's willing. Now, come on, let's forget about Pearl. There's a restaurant on the other side of town you'll just love."

By the end of April, all the men in Omaha were talking about the redhead who sang at the Paradise. By the second week in May, Wade was certain that Stacey was the dealer he'd always been looking for. He was sure that it wouldn't be long before she'd be ready to take over the tables for him, and he was also sure that he had fallen in love with her. Yet, she never gave him any indication that she wanted more than his friendship.

Meanwhile, Stacey was saving as much money as possible from her wages. She concentrated on learning the cards as quickly as possible, so that she could add her earnings at the tables to her nest egg. She hoped to have enough by the end of the summer to take a stagecoach to Portland, if she still hadn't heard from Ben by then. Every day, she stopped by the telegraph office, but the answer was always the same. The telegram was still gathering dust in Portland.

It was Tuesday evening, May 15, a little over three weeks after her arrival in Omaha. Stacey settled herself down in her chair on the small stage and began to sing, unaware of the commotion at the bar where three men stood staring up at her anxiously.

"I said quiet, gents," Ox ordered as he leaned across the bar.

The tallest of the three waved his hand to indicate that they had heard. Ed Larkin stood transfixed as he lowered his hand. His face was pale and his heart was pounding. It couldn't be! He was looking at a ghost! Stacey Clayton! She had died last year when the Indians had attacked the wagon train Ed had been leading to Oregon. Ben Clayton had been there and seen the whole thing. So had the head scout, Bass, who was standing next to Ed right now.

"It's impossible," Bass gasped in astonishment. "She's dead . . . I know she's dead! I saw it with my own eyes."

Ed's cook, Pete Hatcher shook his head, his eyes wide with fear. "Then we're watchin' a ghost, Bass," he muttered half-aloud. " 'Cause the lady on that stage sure as hell is movin' around."

Ox cautioned them again, but this time Ed whispered to him urgently, "How can I speak to her?"

Ox nodded toward Wade, who was standing at the foot of the steps near the stage. "Him."

Ed Larkin was a tall, rugged man with broad shoulders and a tanned, weathered face. He and his two men had just arrived in town that morning. After leaving what remained of the wagon train in Oregon last November, Ed, Bass, and Pete had gone to Sante Fe, then moved up through the Cimarron cutoff to Omaha again, where one of the land agents had gathered settlers together for another wagon train, and the circle started all over again.

When they had decided to wash off the dust in Omaha's fancy new saloon, none of them had dreamed that they would run into a woman who was supposed to be dead.

With his deep blue eyes glued to the stage, Ed stood transfixed until the last note echoed through the chandeliers. Then, while the other men hollered and clapped wildly and Stacey disappeared backstage, Ed and his men headed for the steps where Wade was lounging with a pleased look in his eyes.

Wade watched absentmindedly as the three men pushed their way through the crowd toward him, unaware they were addressing him until the tallest of the three raised his hand to get his attention.

"Sir?" Ed asked. "Excuse me, you're the owner?"

Wade smiled. "Wade Savagge, with two g's, at your service, gentlemen." He held out his hand.

"Ed Larkin, and these are my friends, Bass and Pete," Ed said hurriedly, shaking Wade's hand. "Can we talk alone?"

Wade eyed him curiously. "Is it important? I've got a faro table to handle."

"It's important," Ed said.

There was something about the ominous way he said it that made Wade take a second look at him. His clothing was that of a rough frontiersman, and the steady blue eyes were hard. Although his features were broad, he wasn't bad-looking in an earthy way. The kind of rugged individualist women often liked to mother. Now, what the hell did this man have to say that was so important?

"All right," Wade said, leading Ed and his men upstairs to the landing, then quickly down the other side into the hall where they were out of sight from the barroom. "What's it all about?" he asked.

"Where is she?" Ed asked curtly. "Where does she go after she's through?"

"Where does who go?" Wade asked, bewildered.

"You know damn well who I mean. Where's the dressing room? I've got to talk to her."

"Now, wait a minute. Do you mean Stacey?"

"I mean Stacey Clayton. Bass saw her get killed last September in a raid along the North Platte River, and now suddenly here she is singing on a stage in Omaha. Same face, same name, same woman. Now I gotta know what's goin' on."

"You sure you're talking about Stacey?" Wade asked, dumbfounded.

"Positive!"

"I guess you had better talk to her, then," Wade said, frowning. "Come with me."

Stacey was in the dressing room practicing something Wade had shown her with a deck of cards. She still had on the turquoise dress because there was another performance at ten. All the other girls were out mingling with the customers, so she was alone. She sat at one of the dressing tables, letting the cards flow through her deft fingers, then stopped abruptly when the door opened and Wade stuck his head in. He looked at her curiously, motioning with his head. "Stacey, come here."

She dropped the cards and stood up. There was something about the way he said it. A seriousness, an urgency. As she walked to the door, he opened it farther, and she saw he wasn't alone. As Stacey's eyes fell on the men standing with Wade, her face paled and she gasped in awe.

"Ed! Bass! Pete! Oh, my God! Ed!" Tears sprang to her eyes as she ran toward the tall, rugged frontiersman. "Oh, Ed!"

She flung her arms around him, and Ed instinctively hugged her back, her body soft and warm against him. Then he held her back away from him and stared at her increduously, while she gazed at him, Bass, and Pete with shining eyes.

"How did you find me? Where have you been? Where's Ben?" Stacey's questions came tumbling out, but she quickly realized her mistake. "Oh, damn!" she muttered self-consciously, extricating herself from Ed's arms.

"Jesus Christ, it *is* you, isn't it?" Ed said, his hands running slowly up and down her bare arms as if to make sure she was real. "Where the hell . . . how'd you get here, anyway?"

"I . . . Oh, Ed!" What could she say? Ben would have understood, but not Ed. She had forgotten all about Ed and the other men on the wagon train, and she certainly hadn't expected to run into them. She stared at Ed now, unable to answer him. "Ed, please, may I talk to you alone?" she asked.

He stared at her intently, trying to understand. "I guess so."

"Is it all right if we use your office, Wade?"

Wade shrugged, frowning deeply. He didn't like the idea, but what could he say? "Go ahead."

Stacey led Ed to the office while Wade, Bass, and Pete stood watching and wishing they knew what the hell was going on.

"You gents go tell the bartender the drinks are on me," Wade told the other men. "I've got a faro game to run," and he turned reluctantly, stepping through the doorway to his right, into the gambling room.

Upstairs in Wade's office, Stacey shut the door firmly and offered Ed a drink from Wade's private stock.

Ed glanced at the fancy decanter and eyed Stacey suspiciously, watching the flickering light from the kerosene lamp cast shadows on her face. "Will I need it, or are you just being sociable?" he asked.

"You're going to need it, Ed," she advised.

"Then pour."

She gave him a generous glass full of brandy as he continued to study her curiously.

She had always liked Ed. He was the kind of man you couldn't help liking. She and Ben had both considered him their close friend. Now she was going to have to trust in that friendship and hope he'd understand.

"I think you'd better sit down, too," she said nervously. He walked over and sat in a cushioned chair near the lamp. She watched him, her stomach tied in knots and her hands clammy. She had to tell him the truth. There was no other way.

"Ed, this is going to be terribly hard for me," she said slowly. "But you have to know the whole story. Do you remember the incident at Fort Kearney, when I talked about General Custer and the Little Big Horn. Remember I said that it wouldn't happen until 1876 or so?"

He eyed her warily. "Yeah."

"Didn't you ever wonder what I told Ben that night by the river when you questioned the incident?"

He was too puzzled to answer.

"Ed, that night I told Ben where I was really from and why I know things that won't be happening for years yet. Ben believed me. Now I'm asking you to believe me, too. Ed . . ." She swallowed hard, her heart racing. "I'm from the future. In the year 1975 I dove into my sister's swimming pool and was transported back in time to the year 1865."

For almost an hour she talked, telling Ed her whole story, including her return to 1975 and the events that heralded her coming back. She left nothing out, including her unhappiness with Drew.

"And now I have to find Ben," she said anxiously, her tale finished. "I love him so much, and I know God sent me back to be with him. Please help me, Ed."

He was staring at her dumbfounded, trying to let her strange story sink in. It was the damnedest thing he'd ever heard. Yet, as she had revealed it, all the little things had fallen into place. She had so often seemed different from the other people on the wagon train, even in her mannerisms and the words she used. But for a person to travel through time . . . from another age . . .

"I don't know what to believe, Stacey," he murmured, confused.

She dropped to her knees and gazed up at him, her eyes vibrant and misty with tears. "Ed, you say I was dead. Where was I buried?"

"I . . . You weren't. We didn't find anything to bury."

"That's right, because I wasn't dead. I'd gone ahead in time again. Would I be here now if I'd been killed? Ed, feel me, I'm alive," she cried. Turning her back to him, she pulled on the low neckline of her dress and revealed the scar on her shoulder blade. "Look, Ed, that's where the arrow hit. You know I'm who I say

I am. Now, how else could I be here except the way I told you? Telegraph the jeweler in Cleveland if you want to, he'll tell you I sold my rings to get this far.'' She readjusted her dress and turned to face Ed again. "You have to believe me, Ed," she whispered desperately. "I'm working here to get the money to take a stage to Portland and find Ben."

"He's not in Portland," Ed said, half in a daze.

"Not in Portland? But the man who brought the diary to my hospital room said he lived in Portland."

"Ben stayed in The Dalles," he whispered unsteadily. "Said if he didn't like it there, he'd head for Portland later. He said it looked like a good place to settle."

"No wonder he hasn't answered my telegram," she sighed.

"You sent a telegram?"

"To Portland."

Ed's eyes darkened as he stared at her. "Stacey, I don't know what to believe. I want to believe you, but . . . it's so . . . so damn crazy and absurd!"

Stacey's jaw tightened stubbornly. She had to convince him. "Wait, I know a way," she said hopefully. "You stay here. Right here, don't you dare move. Have another drink while you wait," and she hurried downstairs to the dressing room.

She returned with her brocade handbag. "Now I can prove what I say," she said triumphantly. She reached into the handbag and pulled out a small beaded bag.

He set his glass of brandy down and took the bag from her.

"Inside you'll find two paper dollars," she said. "Look at the dates on them."

He took out a piece of green-and-white paper. It was unlike anything he'd ever seen before, and he carefully examined both sides. "What's this supposed to prove?" he asked.

"Isn't there a date on it?" she asked.

He studied both sides again. "Nope, I don't think so."

"Damn! Well, try the coins," she suggested. She was sure there was a date on the dollar bill, but he had probably missed it. She had three dimes, a penny, and a nickel left.

He leaned closer to the lamp and examined them.

"Look at the dates," she said eagerly.

"They're too small."

She moved to Wade's desk and rummaged around in the drawers until she found a magnifying glass. "Try using this," she said.

He held the glass over the coins. There was a strange man's head on the first coin, along with the words "Liberty" and "In

God We Trust.'' There was also a date: 1973. The next two
coins were identical, except for the dates. One date was 1966,
the other 1975.

"That's a nickel, a five-cent piece," Stacey said as he put a
larger coin beneath the glass.

On one side Ed read the words "Monticello" and "Five
Cents." On the other side was a picture of a man and the date
1964.

"And look at the Lincoln penny," she said.

He held the small copper piece in his fingers, looking at the
picture of Abraham Lincoln on it. The date on it was 1972.

"I had that money in my pocket when I came back through
time, Ed," she said. "How could I possibly have money with
those dates unless I had been there? I didn't mint those coins.
Oh, yes, and I have something else," she said, reaching into her
handbag. "I don't think you've ever seen a watch like this. It's
called a digital watch, and everyone in the 1970's wears them."

He took the watch from her and stared at it incredulously,
watching the seconds tick off. "What the devil . . ."

"It works on a battery, but then, you wouldn't know what a
battery is. Here, watch," she said as she showed him how to
press the tiny button on the side and light up the dial. He
couldn't take his eyes off the watch. "Do you believe me,
now?" she asked hopefully.

He glanced from the strange timepiece to the coins again. His
eyes were hauntingly alive. "If you were anyone else, Stacey,
I'd say you were trying to pull my leg, but . . . I want to
believe you."

"What more can I do to prove it, Ed?"

He sighed. "You know, Ben said something once that . . .
you know that diary you were telling me about? The one you
used to write in all the time?"

"Yes."

"Well, one night, about a week out of Fort Laramie, I saw Ben
writing in it. I knew it had been yours, and I asked what he was
doing. He said the strangest thing." He hesitated.

"What did he say?"

"He said he was writing a letter to you. When I asked him
how he thought you were going to read it, since you were dead,
he said, 'She's not dead, not really, Ed, and I think I know
where she is, and someday, somehow, she's going to read this
and know I still love her.' " Ed flushed. "I thought maybe he'd
lost a few upstairs for a while there, but he never said anything
else to make me doubt him, so I overlooked it as his way of

coping with your death.'' A strange, knowing look crossed his face. ''You know, now that I think of it, he talked about you a lot, as if you were still with him.''

''I was,'' she said softly. ''In the diary. I just wish I had read all the messages he left for me. Then I'd have known he was in The Dalles instead of Portland. You see, Ben knew where I was from, and he suspected that I'd gone back. Please, Ed, believe me now and help me find him,'' she pleaded anxiously.

Ed took his empty glass over to Wade's private stock of liquor and fortified himself again. ''It's a lot to swallow, Stacey,'' he said slowly.

''I know,'' she said. ''But you have to believe me. I'm not crazy, Ed.''

''I know you're not,'' he replied. ''That's just the trouble. After seeing those things you just showed me . . . I don't have much choice, do I?''

''Then you do believe me?''

''I believe you.''

Relief showed on her face.

''But you asked me to help you. How?'' he asked. ''I won't be around. They've got a wagon train all ready for me, and we'll be moving out again in about a week.''

She stared at him thoughtfully as he swirled the remainder of the brandy around in his glass. He knew she was watching him and felt self-conscious. After a few minutes, he downed the last of the brandy, set the glass down, and looked at her. At that moment she made her decision. He saw her eyes light up.

''Take me with you,'' she whispered breathlessly.

''Take you with me?''

''I can drive mules, you know that, And I could help Pete.''

''But I can't have a woman on the lead wagon, Stacey.''

''Why not?''

''I work for the land agency, remember? They have rules. No wives. That's why they hire single men to lead the wagons. We have enough to worry about without families of our own to look after.''

''But it wouldn't be like a family. It'd just be me.''

''No women in the wagon master's wagon,'' he said emphatically. ''If this was a private train, it'd be different. But I'm getting paid by the land office, and I have to go by their rules.''

''That means I have to hang around here until I get enough money to go by stage,'' she said angrily. ''And that could be months.''

"Maybe not," Ed said suddenly. "Would you be willing to work for your passage?"

"What do you think?"

"Let me look around, see what I can come up with. There's almost always someone who wouldn't mind a helping hand, and you'll be one jump ahead of the others because you already know the routine."

"Oh, Ed," she said excitedly. "How can I thank you."

"Don't thank me yet. I may not find anyone. That reminds me," he said. "What about your Mr. Savagge downstairs? I don't think he's going to like losing his biggest drawing card. Everyone in town is talking about the fancy redhead at the Paradise Saloon. He's not going to give you up that easily."

"He'll have to."

Suddenly there was a knock on the office door and Wade stuck his head in. "I hope you're through," he said. "It's almost show time again, and you've been talking for over an hour."

"Speak of the devil," said Stacey, and Wade glanced at her curiously.

"You were talking about me?"

"Maybe you'd better go, Ed," she said. "I'll explain everything to Wade."

Ed wasn't too pleased. "You sure you'll be all right?"

"I'll be fine."

"I'll be downstairs if you need me."

Wade frowned, watching Ed leave. He looked at Stacey and saw that her face was flushed. "What's this all about, anyway?" he asked.

"Ed and I were discussing your reaction to my departure," she said hesitantly.

"What the hell are you talking about?"

She flinched at the anger in his voice. "If he can find someone to take me on, I'm going to join his wagon train."

"The hell you are!"

"What do you mean by that?"

"Just what I said. If you think I'm going to let you just walk out of my life—"

"I've never been in your life!"

"Don't bet on it, Red," he said. "You know damn well how I feel about you. If you think I'm going to sit back and let you leave because some yokel asks you to . . ."

"He didn't ask me, I asked him," she snapped. "My husband's in Oregon and—"

"I don't care where the hell your husband is," he interrupted furiously. "All I care about is you!" He confronted her, his eyes boring into hers. "You owe me more than that, Stacey."

"I owe you nothing!"

"Don't you? What about all the time I've spent teaching you everything I know? I gave you a chance when no one else would. Doesn't that count for anything?" His voice softened, eyes warming seductively as his arm encircled her waist. "And how about all the walks home, the dinners together . . . You owe me for those, Red. I won't let you go until you've paid for them."

"Wade, stop it," she said, pushing him back with her hands against his chest. "You can't keep me here. You know better than that."

"Can't I? All I have to do is lock you in here then tell that overgrown frontiersman you changed your mind."

"He'd never believe you!"

"I'll take my chances!"

"Wade, for God's sake!" she cried heatedly. "Let go of me!" But Wade only held her more tightly, his gray eyes smoldering with desire.

"Never!" he whispered breathlessly. "I'll never let you go, Stacey."

Suddenly she realized how badly she had misjudged him. All the charm was suddenly gone, and in its place was a frightening intensity.

"Dammit, I love you, Red," he said desperately. "I need you, not just for the Paradise, but for me."

"No!" She struggled against him, trying to pull away. "No, Wade, stop it!"

"Please," he whispered passionately, as his lips pressed against her neck. "Let me love you, Red. Don't fight me . . . stay with me . . . please . . ."

"I can't, Wade," she cried helplessly. "I don't love you."

"You will!" His lips moved up her throat to the sensitive nerves below her ear. "I'll make you love me. You already care a little, I know. Let me make love to you, Red, and you'll never need another man."

Stacey's heart sank. He wasn't about to let go, not willingly.

She closed her eyes, forcing herself to ignore his intimate attempts at persuasion. She had to make him understand, but there was no stopping him. His lips crept across her cheek and claimed her mouth in a long, hard kiss. Stacey felt sick. She wanted no part of this, no part of him. When his tongue forced itself between her lips, his hand eased on her waist and Stacey took the chance. Twisting violently, she wrenched herself free of his arms.

"Stacey . . . what the . . ." he cried.

"Stop!" she panted breathlessly. "Don't come near me."

"What's the matter with you?" he gasped. "I know damn well you liked that."

"No!" She shook her head furiously, but he didn't seem to be paying any attention to her protests.

His eyes narrowed passionately, and he reached out like a cat trying to mesmerize a mouse. "Come to me, Red. Let me love you here, now. The bed's so close. Let me show you what love really is." His hand touched her arm, and she let out a wild shriek.

Hands fumbling, he grabbed for her, but she lunged away, stumbling, then tripped on the long skirt of her dress. Startled and off balance, she fell on the chair and knocked it against the stand that held the lamp. Instinctively, she reached out for something to break her fall, but there was nothing, and with a loud, sickening crash, the chair, stand, and kerosene lamp went flying through the air. When Stacey hit the floor, her eyes grew wide with horror as the whole mess crashed around her and flames shot from the shattered lamp. Within seconds, fiery fingers were clawing their way up the drapes, and the whole place burst into flames.

CHAPTER 13

Wade stared at the flames swiftly devouring the curtains, eating across the floor, and creeping up the walls, and his desire for Stacey was abruptly replaced by sheer panic. He let out a startled cry as the fire shot toward Stacey, who still lay prone on the floor. Quickly he pulled her up and brushed out the wayward flames that were blackening her skirt.

Hands shaking, Stacey clung to Wade as he dragged her away from the fire. She looked at him in despair. "My God, Wade! What'll we do?"

Pushing her toward the other side of the room, he grabbed a small rug and started beating the flames, but it was useless. The kerosene had splattered all over the room and now it was feeding the flames.

"Run downstairs and warn the others," he yelled as he dropped the rug and started toward his bedroom.

"You can't stay here alone!"

"I've got papers and my strongbox in the bedroom," he yelled back. "Now, get going. Maybe if we're fast enough we can save a few things. Tell Ox to pull out the roulette tables and get the money from downstairs. This place'll go sky-high!"

Stacey picked up her skirts and ran down the hall. She met Ed halfway down the stairs and grabbed his arm hysterically.

"I heard a scream," he said hurriedly.

"It's fire," she cried. "The lamp shattered and it's spreading fast."

"Wade?"

"He's up there saving what he can."

Ed sent her downstairs, then went up to help Wade.

Within minutes the place was a madhouse. Some men stayed to help, carrying out what they could and forming a bucket brigade in an attempt to soak everything, but the flames were spreading too fast.

The girls all managed to save some of their clothes and money, but they barely made it back downstairs. Pearl almost got caught in the upstairs hall, and Wade had to force her not to go back for a pair of shoes.

Ed carried a small safe while Wade stumbled along with a bunch of ledgers, a wooden box and some clothes, shoving Pearl along in front of him.

There was mass confusion when the three reached the landing halfway down the stairs. Ed saw flames eating through the barroom ceiling, but men were still carrying things out. "It's got the ceiling!" he hollered as he made his way through the thick smoke rolling down the stairs.

Ox gave a roar and waved his arms, and everyone began pushing and shoving out of the burning building.

With her guitar slung over her shoulder, Stacey stood away from the building and watched the holocaust. She knew it was hopeless. The place was going up like a bonfire. She was grateful that so many things had been saved and that no one seemed seriously hurt. But now, as she watched the flames leap into the night, she realized Wade and Ed hadn't come out yet. Nor had Pearl and a couple of the other girls.

Lil was standing nearby with Ellie and Hazel, but there was no sign of the others. Maybe they went out the back door. She was just about to run to the back of the building, when Ginger, Ox, and Mae staggered out the front door. Behind Mae, Pearl was being pushed by Wade. Finally, Ed lumbered through the smoking doorway, carrying a small safe on his shoulders that he tossed to the ground once he was far enough away from the building.

Stacey rushed over and grabbed Ed's arm. "Oh, my Lord, I thought you'd been caught in there!"

He put his arm around her and pulled her close. "We almost were," he said as he watched the building burn. Stacey felt him shudder.

Next to Ed, Wade stood with flames reflected in his eyes. He was watching his dreams go up in smoke and he wanted to cry. Everything he had worked for, everything he had always wanted, gone! He stood watching the fire with his arm around Pearl, who hugged her few belongings and sobbed quietly. In his other arm, Wade held his own few possessions, and suddenly he felt bitter. He turned and gazed at Stacey, who was snuggled close to Ed, and he made a silent vow. It wasn't going to be in vain.

He had lost the Paradise because of her, because she had spurned him. Well, now she owed him for more than just a few dinners and some card lessons. She owed him for the Paradise, and, by God, before he was through, he'd make her pay for it, too. All the way!

Huddling close to Ed, Stacey drew her eyes away from the fire to gaze at Wade. She knew he must be furious, losing everything like this. But it had been his own fault. He had no right to attack her as he had, to try to force her to stay. Now there was nothing to stay for. Suddenly Wade's eyes locked with hers, and the sheer strength of his expression made her cringe. He would never forget that she had knocked over that lamp, and she knew it. But just at that moment, Bass and Pete hurried up to talk to Wade.

"We helped haul out the roulette table for you," Bass said.

"Thanks."

"And most of the things in the dressing room were saved, and a lot of the whiskey and beer. Your bartender carried out most of it. But I guess all that was saved from upstairs was what you folks have."

Wade glanced down at the ledgers, clothes, and safe at his feet. "Well, at least I didn't lose everything," he said.

Bass looked back toward the building as the upstairs gave way and fell into the main floor. "I guess the town can be thankful your saloon sat alone on the corner," he said, his eyes taking in the flying sparks, "or they'd be losing half the town by now."

They watched for a long time, glad there was no wind to feed the flames. Ed turned to Stacey. "What'll you do now?"

"Go back to my hotel room, I guess," she answered. "Then I'll just have to wait and see what you can find out about the wagon train. I saved my guitar, but it won't do me much good now."

His arm tightened about her shoulder. "You weren't staying at the Paradise, then?"

"No. I have a room at the Cromwell House, where Ben and I stayed the last time I was here."

"I'll walk you over."

She smiled up at him wearily, then turned to Wade. She wanted to say something, to apologize somehow, but she could think of nothing appropriate. He was still watching the fire in a daze, and she turned away from his troubled face.

"Ed, could we go back to the hotel now?" she asked.

Wade watched the big frontiersman walk away with his arm around Stacey. He saw the intimacy with which this strange, lumbering man entered into her life, and it hurt. A sharp pang of savage jealousy ran through him. She seemed to have no qualms about letting this man hold her, and they'd been in the office alone for almost an hour. Ánything could have happened between them. Wade frowned, then realized he was still holding Pearl.

"What are we going to do, Wade?" Pearl asked between sobs.

"I don't know. Give me time to think."

Within minutes Lil, Hazel, Ellie, Ginger, and Mae all surrounded him asking the same question, and he stared at them, flustered.

"Dammit, how do I know what we're supposed to do," he said angrily. "Why the hell can't you all think for yourselves?"

Lil stared at her nephew. The front of her fancy blue satin dress had a large scorched hole in the skirt, and it was covered with ash. "How did it start?" she asked. "You were upstairs, what happened?"

"Never mind how, it just started," he fired back at her.

"It was that redhead, wasn't it? You were upstairs with her."

He dropped his arm from around Pearl and wiped perspiration from his forehead, streaking dirt across his face. "So what if I was."

Lil's face went rigid. "I told you she'd cause trouble. I warned you about mixing your women!"

Pearl wiped the tears off her smudged cheeks. "What does Lil mean, mixing your women? You swore you weren't messing around with her."

"I wasn't."

"But Lil said—"

"I don't give a damn what she said. If I say I didn't, I didn't! Now . . ." He gazed around at all the women, then called Ox over. "Did Rundy make it out?" he asked.

Ox motioned with his head, and Wade glanced toward the watering trough where Rundy stood, his clothes soaked to the skin. "He wet his clothes down and was helpin' carry," Ox said. "Put six fellas on the piano and dragged it out the door." Wade glanced beyond Rundy to where the piano sat in the middle of the road with the stool set in front of it as if someone was about to play.

"Tell him to get some men and carry the thing down to . . . Oh, Christ, what do I do with all this?" Wade complained angrily as he surveyed the pile of furniture, kegs, and cases of liquor. "Where the hell do we go?"

"Maybe one of the churches in town will put us up," said Ellie innocently.

Hazel sneered. "You've got to be kidding, love."

"Well, I was just trying."

Wade shushed her up. "Hazel's right. It was a dumb idea. The pious citizens of this town aren't about to help us."

"Why don't we just go to a hotel for the night?" asked Lil.

"That's fine for us," he answered. "But I can't leave all these things lying around. And I sure as hell can't leave a piano sitting in the middle of the road." He turned to Lil. "Take the women and see if you can get rooms somewhere. I'll come by later, after I've figured a way out of this mess."

"Which hotel?" she asked.

"How the hell should I know? If you can't find anything, come back here," he said. "Maybe I can think of something."

Lil herded the women together and they started walking toward the center of town. Meanwhile, Wade and Ox elbowed their way through the crowd that was still watching the Paradise burn.

By the time the last beam had charred through and the last spectator had decided the whole thing wasn't worth watching anymore, Wade had decided what he was going to do.

He had salvaged all the money that had been on hand, which was a considerable amount, and he could sell the whiskey, beer, and furniture. But he'd keep the roulette table and piano. Then he'd use the money to build again. Only not here. Omaha was getting too crowded. The railroad was moving faster now, and in no time cities would be springing up all over the place. The west was full of opportunities, and besides, that way he'd be able to make sure Stacey paid.

By the time dawn came up over the hills and settled on the last smoldering embers of the fire, Wade was on his horse heading toward the edge of town where the wagon train was gathering. After leaving Ox and Rundy to guard what was left of the Paradise, he had sold the whiskey, beer, and furniture, bought a wagon and mules, and signed up with the land agent who sponsored the train. Now all he had to do was get a list of supplies from the wagon master and everything would be set. Only he wondered just how the wagon master was going to take it.

The wagon train was camped beyond Capitol Hill near the Capitol Building for the Nebraska Territory. As he approached the wagons, he realized they were practicing maneuvers, and he sat in the saddle for a long time, listening to Ed Larkin and his men shout orders. When he felt he had watched long enough, he drew a cheroot from his pocket, lit it, and gave his horse a nudge in the ribs.

Wade eased his horse over toward where Ed stood mounted, watching the wagons maneuver into a semblance of a line.

Ed saw him approach out of the corner of his eye and turned to his head scout. "Take over, Bass." He reined his horse in Wade's direction as Bass wheeled his horse about and rode off to direct the wagons.

Ed stopped a few feet from Wade and stared intently as he rode up. Last night, Stacey had told him how the fire had started, and now he studied Wade with a hostile eye.

"What can I do for you, Mr. Savagge?" he asked calmly.

Wade took a deep drag off his cheroot. "The land agent sent me out to tell you I've signed up. He told me to get a list of supplies and find out when you want me to bring my wagons out."

Ed's eyes narrowed. "You signed up?"

"Why not? I've got nothing left here." He looked back toward town. "I was thinking of rebuilding, but then I got to wondering if it might not be best to move farther west."

"What about your ladies?" Ed asked. "How do they like the idea?"

"I haven't told them yet."

"Oh . . . and when you do?"

"Those that want can stay . . . it's up to them. They won't have any trouble taking care of themselves."

"What made you pick this train?" Ed asked, although he knew full well what the man was doing.

"Which one should I have picked?" Wade replied smartly. "The one full of Mormons? You think they'd let my little troupe travel with them? Now you're being ludicrous. Besides, I don't much care to go to Utah. I'm heading for higher stakes than that. Someplace like Virginia City, Nevada. I hear tell there's gold lining the streets."

"If you're heading for Virginia City, you'd be better off going by stage," Ed said. He hated the thought of taking Wade along. "In the first place, you'd get there faster, and in the second place, I'm not going anywhere near Virginia City. We head north from Fort Bridger, and you'd be on your own."

"The land agent said if I stay with you to Fort Hall, I can pick up a party headed down to the Humboldt River and follow the California trail down. He said some of your people are already planning to do that as it is."

Ed eyed him shrewdly. The man certainly didn't let anything get by him. "You've got your wagon already?"

"Two of them. All I need are the supplies."

"Who's driving?"

"Rundy and I'll drive one and Ox'll take the other."

"Rundy?"

"My piano player."

Ed laughed. "You expect that little fella to drive a span of mules?"

"You've got women driving, haven't you? If they can drive, so can he." Wade's eyes hardened. "He'll drive them, and so will any of the women who come along."

Ed leaned back in the saddle. "I presume you can read," he remarked.

Wade's eyes narrowed cruelly. "You trying to be funny?"

"Nope." Ed motioned with his head toward the lead wagon. "Some folks can't. Since I presume your answer meant you can, then as soon as they're through practicing, go over to the lead wagon and tell Pete to give you a list. I'll expect you back here tonight with both wagons. You're going to need all the practice you can get."

Wade nodded and glanced toward the wagons trying vainly to form a circle. He smiled to himself as Ed cantered toward them, shouting at the top of his lungs.

Wade didn't meet the women at their hotel until late afternoon, after he'd bought all the supplies, loaded the wagons, and sent them to the campgrounds with Ox, Rundy, and a couple of men he had hired to drive them to the site.

He had guessed that Lil would pick the cheapest hotel in town, and he was right. Now he stood outside the door to her room, dreading the fight that was coming. He straightened arrogantly, took off his new black hat, and smoothed back his dark curly hair. Well, there was nothing she could do about it now. She would either have to join him or stay here. He didn't think she'd care much for the latter.

To his surprise, Pearl was the one who raised the biggest fuss. "Why can't we just stay here and rebuild?" she fumed. "Why do we have to chance going all the way across that damn wilderness? There are Indians out there. We could get killed!"

Wade's eyes darkened. "You don't have to go," he said. "Nobody's forcing you. Any of you," and he looked about quickly at the rest of the girls.

"Oh, for God's sake, Wade. You know damn well I'm going to stay with you," she said. "But why can't we stay here?"

"Because I don't want to."

Lil eyed him curiously. "Wade, what's Stacey Clayton going to do now that the Paradise is gone?"

He stiffened. "How the hell should I know?"

"It wouldn't be that she's going on that wagon train, would it?" she asked.

"That's right! That's it, isn't it?" Pearl cried, her hazel eyes snapping. "Lil said you were upstairs with her when the fire started. . . . Wade, is she taking that wagon train?"

"How should I know."

"I think you do."

His eyes hardened. "Look, I'll be blunt. Either you go or you don't go, I don't give a damn. I can find what I need once I get there, if that's the way you want it."

Pearl flinched. "Oh, aren't you something," she said sarcastically. "Now I know she's taking that train. You scum!" she cried furiously. "You rotten scum!"

Wade laughed and Lil grabbed Pearl's hand as it headed for his face.

"Don't, Pearl," Lil warned cautiously. "It won't do a bit of good, and you know it. All it'll get you is a black eye and a fat lip."

"I'll kill him," Pearl snarled heatedly as she stared viciously at Wade.

"No you won't," said Lil. "You'll do just what you've always done. Rant and rave, and then fall right into bed with him first chance you get. So why try to make matters worse?"

Pearl relaxed her arm and Lil eased her grip on it. The other girls looked relieved.

Lil eyed Wade disgustedly. "It is the redhead, isn't it, Wade?" she asked sternly.

"That's my concern, not yours," he said. "Now, the important thing is that we have enough money for a good start in Virginia City. We made more here in the past ten months than we made the whole time we were in New York, even with the Paradise gone. And with that kind of capital to back us, we'll have even better luck out there."

"You intend to haul enough cash with us to start over again?" Lil asked.

"I've got two wagons. One for you all and one for Rundy, Ox, and me. And I've still got the safe. It'll ride with us, where I can keep an eye on it."

"You'd better not let anyone besides us know," said Lil.

"I don't intend to." He glanced around the room at the girls, his eyes hard. "And that goes for the rest of you too. Nobody learns about that safe, understand?"

They all nodded and Wade glanced over at Pearl, who was

still pouting. "How much did you manage to save?" he asked her.

She bit her lip. "Not much. Two dresses, a few underthings, a pair of shoes, and the little money I had."

"Enough to replace some of the things you lost?"

"Not everything, but I won't have to go naked."

"How about the rest of you?" he asked, and the women looked at each other expectantly.

"I lost all my money," said Ellie. "But I've got a few clothes left."

"I didn't pay too much attention to what I was grabbing," said Hazel. "I've got my money, but lost half my clothes. I've got a dress, two wrappers, and a little underwear. I didn't even think to grab a pair of shoes."

"I've got my money too," added Mae. "But I only got one dress and"—she looked at him sheepishly—"three pairs of shoes."

He rolled his eyes and shook his head. That was Mae. She and Pearl were the best dancers and both of them were particular about their shoes. He looked at Ginger. "How about you?"

Ginger grinned sheepishly too. "I got myself out," she said, and he looked startled.

"I thought you were upstairs with the rest of the girls," he said. "Didn't you come down just before Pearl and I did?"

"Oh, yeah, I was upstairs," she admitted. "But I dropped my money box and the damn thing broke open. I tried to scoop it up, but there wasn't time. Then, when I was running for the stairs, I ran into Mae. I mean, I literally ran into her. I lost my dresses and didn't even know it. When I got outside, I discovered all I was carrying were two petticoats and a couple pairs of bloomers."

Wade shook his head. He'd have to give her money for clothes. He reached in his pocket and handed some money to Lil. "Here, see that everybody's got decent clothes," he said. "I mean decent. You know, plain clothes. Nothing fancy until we get to where we're going. You're all going with me, aren't you?"

They agreed in unison and he smiled. "See, Pearl," he said, chucking her under the chin. "They know what I can do for them . . ." His eyes glistened. "And so do you, so forget the nonsense and help Lil and I guarantee someday you'll be the toast of Virginia City."

Pearl stared at him with cold, hard eyes, trying to keep his charm from melting her anger. "You told me that last year about Omaha," she reminded him.

He smiled, his handsome face close to hers. "I know," he

said softly. "Isn't it terrible what a man'll do to keep a woman in line." She started to swing at him again, but he caught her arm and planted a firm kiss on her mouth.

"What was that for?" she asked, startled.

His eyes softened and he laughed wickedly. "Wouldn't you like to know." He turned once more to Lil. "After you get the girls all set, hire someone to bring all of you out to the campgrounds. I'll meet you after I settle a few things here in town first."

As Wade left, Pearl stared after him, unsmiling.

"Someday I'm going to kill that bastard," she murmured softly. The others didn't hear her because they were too busy talking about the trip ahead. Only Lil heard, and she didn't like the way Pearl said it. Wade was asking for trouble, but then, he always did.

It was close to noon. Stacey smiled as she greeted Ed in her hotel room, but he declined her offer to stay.

"I'd rather take you for a bite to eat," he said self-consciously. "That is, if you don't mind eating with a man in work clothes."

He was wearing scuffed leather pants, a blue work shirt, a rawhide vest, six-shooters on both hips, and was carrying a large sweat-stained hat. What Stacey didn't know was that he had made a special trip to the local bathhouse before coming over. All she saw was his slicked-back amber hair carefully combed off his ears.

Her eyes warmed. "You know better than that, Ed." She took her handbag off the dresser and stared at it for a minute, suddenly realizing that during the whole ruckus last night she had managed to hang on to it. Of course, she had looped the ties around her wrist, and that had helped. Along with some of the money she had saved, the handbag also contained the money and the watch she had brought back from the future.

She pulled the drawstring tight and turned back to Ed, her eyes alive with hope. "I'd love to have lunch with you, Ed. Only I hope you have good news for me."

"Some good, maybe . . . some bad," he said as he watched her put on her bonnet.

They sat in the dining room of the Cromwell House and Ed watched Stacey eat sparingly. He knew she was still upset over the fire. Her pale yellow calico dress and small straw bonnet made her look nothing like the fancy singer who had entertained at the Paradise. He hoped with all his heart that he was doing the right thing. Especially now, with Wade joining the train.

Stacey was enjoying the soup, but her stomach was still a little fluttery after last night's disaster. She looked over at Ed and realized he was staring at her.

"Is something wrong?" she asked.

He shook his head, embarrassed. "No . . . I just . . . I can't get over the way you sang last night, Stacey. I remember you used to entertain the kids on the train sometimes to keep them out of their mothers' hair. But I guess I just never thought you could do something like what you were doing at the Paradise."

"Neither did I, at first," she confessed. "I was scared to death. But when your stomach's empty and you know the rent's due, it makes it easier."

He flushed. "Have you ever sung before?"

"No, not for pay, anyway. But I've always loved music, and was good at it. I used to entertain at hospital benefits sometimes. Remember, I told you I was a nurse."

He nodded.

"Ed, I don't think you asked me to lunch just to go over my story again, did you?"

"You're right." He swallowed the food in his mouth and took a big swig of coffee. "I think I've got something for you," he said, setting the cup back on the table. "But I don't know if you're going to like it or not. First . . . there's a man and his daughter on the wagon train. I'd say they're probably the least suited for the trip. I think they've had life pretty easy up until now. Neither one of them's doing too good at anything, including driving. I talked to them this morning and they both seemed pleased at the thought of having some help on the trail, especially from someone who's already familiar with the routine. They won't give you any money, but they'll feed you and let you work your way."

"Sounds ideal."

"It would be, except for one thing."

"What's that?"

"Wade Savagge has joined the train. Signed up this morning."

"You're joking."

"I wish I were." His eyes were troubled. "I don't like it, Stacey. He had a look on his face . . . and you said yourself that he said he was in love with you."

"I know." She wiped her mouth and set the napkin down beside the empty soup bowl. "But I have to go, Ed. I have to reach Ben. I don't have enough money for the stage, no job now, and . . . I have to go with you."

He didn't like it. Not one bit. He gazed into her beautiful blue eyes. He was fond of Stacey. Maybe a little too fond. "You think you can handle Wade Savagge?" he asked.

"With your help, yes. You will help me, won't you?"

"As much as I can. But there'll be times I won't be around, Stacey. Can you handle it then?"

"I'll have to, because I'm not backing out, Ed. If those people will have me, I'm going."

He finished the last of his coffee, and his tanned face wrinkled into a slow smile. "Then I guess I'd better take you out and introduce you."

"Do they know who I am?"

"Nope. I didn't tell them your name. I was afraid they might have been in town and heard it around. I just told them you were on your way to your husband and needed some help."

"Good," she said. She downed the rest of her own coffee. "Then shall we go?"

A short time later, Ed maneuvered a rented buggy through the cottonwood trees and onto the path that circled the camp.

"It all looks so familiar," Stacey said as they neared the wagons. "I can remember it all as if it were yesterday. Ed, you don't think I'm making a mistake, do you?" she asked suddenly.

"It's your decision, and yours alone, Stacey," he said slowly. "If you feel it's right, then it's right. Now, come on." He took her hand and helped her down from the buggy. "Let's see if the Tanners are willing to take you on."

As her feet hit the ground, Stacey suddenly realized what Ed had just said and a knot balled up in the pit of her stomach. "What did you just say their name was?" she asked hesitantly.

"The Tanners, why?"

"Oh, my God!" She stared at him in dismay. "That's the name of Ben's . . ."

It was as far as she got. At that moment, a stout man with a heavily jowled face that was registering shocked surprise emerged from behind his wagon and stopped stock-still, staring at her. His voice broke with emotion as he murmured, "Good heavens, Mrs. Gordon!"

Stacey was speechless. It was Ben's father-in-law, J. D. Tanner, and behind him, climbing down from the seat on the wagon, was his daughter Paula Tanner.

Paula was in her middle thirties and still single, a fact that was a surprise to most people because of her looks. She was quite beautiful in a sophisticated way, but her nose was carried a little too high and her insistence on money as well as looks and charm scared away more suitors than her father wanted to admit. But she had had her eye on Ben for years.

Paula was as dumbfounded as her father to see Stacey standing in front of them. "It is Mrs. Gordon, isn't it?" Paula said, her green eyes flashing. "Father is right?"

Ed glanced at Stacey, noting the shocked look on her face. "What . . . what's going on, Stacey?" he asked.

She swallowed hard and forced her knees to stop shaking as she turned to him. "Mr. Tanner and Paula are Ben's first wife's father and sister," she explained hesitantly.

"What do you mean, his *first* wife?" Paula asked.

"Because I'm his wife now," Stacey answered slowly, and saw Paula's eyes narrow.

"You're lying!" she gasped.

"Am I? Ask Ed Larkin."

"She's right," Ed replied, surprised at this new turn of events. "I performed the ceremony myself."

"Then why isn't Ben with you?"

Stacey held her breath. Uh-oh. Now she was in a pickle. How could she explain? She turned to Ed, her eyes warning him to let her think of something. "There was some trouble with Indians," she said. "Ben thinks I'm dead."

Paula stared at her with cold eyes. "If you and Ben were married, why didn't he let us know? He's written since he's been out there, and when we wired to tell him we were coming out, he never mentioned a word about you."

"You've heard from him since he's been in The Dalles?" asked Stacey.

"Haven't you?"

"I told you, he doesn't know I'm alive."

Mr. Tanner gazed at her curiously. "He's been in The Dalles since November. How come he doesn't know you're alive?"

"Because I didn't know where he was until yesterday," she explained. "I thought he was in Portland."

J.D. wasn't convinced. "It took you this long to find out? How come he thinks you're dead?"

"Does it matter?" she asked.

"It might."

"There was an Indian attack, I was hit and the place was overrun. He was certain I was dead, but some friendly Indians found me and nursed me back to health, then some men came along and brought me back here. Now I'm trying to reach him."

Both Paula and J.D. looked at her skeptically.

"Is that true, Mr. Larkin?" J.D. asked.

Ed nodded. "Much as I know of it."

A sardonic smile curved Paula's full, rosy lips. "And now you need passage so you can get to Ben, right?"

"That's right," Stacey confirmed.

"Well, well. And what if we decide we don't need you?" she asked.

"You need her, Miss Tanner, make no mistake about that," said Ed, watching the sharp way the woman was treating Stacey. "Stacey can drive a team as well as I can, and she knows the routine. Unless the two of you can improve a hundredfold between now and the day we leave, I don't intend to take you with me without someone like her along."

"You mean you'd leave us here?"

"You can't do that," said J.D. "I paid our way."

"It's either her or someone else," he said. "Money or no money, I don't take anyone who can't drive. Even the land office will support me in that. And I must say, from what I could see this morning, the two of you don't have the faintest notion what you're doing with those reins. Jim Dugal, the man who's been keeping his eye on all of you, said everybody's been practicing for darn near two weeks now. Seems to me you should know a little of what you're doing by now."

Flustered, J.D. cleared his throat. "You have to remember, Mr. Larkin, I'm a businessman," he said pompously. "My daughter and I aren't used to this sort of life. We've always had servants, and the most we've had to handle is a one-horse buggy."

"That's the point," Ed replied. "You'd be foolish not to take on Stacey. It won't be easy to find somebody else at this stage of the game. We leave the twenty-fifth of May. Now, does she go with you or do I find another place for her on the train?"

Stacey stared at Mr. Tanner and Paula. She wasn't sure whether she wanted to be on their wagon. But Ed had told her they were the only ones who needed help. That meant he was throwing a bluff at them. If they didn't take her on, there wasn't much she could do.

"Can we think it over?" Paula asked deliberately.

Stacey shrugged. "If you want. In the meantime, I think Ed and I will go to the telegraph office. Since I know Ben's in The Dalles now, maybe I can reach him, and I might not have to join you after all. He might think of a better way for me to reach him."

Ed held out his arm and Stacey took it. He frowned as they

reached the buggy. "I take it you don't care much for the Tanners, nor they for you."

"That's about it," she said. "I'm afraid Paula Tanner's been in love with Ben for a long time. That should clarify the situation."

Ed flicked the reins and headed back toward town. "Did you mean that about the telegram?" he asked.

"I thought it might help if I could reach Ben."

But she didn't reach Ben. By the next afternoon, there was still no answer to the telegram, and she wanted to cry. For a few brief moments, she almost doubted Ben's love, but then she remembered the diary and the words of love, and instead of doubt, fear gripped her. What if something had happened to him? It was the only explanation. Two hours later, when Ed told her the Tanners had decided to take her on, she jumped at the chance.

For the next ten days the atmosphere in the campgrounds was strained. Wade Savagge and his troupe of performers, as he called them, joined the train and raised a stir, but there was no proof that Pearl, Hazel, Ellie, Ginger, and Mae were anything other than the singers, dancers, and actresses they purported to be. In addition, Rundy, who was a likeable fellow, and Ox, who made Hercules look like a weakling, helped convince the people on the train to take Wade at his word.

Paula seemed really pleased to have Stacey along, which surprised Ed until he discovered the way she was ordering her around.

The afternoon before their departure, Ed confronted Paula, who had just sent Stacey into town for some more supplies. "Look, Miss Tanner, Stacey's here to help you learn the routine and give you an extra hand. She's not here just to cater to all your whims. We've got long miles ahead of us. What if something happens to her on the trail? What will you do then?" he asked.

"I've learned to drive," Paula replied haughtily. "How do you think I got these blisters on my hands? And I can build a fire as well as she can, if I have to. And I've learned to do all the other things I need to know. I don't even really need her anymore, so don't get funny with me, Mr. Larkin. She needs this job. Without it, she stays in Omaha and rots."

Ed set his jaw stubbornly. "I can always find her a place with someone else."

"Can you?" She laughed cynically. "I doubt that. You see,

I've discovered how she made her money in Omaha, Mr. Larkin. She was one of Wade Savagge's girls, and the whole train knows it. Now, who else would be willing to let her travel with them? No one. And she hasn't heard from Ben, either. He doesn't care about her. Never did, in fact. When he heard Father and I were heading for Oregon, he seemed quite pleased. No, I think Ben Clayton's probably forgotten all about Stacey Gordon. Oh, yes, you do call her Stacey Clayton. I'm sorry about that. I guess I'll have to get used to it. But no, Mr. Larkin, don't tell me how to treat her while she's working passage on my wagon. Remember, she is working her way to Oregon. It's as simple as that.''

"You hate her, don't you?"

Paula sneered. "How did you guess?"

"Then why did you consent to her joining your wagon?"

"Why?" She laughed, her voice soft and sultry. "Oh, come now, Mr. Larkin, you can't be that naive," she said. "I can hardly wait until we reach Oregon and Ben discovers that his dear, precious wife is not only alive, but was entertaining the male populace of Omaha at the Paradise saloon and was working as one of Wade Savagge's paid whores.''

Ed's eyes narrowed as he stared at Paula. She was beautiful, true. She had the looks that made men stare, but her beauty held no warmth. Beneath the stylish hairdos and fancy clothes, she was a spoiled woman who would do anything to get her own way. Suddenly Ed wished there had been another choice for Stacey.

On May 25, 1866, Stacey once more left Omaha on a wagon train headed west. There were close to forty wagons this time. Both the Tanner wagon and Wade's two wagons were buried somewhere in the middle of the line. The afternoon before leaving, Stacey stopped by the telegraph office one last time, but there was still no answer from Ben.

"Don't worry, if an answer comes, I'll see you get it," the telegrapher said, seeing the sadness in her eyes.

"There won't be an answer," she said, discouraged. "Besides, I'm leaving Omaha . . . but I was so sure . . . they said he was there. . . ." She left the telegraph office in tears. She figured it would be pointless to change her telegram and tell Ben she was leaving, because it was obvious the message would never reach him.

Now, as she whipped the mules up and pulled into line with J. D. Tanner watching her appreciatively and Paula complaining about the hard seat, Stacey wondered what might have happened to Ben.

But she didn't have time to worry now. Her mind's wanderings were lost in the anxiety and excitement of the moment as Ed hollered, "Catch up!" and the wagons began to roll. She was on her way.

CHAPTER 14

It was Friday, June 1, 1866. Ben Clayton pushed open the door to the house and held it for his housekeeper, Frieda Evers, who was followed by Charlotte, Becky, and Ethan.

"Well, how do you like it?" he asked as he strolled through the entrance hall into the empty parlor, then walked over to the staircase.

"It's rather big, isn't it, Father?" said Charlotte as she looked up at the high ceilings.

"A little, maybe," he answered. He smiled, his mustache almost hiding the deep dimples in his cheeks, and his dark eyes studied Charlotte.

She was growing into quite a woman. She was sixteen already. It wouldn't be long before Ethan would probably ask her to marry him. Ben wasn't sure he liked the idea of maybe being a grandfather so soon. But Charlotte was attractive, there was no getting around that. With her dark hair and eyes, she reminded him of his mother. His mother had died when he was only fourteen, and Frieda had raised him, but he had never forgotten how pretty she had been. Charlotte always brought memories of her back to life.

At first it had been hard to forgive Charlotte for the way she had treated Stacey all those months on the trail. But it was equally hard to stay angry with someone you loved, and after Stacey's death, or disappearance, there was no reason to remain angry, and he tried to understand how Charlotte must have felt.

Now Charlotte moved from room to room with Ethan, who was pointing out the advantages of the window seat in the dining room and the fireplace in the kitchen. They asked Frieda questions about where the furniture would go while Becky oohed and aahed over everything. Watching them, Ben felt a deep pain that lingered longer than usual in his breast. He turned away and ascended the stairs, then walked slowly down the hall to his room. He'd chosen it when he'd first looked at the house. Stepping over the threshold, he stared at the stone fireplace and imagined where the bed and dresser would go. Suddenly, he cursed softly to himself and walked to the window overlooking the dirt road out front, looking down he saw the carriage and the freight wagons piled high with furniture, and his heart was heavy.

Why? Why couldn't Stacey have stayed with him? And why couldn't he forget? The pain hurt as deeply now as it had that night on the banks of the North Platte River, when he knew she was gone forever.

Stacey! Stacey! Closing his eyes, he leaned against the window frame, then took a deep breath, straightening and opened them quickly when he heard footsteps in the hall.

"Oh, here you are," Becky said. Her gold-flecked brown eyes were animated. "Is this going to be your room?" she asked.

He smiled at his younger daughter, trying to forget the ache in his heart. "Do you think the furniture will look all right in it?"

She gave him a big grin as she pushed her riotous coppery curls to the back of her head. She had gotten used to wearing dresses without pantalets on the wagon train, and she had refused to put them on again after their arrival in The Dalles. Now, at thirteen, she was wearing floor-length dresses. Charlotte protested because she had had to wait until she was fifteen, but Becky had sprouted up almost four inches over the winter and Ben was convinced it would be all right if she gave up the pantalets. Becky had been pleased with her victory, and now her blossoming body was fit snugly in one of Charlotte's cast-off dresses.

Becky studied her father's face, instinctively knowing he was upset. "You were thinking of Stacey, weren't you?" she asked softly.

"How did you know?"

"Because you always get that look in your eyes."

Embarrassed at his daughter's candor, he flushed. "I suppose I should have forgotten her by now. But instead of becoming easier with time, it seems to be getting more difficult." He looked around the room. "She would have liked this room, don't you think?"

"Do you like it, Father?"

"Yes."

"Then I think she would have too." She saw him fight the tears that quickly sprang to his eyes.

"Do you think Charlotte and Ethan like the house?" he asked.

"Uh-huh. And Frieda's in love with the kitchen. It's so big and roomy."

He put his arm around Becky's shoulder. "Come on, I'll show you your room," he said, trying to forget. As they walked down the hall, they were joined by the others, and Ben showed them all their bedrooms. Everyone except Ethan, that is. His bedroom wasn't in the house.

In fact, that was one thing that had helped convince Ben to buy the place. He had come to Portland by himself to look at the house. It had the size, and the living quarters above the carriage house, he had been looking for.

Ethan hadn't liked living in the same house with them, and Ben knew it. Ethan didn't like feeling too beholden. It was enough that Ben had taken him in after his parents were killed. He didn't want to owe him everything. He was a proud nineteen-year-old who insisted on working to earn his keep. He drove the carriages, took care of the grounds, and did anything else Ben wanted in pay for his board.

Ben agreed, but he wanted more for Ethan. The boy was smart. His education had been limited, but he had taught himself as much as he could and when Ben pulled up stakes in The Dalles and moved to Portland as part-owner of a lumber mill, he made Ethan promise to come along and learn the business from the ground floor up. Eventually Ben planned to let Ethan work at the office as his personal assistant. Ben was certain that, with a little tutoring, Ethan would prove to be a decided asset.

Ethan consented to Ben's plan, but he had one condition. He insisted on working as a handyman around the house while he was learning so he could earn a salary to pay his own room and board. Ben agreed, but he wanted the young man nearby, so living quarters above the carriage house were ideal.

After looking through the house, they all went to look at the rooms above the carriage house. Charlotte was delighted and immediately started setting imaginary furniture in place.

"Hey," said Ethan as he watched her. "Don't I have any say-so in what goes where?"

"As the woman of the house, I think the furnishings should be my problem," she said, looking at him coyly. She turned to Ben. "Father?"

"Don't get me in on it," Ben said, amused. "What goes into the place is up to you two."

"See," said Charlotte. She pulled Ethan toward the room he was going to use for sleeping quarters, while Ben, Becky, and Frieda disappeared down the rickety stairs that clung to the side of the carriage house. "You'll still have to eat with us, Ethan," Charlotte said as she pulled him to the window overlooking the valley. "But just look at that view 'you're going to have every morning."

"I like the view I'm getting now," he teased. When she glanced at him, his eyes were intent on her face.

"Will you be serious?" she asked.

"I am." He pulled her into his arms and caressed her back. "I haven't had you alone the whole trip here from The Dalles," he said slowly. "That's over two weeks. You can't expect me to have my mind on trees and hills when I finally get you alone, can you?"

She stared up at him. He was tall, almost six feet already, but his shoulders hadn't filled out yet and the fuzz on his chin was a little too light to be shaved. She ran a finger across the deep cleft in his chin, feeling the trace of whisker stubble.

"You'd better not let Father catch you taking liberties with me, Ethan," she said. "He might change his good opinion of you."

"I think your father already knows," he said, smiling.

"What makes you think so?"

"He's not dumb, Charlotte," he said as his hand moved up to touch the curls at the nape of her neck. "Besides, he's different. Most fathers forget what it was like to be young, but he hasn't. He knows I'd never hurt you. Maybe because he's not like most men." He looked into her eyes. "Did you ever wonder why most fathers worry so much about their daughters?" he asked.

"No."

"Well, I have. And I've come to the conclusion that the ones who worry the most are the ones who were the worst when they were young. They're afraid the man courting their daughter is going to try the same things."

"Ethan!"

"Well, doesn't it make sense?" He smiled. "I bet your father never tried to compromise your mother before he married her."

"Don't be too sure about that. He's a man, isn't he? Look what happened with Stacey."

Ethan clamped his mouth tight and made a disgruntled noise. "Sometimes I could throttle you, Charlotte," he said angrily. "You still haven't forgiven him for marrying her, have you? Even though she's dead."

"Is she?" she asked with a brittle voice. "You wouldn't know it by the way he acts. He never mourned Mother like this. He even writes in that stupid diary of hers all the time. He thinks we don't know it, but I saw him off by himself on the way here. Sometimes I wish I hadn't given him the diary when I found it after the Indian attack. I know it's out front right now, stuffed in one of his suitcases somewhere.''

''Are you sure?''

''Positive. And Father's not a saint either, Ethan. Remember Omaha.''

''You don't know for sure that anything happened in his hotel room that night.''

''Don't I? I heard them discussing it with my own ears. . . . What did she do to him to make him act like that, Ethan? Why can't he just forget her?''

''He was in love with her.''

''He was in love with Mother too, but he certainly forgot her quick enough when Stacey came along.''

''For God's sake, Charlotte, let it rest,'' Ethan finally said. ''Give him time . . . let him work it out his own way.''

''That's what I've been doing,'' she said. ''But it's not working. You've seen for yourself. He hardly ever laughs anymore and . . . I don't know, he's just not the same.''

''Well, I haven't changed,'' Ethan said huskily. ''I still enjoy kissing you.'' His lips came down on hers hungrily as they both heard Becky calling from downstairs for them to come and help unload the furniture.

Ben hadn't cared too much for The Dalles. Everyone seemed to end up there. It was overcrowded and there were already enough lawyers to handle what business came along. Besides, he had suddenly become restless, and when he had unexpectedly found the chance to buy into a lumber company in Portland, he had jumped at it. Portland seemed to be everything The Dalles wasn't, and he was certain he was going to like it.

For the rest of the day, he hummed softly as they all worked, carrying in the furniture, putting up the beds, and laying the rugs. By nightfall the house began to look lived in. They had some furniture from The Dalles, but it was lost in these big rooms. The place was a little larger than their old house in Cleveland. It had fireplaces in almost every room and a front porch that ran the width of the house. Over the porch was a roofed-in balcony adjoining two of the four large bedrooms upstairs. Ben had fallen in love with the house on sight.

It had been built in Portland's early days and was on the outskirts of the city, with a view of the forests and mountains that was breathtaking, especially in the spring. On a clear day, the snowcapped mountains along the distant Cascade Range were a dramatic contrast to the sparkling waters of the Willamette River that flowed through the valley. The whole panorama could be seen from the upstairs balcony, like a huge painting.

That evening, tired and dirty from the day's work, Ben soaked in a warm tub, slipped on his robe, then stood on the balcony outside the bedroom. He glanced back, staring. Inside the bedroom, his big four-poster bed stood empty, the sheets cold and crisp. He turned from it reluctantly, gazing into the night, and wondered where Stacey was and what was happening to her.

He caressed the diary in his hands as he watched the crescent moon rise above the mountains and turn the treetops silver. He had read the diary over so many times, yet each time brought her to him more vividly. That was the part of it he could never quite understand. He had loved his first wife, Ann. It had been the love that comes with youth and grows comfortable and warm with age. Ann had been his first real love, the first woman to stir his slumbering loins to a fever pitch. Yet, he'd realized after loving Stacey that his life with Ann hadn't been complete.

Now, as he stood staring into the night, he realized the emptiness he'd felt after Ann's death was only a shadow of the loneliness he felt now. From the first moment he had looked into Stacey's passionate blue eyes, and felt the sparks of love ignite deep down inside him, he had known he would never be the same. His love for Ann had grown with time, but it was as if his love for Stacey had been there always, even before he knew her. He had fought against it for weeks, telling himself he had no right to love again, yet knowing the battle had been lost before it had really begun.

He took a deep breath and returned to his room. He walked over to the desk, lit a lamp, and opened the diary. Sitting down, he skimmed the pages slowly.

At times, he cursed his own foolishness. He had let the diary become too much a part of his life, yet every time he tried to put it aside, an inner voice would cry out to him and he just couldn't do it. He'd think of her reading it years from now and still loving him. She had to have something of him, and again he'd sit and share his life with her at the end of the day.

Tears flooded his eyes. Sometimes he felt so strongly that she was still alive that he trembled inside. All he had to do was close his eyes and he could feel her presence. She wasn't dead, he knew. He couldn't feel like this unless she was alive somewhere. Lost to him, yes, but as long as he had the diary she wasn't lost to him completely.

"Someday my love, you'll know you weren't forgotten," he whispered softly. Fighting back the tears, he wrote on the empty page:

June 1, 1866 Friday.

My Darling Stacey,

    We finally reached Portland . . .

The next morning, Frieda watched Ben wander off toward the stables to saddle a horse and head for town. He didn't look good this morning, and she knew he hadn't slept well. It was nothing new. Some nights were worse for him than others, but that was understandable. The more idle time to think, the harder the memories were to conquer.

If only Stacey hadn't been killed. She had been such a delightful person and he had loved her so much. Frieda shook her head as she watched him disappear into the barn. Poor love, why did happiness always elude him?

She walked back into the kitchen and was washing the dishes when Charlotte came in. Her hair was pinned back, her wrapper still on, and she was shuffling across the wooden floor in her slippers.

"Where's Father going so early?" she asked.

"Into town. He told that man, his new partner, what's his name . . .?"

"Mr. Jaquette?"

"That's it. He told him he'd stop by first thing."

"Oh." Charlotte stared out the window after Ben for a few minutes, then turned to Frieda.

Frieda wore her graying hair in a neat bun at the nape of her neck, and her warm brown eyes crinkled affectionately as she stared back at Charlotte. "All right, out with it. What's the matter, Miss Prissy?" she asked matter-of-factly.

"Do you have to call me 'Miss Prissy'?" Charlotte asked. "You do that all the time lately. You used to call me Char."

"And you used to act like Char, too," said Frieda. "I only call you 'Miss Prissy' when you get that look in your eyes. What is it now?"

Charlotte flushed. She loved Frieda, but sometimes she could be so exasperating. What with the weight she had lost on the trip west and the way she treated her, Frieda almost seemed like a stranger.

"Well?" Frieda asked again.

"Well what?" countered Charlotte.

"Look, honey, something's bothering you. What is it? The move? Ethan?"

"It's Father."

"What's he done?"

"You know very well what it is, Frieda. Stacey's been gone for nine months and he's still pacing the floor half the night. And on the way here I noticed he still has that stupid diary. I bet he was reading it again last night. I'd like to throw it out."

"You'd better not, Charlotte," Frieda said sternly. "That diary's your father's business. He'll throw it out when he's good and ready."

"That'll probably be never."

"Then it'll be never." She picked up some cups to put in the cupboard. "I don't understand you, Char. If your father did forget all about Stacey and started seeing other women again, you wouldn't be happy, would you?"

Charlotte's mouth pursed stubbornly.

"See," said Frieda. "I knew it. Charlotte, your father's a human being, a man. He loves, hates, feels . . . don't try to take the place of a woman in his life. You're only sixteen and his daughter, not his wife. He lets you run the house, isn't that enough?"

Charlotte's eyes darkened. "No, it's not enough," she said, bitterly. "Father had no right to marry Stacey. He had an obligation to Mother."

"Charlotte, your mother's dead."

"And now Stacey's dead, but does that bother him? He forgot about Mother. She'd been dead only four months when he took that woman to the opera."

"And every time he took someone out after that, you made him miserable, didn't you?"

"That's beside the point," Charlotte said. "The point is, he has no right to moon over Stacey like this. It isn't fair to Mother's memory."

"Well, there's nothing you can do about it, young lady," said Frieda firmly. "So go wake up Becky and get dressed so you can give me a hand. We have a lot of work to do today."

Charlotte gave Frieda a disgusted look as she left the kitchen, but it was lost on the housekeeper, who was already busy hanging cups in the cupboard.

* * *

Ben reined up outside the office on Front Street and gazed around thoughtfully. He dismounted, tied up the reins to the hitching post, and pulling down the sleeves on his gray business suit, opened the glass-windowed door that read "JAQUETTE BROTHERS LUMBER COMPANY." He had been to the office only twice before. Once when he had come to Portland and made his momentous decision, and again when he signed the papers giving him part-ownership.

The office smelled of old papers and varnished wood, and he gazed around at the familiar surroundings until a lone figure standing at the large mahogany desk made him suddenly catch his breath. Her back was to him, but he stared transfixed at her hair. It was red, the same shade, long, lustrous and curly, and all the memories came flooding back to him. He could hardly breathe as he shut the door behind him.

The click of the door echoed through the quiet office and the woman turned. Ben wanted to cry. The figure, the hair, the blue eyes were all so like Stacey. But it wasn't Stacey. The eyes were an icier, paler blue, the face was a trifle fuller. She was quite pretty.

Her full lips curved into a smile as she looked into his dark eyes. "You have to be Ben Clayton," she said as she studied him.

He removed his hat and ran a hand through his dark, wavy hair, disappointment showing strongly on his face. "Is Mr. Jaquette in?" he asked.

"My brother-in-law's in the back room."

Staring at her black dress, Ben realized who she must be. He hadn't met her on his other visits, but Mr. Jaquette did say she was helping out in the office. She walked over to a door that opened into some sort of storeroom in the back.

"Steven!" she called quickly. "Steven, I believe Mr. Clayton's finally arrived." She turned back to Ben and ran her eyes over him flirtatiously. That was something he hadn't expected from a woman whose husband had been dead only a few months. "You didn't answer my question before, but I assume you are Ben Clayton?"

He forced a semblance of a smile. "What gave me away?"

Her eyes settled on his face, taking in his dark, aloof eyes and the full mustache that enhanced his looks. "When I asked Steven what you were like, he said you were one of the handsomest men he'd ever seen." Her eyes twinkled mischievously. "And I must say, he was right."

Ben turned crimson. He was used to Paula Tanner flirting with him, but he'd known Paula for years. To have a strange woman be so obviously attracted was embarrassing. "Is Steven coming out?" he asked to change the subject.

"I heard him grunt something about being right here," she said.

At that moment, Steven Jaquette appeared in the doorway, brushing dust from his clothes. He was middle-aged and had graying hair, but he was still well-built. He had a broad, clean-shaven face and piercing green eyes, with brows that were a little too bushy. And he was at least five inches short of Ben's six-foot-four.

"Ben," he said jovially. "You finally made it." He hurried forward to shake Ben's hand, then turned to his sister-in-law. "I see you've met my late brother's wife, Caroline."

"He didn't introduce himself," she said. "But the description you gave me was very apropos, Steven."

He smiled as he saw Ben's discomfiture. "You'll have to excuse Caroline, Ben," he said. "There are times when I think she's glad my brother died."

"Steven!" she exclaimed in surprise. "How can you say that? You know I cried for weeks. And I miss Robert terribly. But it has been some time and I am a woman. After all, Robert died, I didn't."

Steven Jaquette laughed. "You see what I mean, Ben? Oh, well, we all love Caroline. Now, I presume you came to look things over." He grabbed his hat off the hook behind the door. "Come along. I'll take you out to the camps and show you the new equipment that you made it possible for us to buy. It arrived two days ago and the men have already quit complaining." He glanced across the room to Caroline. "Answer that letter I was telling you about this morning, then check the figures on that deal with the shipyard. It seems a bit low. There may be a mistake."

"Are you going to be back by lunchtime?" she asked.

"Might be, but don't expect us. I may take Ben out to the house for lunch. I'd like him to meet Phoebe and the boy."

"The doting father," she said, smiling. "All right, I'll eat alone if you're not back. But remember, you have a meeting with Henry Washburn at two."

"Ah, that's right," said Steven. "Good, it'll be a chance for Ben to meet him." He and Ben tipped their hats to Caroline and left, heading for their horses.

They headed north from town. Ben loved the countryside around Portland, and as they rode along, he drank in the wonder of the windswept trees and fresh air that carried through the forests.

They toured the Jaquette Brothers Company's various logging camps, looking over the new equipment and taking stock of the overall operation. Ben was not only impressed but also fascinated as he watched the huge trees felled. He felt an overpowering sensation of awe as they crashed to the forest floor. Majestic and towering one moment, helpless and defeated the next. He listened to the various sounds of the work: the lumberjacks calling to one another, the noise of the axes and saws, the bellowing of the mules and oxen as they strained to drag what was left of the once-mighty giants to wagons to be hauled to town. He watched in wonder, thinking of all the houses and ships that could be made from all this and he was glad to be a part of something so big.

"What do you think?" asked Steven as they watched some men preparing to fell a tree.

"Makes a man feel rather insignificant, doesn't it?" Ben answered.

Steven grinned and suggested they move on.

They left the high country and went to one of the mills where the logs were cut into lumber. From here, the wood either would be shipped out or kept in Portland for local building. The operation was a good one and the opportunities were immense.

The only hitch for Steven had come when his brother Robert died unexpectedly, leaving debts Caroline and Steven had known nothing about. They were gambling debts that Robert had contracted at the various casinos that had sprung up in Portland over the past few years. He had borrowed against the company to pay the debts, but he had gone above and beyond what the company could safely afford. Thrown into a financial bind he hadn't expected, Steven was forced to seek a partner with enough capital to swing in the balance. Ben had come along just in time.

Ben's arrival hadn't been all luck, however. Bad news travels fast, and Ben had heard about the Jaquette Company's dire straits in The Dalles. Now he was part-owner and the lettering on the office door would soon read "JAQUETTE-CLAYTON LUMBER COMPANY."

Ben straightened tall in the saddle as they finally headed back toward town, stopping off at Mr. Jaquette's home on the way where Ben met Steven's wife, Phoebe.

She was a lovely little thing. A petite brunette, she had big brown eyes, a petulant mouth, and a nervous habit of wrinkling her nose whenever she was excited. Apparently, meeting her husband's new business partner excited her a little more than usual. Ben took her obviously flustered emotions in stride, since he had become used to women ogling over him over the years. It was much easier to handle then Caroline's blatant remarks. But Phoebe was a delightfully friendly woman and Steven seemed devoted to both her and their son.

Steve Jr. was twenty and good-looking. Both heavier and a bit shorter than Ethan, he had hazel eyes and light brown hair streaked with gold. He was studiously hesitant as he was introduced to Ben. Ben wasn't surprised to learn that he had just returned from a couple years at a Boston college.

"Father was hoping I'd go into the business with him," he said during lunch on the Jaquettes' veranda overlooking the Willamette River north of the city. "But I'm not sure yet what I want to do. Lumber doesn't really sound all that exciting."

Ben disagreed. He had found the business fascinating, and both Phoebe and Steve Jr. were forced to listen patiently while Steven and Ben discussed more business over lunch. But before he left, Phoebe invited Ben and his family, including Ethan, over for Sunday dinner the next day. She was certain Steve Jr. would be happy to meet Ethan and introduce all the young people to his friends in town.

That night when Ben sat down to write in the diary, he wore a worried expression. How should he tell Stacey about Caroline Jaquette? And yet, he had to. There was something about the woman. She reminded him a great deal of Stacey, except for her boldly flirtatious manners. Stacey had never been like that. Yet, like Stacey, Caroline seemed genuine, not fluttery and coquettish. She wasn't nauseatingly coy like other women who constantly flapped their fans and rolled their eyes. Caroline's flirtation was just open admiration. She wasn't playing a game, she was being herself. But at times it was disconcerting.

His thoughts wandered to the moment he had first laid eyes on Caroline. She had so strongly reminded him of Stacey. The turbulent stirring in his loins had taken his breath away, then when she had turned around, disappointment had gripped him and squelched the surge of passion, but there had still been a gentle rumbling of warm throbs pulsating through his flesh. She wasn't Stacey, but for a moment his body had felt as though she could take Stacey's place. It was almost a year since he had made love to Stacey, since he had even wanted to hold a woman in his arms. But in that brief moment, he had wanted to hold Caroline, if only because it would have been the closest thing to holding Stacey.

He closed his eyes for a minute, wondering. Would it be wrong to try to recapture a little of what he had once had? He knew that it wouldn't be too hard for Caroline to still the ache that made him only half a man. After all, she had been the first woman to affect him since he'd lost Stacey. Naturally, the fact that she reminded him of Stacey had a great deal to do with it. She could never be more than a substitute for the woman his heart and body really craved, but perhaps it wouldn't be so bad.

He opened his eyes again and slowly began writing. He would decide what to do after he got to know Caroline better. And he wouldn't let her resemblance to Stacey sway his thinking too much. Besides, his first impression of her might be completely wrong. He would wait to see before worrying about it anymore.

Sunday dinner the next day was extremely pleasant. The Jaquette home was beautifully furnished. Their dining room was elegant, their tableware expensive, the food was delicious, and for the first time in a while, Ben enjoyed himself. The conversation was stimulating, ranging from talk about business to discussions of the present condition of the South and the expanding railroads.

But the afternoon was especially interesting because Caroline, who had just sold her home and moved in with the Jacquettes, joined them for dinner.

"I've been thinking of going back East," she said as they sat on the back terrace after dinner, while the young folks took a walk along the river.

They were all enjoying a glass of after-dinner wine. After watching the young people disappear down the path, Ben glanced over at Caroline.

She was still wearing black, but her dress was as daring as possible under the circumstances. Her décolleté was low and the waist was nipped in tight, pushing her breasts high. Black velvet ribbons held her red hair high on her head, and onyx earrings dangled from her ears.

"Do you have family back East?" Ben asked, picking up on her remark.

"Two married sisters. But I'm not sure I want to impose on them," she said. "They both have children, and I'm not used to having children around." She looked into Ben's dark eyes inquisitively. "Your daughters are quite lovely, Ben," she remarked. "Of course it's clear who Charlotte resembles. With her dark hair and eyes, you could never deny her. But Becky's so different."

"Becky looks like her mother," he said. "Ann's hair was like golden copper and she had freckles scattered across her nose."

"I hope I'm not prying, but how long has she been gone?"

His jaw tightened. "It was two years in the spring."

She smiled warmly. "Well, at least you still have part of her with you in the children. Sometimes I wish Robert and I could have had at least one." She sipped at her wine, then turned to her sister-in-law. "Do you think I should go back East, Phoebe? Or should I go to California? I might be able to find one of those wealthy Spanish dons with a land grant and live in luxury for a while."

"Caroline!" Phoebe exclaimed, mildly shocked. "My heavens, Mr. Clayton's going to think you're a terrible hussy, going on so."

"I think Mr. Clayton's going to think I'm exactly what I am, Phoebe, dear," she said warmly. "An unfortunate widow, too young to give up men for the rest of my life, and not ashamed to admit it. After all, I didn't marry Robert just for security. We had a good twelve years together and I miss his attentions desperately."

"Caroline, for heaven's sake!" Phoebe was mortified. "Do change the subject. Can't we talk about the weather . . . or something less embarrassing?"

Caroline laughed, then glanced over at Ben. "Poor Phoebe, and she was simply outraged when I started working at the office after Robert's death. But why shouldn't I? I had to have something to do. Besides, after the mess Robert left dear Steven with, I felt it was my duty to help straighten things out."

"Then you work for Steven?"

"Almost every day now. I answer all the correspondence, go over contracts to make sure everything's spelled right, and recheck the books after Steven's been dabbling with them."

"She's a real asset to me, Ben," Steven added from his wicker chair. "She's the one who originally came up with the idea to let somebody else buy in. I was all set to give up."

"Where did you learn about running a business?" Ben asked her.

"From Robert. He was always bringing work home, and I'd go over it with him. It wasn't that hard to catch on."

"Do we have to talk business?" Phoebe said, her nose twitching. "I know, let's play some backgammon. You do know how to play, don't you, Mr. Clayton?"

Ben finished his wine. "Not too well, I'm afraid. But if everyone's willing, I'll try."

They all went into the parlor, where they spent the rest of the afternoon playing backgammon and dominoes.

*   *   *

By the end of their first week in Portland, the gold lettering on the office door had been changed and Ben had been thoroughly initiated into the lumber business. He spent a great deal of time at the office, which meant he saw Caroline every day. But he didn't really mind. In fact, she was good company. She was extremely witty, even if she was occasionally a little too cynical. Ben guessed she was probably in her late thirties, although her age was never mentioned.

At first, her open interest in him was embarrassing and he avoided direct encounters with her as much as possible. But he soon learned that it was impossible to avoid someone like Caroline. So he began to accept her little attentions in the same offhand manner in which she gave them. One minute she would look at him with blatantly inviting eyes, and the next she'd suddenly be talking about the price of lumber in San Francisco. It actually became frustrating for him to try to anticipate her next move. More and more when he came home, Ben found himself thinking about her. She was a strange, exciting, and attractive woman, yet he just wasn't sure whether or not he liked her.

On Friday evening, June 15, Steven gave a party to celebrate Phoebe's birthday. It was a gala affair and for the first time Ben met what was lightly referred to as Portland Society. A small string orchestra played on the terrace at the back of the big white house, and everyone danced under the stars.

Ben wore evening clothes for the first time since leaving Cleveland. Earlier in the evening, when he was dressing, he remembered that he had last worn them when he and Stacey had gone to the theater the Thursday before leaving Cleveland, and the memory of that night made him ache inside. She had looked so lovely that he'd had a hard time concentrating on the play. If the girls hadn't been with them that night, anything might have happened on the way home. Remembering, Ben sighed. The memories were sweet and good, but, God, could he live on memories forever?

Ben had arrived at the party a little late, but the evening was going well. He mixed in as best he could, dancing with business associates' wives, talking business when the subject arose, and just trying to be friendly. After finishing a dance with Phoebe, Ben made his way to the terrace for a glass of fruit punch laced with brandy.

"Phoebe said I'm not to have any more punch," Caroline said, peeking around from behind him as he was raising his glass to drink.

He looked at her, startled. The few times he had seen her at the party, Caroline had been surrounded by admirers, so he had kept his distance.

Now she gave him a rare warm smile that was nothing like her usual teasing manner.

"Do you think I've had too much punch, Ben?" she asked softly.

"I wouldn't know. I haven't seen enough of you since I arrived to make a fair judgment."

"Then you shall see more of me," she whispered softly. "Drink up and we'll take a walk down by the river. How does that sound?"

"To clear your head?" he asked.

Her eyes smoldered. "To clear my head."

He drained the small round goblet and held out his arm for her. They made their way through the crowd and moved off toward the path to the river.

As they walked along, the strains of the music and the talking and laughter faded until they couldn't hear them anymore. The path was a little uneven and Caroline held Ben's arm tightly, laughing softly once or twice when she stumbled over a clump of grass.

"Goodness, it's been ages since I've walked down here," she said as they followed the path through the trees.

Ben's arm tightened and he pulled her a little closer. Her footing faltered again and she laughed and picked up the skirt of her black lace dress.

"Are you all right?" he asked.

Her voice was a little unsteady. "I guess Phoebe was right. At this point I don't know if it's me or the rough ground."

"Perhaps a little of both?"

Her hand tightened on his arm. "Maybe."

A few minutes later they stepped from the path into the bright moonlight shining on the riverbank. The river wound before them like a silver road.

"It's so beautiful, isn't it?" Caroline said softly. "It almost takes your breath away."

Ben glanced down at her as she stood marveling at the scene. He couldn't see her face clearly, but what he did see caused a surging warmth to spread through his loins. He trembled. She was so like Stacey.

He touched the silky auburn hair at the nape of her neck, and she suddenly froze. Stacey's hair had felt like this, he thought.

His hand moved to caress her shoulder, and he felt her tremble. Stacey had always trembled at his touch.

He turned her to face him, all the while telling himself she wasn't Stacey, but it wasn't doing much good. The resemblance was more than he could bear.

Caroline was warm and pliable. He drew her toward him, his arm encircling her waist, and before he realized what he was doing, his lips lowered to meet hers and with the kiss came all the wonderful, aching passion that had consumed him the past few months.

Her lips were warm beneath his as they answered him back, her body molding close to his, and Ben no longer fought the feelings awakening within him. As the kiss deepened, his heart took flight and the dam of love within him burst. His hands kneaded the flesh beneath her lacy gown and his lips ran fervently across her flesh, claiming her mouth, her eyes, and her neck, then he groaned, and murmured against her ear, "Stacey, Stacey! My darling Stacey!"

Caroline stiffened. Ben slowly opened his eyes, staring at her in the moonlight. It wasn't Stacey, and a sob escaped him.

"I'm sorry, Caroline," he whispered softly, still holding her close. "Oh, my God, I'm sorry. I had no right to do that." Slowly he stepped back and stared up at the night sky, the ache inside him hurting like hell.

"Who is she, Ben?" Caroline asked softly, her lips quivering. "You said your wife's name was Ann, not Stacey."

"She was my second wife," he said slowly. "We were married last August on the way out here. She was lost in an Indian raid."

"And you still love her that much?"

"I'm sorry, Caroline. You see . . ." He flushed, embarrassed. "She had red hair like yours." He reached up and touched her hair, then let his hand drop. "And blue eyes. And her figure was much like yours." His eyes were dark and stormy. "I apologize, Caroline. I was using you as a substitute for what I'd once had with her."

Her eyes softened. "Is that so bad?"

"It isn't fair to you."

"Life has never been fair to me, Ben," she said, bitterness tingeing her voice. "I wouldn't mind sharing you with her memory. After all, I shared Robert with half the whores in Portland."

He frowned.

"Don't look so shocked," she said, unsmiling. "It's true, and

I knew it. So did the whole town. That's why I act the way I do, I guess."

"You put up with it?"

"Oh, how rare you are, Ben Clayton," she said candidly. "Pray what was I to do? This is a man's world. Besides becoming a shrew, there wasn't anything I could do. But I must say one thing for him. Robert never cheated me. I got the same as all the others, perhaps a little more. I can't be quite sure, but I do know he never left me wanting. Except in here," she said as she touched her heart. "But I think it would be easier to share a man with a woman's memory than with a woman in the flesh." She reached out and touched his arm. "Don't be afraid of me, Ben. I'm not a dewy-eyed maiden with stars in my eyes. That part of me died long ago, after my first tumble in the hay. I wouldn't expect fidelity, nor would I demand love. To be near you whenever you wanted would be enough. It would be all I'd ask."

He studied her face in the moonlight. Her eyes were sad, yet there was a hardness about them. She was offering herself, although she knew there was no love in the bargain.

"Do you know what you're saying, Caroline?" he asked softly. "Do you have any idea what you're asking?"

"I know my husband's been dead for over four months, Ben. No man has touched me since, and I feel it. If it's wrong to miss his body next to mine, then I guess I'm wrong. But I can't hold out much longer. When you kissed me just now I knew I'd lost my fight completely. I don't care anymore, Ben. I'd rather share your arms with a memory than have nothing at all. And after that kiss, Ben Clayton, if you don't take me to bed soon, I'm liable to do something drastic."

Her tone was the same teasing banter she always used at the office, but her eyes were sincere.

Ben studied her carefully. He didn't love Caroline. In fact, if it weren't for her physical resemblance to Stacey, he probably would have paid little attention to her. There was something about the cold calculating look in her pale blue eyes that disturbed him. But her lips were full and had managed to ignite the smoldering fire within him.

True, he had just pretended she was Stacey, but for a few brief moments it had sufficed. Could he make love to her the same way? He had realized the hard way that he was different from most men. No matter how strong his desire, without feelings for the woman, the act became a sham. He had tried once, shortly after Ann's death, and the results had been disastrous. Yet he knew the moment he saw Stacey that she would be different. He had seen the love and desire in her eyes from the very first moment, but he had never seen them in Caroline's eyes.

He touched Caroline's face as he stared at her. Her eyes gave him want, need, hunger, and passionate desire, but not the unselfish warmth of love. "I don't love you, Caroline. I don't think I'll ever love again," he said softly. "I don't even know if I could make love to you. I'm not like Robert, I'm afraid, I'm . . . well, let's just say I need more than just a woman's body."

"I'll give you more than just my body, Ben," she said eagerly, turning her head to kiss his hand where it touched her cheek. "Make love to me . . . please . . ."

Her lips were warm against his hand. He buried his fingers in her hair and watched the moonbeams bring it to life. Once more memories of Stacey flowed through him. God, he missed her so. He had to feel that fierce exploding passion once more. A soft body beneath his hands. It would be like holding Stacey again. His lips brushed hers, and with his eyes closed he could pretend he was kissing Stacey.

He pulled his mouth from hers, breathing heavily. "Where?" he asked softly.

Her breath caught. "Here, come . . ."

Taking his hand, she walked away from the riverbank and deeper into the trees. When they reached a spot where the grass was soft and the trees screened them, she circled his neck with her arms and pulled his mouth down to meet hers.

"Here, take me here, Ben," she whispered huskily against his lips, and kissed him again, her mouth opening beneath his, inviting him.

Ben was lost in his quest for Stacey. He wanted her so badly that every curve of Caroline's body made it possible for him to pretend he was holding Stacey once more.

He kissed her slowly, unfastening her dress, and covered her flesh with his lips. At the same time, she gently removed his clothes, until they both stood naked in the dark shadows beneath the trees.

He pulled her to the soft grass, remembering another time, another river, another place, and once more he was with Stacey beside the North Platte River. She had just become his wife, and he was loving her as he'd loved her from the very start. Her memory intoxicated him, and his head reeled as he played upon Caroline's body, his pent-up desires driving him on, and the only sound from Caroline was the gentle moaning of a woman being satisfied, the ecstatic cry of pleasure that tore from deep inside her as he entered and took her flesh.

As quickly as it had started, it was over. Ben shuddered with his release, and then reality reasserted itself like lightning splitting the sky. He lay quietly on top of her, blades of grass tickling the sensitive skin on his legs and listened to the night sounds in the darkened glade. He hadn't noticed them before. Nor had he felt the hardness of the earth beneath the grass and the tiny sticks that scratched his hands as he lifted himself from her. He rolled over and fell onto his back, sensitive to everything in the night around him. He closed his eyes, a wave of utter despair washing over him.

He heard a movement in the grass beside him and felt her hand on his chest. Her fingers gently eased through his curly hairs, and he felt her hot breath near his lips. His eyes flew open and he caught her by the shoulders and pushed her away, the pretense over.

"No!" he cried bitterly. His voice was deep with emotion. "Don't, please . . . let me handle it my own way."

Her voice was rich, vibrant. "I don't think you're handling it at all."

He stood up, suddenly all too aware of his nakedness, and felt as if his very soul was bared. Quickly he snatched his clothes from the ground, brushed them off, and began slipping them on, realizing that she too was getting dressed.

"Will you fasten my corset?" she asked softly. He hitched up his pants, and reached out in the dark, hands fumbling. He found the ties and pulled them, fastening the back of the boned corset. When he was finished, she turned to face him in the darkness. "Was it that terrible, Ben?" she asked softly.

"It wasn't you," he said as he buttoned his shirt. When he finished dressing, he smoothed back his hair and gazed at Caroline's vague silhouette. As he watched her pin up her hair, he felt an overwhelming sense of remorse.

It hadn't been the same. Pretending didn't work, because the one ingredient that made the whole act worthwhile was missing. Now he felt awkward and self-conscious as she turned to him again in the dark.

"Are you sorry now?" she asked.

"It didn't work," he said huskily. "I told you it wouldn't."

"Didn't work?" She laughed lightly. "My God, Ben, if what you gave me wasn't as complete a love as any woman could want . . ."

"That's just it, Caroline," he said. "It wasn't you. I didn't

give you anything . . . I was making love to her. It isn't
right . . . it wasn't the same.''

"Oh, Ben, you're acting like a guilty husband. Your wife's
dead.''

"Not for me she isn't.'' He took a deep breath and held out
his arm for Caroline to take. "I think we'd better get back to the
others,'' he said unsteadily. "We've been gone too long already.''

She stared at him for a minute, then took his arm and let him
lead her back into the bright moonlight. The moon was full on
his face and her heart skipped a beat. This gorgeous man had just
made love to her as no man had ever done before. She trembled

"What is it?'' he asked. "Are you cold?''

"No, I was just remembering,'' she said.

He scowled. "I was hoping you'd forget.''

She stopped walking and stared up into his face. "I'll never
forget, Ben Clayton,'' she said, her voice filled with emotion.
"I'll never be able to forget what you did to me tonight.''

He saw her face clearly now and she looked nothing like
Stacey. She was pretty in her own right, but she just wasn't
Stacey. His eyes darkened. "I'm sorry you feel that way, Caro-
line,'' he said. "Because it should never have happened. I guess
I'm just not ready yet to let her go.''

"Well, when you are, Ben, don't forget I'm here,'' she
whispered seductively. Suddenly she laughed. "Well, now that
we've cleared my head, maybe Phoebe won't mind if I have a
little more punch. How about you?''

"Sounds good,'' he said, his voice steady again. "I think I
could use a drink about now,'' and they headed back toward the
house, hoping they looked presentable enough to hide what they
had been up to.

Surprisingly, only Phoebe had missed them, and she innocently believed their story about taking a long walk. She wasn't
even surprised when Ben left early. But she did catch the knowing look Caroline gave Ben when he said good-bye.

"You like him, don't you?'' said Phoebe teasingly as they
watched Ben leave.

"Someday he's going to be mine, Phoebe,'' Caroline answered confidently. "All mine.'' Her eyes glistened with unbridled desire as she watched Ben disappear from sight.

Later, Ben stood on the balcony in his quilted robe. Frieda had
been surprised to see him home so early, but she said little about
it. Now he was holding the diary and staring across the valley at
the snowcapped mountains visible in the moonlight. The same

moonlight he had hidden from while trying to bring Stacey's memory to life in Caroline's arms. It had been so real at first, but only because he had wanted it so badly. Now the remembrance of the pain that had swept through him when it was over made him hurt all the more.

He had cheated not only himself but also Caroline. And Stacey. He lifted the diary and ran a hand across the front of the black ledger, as if caressing all the words of love that filled it. Someday, somewhere in the future, Stacey would read his words and know that there had been no end to their love. He had shared every day with her since she'd been gone, but how could he share tonight? He couldn't! And yet, he couldn't lie either.

He took a deep breath and walked back into his dimly lit room. Setting the ledger down on the desk, he stared for a long time at the empty page and then slowly closed the book. He couldn't write in it, not tonight. Betraying her memory was bad enough without making a mockery of their love as well. With a heavy heart he blew out the lamp and went to bed.

The next day, Saturday, was business as usual at the office. Both Steven and Caroline were already hard at work when Ben arrived. The thought of facing Caroline this morning had bothered Ben all night and he hadn't slept well. His eyes were a little bloodshot as he hung up his hat and headed for his desk.

After greeting Ben courteously, Steven unfolded his plan for introducing Ben to their business associates.

"I'll let you send the telegram to Crocker at the Southern Pacific in Sacramento about the shipment of railroad ties," he said. "It'll get them used to hearing your name. So far, you've been more of a silent partner, but I think you know the routine well enough now to get actively involved. By the way, did you study that new Martin contract for the timber at camp number three? Is it all right?"

Ben nodded and shuffled around the papers on his desk, conscious that Caroline was surreptitiously watching him. "It would be," he said handing Steven the papers, "if it wasn't for the fine print I've underlined. Take a look. I suggest you have a talk with Mr. Martin and his lawyers. The way it reads now, you're paying for the timber rights, plus a percentage on each log hauled out, whether sold or not. I don't think that's what you agreed on, is it?"

Steven's eyes narrowed. "You're damn right it's not. He agreed on a flat rate, no percentages."

"Then I suggest you don't sign until you get it straightened out."

Steven fumed as he rolled the contract into a cylinder, grabbed his hat, and called Caroline over. "I'm going out to see old man Martin," he said hurriedly. "Then I'll swing around by the sawmill and make sure that shipment's going to be ready by Wednesday. If I'm not back, close up at five as usual." He glanced at Ben. "And don't forget that telegram, Ben. He's waiting for a confirmation on those ties."

Steven rushed out, closing the door behind him. Ben put both hands on his desk and sat staring at the closed door.

"You're not still upset, are you?" asked Caroline as she walked toward him.

Ben studied her as she approached. She was still in black. Her neckline was high and her sleeves were long, but the dress molded to her figure like a glove. Her red hair was loose this morning, held back with two large combs, and once more the resemblance to Stacey was overwhelming.

Caroline stood before his desk, her smile inviting. "I was hoping that by this morning you'd have gotten over the ridiculous notion that what we did last night was wrong," she said.

His eyes hardened. "I didn't say it was wrong. I said it shouldn't have happened."

Her eyes bored into his. "You know, I got to thinking last night," she said. "You told me your wife Ann had been dead a little over two years. Why didn't you mention that you had been married again?"

"Would it have mattered?"

"It might have." She glanced down at his desktop. "You have to forget her sometime, Ben, you know that."

"I know."

"Then why not now? Why are you so afraid to try?"

He pushed back his chair and stood up. He hated Caroline for knowing the truth about him, for realizing that Stacey had bound him to her so strongly that he felt he'd never escape. Yet, did he want to? He hadn't written in the diary last night. Not just because he didn't know what to say, but because for a few brief moments with Caroline he had felt alive again. He had to give her credit for that. Even though Stacey's memory had inspired him, it was Caroline's body that had answered his hunger and appeased it. If only for those few brief moments.

He turned from her and walked over to the front window, but she followed him.

"Forget her, Ben," she whispered softly. "Or at least remember that she's gone and will never be yours again. Keep your memories if you must—there's nothing wrong with that. But you deserve a woman's arms, a woman's love. Let me try to be that woman, Ben, let me try . . . it was so wonderful last night.''

He closed his eyes. Maybe with time . . . He could never give Caroline the love that would always be Stacey's, but perhaps if he'd let go a little, it wouldn't be too bad. Caroline wasn't Stacey, but she was a woman. He opened his eyes and turned, looking down at Caroline, his heart in torment. "You're right, I guess. I should forget," he said softly. "Only I'm afraid it won't be easy."

"I'll help, if you'll let me," she whispered.

He touched her hair gently, and a twinge of pain settled in his breast. "You'll give me time?"

Her eyes grew warm, triumphant. "All the time you need," she answered. She leaned toward him, knowing he was vulnerable, and as their lips met, he told himself again that he couldn't live on only memories.

Half an hour later, Ben hitched his horse and strolled into the telegraph office to send the wire for Steven. He had ridden around a bit after leaving Caroline at the office, and his head had cleared some in the fresh air of Portland's streets. No, Caroline wasn't Stacey, but she was fun and interesting, and eventually he was sure he'd be able to stop pretending when she was in his arms. If not, then that was his problem.

Ben was the only customer in the telegraph office. He wrote out his message to Mr. Crocker of the Southern Pacific Railroad in Sacramento, signed his own name and the company address, then handed it to the telegrapher.

The telegrapher was a short, wiry man with glasses and a partially bald head. He slipped his glasses down to read Ben's telegram, then scowled and read it again. He glanced at Ben. "Your name Ben Clayton?" he asked, a puzzled look creasing his forehead.

"That's right."

He bit the inside part of his mouth as he studied Ben some more. "Seems I should know that name," he said thoughtfully. Suddenly his eyes grew wide with recognition. "Aha! I remember now," he said, pleased with himself. "I think I've got a telegram for you."

"A what?" Ben asked.

"A telegram," the man said as he hopped off his stool and

walked to the end of the counter. "It came in well over a month ago. Somebody in Omaha kept checking to see if it had been picked up. Since they seemed so sure you'd be here, I kept it around."

Bewildered, Ben watched the man as he rummaged around in a drawer. Finally he came up with an envelope with Ben's name written across the front. Ben looked it over, puzzled, and then tore it open.

As he began to read the telegram a shocked expression spread over his face and he went white. His mouth went as dry as cotton and tears welled up in his eyes. With his heart pounding and the world suddenly whirling around him, he slowly read the words over once more, unable to believe his eyes. It read:

Dearest Ben,
I have come back through time to you. I am in Omaha. Come for me. I love you.

Yours forever,
Stacey

CHAPTER 15

Scenery along the Oregon Trail was beautiful but dry. The rutted roadbed, which had been well worn by hundreds of wagons, was kicking up an unusual amount of dust. Since leaving Omaha three weeks ago, they had had only one light rain that hadn't even wet the canvas on the wagons. The dry spell was unusual for this time of year and everyone felt the heat, picking at each other irritably.

Stacey sat at the front of the Tanner wagon wearing an old pair of pants, a faded shirt, and a cowhide vest. She yelled at the mules, but the scarf covering her mouth against the dust and dirt muffled her words. Meanwhile, Paula and J.D. sat in the back of the wagon on comfortable pillows, watching the trail behind them. Stacey's hair was powdered with dust and her hands were callused and grimy. Her gloves had worn out long ago and her once beautifully manicured nails were broken and uneven.

Exasperated, she shoved her wide-brimmed hat lower on her head to keep out the sun, and let her mind wander back over the past few weeks, anger at Paula giving her the strength to keep the mules in line. From the very start, Paula had been impossible. Both Paula and J.D. had managed to learn to handle the mules, but that's as far as it went. Once out on the trail, the blisters on their hands healed without forming calluses because neither of them bothered to drive after the fourth day.

At times, the driving wasn't too bad. Sometimes the trail wound along a shaded river or across a lovely meadow and Stacey could relax and let the mules follow the leading wagon. But most of the time, driving was hard work and by the end of the day she was exhausted. Unfortunately, Paula didn't seem to care. She still insisted that Stacey build the fire, cook the meals, and take care of the clothes. All Paula did was walk around looking pretty. Occasionally she'd pretend to be busy when one of the women strolled by throwing dagger eyes her way, but most of the time she managed to avoid doing anything constructive.

Her favorite pastime seemed to be thinking up things for

Stacey to do so that by bedtime she was ready to drop. At least, that's the way things went for the first week or so. But after three weeks on the trail, Stacey had managed to perfect her routine so that she actually had time once in a while to visit people in the evening. Paula found this quite disconcerting.

Stacey thought back to the first night she had found herself with free time and she and Paula had tangled. After washing the supper dishes, gathering wood for the next day, and mending one of Paula's dresses, Stacey had been unable to find anything else to do, so she decided to take a walk and see if she could find Ed. She needed to talk to somebody besides the Tanners. She had to get away from Paula's scalding green eyes and J.D.'s disapproving frowns and lectures about loose women.

She jumped down from the back of the wagon, straightened her skirt, and started to walk away when Paula's voice stopped her.

"Just where do you think you're going?" she asked tartly.

Stacey whirled around. Paula was standing next to the wagon, wearing a pink silk dress that was so out of place it looked ridiculous. It was more suited to an afternoon tea, not an evening on a wagon train.

"I'm going for a walk," Stacey answered calmly.

"You have everything done?"

"Yes."

Paula's eyes narrowed. "You couldn't have."

"Well, I do."

"Even my dress?"

"Even your dress."

Paula stared at her, unwilling to give in. "I didn't hear you ask if you could leave."

Stacey stared right back, a fury beginning to smolder inside her. "That's right, I didn't ask. I didn't think it was necessary."

"Well, it is," Paula snapped, ignoring the anger in Stacey's eyes. "I might have something else for you to do."

"Like what?"

"I'm sure if I think about it for a few minutes I can come up with something," she answered.

Stacey's jaw tightened. "Well, while you're thinking, I'll take my walk. You can let me know when I get back." She turned away but was stopped once more by Paula's sultry voice.

"I just thought of something," she said.

"The hell you have."

Paula raised her chin stubbornly. "My bed has to be made up."

Stacey didn't answer at first. She was weighing her reply, but the vicious smile on Paula's lips decided it for her. "Than make it up yourself."

"Stacey, we promised you passage in exchange for your services," Paula countered. "Well, I have need of those services."

"You would, wouldn't you," Stacey said, finally exploding. "You'd think of anything to keep me busy. Well, I'll tell you, Miss Tanner, I don't take any more orders from you today. Do you understand? I've driven your wagon, cooked your supper, cleaned up your things, mended your dress, and now, if you want the same services done tomorrow, I'd suggest you make your own bed. Is that clear?"

"You wouldn't dare!"

"Don't tempt me," she said through clenched teeth. "I'll walk to Oregon and beg, borrow, or steal my meals rather than work for you unless you get off my back!"

Paula knew Stacey meant every word, and she also knew that without Stacey she and her father would have to drive the wagon. She clasped her hands together, feeling her own soft, smooth skin. Oh, how she hated the woman! But there was nothing she could do. If Stacey quit their wagon . . . She could never do all those things for herself and her father. She retreated, telling herself she'd have her day.

"All right," she consented grudgingly. "If you're going to be unreasonable about it. Go ahead, go for your walk. It won't do you any good, though. Who's going to talk to you, Miss Lady of the Evening?"

Stacey exhaled disgustedly. Her anger at Paula spoiled whatever triumphant feeling she might have enjoyed.

"I'll be back later," was all Stacey said as she turned and briskly walked away, trying to let her anger simmer down to a slow boil.

It was so hot and dry, even the grass beneath her feet lay limp against the parched earth. Some of the people she passed nodded, but many recognized her and averted their eyes. They all believed she had worked as one of Wade's whores, a story Paula had made certain was kept alive. But she didn't care. She was on her way to Ben, and that's all that mattered. She'd get there in spite of Paula and the other self-righteous people on the train.

As she neared Ed's wagon she saw Pete sitting by the fire whittling.

"Where's Ed?" she asked, startling him. He looked up and squinted to see who it was in the dim firelight.

"Who's there?" he asked hesitantly.

Stacey stepped into view, and he smiled.

"Well, dang if it ain't Stacey," he exclaimed. "Did the slave driver you're working for finally give you a night off?"

"I took it."

He laughed. "Good for you."

"Where is he?" she asked again.

He motioned with his head toward the open field beyond the wagons where they were keeping the cattle and livestock for the night. "He's over talking to some of the men, making sure everything's tight and the guards are set."

"Thanks." She climbed over the wagon tongue, careful not to catch her skirt on the single trees where the horses were usually hitched.

"You goin' over there?" he asked.

"It'll be all right, won't it?"

"Just be careful. There's lots of men in this camp who believe those stories about you workin' in Wade Savagge's upstairs rooms. It's dark out there." He started to put his whittling away. "Maybe I'd best go with you."

"Oh, no, Pete, please. I'll be all right."

But he finished setting down the wood and shoved his knife into its sheath. "Don't argue. I was right the first time," he said. His eyes crinkled warmly. "I'll feel better goin' with you."

They had no trouble finding Ed. Pete was glad, and he cautioned her not to wander off alone before he said good night.

"How's it going?" Ed asked when Pete was gone.

She shrugged. "I don't mind the work too much, Ed. It makes the time go faster. But I can't stand Paula or her father. I'm thankful for the few times you've stopped by to talk."

"I'd come more often, but besides being short on time, I don't get too warm a welcome from the Tanners."

"I know."

"How about a walk?" he asked, smiling. "It'll do you good."

"Is it safe?"

"Few Indians are this far east," he said. "The guards are just a precaution right now. And they keep the livestock from wandering off. We'd be in a hell of a mess in the morning with mules and oxen missing. There are a few Indians around, but we should be safe enough."

They headed off toward the woods. Stacey walked silently beside Ed for a long time, enjoying the warmth of his friendship.

"You look tired," Ed finally said.

"I am, a little," she agreed. "Even though I know what to

do, I'm not used to this sort of work. Where I come from, Ed, we have machines to do most of the heavy work for us. I even had a woman who came in and cleaned the house for me once a week. So this is something new for me."

"Paula has no right to work you like that."

"As she puts it, she has every right."

"Damn highfaluting dame, that's all she is. No better'n those girls of Savagge's, I'd wager," he said disgustedly. "Acts like she never had a man." He looked at Stacey quickly. "Sorry, Stacey. But I've seen the likes of her a hundred times. All prim and proper, acting so outraged and all, and just because she doesn't charge a fee she thinks it's different. I'll wager the only difference between her and Savagge's girls is that she gives hers away. That is, if she can find a fool dumb enough to take it."

"I think you've been around a little more than I figured, Ed," she said, and he heard the laughter in her voice.

"You think I'm right too, don't you?" he asked.

Her laughter was soft, warm. "I'm sure you're right, but I also think that she's letting her love for Ben drive her off the deep end. . . . Do you know what I mean?"

"If that's the case, then be careful, Stacey," he cautioned. "A woman scorned . . ."

"Don't worry," she said confidently. "I can handle Paula . . . in fact, I think you'd be real proud of me, Ed," she said, her eyes shining as she told him about her encounter with Paula.

They were close to the river now, and he glanced at her, feeling uneasy. "What if she takes you up on your threat?"

"She won't." Stacey laughed smugly. It was unusual for her to be vindictive, but she couldn't help it. "You should have seen her face. You know, I finally have Paula over a barrel. I don't intend to push it, but I think she knows she needs me now." She moved closer to the river's edge and gazed at the wide expanse of water. She picked up a stick and threw it as far as she could, watching it land with a splash. Then she took a deep breath and glanced over at Ed. She just had to ask. He might not know the answer, but she had to talk to someone. "Ed, why do you think Ben didn't answer my telegram?" she asked hesitantly.

He looked at her, surprised. "You mean the one you sent to The Dalles?"

"You and Paula both said he was there," she murmured softly.

His eyes softened. "The Dalles is a big place, Stacey."

"Paula got through."

"I know, but that doesn't mean anything. Don't worry about

it. There could be a dozen reasons. You didn't have a definite address, and if he didn't stop by the telegraph office, they wouldn't know where to deliver it."

"You don't think anything could have happened, do you?" she asked, her voice a little unsteady.

"Not to Ben. He may be a lawyer, but he proved himself along the trail, Stacey. By the time we reached Oregon, he was far from being a greenhorn. No, I don't think anything happened to Ben. I think he'll be waiting when you get there."

"Oh, God, I hope so, Ed," she said, her voice breaking. "If I didn't think so, I couldn't go on. Sometimes I miss my daughters so much, and there are times I think of Drew and everything I left behind. But I know once I'm with Ben the hurt will go away and it'll all be worth it. It just has to work out. He has to be there. I've given up too much."

"Well, I'll tell you one thing," he said firmly, trying to lead her away from bad memories. "If you intend to do all the driving for the Tanners, you have to get a better hat than the one you're wearing. You don't want to end up as dried and wrinkled as a prune, do you? By the time we get to Oregon, Ben won't even recognize you."

She touched the end of her nose and peeled away some of the sunburned skin.

"That little bonnet you wear barely keeps the sun off your forehead," he went on.

"You don't happen to have an extra hat, do you?" she asked, rubbing a piece of flaky dried skin off her cheek.

"Bass does, and he'd be more your size. I've got a big head."

She studied him for a minute in the darkness, conscious of the unsightly dirt and grime on her yellow calico dress from the day's driving. "Do you think you could find something else for me too, Ed?" she asked.

"What's that?"

"A pair of pants and a shirt. And a pair of boots."

"Hey, wait a minute. What are you up to?"

"You never had to drive mules wearing a dress," she said unhappily. "I have. It's awkward. The skirts get in the way."

"You intend to wear breeches?"

"If you can find any that'll fit."

He smiled. "I'll see what I can do."

"Thanks, you're an angel."

Ed looked down at her face in the moonlight. Even with the peeling sunburn, she was beautiful. He envied Ben. "Ready to walk back?" he asked.

She gazed around. "It's so beautiful here."

"We can stay awhile longer if you'd like."

They sat on a couple of logs and talked about the last trip, and this trip, and the weather, and Ben and a variety of other things, and it was exceptionally late when they finally went back to camp.

Paula was still awake, but she said little to either of them. She studied Ed curiously while he talked to Stacey for a few minutes before saying good night, then she continued watching him as he walked back to his own wagon, while Stacey went inside and got ready for bed.

Ed was a good-looking man in a rugged way. But his eyes could be so hard and demanding. Their blue depths only softened when he looked at Stacey. As Paula watched his broad back fade into the dark night, she wondered just how fond of Stacey the man really was. It might be interesting to find out.

She glanced over at her father. J.D. was already asleep under the wagon, his wheezing snore mingling with the chirping of the crickets. The old fool, she thought. He sure had bungled things. They were lucky they got out with the little they did. At the time, she had been so afraid that he would end up in prison and leave her to shift for herself. It was only pure luck and a few connections in the right places that had saved his neck. Why on earth he had insisted on joining a wagon train was beyond her. They could have easily made it to Oregon by stage. Sometimes she thought he was getting senile. It was true that they couldn't have taken all their clothes and valuables on the stage, but she hated this godforsaken country with its dust and heat. Hated it!

She sat on the ground in front of the fire and hugged her knees, feeling her pink silk dress sliding against her satin petticoat. Her green eyes stared at the fire, but she didn't see the flames. She only saw the dark eyes of the man she had coveted for so many years. She smiled wickedly. And now Ann wasn't around anymore. She glanced toward the wagon, tilting her blond head angrily. But Stacey was! Well, that wouldn't last long. As soon as they reached Oregon, things would be different. Ben would learn just how he'd been taken in by Stacey Gordon, and when that happened, he'd turn to her. He had to. Hadn't she forgiven him for letting Ann trap him? She'd forgive him for Stacey, too. After all, it wasn't really his fault. She had been in New York when Stacey had wangled her way into his life. If she had been in Cleveland, things might have been different. Well, she had learned from her mistakes, and she wasn't going to make another one.

She watched the fire until the flames died down to glowing embers and then headed for the wagon, determined to open Ben's eyes to the kind of woman Stacey really was when they reached Oregon.

The evening after her argument with Paula, Stacey had her first real encounter with Wade since their departure from Omaha.

Stacey had finished almost all her chores for the day, and only had to gather wood for the morning. Grabbing her old cotton bedspread to carry the wood, she headed for some trees a hundred or so yards away at the foot of a small hill. The place was a tangled mess of underbrush and half-rotted trees, with grass and some scraggly blackberry bushes scattered about. Much of it was tramped down already. The others had been there earlier, while she had been washing up the supper dishes, and she hoped there'd be something left.

Most of the others gathered the wood in their arms, but most wagons had more than one person gathering wood. Since she worked alone, it would take Stacey three or four trips if she just carried the wood in her arms. So, instead, she piled the sticks for kindling and the large branches in the middle of the old bedspread. When there was enough, she'd tie the ends together and haul the whole bundle back to camp. Sometimes, however, the bundle was so heavy she'd have to drag it most of the way. But it was better than going back and forth a half-dozen times.

Tonight Stacey had gotten the old spread half-full when she heard twigs crack behind her. She turned abruptly, frightened at the sound.

She was only a little relieved when she found herself staring straight into the intense gray eyes of Wade Savagge.

"Need some help?" he asked politely.

She eyed him warily. He looked as handsome and composed as ever. Certainly he looked nothing like the angry man she had spurned back in Omaha. He surveyed her pleasantly, making her all too aware of the dirty yellow calico dress she was still wearing and the strands of auburn hair falling across her face. She brushed her hair back and said, "Hello, Wade."

He was holding a stick in his hand and he dropped it in the middle of the old bedspread. "I missed you," he said softly.

"Wade . . . !"

"All right. All right." He held out his hands as if to ward her off. "So I didn't miss you, so I won't say it anymore. But I do want you to know that I don't blame you," he said seriously. "It was my own damn fault. I got carried away . . . but when you said you were leaving . . . it was such a shock, such a surprise. Can you forgive me for being such a fool?''

She eyed him skeptically. ''Are you serious?''

''Very,'' he answered, giving her the same intimate smile she'd seen on his face a hundred times before. ''Can we still be friends?''

She didn't know what to make of him. The night of the fire, he had stared at her with hate-filled eyes. Or was it something worse? The look had certainly been weird enough to frighten her. But now he actually looked penitent. Was he truly ashamed of his actions?

''Are you willing to be just friends?'' she asked slowly.

''If you can accept me as a friend after the way I treated you. But there's one thing I want you to understand, Red. I never would have hurt you,'' he said slowly, seriously. ''I never would have forced you.''

Was he telling the truth? It was hard to tell. A man who could cheat at cards without changing his expression could probably lie with the same ease. Yet, she wanted to believe him. There had always been something likable about Wade. His easy humor reminded her of the way Drew always kidded around. She probably should tell him to stay away, but it was a long way to Oregon and she didn't want the friction that would be ignited between them if she said no. She hated dissension. It was bad enough having to put up with Paula's antagonism. One enemy on the wagon train was enough.

Her eyes softened. He said he wouldn't have forced her. His statement was debatable, but she was willing to give him the benefit of the doubt. Her bright blue eyes mellowed and she smiled. ''Well, if you want, lend a hand,'' she said.

''And if you still want to learn how to deal, I'm willing,'' he offered.

''I wouldn't have any use for it anymore.''

''It'd make the time go faster. If nothing else, we could just play a few hands once in a while.''

She glanced down at her hands. They were dirty and sore and the blisters were healing into hard calluses. They were also red and skinned from doing the dishes and laundry. ''I'm afraid my hands aren't exactly the hands of a dealer anymore,'' she said self-consciously.

He glanced at them quickly, and his jaw tightened. ''Miss Tanner should be horsewhipped,'' he said angrily. ''Tell me, is it true she's related somehow to your husband?''

"His former sister-in-law. Ben was a widower when I married him."

"I'd heard talk."

"What kind of talk?"

"That Paula Tanner makes you do all the work while she sits around enjoying herself. The girls took a liking to you. They've been watching the lady operate."

"The girls? You mean Ginger, Hazel, Mae, and Ellie. Surely you're not including Pearl?"

He flushed. There was no use pretending. "No, I'm not including Pearl."

"I didn't think so."

He smiled guiltily, then picked up some sticks and added them to her pile. "Come on, I'll help you finish, then carry it to the wagon for you."

"You don't have to."

"Well, now, I know that." His smile lost its guilty curve and became more pleading. "Friends help friends, right?"

How could she refuse? It took almost half an hour between talking and laughing to fill the old bedspread. Wade was his old self, teasing her and telling her about some of his adventures in New York, and she hadn't realized how much she had missed his easy banter. Neither of them mentioned the fire again, and Stacey was glad. As they headed back toward camp, Wade carrying the heavy bundle of sticks on his back, she wondered if she had panicked too quickly. Maybe he wouldn't have done anything that night. Yet, when she thought back to those brief moments, remembering the look in his eyes, the sinister way his hands had reached for her . . . She brushed the thoughts aside as he spoke.

"It looks like your Simon Legree's getting ready to tangle," he said as they neared the circle of wagons. Stacey glanced up.

Paula was leaning against her wagon, waiting for them.

"Ah, Miss Tanner," Wade said, swinging down the bundle of firewood. "What a lovely surprise." The smile he bestowed on her was meant to melt the coldest heart, but he wasn't certain of the effect it would have on Paula.

She stared at him, seemingly oblivious of his charm. She was wearing a bright blue cotton dress that clashed with her green eyes and made them look menacing. "Just what do you think you're doing?" she asked, her eyes moving from the bundle of firewood to Stacey and Wade.

"Why, Miss Tanner, surely you wouldn't begrudge me the opportunity of bringing your firewood?" he asked.

"That all depends," Paula said deliberately. "Getting the firewood's supposed to be Stacey's job."

"I know," he said congenially. "But you see, Stacey's a friend of mine, and I thought it might be nice to give her a hand."

Paula stared at his black curly hair, conscious of his obvious good looks. The man literally exuded an animal magnetism that was unnerving, and she wondered just how happy Ben would be with this sort of arrangement. It was thought-provoking, to say the least. She smiled smugly. "Oh, then, if that's the reason you're bringing my firewood, forgive me, Mr. Savagge," she said, warming to the situation. "Help Stacey, if you want, all you want. In fact, you can visit her anytime you please, as long as she gets her work done. Far be it from me to interfere with your love life." Her eyes shifted to Stacey's face for a moment to gauge her reaction before she addressed Wade again. "Stacey can show you where the wood goes, then she can have the rest of the evening off if you'd care to go for a walk or something. Now, if you don't mind, I have some things to do. Don't be too late, Stacey, dear," she said sarcastically.

"As I said before, that woman should be horsewhipped," Wade mumbled as he watched Paula climb back over the wagon tongue.

"Maybe you'd better let me carry the wood after all, Wade," Stacey suggested. "And maybe you'd better not stop by the wagon too much. People could get the wrong idea."

He turned to her, eyes intent on her face. "If you think I'm going to let what she said scare me off . . ."

"Wade . . . it isn't just what she said, it's what she's going to tell Ben," Stacey said. "I know Paula. This is just what she's been waiting for."

"Let her say what she wants. I can deny whatever she makes up, can't I? And I'm sure Ed Larkin will vouch for your fidelity. Let her go. She can't hurt you, Red, not if this husband of yours really loves you. Hey," he said, hefting the bundle of firewood onto his back again, "if anybody's going to be in trouble with your husband when we get to Oregon, it's going to be Miss Tanner. Wait until he finds out how she's been treating you. Now, buck up, smile. We're on our way to new pastures and new places, so why don't you take her up on her offer. Come back to the wagon with me. Lil and the girls will be glad to see you. Maybe we can get Rundy to play, and you can sing a little for us. Let your hair down, enjoy yourself a little for a change. It'll do you good."

She weighed the consequences of an evening of fun, then shrugged. Why not? Ben loved her, and he knew she'd never do anything wrong. Besides, it wasn't like she was wandering off alone with Wade.

"You know, I think I will take you up on that," she said. After putting the firewood away, she had him wait while she slipped on her clean blue calico dress, and then they went to his wagon. If nothing else, Stacey was glad to get away from Paula's and J.D.'s prying eyes for a while.

It had been good to see the girls again. She wasn't too fond of Lil, who could be ruthless and callous at times. But Ginger was always friendly, and Ellie's look of innocence always awed Stacey. Especially now. Wade had ordered them to get plain dresses, nothing fancy. In her brown cotton with the white collar and little white buttons down the front, Ellie looked as pure and chaste as a newborn babe. Even Hazel didn't look as garish, and seemed glad to see Stacey. But her thin face was still sad and her eyes were pitifully forlorn. Stacey wondered if Hazel would ever get used to the life she was forced to lead. Mae made up for Hazel's unsmiling presence, even flirting with Wade because Pearl wasn't around.

"Where's Pearl tonight?" Stacey asked.

"Probably still getting the firewood," offered Mae. "It's her and Rundy's turn tonight. I saw them head off toward the river, where some of the folks found some pretty good wood."

Stacey glanced up at Wade. "You mean you came to help me carry wood and let Pearl carry her own?"

"Pearl's not going to like that, Wade," cooed Ginger.

Wade's eyes snapped. "Rundy's helping her."

"But she's still not going to like it."

"Shut up, Ginger," he snarled, exasperated. But Ginger only grinned broader as she studied Wade's face.

And Ginger was right. When Pearl and Rundy returned with their armloads of wood, Stacey felt the air literally vibrating with Pearl's anger. Although nothing was said, the conversation suddenly lost its relaxed atmosphere and the tension quickly became too much for Stacey, but she couldn't talk Wade out of walking her back to her own wagon. She could feel Pearl's hate-filled eyes on the back of her neck as they walked away, but she was reluctant to mention it to Wade. She didn't have to. He mentioned it first, apologizing for Pearl's sarcastic remarks and rudeness.

When he said good night, he once more assured Stacey that all was forgiven, promised to soothe Pearl's anger as soon as he got back to the wagon, and vowed that all he wanted to be was friends.

After he left, Paula informed Stacey that Ed had dropped by and left a bundle for her. Stacey was pleased, and the next morning everyone was surprised when she emerged from the Tanner wagon wearing an old pair of men's brown pants, a faded blue work shirt, patched cowhide vest, and a floppy wide-brimmed hat. Ed hadn't been able to find boots, so she wore the brown suede loafers she had been wearing the night she'd come back. The digital watch was shoved in her pocket, and she used it all the time. She didn't dare wear it out in plain sight, yet felt lost without it, and that morning at seven, when the wagons rolled, she felt better about the rest of the trip.

But now, three unseasonably dry weeks out of Omaha, some of her optimism had flown. As she rode along, going over the incidents in her mind, she wondered if she was doing the right thing by remaining friends with Wade. Of course, he hadn't tried anything and he didn't stop by the wagon too often. It was just a hunch she had, a sixth sense that told her to keep her eyes open.

She glanced back into the wagon where J.D. and Paula were sitting, enthroned on their pillows. At least they got to enjoy the scenery. Up front, the dust stirred up by the wagon in front of them was so thick that it was hard to see at times. If it would only rain.

She pushed the brim of her hat back and gazed at the cloudless sky, watching a buzzard circling off in the distance. Soon it was joined by another, and then another. She wondered what it could be. An animal? Maybe an Indian or trapper, or a settler who hadn't made it? She shivered at the thought. Well, it was too far off to worry about. She checked the sun, then pulled her hat back down and pulled out her digital watch. It was getting close to noon, and they'd be resting soon. She shoved the watch back in her pocket and yelled again at the mules, but not with the same gusto.

They were about a day's ride from Fort Kearney, and so far everything was going all right. Stacey had been afraid the Loup River crossing would bring back memories of Reith Stark, but they had been so busy with the wagons that his attempted rape of her the last time she was through here, had barely crossed her mind.

The only awkward part about the whole trip was Bass's reaction to her reappearance. Pete hadn't seen Stacey's supposed death, so her return wasn't hard for him to accept. But Bass had witnessed the whole thing, and Stacey knew that he didn't believe Ed's explanation of her reappearance in Omaha. Only his trust in Ed, and his affection for Stacey, kept him appeased. Yet there were times she would catch him staring at her curiously, and she'd feel self-conscious. She wished she could tell him the truth, but she didn't dare take the chance. It was enough that Ed knew.

Although there were too many people on the train to become really good friends with any of them, there were a few who were nice to her. But her friendship with Wade Savagge's "questionable ladies" and her tendency to wear men's clothes and keep to herself made her a subject for gossip and skepticism. Most people didn't know quite what to make of her, so they avoided her. When she had saved a young man's life by using the Heimlich Method to dislodge a piece of venison from his throat, she became even more a topic of conversation and speculation. No one knew how to accept this strange woman. Even the way she talked was different. There were times when the things she said didn't even make sense, and once more, as they had on Stacey's last trip, people began to question and wonder. Some almost feared her, others stared at her in awe, but few wanted to call this strange, beautiful woman, with the grace of a gazelle and the strength of a man, friend.

Stacey put aside her daydreaming about the past few weeks and watched the wagons ahead as they began to pull four abreast for the noon break. She was tired and hungry, and her mouth was dry with dust.

J.D. and Paula felt the wagon jerk as the span of mules pulled into line along the riverbank, and they stretched. Stacey had thought they were following the North Platte here until Ed had told her that they had left the North Platte some twenty-five miles back and were now making their way along the Wood River. After the nooning today, they'd cross the Wood River and move on toward Fort Kearney, so this would be the last they'd see of water for a while.

So while the mules grazed and J.D. and Paula ate lunch, Stacey took advantage of the break. Slipping away unnoticed, she plunged through the cottonwoods beside the trail and made her way to the river's edge. When she was out of sight of the wagons, she washed her hair, face, arms, and feet. She did everything except strip in the shallow water, and it felt heavenly. When she returned to her seat on the wagon, hair shining in the sun and face clean of the grime from the dusty trail, Paula stared at her with not only surprise but also envy. How any woman could dare to look so fresh and alive after what they had just been through was beyond her. Paula's eyes were filled with jealousy as she watched Stacey get settled for the afternoon drive.

Seeing the coldness in his daughter's eyes, J.D. cringed. He hated to see Paula like this, yet he knew what she was going through. She had always been his favorite. Ann was more like her mother—sweet and generous to a fault. Paula had a little more larceny in her heart and J.D. felt more akin to her, and he knew she'd been hurt when Ben had married Ann. It hadn't been fair of Ben to ignore Paula the way he had after Ann's death. Paula would have made him a good wife. He glanced over at Stacey, as he tried to get comfortable on the cushions again. His rheumatism was bothering him, his back was sore, and, by God, there were times when he wondered why he had decided to make the trip. But when he got to thinking about the mess back in Cleveland, he was thankful he had wormed his way out of it as easily as he had. And in Oregon Paula would have a chance with Ben again. Besides, a stagecoach would be just as bumpy and far more dangerous. He would rather take his chances against a horde of Indians on a wagon train than on a stagecoach with a single driver and only a shotgun guard.

He watched Paula settle down beside him and hoped he didn't have to listen to her complaining about Stacey for the rest of the afternoon, then he braced himself as the wagon once more began to roll.

That evening after supper, when all the chores were done, Stacey washed her face and put on her clean yellow calico dress. She was just climbing down from the wagon when two strong hands circled her waist, picked her up, and set her firmly on the ground. She whirled around quickly, then laughed, embarrassed, as Ed's deep blue eyes assured her he hadn't meant any harm.

"How about a walk?" he asked hesitantly.

She smiled. "I'd love to."

They climbed over the wagon tongues and left the circle, neither of them noticing Wade as he watched them, his eyes narrowing curiously. He had been on his way to the Tanner wagon himself.

"You look pretty refreshed tonight," Ed said gently. "Especially for somebody who's been behind a team of mules all day."

"I washed my hair during the nooning."

"It looks nice."

"You haven't been stopping by much, Ed," she said curiously. "Last night was the first time in about three or four days. How come? Busy?"

"That, and I don't relish bumping into Wade Savagge," he said. "I have to have him on the train, Stacey, but I don't have to like him."

"He's not really bad, Ed, honest," she replied. "In fact, he can be fun when he wants to be. We played three-card monte the other night and he didn't even cheat."

"That's supposed to be an asset to his character?"

She laughed as they stepped onto the rutted trail and walked along it, as the shadows deepened and night began to surround them.

"How can I explain Wade?" she said lightheartedly. "He's like a little boy who hasn't grown up. There's always that dream around the corner, and a fast way to get it. He won his big stake to move west in a poker game one night. That's where he got the money to build the Paradise."

"I don't know, Stacey. I don't quite trust a man who lives solely by his wits. They're unpredictable, and he likes you too much."

"He's been warned, Ed," she assured him. "He knows we're just friends. I've told him that over and over again, and I've made it very clear that my heart's in Oregon with Ben."

"Knowing and feeling are two different things, Stacey," Ed said with a timbre in his voice that Stacey hadn't heard before.

She glanced over at him. He had taken time tonight to change his shirt and clean up, washing his hair and shaving off his half-day's growth of beard.

"What are you getting at, Ed?" she asked hesitantly.

"Can we talk?" he asked. He stopped and glanced back toward the nearby circle of wagons. "Away from the wagons, I mean."

She nodded and he helped her make her way into a small grove of trees just off the path. When they were deep in the trees, away from any prying eyes, he sighed.

"Well?" she asked as she stopped close beside him.

He cleared his throat. "Stacey, I'm not much for words. You know that . . . and I've . . . well, I've never been in this predicament before, but don't tell me the fact that Wade knows Ben's waiting for you in Oregon makes any difference. It doesn't, not a bit. You could be in love with a dozen men in Oregon and that wouldn't change his feelings for you in any way. I know."

Her eyes darkened, puzzled. "What do you mean?"

"I mean just because you're another man's wife doesn't mean

a thing to him. The man doesn't have scruples. A man like that isn't about to just sit back and let things ride, and it scares me, Stacey." His eyes settled on her face, vaguely visible beneath the shadows from the tree branches. "Stacey, I think too much of you, and I don't want to see you hurt."

She stared at him uneasily.

"Don't look so shocked," he said, his voice deep, resonant. "I think you knew last year when you married Ben that you meant a little more to me than just a friend. But that's beside the point. What's important now is that you have no idea what you're doing to the man, Stacey. I've watched his face when you're not looking, and I swear he hasn't forgiven you for the Paradise. I think he's just waiting for the right moment, the right time. We'll be at Fort Kearney tomorrow. Remember Fort Kearney?"

"How could I forget. That's when I talked about Custer and the Little Big Horn."

He frowned. "You know, I always meant to ask you. Is that really true? Will Custer be killed at the Little Big Horn?"

"Sitting Bull's tribe is going to massacre his whole outfit," she said. "But not for about ten years yet."

"It must be strange knowing the future. Doesn't it ever frighten you?"

"No. If I knew it without having lived in the future, it probably would, but no . . . it's only that sometimes I can make mistakes, like last year at Fort Kearney. But this time I think I'll stay clear of the fort. I don't want to be recognized."

"That's why I wanted to warn you," he said. "If the Tanners need any supplies, let Pete know and he'll pick them up for you. And remember, at the fort it's easier to move around, so don't let Wade talk you into any strolls down by the river, where you'd be out of earshot. Things can be a little different at the fort. I had to warn you. I just don't trust the man."

"I'll remember, Ed, but I don't think he's going to try anything. Not anymore," she said. "He promised we'd just be friends."

"I hope so," he said thoughtfully. "But I wouldn't put anything past him."

"You worry too much," she said casually. "But I thank you for it." She took his arm. "You're a good friend, Ed. The best kind to have."

"Ready to go back?" he asked, flushing.

She wound her arm through his, picked up her skirt, and they headed back toward camp.

Ed squeezed her arm close to him. His heart felt as if it would explode. He knew before the night was over he'd be escorting Ginger or one of Wade's other girls into the cottonwoods to soothe the frustrating emotions that were running rampant inside him. He gazed down at Stacey and told himself again what a lucky man Ben Clayton was, and cursed himself for liking the man's wife a little too much.

While Stacey and Ed were talking in the cottonwoods, across the camp where the cattle were picketed, two men sat quietly by a fire waiting to go on watch. One was Jed Cato and the other was Will Harris.

Cato was a tall, stocky man with wiry hair the color of seasoned wood, broad features, and a slightly pockmarked face. His pale blue eyes studied the man beside him at length.

Harris's hair was dark brown and hung limply to just above his collar. Both men wore work clothes appropriate for the trail: leather pants, six-shooters, cowhide vests, and wide-brimmed hats. As Harris rolled a cigarette in his scarred hands, his brown eyes looked up occasionally and surveyed his surroundings.

Harris shoved the cigarette between his thick lips and lighted it with a stick from the fire. The flame from the stick illuminated wide nostrils, an exceptionally long, thin nose, and small dark eyes. He threw the stick on the fire, then sat back and let out a stream of smoke before he spoke.

"I'm telling you what I've decided we're going to do," Harris said, watching the look on his friend's face. Both men had been hired at the last minute to help herd the cattle. Ed hadn't liked their looks, but the land agent said they had worked for other trail bosses, and he was short of hands. "We're not going to do anything until after we leave Fort Hall," Harris said thoughtfully. "We'd be stupid to pull anything this side of Laramie. Two men alone wouldn't have a chance against Indians on the trail. And we'd be just as stupid to cut out between Fort Laramie and Fort Hall. There's too many empty miles out there. But after we leave Fort Hall, we can make our play and cut out toward the mountains to the south. We can take the main trail to Salt Lake City, and they won't know where we've gone. Besides, nobody's gonna care about goin' after that gambler's money, nohow. Folks on this train don't think much of him and his women as it is, and they ain't gonna care if he loses out."

Cato watched his companion closely. "You sure you saw him pack that safe in the same wagon with the piano?"

Harris grinned. "Big as life. He and that big fella he calls Ox, did it, but first he opened it up and stuffed in that whole passel

' bills that we saw him draw out of the bank. We both heard the
teller count out twenty thousand for him, and you know damn
well there was money in that safe when they hauled it out of the
fire. Now, that's a big cut to split two ways.''

Cato smiled, showing yellowed teeth. "Ain't it, though.''

Harris stared at his companion with small, shining dark eyes.
"In the meantime, between here and Fort Hall we just keep a
good eye on that wagon so nothin' unforeseen happens to it.
Understand?''

"Don't worry, Harris, there ain't nothin' gonna happen to that
wagon, not on your life. Not with over twenty thousand dollars
ridin' in it. That's one wagon that's gonna have a charmed life.''
Cato stretched and stood up, then froze as he saw two lone
figures emerging from a grove of cottonwoods on the other side
of the trail.

"Looks like the boss has found himself a lady," Cato said,
frowning. "The same lady our gamblin' man's sweet on, if I
ain't mistaken. This should prove interestin'.''

"And it's such a long way to Fort Hall!'' said Harris. "I
wonder who's gonna win.'' Both men laughed as they grabbed
their rifles and left the fire to go relieve the cattle guards. They
spent that night standing watch and dreaming of what all they
were going to do with Wade Savagge's money, money they were
very sure would be theirs in the not-too-distant future.

CHAPTER 16

Ben Clayton grabbed the counter and held on with white knuckles, still unable to accept the words before him. He forced himself to read the telegram for a third time, burning the message indelibly into his mind.

There was no mistaking the words, nor what they meant. His face was still pale, but at least his knees were once more strong enough to hold him. For a minute he had been sure he was going to hit the floor.

The telegrapher was staring at him curiously. "Are you all right, Mr. Clayton?" the man asked, concerned.

Ben nodded, trying to find his voice. "I think so."

"I didn't know the telegram was going to do that to you, sir," he apologized. "Is there anything I can do? Is it bad news? Good news?"

Suddenly Ben took a deep breath, tears rimming his eyes. "I guess it's about the best news a man could have," he said dreamily. "She's alive. She's come back, and she's alive."

"Pardon, sir?"

Ben straightened and wiped his fingers across the top of his mustache. To the telegrapher, it looked as if the man named Ben Clayton had forgotten he was there.

"You say this came in a few weeks back?" Ben finally asked.

"You can see the date there." He pointed to the heading. "April 26, to be exact."

Excitement tensed every nerve in Ben's long, muscular body. He glanced at the return address. "I'd like to send an answer," he said hopefully.

The man handed Ben a message blank.

Ben took the paper with a shaky hand, then stared at it dumbfounded. What should he say? His mind tried to grasp the reality of the situation, and he shuddered unexpectedly. Slowly he placed the paper on the counter, picked up a pen, and wrote Stacey's name and the address of the Cromwell House on the telegram. This done, he took a deep breath and wrote:

Dearest Stacey,

    I love you. Wait for me there. I am on my way.

Yours forever,
Ben

He read the message over carefully, making certain it was what he wanted to say, and then handed it to the man. "I'll wait for an answer," he said anxiously.

"It may be a long wait," the man said reluctantly, hating to take the sparkle from the customer's eyes. But he knew that because the telegram was so old, the chances of an answer weren't too keen.

But Ben refused to leave. He walked to the front of the shop and stared out at the warm Saturday afternoon, his heart fluttering like a butterfly. He listened attentively to the clicking instrument behind him as it sent his words across the country.

When the clicking stopped momentarily and then started up again, Ben hurried to the counter and watched the telegrapher jot something down.

When he finished, the man's face was creased in a frown. "Sorry, Mr. Clayton. The line's down again somewhere between Fort Bridger and Omaha. They're workin' on it, but no idea when it'll be clear. The Indians raise hell on the lines down there. Keeps the men busier than a month of Sundays just tryin' to keep them spliced together. I guess they got a fool notion that if we can't send telegrams, we'll quit coming into their territory. Beats all, don't it?"

"Do you think it'll be fixed today?" Ben asked.

"Could be, but sometimes it's down for a couple of days. All depends on where the break is and if the Indians are still around."

Ben rubbed his mustache, trying to think of what to do. He had to have an answer. Her telegram was two months old. He had to be sure she was still all right.

The telegrapher saw the pain and anticipation in his eyes. "Look, Mr. Clayton, if you wouldn't mind . . . you evidently live around here . . ."

Ben gave the man his address.

"Good," he said. "When I get an answer, I'll send someone out to the house with it, how's that? Of course, there's an extra charge."

"I don't care about the extra charge. You sure you can find someone to deliver the message?"

"Young man next door, works in his father's store. He's used to running telegrams for me when I need him. You go home and take it easy." The telegrapher thought Ben still looked a little pale under his suntan. "I think you should rest a bit. You look as if you'd been kicked by a mule."

"I feel like I have been," Ben said. "Now, you'll be sure to send it right out to the house the minute an answer comes? No matter what hour of the day or night?"

The man nodded, and Ben paid for the telegrams and left, Stacey's telegram still clutched in his sweaty hand. He stood on the sidewalk for a long time and stared at it, tears filling his eyes. Finally he glanced up self-consciously, realizing people were staring at him.

After all, what did he expect? A man his size was conspicuous enough without crying out in front of the telegraph office. He sniffed back the tears, stuffed the telegram in his pocket, and rode out of town toward the hills.

His first instinct was to yell, shout, scream, and jump up and down. But grown men weren't supposed to act like ten-year-olds. But he had to do something! He sat tall in the saddle, closed his dark eyes, tilted his head back, and took a deep breath, her name echoing on his lips like a prayer. She was here, back where he could reach her again, touch her, love her. . . . All he had to do was get to her. How or why she had come back, he didn't know, nor did he care. All that mattered was that she was no longer lost to him. He felt crazy, like a kid again.

He grabbed his hat from his head and let out a wild whoop that startled a few others on the road, and they stared after him curiously as he nudged his horse in the ribs and took off like a wild man toward home.

Frieda was upstairs dusting, Becky was in the sewing room, and Charlotte was helping Ethan with some paperwork in the study when Ben came bounding in the back door. "Where is everybody!" he yelled as the door slammed behind him.

Charlotte looked at Ethan, startled. "Father?" she asked. She checked the clock on the mantel. "It's just a little past noon. The office doesn't close until five on Saturday."

Ethan set his papers down. "Something's wrong, can't you tell by the sound of his voice?" he said anxiously. He grabbed her hand and pulled her from the chair. "Come on!"

They rushed from the library and met Becky at the sewing-room door.

"What do you think's the matter?" Becky asked as Ben yelled for them again.

At that moment, Frieda rushed down the steps into the parlor, wringing the dustcloth in her hands. "Let me go in first," she said quickly as they all moved toward the kitchen. "If it's bad news, I'd rather let him take it out on me."

They all agreed, forming a skirmish line behind Frieda. Frieda straightened her white apron and took a deep breath. She was primed for battle as she opened the kitchen door, but she certainly wasn't prepared for what hit her when she stepped inside.

Ben let out what sounded like a war whoop and swept Frieda into his arms.

"She's back . . . she's back! Oh, God, Frieda, she's back!" he cried passionately as he twirled her around the kitchen like a madman.

"Ben!" she yelled, holding on to his broad shoulders. "Land's sake, Ben, what's got into you!" He stopped twirling and set her down. Holding her by the shoulders, he looked deep into her warm, motherly eyes.

His own eyes filled with tears as he spoke. "She's back, Frieda," he whispered ecstatically. "Stacey's back."

"What . . . what are you talking about, Ben?" she asked breathlessly, her face suddenly white.

He pulled out the telegram and showed it to Frieda, while Charlotte, Ethan, and Becky hovered curiously outside the kitchen door.

Frieda read the words, looked up at Ben's glowing face, and read them again. "What is this, some sort of cruel joke?" she asked anxiously.

"It's not a joke," he said, his voice breaking. "It's from Stacey. You can see for yourself, she was in Omaha. The telegram was sent in April."

"But, Ben, she's dead," Frieda cried helplessly. "Stacey's dead!"

"No . . . she's not dead. I know she's not. I knew it all along. I can't explain how, but I did. That's why I could never let go, and now she's coming back to me, don't you see?"

"You believe this?" she asked.

He straightened, and his dark eyes glistened with eagerness. "I've already sent a telegram to tell her I'm coming for her," he said as Charlotte, Ethan, and Becky finally stepped into the room. "As soon as I get an answer, I'll be leaving."

"Leaving for where?" Charlotte asked abruptly.

Seeing his daughter's puzzled face, Ben suddenly realized what this was going to mean to her. But he couldn't avoid it. Nothing and no one was going to keep him from Stacey. "Stacey's alive," he announced carefully. "She's in Omaha, and I'm going to go after her."

All three of them stared at him dumbfounded, but it was Charlotte who spoke. "It can't be, Father," she said angrily. "Someone's playing a cruel trick on you. She can't be alive."

"But she is." He took the telegram from Frieda and handed it to Charlotte, who read it with wary eyes. "See for yourself," he said firmly. "Only Stacey could have sent that telegram."

Charlotte read it, then stared up at her father. "Only Stacey? Father, anyone could have sent you a telegram from Omaha and signed it with Stacey's name. She's dead, you saw her die. Don't let yourself be hurt like this."

Ben's face hardened, the uncontrollable joy he had felt only moments ago held in check. "Did we bury a body, Charlotte?" he asked solemnly.

"No, but that doesn't mean—"

"It means that what we saw, what we were certain had happened, didn't happen. She's still alive. Don't ask me how I know, I can't tell you." He could hardly explain that only Stacey would have written "I came back through time." "I'm going to Omaha for her, Charlotte," he said forcefully. "And nothing's going to stop me."

"What about the company? What will Mr. Jacquette say?"

"He can take care of things while I'm gone, and Ethan can run things for you all here. I'll only be gone a couple of months, three at the most. It takes about twenty days to reach Omaha by stage. I'll leave power of attorney at the bank until I get back, so none of you will want for anything."

"Father!" Charlotte was aghast. "Father, you can't just go off like this. You can't just leave."

"Can't? Charlotte, Stacey's my wife. What do you expect me to do, sit back and do nothing? Just act like the telegram never came?"

"I think he should go," Becky said. For the first time in almost a year, Becky saw hope in her father's eyes. "If there's the slightest chance that Stacey's there, I don't think we have any right to ask him to stay, Charlotte."

Charlotte whirled on her, her white muslin dress highlighting her flushed face. "You would like that, wouldn't you?" she said, looking at her sister with loathing. "Ever since Stacey saved your life with that stupid operation, you've thought she was some kind of a saint."

"No, I haven't," Becky argued back. "But I don't think either you or I have any right to tell Father what to do. This is his house, she was his wife, and we have no right to interfere."

"Hurrah for you," said Ethan from behind Charlotte.

Charlotte caught his eyes in an angry embrace. "I might have known you'd agree with Becky," she said bitterly. "You always have. Well, there's no law says I have to. I don't believe Stacey's alive, and I don't think Father should risk going back to Omaha, but I know my feelings won't count." She turned back to her father, her eyes misty. "And what do we do if you don't come back?" she asked helplessly. "What if you're killed . . . anything could happen. Why do you have to risk your life on something so crazy?"

"Because it isn't crazy," he explained slowly. "When you gave me Stacey's diary, Charlotte, you told me you were sorry. Remember? You asked me to forgive you for treating her the way you did, and I forgave you. Now I'm asking, did you really mean what you said, or were they just words?"

She stared at him. It had been so easy to ask forgiveness at the time. After all, Stacey was dead and she would never have to see her again, but now . . .

"I guess I meant them at the time," she said, anger smoldering in her eyes. "But that was before I realized that you thought more of her than you did of Mother. You never grieved for Mother the way you've mourned for Stacey. Tell me, Father, if Mother came back too, who would you pick?" she asked bitterly. "Her or Stacey?"

Ben held his breath. What a question for her to ask. But she had asked it, and it was a question he had even asked himself. He looked deep into her dark eyes. "Do you want the truth, Charlotte?" he asked solemnly. "Do you really want the truth?"

She stared at him, her face white. "Yes," she whispered breathlessly. "Yes, I want the truth."

"I don't know," he said dismally. "That's something I can't answer, because I just don't know. But I do know that I love Stacey and she did come back. If you think I'm betraying your mother because of it, then I'm sorry. There's no way I can convince you otherwise. But I can't give her up. Not for you or anyone else. Hate me if you must, but that's the way it has to be. We all have our lives to live, and this is mine. I have to do what my heart tells me. Frieda understands, and so do Ethan and Becky. I only wish to God you did."

"I do," she said, tears welling up in her eyes. "That's why it hurts so much. I understand only too well, and I hate Stacey for it. She made you love her more than you love any of us. Go ahead, go to her, Father, only don't expect me to rejoice about it." She crumpled up the telegram as she spoke. "I'll curse the day she walks into this house!" She threw the crumpled telegram at Ben and left the kitchen, slamming the door to her room upstairs. Frieda, Becky, and Ethan tried to make Ben feel better, but dinner was strained. Charlotte was there, but she was silent and her eyes were red from crying.

It was almost bedtime when a young man showed up on the doorstep with the answer to Ben's telegram. It wasn't what he had expected. The telegrapher in Omaha had stated that the party sending the telegram had notified their office that she was leaving town. But there was a small note on the bottom of the message from the telegrapher in Portland.

"Just from me to you, Mr. Clayton," the telegrapher had written, "our man in Omaha said he was quite certain that the woman named Stacey Clayton had joined a wagon train heading for Oregon and that she should be well along the Oregon Trail by now." He had signed it "Bud."

Ben stared at the message, tensing with new hope. He went to the library, took out a map, and studied it intently. If he could figure out approximately how many miles they had already traveled, then he could take a stage to the nearest town or fort or whatever, get a horse, and head east along the trail until he found the right wagon train.

But first he had to know when she had left Omaha. He stared at the map for a long time, then went into the kitchen, where he found Frieda.

"I'm going out, Frieda," he said, grabbing a lightweight leather jacket off a hook behind the door. At the last minute, he also took his gunbelt and six-shooters off the hook and put them on.

"You really need those things?" Frieda asked.

He hefted the guns more comfortably onto his hips. "I hope not," he said. "But it's a long way to town this time of night, and a lone man's too good a temptation. Even out here."

"I was hoping we had left that custom back on the plains," she said thoughtfully. "But I guess they're even wearing them in San Francisco, or so Ethan says." She eyed Ben curiously. "Have you figured out just what you're going to do yet?"

"One way or another, I'm going to find Stacey," he said. "I'm going in to the telegraph office again. There ought to be a sheriff or marshal in Omaha, since it's the capital of the Nebraska Territory. I thought I could get him to check with the hotel and find out when she left, so I'd know about how far they've traveled already."

"Why don't you just wait until she gets here?" she asked hesitantly.

He glanced at her sharply. "I can't, Frieda. When you love somebody so damn much that it's tearing you apart inside, you can't just sit back and wait." There were tears in his eyes. "I know it's hurting Charlotte, and I don't mean to, Frieda, you know that. I loved Ann. I'll admit I don't think I loved her quite as deeply as I love Stacey. Ann and I were young when we married, we grew up together. But Stacey's different, Frieda. I think you sensed it right from the start. There's just something between us . . . Without her, I don't feel whole. God help me, if Stacey had come into my life while Ann was still alive . . . Frieda, Charlotte's question today actually scared me, because I don't know what would have happened. Can you understand that? Sometimes it's frightening because my feelings for her are so strong. I have to go, Frieda. All I have to find out now is when and how I'll go, and I won't be able to sleep until I do."

Frieda nodded, sighing. Poor Ben. Was he chasing a dream, or was the telegram authentic? She frowned as he kissed her on the cheek and left.

Half an hour later, Ben rode up in front of the telegraph office. There was a different man on nights, and he was sitting behind the counter in a wicker chair reading when Ben walked in.

"Help you?" he asked, pulling himself up from the chair. He was heavier than the day man and had pudgy cheeks and a small potbelly.

"Are you Bud?" asked Ben.

"Yup."

"I'm Ben Clayton. You sent a telegram out to the house a while ago."

"Oh, yes, Mr. Clayton," he said congenially. "Ralph on days said you were expecting it. Everything all right? I hope that note I sent with it wasn't being too forward. But our man in Omaha likes to talk some over the keys, and Ralph said you were pretty upset."

"No . . . no, in fact, I'm glad you added it. Now, you can help me a little more, if you will. Is there any way I can find out what day she left? Maybe there's a sheriff who could check the hotel register, anything like that. I'm willing to pay for another telegram, a dozen if I have to, but I have to find out."

"Let's see what we can do for you," he said amiably. "I'm not really supposed to do this, but, well, folks get lost sometimes. It's a big country. For twenty dollars I can find her for you. Sound fair?"

Ben couldn't help smiling. There was a bit of larceny in everyone's heart when it came right down to it. "You find her and the twenty's yours."

The man began transmitting while Ben paced the floor, occasionally staring at him with alert eyes.

Finally, after half an hour, the man triumphantly turned to Ben.

"You've got it?" Ben asked.

"She's on a wagon train. The wagon master's Ed Larkin out of the Omaha land office, and they left Fort Kearney yesterday morning, headed for Fort Laramie."

"You're sure?" Ben asked.

"That's what the man says."

"Is there any way I could get a telegram to her?" he asked. "Could someone ride out to catch the wagon train, see that she gets it?"

"I don't think you're going to find anybody willing to do that, Mr. Clayton," he offered. "The Indians are getting skittish lately about so many wagons going through, and a lone rider would be a real target. But if you want, I can send a message ahead to Fort Laramie telling them to get word to Ed Larkin's train when it arrives."

"No thanks. By the time they get to Fort Laramie, I can be there myself, waiting for them."

He paid the man his twenty dollars and left. He frowned as he mounted his horse, remembering the long miles from Fort Kearney to Fort Laramie and the Indian attack that had taken Stacey from him in the first place. Now, according to the telegrapher, the Indians were being especially skittish. He prayed hard that she'd make it through all right. As he dug his horse in the ribs and headed home, he let his thoughts wander. The man said she was on Ed Larkin's train. At least that was reassuring. Although it seemed ironic that she should end up with Ed as wagon master.

Suddenly Ben remembered something else. Paula and J.D. were on their way west too. Just before leaving The Dalles, he had received a telegram from them which said they would be heading out on the next wagon train. Wouldn't it be a coincidence if they were all on the same train? But no, it wasn't possible. Things like that didn't happen. Besides, the way Paula despised Stacey, he'd hate to think of them being on the same train together. In fact, the more he thought of it, the more he hoped they were no where near each other.

And another thing bothered him. What had she told Ed? What explanation could she possibly give for being resurrected from the dead? He hated to think of what she might be going through. Now more than ever, he knew he had no time to spare in reaching her.

His thoughts continued to wander as he rode along. Sometimes he was afraid he was going to wake up and discover it was all a dream. But he knew it wasn't. He closed his eyes for a minute and saw her blue eyes before him, so full of life and love. She was so beautiful and warm. Was it any wonder he could never forget her?

Suddenly his stomach tightened as a fleeting glimpse of another woman's face swam through his thoughts. Caroline! My God, last night! He trembled, remembering making love to her. And this morning in the office he had made plans to see her tonight. Steven, Phoebe, and Steve Jr. were going out, and they'd have the house all to themselves.

"Except for the servants, that is," she had whispered in his ear. "But then, we can always get rid of them, too."

He was supposed to have been there for dinner at eight o'clock, and it was almost midnight already. He had completely forgotten about it.

Remembering last night, he felt sick. His mouth was dry and his hands were clammy on the reins. How could he have accepted Caroline as a substitute for Stacey? If only he had gotten the telegram from Stacey yesterday. But he hadn't. Before the telegram, it had seemed so right. The logical result of their friendship. She was a desirable woman and he was a lonely man. But now!

It was too late to go explain to Caroline tonight, and he hated the thought of facing her tomorrow. Pushing the thoughts of Caroline aside, he gazed up at the full moon and wondered if Stacey saw it too. Then other thoughts flooded in on him as he began to theorize how she might have ended up in Omaha? The whole thing was so bizarre. If he didn't know where Stacey was from, he might be tempted, as Frieda and the rest were, to think someone was playing a cruel trick on him. But he knew the truth. It wasn't a dream or a grim joke. It was reality. Somewhere along the Oregon Trail, Stacey was on her way to him.

Everyone was in bed when he reached the house. He bedded down his horse himself, and made his way through the darkened house to his room without bothering to light a lamp. Once inside, he leaned against the door, his heart in a turmoil. So near, yet so far.

He lit the lamp and threw off his coat, hat, and gunbelt. He was weary from the day's excitement, but he was still determined to follow the course he had set for himself. But Charlotte was right about one thing: he couldn't just take off. There were things he had to settle first.

Tomorrow he'd explain everything to Steven, and he'd face Caroline. That part was going to be the hardest. She had looked so enraptured today, so content when he had held her in his arms.

Damn! How could he have gotten himself into such a mess? And what was Stacey going to say about it? Well, dammit, he hadn't really done anything wrong. Stacey hadn't been here for him to make love to.

He stood by the bed in his underwear and glanced at the desk drawer where the diary was, remembering why he hadn't written in it the night before. He had promised himself to forget Stacey and start living again. Tears came to his eyes as the impact of the day overwhelmed him.

He blew out the lamp and climbed into bed. The tears washed down his face onto the pillow and he tried to choke them back.

He wouldn't need the diary anymore; he was going to have her with him once again, and through a restless night of tossing and turning, anxiety keeping him from a sound sleep, he dreamed of Stacey over and over again. He woke up with thoughts of her and fell asleep again with thoughts of her, until the first rays of the sun finally crept through his window.

He lay in bed for a long time, contemplating the day before him. His carefree joy of the afternoon before was replaced now by a quiet urgency. He slipped from the bed, put on his robe, and hurried downstairs to see if anyone was up and about.

It was just dawn and the house was quiet. It was Sunday, and they hadn't found a church to attend as yet, so everyone took advantage of the restful day and slept late. But Ben couldn't sleep any longer. There was too much to do. He was just getting a fire started in the woodburning stove when Frieda came in.

She was still in her nightgown and wrapper, her gray hair hanging down her back in a long thick braid. She was surprised to see Ben up so early, and scolded him for doing what she considered her work, making him sit down at the table, then she began getting him some breakfast.

She threw some bacon in the frying pan and set the coffee away from the hottest part of the fire to let it perk.

"Well, have you decided yet just what you're going to do?" she asked Ben.

"I'm still going," he replied thoughtfully. "There's a stage leaving tomorrow morning at ten. The bank opens at nine and I can take care of my business there before I leave. I'll pack some things today. But first I'll ride over this afternoon and tell Steven Jaquette."

Frieda brought a loaf of bread to the table and cut two slices, then looked at him anxiously. "Ben, are you absolutely positive there hasn't been some mistake? I've been tossing and turning all night. I liked Stacey very much, you know that, but when she fell off that cliff with the arrow in her back, no one who saw it—not you, or the scout Bass, or any of the other men who tried to rescue her from that Indian—no one believed there was even the remotest possibility of her having survived. Ben, why are you so certain she's alive?"

"I wish I could tell you, Frieda," he said. "But I can't. All I know is that no one except Stacey could have sent that telegram. I know it seems impossible, but there's no other explanation. But, Frieda, even if I had doubts, I'd have to go."

"I suppose so. It's just that you're like my own son, Ben, and I don't want to see you hurt anymore."

He tried to reassure her while he ate his breakfast, and then he went upstairs to dress. By the time he came back down, Frieda was dressed and the whole household was up. Even Ethan had come over for breakfast.

Charlotte was still bristling. She spoke only when spoken to, and her answers were cold and abrupt. Ben spent the morning in the library going over maps, estimating where he would intercept the wagon train. He tried to pretend Charlotte's anger didn't matter, but it did. Her attitude was putting a damper on his newfound joy, and he felt it deep inside. He loved Charlotte, but he loved Stacey too, and in a way that warred with his emotions as a father. He needed Stacey to be a part of his life, but Charlotte wasn't even willing to acknowledge that Ben had such needs. Maybe by the time she really grew up and learned what love was all about, she'd be able to understand. He could only hope.

After a late lunch, Ben saddled his horse and headed over to the Jaquettes'. It was a beautiful, warm summer day. The leaves barely rustled in the hot breeze, but there were small whirlpools of dust on the road as he jogged along on his dappled mare. He had dressed casually today in a pair of dark blue pants, a white shirt, and a tan hat. His shirt was open at the front because of the heat, and he had to fan himself to keep the material from sticking to him. Nonetheless, the warmth felt good after the cold, drizzly winter.

Unlike Cleveland, there was no heavy snow in Oregon during the winter months. Occasionally the sky would spit a few flakes, but the temperature was never too cold and the snow never stuck. But winter was still winter. There were cold rains and chills that hung on for weeks on end. It was good to ride along basking in the sun's heat again.

Only one thing bothered Ben about confronting Steven. He had never mentioned Stacey to him. It wasn't until he had inadvertently murmured her name while kissing Caroline that anyone in the Jaquette family even knew she had existed, and he dreaded having to go over the whole story with them. He would have to justify his reasons for believing she was alive when they hadn't even known she had existed.

By the time he reached the Jaquettes' beautiful white house on the banks of the Willamette River, he had rehearsed his conversation with them over a dozen times. But each time he repeated it, it sounded a little less convincing.

Ben dismounted and headed for the front door. He arrived just in time to catch Phoebe and Steven. They were due at a friend's house for afternoon tea and were already on their way out when the maid ushered Ben in.

"I'll only keep you a few minutes, Steven," Ben said as they stood in the large foyer. "It is important, however, and I have to tell you today because I won't be in Portland tomorrow."

"You're leaving?" Steven asked, surprised. "A short trip? Business? What . . . ?"

"I've had some marvelous news. Rather shocking . . . but . . . my wife's alive. There's been a telegram from Omaha and . . . well, I have to go back east to get her."

Phoebe stared at him, puzzled. "But you said she'd been dead two years. How could she suddenly be alive?"

He inhaled sharply. "I assume Caroline hasn't told you?"

"Told us what?" Steven said, frowning.

"I told her about Stacey Friday night," he explained. "Ann was my first wife. She died back in Cleveland two years ago. I was married to Stacey on the wagon train coming out here. We thought she'd been killed in an Indian raid, but I learned yesterday afternoon that she's still alive."

Phoebe's hand flew to her breast. "You mean she's been a captive of those savages all this time? Oh, good heavens!" Her eyes were like saucers.

"Not exactly." He cleared his throat and straightened his broad shoulders. "It's a rather long story, but the point is, I have to leave tomorrow morning for Fort Laramie. She's on her way here on a wagon train, and if I leave for Fort Laramie now, I can be waiting when she gets there. I'll go to Boise, then down to Salt Lake City, and take the overland stage from there."

"You're sure there's been no mistake?" asked Steven.

Ben shook his head. "No . . . no mistake. The telegram I got was directly from her."

Steven's eyes studied Ben carefully. "If she's on her way here, why don't you just wait for her, Ben?"

"I can't." His voice was deep with emotion. "In the first place, I can't take a chance on anything happening to her again. But most of all, we've been separated too long already. I have to go." He frowned. "I know you can handle things while I'm gone, but I'd like to ask a favor it it's at all possible."

"What's that?"

"I was hoping that while I'm gone, you might take Ethan under your wing a little. Let him use my desk at the office and help out in my place. He's a smart lad, picks up things quickly. I'd really appreciate it and I know he'd be a big help to you. I should only be gone about two months, maybe a little longer."

"If you think the young man's able, I'll be happy to get his help," he said. "Only I'd much rather have your experience."

"I know," said Ben. "And I wish there was some other way, but I have to go."

The three of them hadn't noticed Caroline coming down the hall from the back of the house. She reached the foyer just in time to catch Ben's last words.

"Go?" she asked, staring at him curiously. "Go where?"

Ben turned to face her, his eyes guarded. She was wearing an afternoon dress of black silk, with lace trimming the low neckline and lace sleeves reaching to her elbows. Her hair was fastened atop her head with a black lace coiffure perched on it, the black grosgrain ribbons falling partway down the back of her deep red curls. Her pale blue eyes were intense, agitated.

"I'm leaving for Fort Laramie tomorrow morning," he began.

"He's going after his wife," Phoebe blurted out excitedly. "Can you imagine, Caroline, she's been held captive by Indians all this time. Steven and I didn't even know he had a second wife. My heavens, things are happening so quickly these days. It's all so unsettling!"

"What on earth is she jabbering about, Ben?" Caroline asked testily. "And what happened to you last night?"

Steven glanced abruptly at his sister-in-law and noted the high color on her cheeks and the grim set to her mouth. He had been very aware of the byplay between Ben and Caroline the past few weeks, and as he watched them now, he realized more was going on than met the eye. His face flushed slightly and he addressed Ben, hoping to clear the air a little. "I'll be glad to take the boy on, Ben," he said, checking his pocket watch. "But if we don't get going, Phoebe and I will be terribly late for our visit. Do you mind?"

"You go ahead," Ben said, realizing Steven was trying to give him time alone with Caroline. "The stage doesn't leave until ten in the morning, so I'll stop by the office with a paper giving you permission to do what you see fit during my absence. That way, if something comes up, you'll be able to handle it without my signature. And I'll bring Ethan in with me. You and Caroline can get him started. I think that should cover everything. Is that all right with you?"

"Sounds fine." Steven frowned again. "But I wish there was some other way . . . What if I make the wrong decision on something?"

"That's one thing that hasn't crossed my mind, Steven," Ben said smiling. "You're teaching me the business, remember?"

Steven looked more relieved. "If you're willing—"

"No," Ben said. "If you're willing. After all, I'm throwing the load on your shoulders."

"All right. Now we'd better go. I'll see you in the morning?"

"Early."

They said good-bye and Ben watched the door close behind them, then turned to Caroline, who was still watching him intently.

"Are you ready to explain what's going on?" she asked.

His eyes locked with hers. "I'm sorry about last night," he said. "Isn't there someplace we can talk besides the foyer?"

She led him through the house and out onto the terrace, and a flood of unwanted memories assailed him. He threw his hat on a wicker stand and gazed across the long expanse of lawn toward the river.

"Well?" she asked.

He looked at her, once more caught up in her resemblance to Stacey. Only Stacey was here again. He didn't need Caroline anymore.

"What Phoebe said . . . most of it is right, Caroline," he said slowly. "My wife, Stacey, is alive. She didn't die in the Indian raid."

"I don't believe you."

"It's true. When I went to the telegraph office to send that wire to Crocker in Sacramento yesterday, there was a telegram waiting for me. It had been sent almost two months ago. I had no idea it was there, but the minute I read it I forgot everything, including my promise to come over last night."

She stood for a minute in a daze, unable to grasp the full portent of his strange explanation. "Now, wait a minute. Let me get this straight," she said, rubbing her forehead. "You mean the telegram was about your wife being alive?"

"The telegram was *from* my wife!"

"You can't be serious."

"I am . . . very serious."

"But how? Where has she been all this time?"

"I don't know. I won't know all the answers until I see her. It only said she was there. I spent most of last evening at the telegraph office and discovered she's headed this way on a wagon train. The train she's on left Fort Kearney on Friday morning. If I leave right away, I can reach Fort Laramie in time to meet her."

"What about us?" Caroline asked, seeing all her dreams fading into nothing. "What about me, Ben? Where do I stand in all this?"

"I was hoping you'd understand."

"Understand? What am I supposed to understand?" She moved close to him, her hand moving up to rest on his shirtfront. "Yesterday you were ready to forget her, Ben. I know you were," she whispered softly. "Friday night you did forget her for a while."

His eyes darkened. "You weren't listening to me Friday night, were you, Caroline?"

"Yes, I was listening. But I was feeling too, Ben." Her eyes softened seductively. "Maybe you thought you were pretending, but you were enjoying it as much as I was. It wasn't your wife who made you feel like that, Ben, it was me, my body. You don't need her. Not really."

"Now I know you weren't listening." He took her hands from his chest. "Yes, I enjoyed your body, Caroline. I'd have enjoyed any woman's body Friday night. Can't you understand that? I was starved for Stacey."

"What about yesterday at the office?" she challenged. "You weren't pretending I was Stacey then."

"Wasn't I?"

"You couldn't have been!"

"Caroline, I'm sorry. I should never have let things get this far. My feelings for you have never been separated from my feelings for Stacey. I tried being honest with you, but I guess you just weren't in the mood to accept it. When I left the office Saturday, I prayed that the day would come when I could kiss you without pretending I was kissing Stacey. But I only kissed you in the first place because I thought I'd never have Stacey to love again."

"And now you think you will?" Her eyes hardened. "It doesn't make sense."

"It does to me."

"Phoebe said she'd been captured by Indians. If she's been with them, you won't want her back, can't you see that? Do you know what they do to white women, Ben? Could you accept her after she'd been passed around from one brave to another?"

"Phoebe was wrong," he insisted firmly. "She wasn't captured."

"How do you know?"

"I just do."

His eyes were cold and reserved as he watched the expression on her face.

"You're a fool," she said bitterly. "You're chasing a dream."

"Stacey's my wife."

"Well, fine, go to her then," she said. "Make a fool of yourself. Let her know she's got you wrapped around her little finger." She sneered. "And I thought you were a man!"

"You're pushing, Caroline."

"Good," she said defensively. "Then maybe I can push some sense into your head. Ben, why do you have to go on such a wild-goose chase? What if you get there and it was all a mistake?"

"It won't be."

"How can you be so damned sure? I know you loved her, that was obvious Friday night, but anyone could have sent that telegram and signed her name to it."

"No, that's where you're wrong. You see, there was something only Stacey and I knew, and the way she worded the telegram, there couldn't be any mistake. The telegram was from Stacey."

"But where has she been? Ben, oh, Ben, if she really, truly loved you, wouldn't she have reached you before this?"

He stared at her, understanding her logic, yet unable to reply to her. He knew where Stacey had been. She had been somewhere in the future, trying to pick up the threads of her life again. Evidently it either didn't work or . . . Whatever went wrong, she had come back again. Back to him. But how could he explain that to Caroline? She'd think he was crazy. No, she'd just have to believe whatever she wanted.

"I came over today to let you know why I wasn't here last night and to ask you to forget what's happened between us, for my sake, if not for Stacey's. I know you're hurt," he said, seeing her tense. "If you weren't, you wouldn't have tried to make me resent the hold I know Stacey has on me, but I can't help that."

He saw her look of surprise. "What's the matter?" he went on. "Does it shock you to hear me admit you're right. You see, she does have me wrapped around her little finger, if that's the way you want to put it. What better way to describe love? I'd fight my way to the ends of the earth if I knew she'd be waiting when I got there. What's wrong with love like that, Caroline?"

She stared back at him, realizing the hurt was stronger than she dreamed it would be. She had really begun to love this tall, handsome man. He was different from any other man she had known. Not just because of his good looks, but because she had never before met a man with the capacity to love that Ben possessed. Women weren't just objects to him. If they had been, he'd have turned to one long ago to fill the void his wife's death had left. Her death. What a laugh. He was so sure he'd find his wife at the end of his wild search. She wondered.

"All right, so you love her," Caroline said. "But that doesn't mean you can just pick up where you left off, Ben. Can't you see that? Things are never the same. What happens if you get out there and discover everything's different?"

"It won't be."

"How can you be sure?"

"Because I know Stacey and I know myself. Nothing could ever change the way we feel about each other. It's something only she and I understand. No matter what's happened to either of us, it can't change what we feel."

"I hope you're right, Ben," she said. "I certainly hope you're right, because if you're not, you've got a big hurt coming."

"I know I'm right. Stacey could never change, any more than I could. That's one thing I don't have to worry about." He gazed at her thoughtfully. "The only thing I have to worry about is you, Caroline," he said quietly. "I want you to promise not to interfere with my reunion with Stacey. I don't want her hurt, and

I think it'd hurt her if she had to see you all the time, knowing I'd made love to you.''

"I won't forget, Ben, I can't."

"Then don't. But for God's sake, Caroline, promise me you won't tell her."

"Promise? You drive a hard bargain, Ben." She watched the anger and anxiety mixed in his dark eyes. Was it really that important to him? She wondered. "All right, you want to bargain, I'll bargain with you, Ben," she said, her voice low and sultry. "I'll promise not to tell her, on one condition."

"And that is?"

She stepped closer to him and once more caressed his chest, her hand fingering the hollow at the base of his throat. Her eyes were warm, inviting. "Take me to bed, Ben," she whispered seductively. "Steven and Phoebe are gone, so is Steve Jr. No one will ever know but the two of us."

He stared at her hard, eyes glistening with anger.

"I promise, Ben. Once more, just one more time, darling, and I'll never breathe a word about it to your lovely little bride."

His eyes blazed and he threw her hand from his chest, as if getting rid of something distasteful. Now he knew what had always bothered him about Caroline. What he'd seen in her eyes so many times that had made him wary. She was a conniving little bitch.

He wanted to hit her, but the words that came out of his mouth had the same effect. In fact, it might have been kinder if he had slapped her.

"Go to hell!" he said furiously. Turning, he grabbed his hat and headed toward the front door.

"Ben, don't!" Caroline yelled as she followed him into the house. "Please, Ben, I'm sorry. Don't turn away!" she cried, but he kept on going.

He reached the foyer, threw open the front door, and stepped outside. Caroline was close at his heels, her face white. She hadn't expected such a violent reaction.

Her voice was quivering, unsteady. "Please, Ben. Please stop. I didn't mean it like it sounded . . . you don't understand. All I wanted was to feel your love again, if only for a few brief moments. Is that so terribly wrong?"

He mounted his horse, then looked down at her from the saddle. "Yes, when you know I have no love to give," he said angrily. "I don't make bargains like that, Caroline." He whirled his horse around, then glanced down at her one last time. "And you reminded me of Stacey," he said bitterly. "How could I have been so wrong." Digging his horse in the ribs, he headed down the drive, leaving Caroline standing next to the hitching post with tears in her eyes.

She watched him until he rode out of sight, then gradually the rigid lines around her mouth faded into a smug smile. Her eyes narrowed, flecks of silver shining in her pale blue orbs, and she walked slowly back into the house.

"Ben Clayton," she whispered to herself as she entered the foyer and leaned against the door calmly. "Tomorrow morning I think you're going to be in for a big surprise," and her mind made up, she pursed her lips stubbornly, heading toward the stairs.

Early the next morning Ben hurriedly reined in his horse and tied her up outside the office on Front Street. Behind him, Ethan drove Frieda, Charlotte, and Becky in the carriage. They had been to the bank already and straightened things out with the manager. Ben left Frieda in charge of household expenditures and drew up papers authorizing Steven to take care of the business during his absence, however long that might be. Now all he had to do before heading for the stage depot was show Ethan the routine at the office.

Ben was dressed in soft brown buckskin pants with a matching jacket and vest trimmed with fringe, an outfit he'd worn often on the trail to Oregon. He wore his pink cotton shirt open at the throat and his money belt securely, and discreetly, wrapped about his midriff. His jacket pockets held his razor, soap, socks, and handkerchiefs so that the carpet bag he'd brought wouldn't weigh over the twenty-five-pound limit allowed each stage passenger. Having ridden the stage before, between The Dalles and Portland, he didn't relish the idea of the long bumpy ride to Fort Laramie, but there was no question of trying to make it by himself on horseback. Besides the danger of traveling alone, he wasn't sure he knew the way and he didn't have time to find a guide. So he'd put up with the stage and hope all went well.

While the ladies waited in the buggy, Ben ushered Ethan into the office. Steven was at his desk and he smiled at Ethan, who was slicked out in a blue suit, white shirt, and new black hat. As Steven greeted them, Ben was aware that Caroline was nowhere in sight, but he wasn't about to inquire about her. If she wanted to make herself scarce until he was gone, that was up to her. He didn't care one way or another. In fact, he preferred it this way.

If he had seen her, he probably would have said something he'd regret.

He showed Ethan around, gave Steven the papers from the bank, and then bid Steven farewell, promising to return as soon as possible. When they reached the stage office, Ben had just enough time to buy his ticket, throw his carpet bag in the boot, and say good-bye.

Frieda, Becky, Charlotte, and Ethan lined up in the dusty road beside the boldly painted Concord stage that had scenic landscapes decorating its doors. Its familiar vermilion, yellow, and black colors were meant to convey the awe-inspiring strength and durability of the coaches. Two other passengers had already boarded the cumbersome coach as Ben started to say good-bye.

He hated leaving them, but it was the only way. He couldn't let Stacey travel alone all that way. He gave Frieda a big hug and assured her that she'd be able to handle things. After all, she had practically run the household single-handedly for Ann while he was in the army during the war.

"It's no different now, except that you have Ethan, instead of Ann, to share the responsibility," he said. "And the girls are old enough to help too."

"Be careful," she cautioned as he kissed her on the cheek.

He reminded her that he had strapped on his gunbelt.

"That doesn't mean you're going to be careful," she admonished quickly, wiping a tear away. "It only means you have a chance of being shot."

He assured her again that he'd be fine and turned to Becky. For a moment he was reminded of Ann the way she had looked the day he'd left for the army. Becky was like her mother in so many ways. Her brown eyes warmed as she hugged him and wished him luck.

"I can hardly wait to see Stacey again," she said as he released her. He winked at her and turned to Charlotte.

His elder daughter had been aloof and reserved all morning, but now that the moment of good-byes had arrived, the anger in her eyes wavered. It was hard to love someone as much as she loved her father and understand how he could purposely hurt her so terribly. She gazed at him and suddenly realized what an attractive man he really was. No wonder Stacey had latched onto him. Still, that didn't make it right. Now he was going to Stacey, even though it meant that they might never see him again. Abruptly, at the thought of never seeing him again, Charlotte let out a small cry and flung herself into his arms.

"Oh, Daddy!" she said tearfully, burying her head in his shoulder. "Why do you have to go?"

She hadn't called him "Daddy" for a long time. It was usually "Father," with an air of haughtiness. For a moment, the plea clung to him, tugging at his heart.

"I have to go, Charlotte," he said hurriedly, his voice break-ing. "Please, understand." He tightened his arms about her and kissed her cheek before he released her. He grabbed the hand Ethan offered, avoiding Charlotte's dark, pleading eyes.

"Take care of everything for me, Ethan," he said quickly. "And if you need any answers, check the lawbooks. I think we've been over a lot already that'll be of help. I've left a map marked with my route. Just in case anything happens, I'll check in at telegraph offices along the way. But things should be all right."

Ethan nodded and promised to keep things running smoothly. Ben glanced around at his family. His heart was torn. There was no question in his mind that he had to go, but it wasn't easy.

The stage driver had gathered up the reins and climbed up into his box. It was time. Ben took one last look, set his hat on his head, and turned to the coach.

The foursome stood aside and watched him open the door of the Concord stage and pull himself in. Charlotte wanted to shout, begging him to come back, but she knew it would be no use.

"I wonder," she said softly to Ethan, "just what kind of a woman makes a man like my father leave all he loves just to be with her."

Ethan drew his eyes from the coach and frowned at Charlotte. "What do you mean?"

"Just what I said," she whispered. "You know, Ethan, I don't think Father took the diary with him. In fact, I'm sure he didn't, and you know, I think it just might have the answer I'm looking for," and her eyes glistened eagerly.

As Ben settled into his seat, his thoughts were with the four people he loved standing at the edge of the dusty road. His eyes were clouded with tears and he looked back out the window. Then as the coach gave a lurch, jerked for-ward, and started to head toward the edge of town, he looked over into the face of the passenger sitting beside him and gasped.

"Caroline!"

"Hello, Ben," she said smugly, her pale blue eyes steadily watching him. She'd been seated in the coach all this time waiting. "Aren't you pleased?" she said softly, enjoying her little surprise. "I'm going back East after all, and we'll be riding together all the way to Fort Laramie." The smile on her face made his heart turn to lead.

CHAPTER 17

Dark clouds had been hanging low on the horizon all morning as the wagon train moved along the trail, stretched out like a snake inching its way across the countryside. Two days earlier, they had had a brief skirmish with a few Indians, but no one had been hurt. Since then, Ed's scouts had been exceptionally alert, aware that the same Indians could return with a larger force.

Fort Kearney was well over three weeks behind them now and they had left Cottonwood Springs, where the North Platte River branches off, six days before. Stacey and Ben had come through the area the year before only a few months after an Indian raid had all but annihilated everyone and everything in the area, but, as usual, everything had built up again and Stacey had been pleased to see Cottonwood Springs alive with people.

Wagon after wagon had slowly moved through the town, taking advantage of the chance to replenish supplies. When they had finally pulled out of the town, a lonely feeling had swept over Stacey as she watched the buildings fade into the distance. Now, almost a week later, she gazed up at the sky. The dark clouds that had plagued them all morning had begun to swirl about, and she felt the wind picking up.

The weather was still extremely dry and overly hot. Sweat poured down inside her clothes and the seat beneath her was damp. Everything she wore felt sticky and thick with dust. She washed the pants and shirt as often as possible, but soap was scarce and they didn't always camp next to a river. It had been three days now since they'd been cleaned.

By late afternoon, a storm was clearly brewing. Ed kept them on the move as long as he could, trying to find the best place to weather it. They finally made a circle in an open field. The land was flat there, but nearby, stony bluffs rose on the horizon. Between the trail and the river, there was almost two miles of cottonwoods and underbrush where kindling could be found. So many wagons had passed this way over the years that it was hard to find such a good supply of wood.

As the night darkened and sharp spurts of lightning licked the sky, Stacey looked around apprehensively. The air was still and felt like it had been robbed of its strength. The oxygen filling her lungs starved them a little with each breath. It wasn't only the heat. Something else was the matter. It was like being in an airless vacuum. Even the mules had been edgy when she had worked them out of their harnesses earlier and driven them to the livestock corral.

Now, wearing her blue calico dress instead of her dirty riding clothes, she stood near the wagon and watched the sky, aware that Paula was sitting on a box near the fire staring at her. It was well past bedtime, but neither was ready for sleep.

"What's the matter?" Paula asked, watching the expression on Stacey's face as the sky once more burst forth with a white light that made it seem like day.

"Nothing," answered Stacey. Her words were followed by a low rumbling that vibrated the earth beneath her feet.

"It's only heat lightning," Paula said. "Surely you've seen heat lightning before."

"Not like this," Stacey replied. "Not for a long time, anyway." She remembered when, back in Cleveland, the weather had carried on like this all night and the next morning they had learned that tornadoes had touched down in the area.

She rubbed her arms unconsciously, feeling a chill run through her. "Where's J.D.?" she asked Paula.

"He's talking politics with old Mr. Bascomb. Said he'd be back late."

Stacey glanced off in the direction of the Bascomb wagon. Harold Bascomb and J. D. Tanner had discovered that they had a lot in common. They shared both a love for checkers and the same political views. Old Mr. Bascomb was quite ignorant of J.D.'s former questionable dealings, and the men spent hours together. Stacey was glad, because it kept J.D. out of her hair. The man was impossible. He wanted everything done his way, even though he knew nothing about anything constructive. He was what Drew would have called a "perfect sidewalk superintendent."

She tensed as she continued to watch the sky. Strange she should think of Drew. It had been days since he had entered her thoughts. Now she wondered if he had realized where she was and what had happened. Too many times in the past few weeks she had lain in her bed and wondered if he and Leslie were together. Did he ever miss her or feel sorry about what had happened? It was hard to watch a love die as theirs had. They had been so close once. Yet he had put an end to it. Or had he?

Wasn't she partially to blame? There was no cut-and-dried answer, but the hurt was there just the same and only one man could soothe that hurt.

Ben! She closed her eyes as more lightning split the sky, trembling at the thought of seeing him again. Suddenly a voice spoke from behind her and she jumped.

"Are you cold?" asked Ed.

She whirled around and smiled. "No, I was thinking of Ben," she said softly. Glancing up again at the sky, she added, "And wondering what we might be in for too."

Ed's own eyes were worried. "I'm afraid we're in for a bad one. But who knows when it'll hit. I've seen the sky carry on like this for days before a storm."

The sky was exploding almost constantly now with bursts of light that were followed by rumblings or ear-splitting claps that made the air vibrate.

"Sleep under the wagon tonight, Stacey," he said softly. "I've warned everyone. If we get a good blow, you'll be safer on the ground. If it doesn't hit tonight, there's every chance it'll hit while we're on the trail tomorrow. If it does, leave the wagon seat and lay flat on the ground under the wagon. You'll get wet, but you'll be safer in the open. Better yet, if you can find an indentation in the ground, like a ditch, get into it. I've seen these things before. They tear down a brick building as if it was made of feathers."

"Are you trying to scare us, Mr. Larkin?" asked Paula, who had joined them.

He eyed her curiously. She was still trying to look like she was ready for afternoon tea, but the effect had become less convincing. Without proper laundry facilities, her silks and satins were showing wear. Wrinkles refused to come out beneath the heat of Stacey's flat iron, and there were spots that lye soap and river water just couldn't remove. Ed had to give Paula credit, though. She held her head high, even though her gorgeous gowns were ruined and her hair was lifeless and in need of washing.

"No, I'm not trying to scare anyone," he said matter-of-factly. "The storm could blow itself out. But we've had little rain since we've been on the trail, and it can't last forever. I'd rather warn everyone and have nothing happen, than not warn anyone and end up with a catastrophe on my hands."

Paula smiled. "How nice of you." She noticed that he had slicked himself up again tonight before coming over to talk to

Stacey. "But then, have you told everyone, or are your warnings just for Stacey?"

"A wagon master has a responsibility to everyone, Miss Tanner," he answered firmly. "The whole train has been alerted."

"Oh." Her smile became coquettish. "Forgive me, Mr. Larkin," she said sweetly. "It's just that you do come over so often. But then, so does Mr. Savagge. It's really hard to keep up with Stacey's gentlemen friends."

"That's all we are, Miss Tanner. Just friends," he said quickly, before turning to Stacey. "Want to go for a walk?" he asked wanting to get away from Paula.

"What about the rain?"

"I think it'll hold off."

"And the Indians?"

He touched the butt of his gun. "I'll keep my eyes and ears open." He studied her affectionately. "It'll do you good."

"Maybe you're right."

He helped her over the wagon tongue and they moved away from the camp. When they were about four hundred feet away, Stacey looked back at the circle of wagons silhouetted in the light of the campfires. "It's a little frightening, isn't it?" she said.

"What is?"

"We make such a good target when we're bedded down at night. I don't know which is worse, being strung out in the daytime like sitting ducks or being tucked away at night like that, just waiting."

"We may get through without seeing Indians again," he said, trying to reassure her.

"We didn't last year."

"Are you really that scared, Stacey?"

"I've been through it once, Ed. I'm petrified."

"Yet you came."

"I had to . . . it was the only way I could reach Ben."

"You could have gone to New York or someplace on the coast and sailed."

"Sailed?"

"Around the Horn. Ships are doing it every day. A lot of people would rather brave the sea than the Indians."

"It hadn't even crossed my mind," she said, amazed. "But that probably would have been expensive. I couldn't have afforded it." She shivered again as lightning continued to streak the sky and the low rumblings came closer.

"It's not too far off," Ed said anxiously. "I'd say an hour, maybe a little longer."

Up ahead, a breeze suddenly rustled the leaves on some scrub bushes. Stacey's step picked up as the breeze reached them seconds later.

"It's really going to blow, isn't it?" she said, lifting her head into the wind. "But it feels so good."

She spread her arms and let out a soft cry of pleasure. She was about to shut her eyes when two Indians suddenly emerged from behind the bushes with rifles aimed right at Stacey and Ed.

They froze in their tracks and held their breath as the Indians bore down on them.

"What do they want?" Stacey asked cautiously, her heart pounding.

Ed's voice was harsh, barely above a whisper. "Probably scouts. Just stand here, don't move."

Stacey couldn't have moved if she had wanted to. Her feet felt like lead weights.

The braves moved closer and Ed whispered, "Sioux!"

Both Indians stopped and stared at them, then one of them hefted his rifle and aimed it directly at Ed's chest as the other motioned for Ed and Stacey to move behind the bushes.

"Do as he says," said Ed hurriedly.

Stacey hesitated.

"Move, Stacey," he said again. "Go behind the bushes. I don't think he's in any mood to argue." Ed said something to the Indians in a language Stacey had never heard before, and the Indian answered back as he shoved Ed along.

When they were hidden from the camp, the Indians grabbed both captives by the shoulder and stopped them. They took Ed's guns and stuffed them into their breechclouts; then Ed began to speak to them again. His words were faltering, but the Indians seemed to understand him.

When the conversation was finally over, Ed swore. "Damn," he said angrily. "They're after the livestock."

Stacey was surprised. "Only two of them?"

"The rest are hiding, waiting for the rain to start. They'll move in under cover of the storm."

"They can't do that!"

"Don't bet on it," he said. "It's one of their favorite tricks. The animals spook easy and it's hard to see in the rain."

One of the Indians poked Stacey with his rifle, and they were both prodded into moving farther away from the camp.

"Where are they taking us?" Stacey asked as they stumbled along the dusty trail.

"They haven't recognized me as the wagon master yet," Ed

replied softly. "Their only interest in us right now is to keep us from warning the others."

"Why did they bother with us at all? Why didn't they just let us walk by?"

"When you threw your arms up and let out that cry, they thought they had been spotted."

"Oh, my God!" she blurted disgustedly. At that point, the Indian holding the rifle on Ed prodded them both into silence.

For a good two hours they stumbled along in the darkness, shoved on by the Indians' rifles at their backs. The rough trail made its way between two hills and then moved down a hillside that was so steep Stacey had to hold on to Ed to keep from falling. As they clung to the side of the hill, Stacey glanced back into the darkness and saw the lightning flash over the peak.

"Ash Hollow," whispered Ed close to her ear. Suddenly the wind picked up, and he felt a few drops of rain on his face. "And here comes the rain."

By the time they reached the bottom of the long hill, it was pouring, but the Indians didn't seem bothered by it. They continued to shove Stacey and Ed on for another half-mile, until they suddenly saw about ten or more Indians some distance ahead, waiting with horses.

"The rest of the raiding party," Ed whispered to Stacey, hoping she could hear him above the rain, wind, and rumbling thunder. As he spoke, a sheet of rain drove across the trail and almost knocked him off balance.

He grabbed Stacey to keep her from falling, and in that split second he realized that the Indians were in as much trouble as they were. The rain was like a wall of water, and he could feel the welting sting of hail on his back.

Quickly he pulled Stacey against him and ducked back, dragging her with him. Keeping the water at his back, he ran and stumbled toward the woods at the side of the trail. When they reached the cover of the trees, Ed released his hold on Stacey's waist and grabbed her hand, and they ran on, trying to ignore the shouts of the Sioux behind them.

Half-dragging Stacey by one arm, Ed forced his way over the uneven ground in the direction of the river. He was more than just familiar with Ash Hollow. Every wagon master who rode through this area knew Ash Hollow and Windlass Hill, with its steep inclines that could scare the lifeblood out of any driver trying to come down it. As they reached the river, the rain began to let up, and he glanced quickly at Stacey, who was wiping the water from her face and eyes.

"I was afraid I'd lose you back there," he said quickly.

She shook her head. "Not me. I don't want any part of them!"

Ed looked about quickly, then pulled her over behind a huge fallen log. Falling to the ground, she leaned against it, breathing hard.

"The rain's letting up," he whispered softly. With no rain to hinder them, the Sioux would begin to search for them.

Ed peered over the top of the log as a series of lightning flashes lit up the sky like a chain of lights popping off against the dark clouds that swirled overhead. He caught a quick glimpse of the Sioux heading toward them.

He leaned against Stacey, hoping to shield her from both the rain and the Sioux's searching eyes. As they lay quietly, Stacey heard the familiar grunts of the Sioux's unintelligible language and she knew they were nearby.

Suddenly the voices grew excited, and Ed eased away from her and raised his head to peer over the top of the log.

"What is it?" she gasped breathlessly, but he put his hand on her face in the darkness, warning her not to talk. She raised herself onto her knees and stuck her head beside Ed's, looking over the log in time to see the Indians suddenly stand stock-still, listening. They listened no more than a few seconds; then, without warning, they all shouted something and ran out of the woods, back to their horses. Lightning crashed across the sky and Ed and Stacey strained their eyes to see through the trees, watching as the Indians galloped away as if chased by the devil himself.

"Ed?" Stacey asked, puzzled.

Pulling her with him, he stood up and cocked his head toward the sky. "Listen!" he said quickly.

Stacey strained her ears and then she heard it too. It was a low rumbling that sounded like a train or stampede in the distance.

"Buffalo?" she asked, bewildered.

Ed shook his head. "The Indians call it the Devil Wind. It's a twister, and it's getting close."

Stacey's heart leaped into her mouth and she trembled as the noise swelled and the wind began to tug and suck at her clothes.

Ed didn't have a second to spare. Grabbing Stacey's hand, he pulled her away from the fallen log and closer to the river, his eyes searching the ground quickly as flashes of lightning lit the sky. It took only a few minutes to find what he wanted, and as he pulled Stacey toward an overhang on the riverbank, she glanced up at the sky, letting out a startled cry. A funnel cloud was swirling down from the dark clouds, weaving back and forth as if trying to catch whatever it could. Silhouetted by the lightning, it dipped up and down, swaying ominously.

Ed saw it too and knew they had run out of time. He grabbed Stacey and fell to the ground with her, rolling her under the overhang, pushing her back beneath the grass-covered earth, feeling roots and dirt against his bare head as he ducked under with her. He had lost his hat somewhere and hadn't even realized it until now.

He pulled his shirt collar up and shielded Stacey's eyes from the dirt as best he could, then lowered his head, burying his face against her hair with his lips close to her ear.

"Say a prayer, honey," he said softly. As the words left his lips, the air above them was filled with the noise of a hundred jets taking off. Stacey's head was filled with the awful sound. The earth above them vibrated and dirt filtered onto them, as Stacey clutched Ed's shirtfront desperately, her arms pressed against his chest. The noise was deafening, and she held her breath, praying for it to stop.

Suddenly it was over. Quickly, almost as if it had never been. The noise became a faint whisper and all they could hear was the rain hitting the earth above their heads, dripping down in streams from the grass at the edge of the overhang.

"It's so quiet," Stacey whispered after a few uneasy minutes. Ed inhaled. "Are you all right?"

"A little dirty, but that's all."

She waited for him to move, but he didn't and she trembled.

"Cold?" he asked.

"No."

Her answer was soft and unsteady. He heard her hesitancy and realized at the same time what was causing it. Her clothes were soaked, yet he could feel the heat of her body through her dress. It was as if the clothes separating them didn't exist. She was molded to him and her softness warmed him until his own flesh began to tingle.

His lips were barely touching her ear, and the sensation was unnerving. He flushed as he felt himself harden against her. It was pitch black beneath the overhang. Neither of them could see, but they were both very aware of the contact between them.

It had been so long since Stacey had been in a man's arms and her body was responding to Ed in a way that surprised her. He was attractive, true, but she had never been attracted to him. She had never seen the same kind of animal magnetism in Ed that she had sensed in Wade or John. Yet, lying here with his breath hot on her ear and his body almost overpowering her, she felt as if she were with Ben again. She couldn't see, but she could feel, and it was disastrous.

The more she tried to shake it from her mind, the stronger her awareness of Ed became, and suddenly she felt a throbbing begin near her pelvis. It radiated lower and spread through her loins like a flood of warm water.

Her face was still half-hidden beneath his shirt, and she caught his faint masculine smell mingling with the damp smell of the earth surrounding them. This was crazy, insane—her body was on fire. She held her breath, trying to fight it, then very softly, his lips whispered low against her ear, "How long has it been, Stacey?"

She let out a low half-sob. "Too long."

"Well, it's either stay here like this until the rain lets up or try to find our way back to camp in that downpour, which I can't guarantee. What'll it be?" he asked hesitantly.

She lay quietly for a few minutes, trying to decide. She didn't like the feelings that were reawakening in her, and yet . . . even though the tornado had passed them already, she could hear that there was still heavy rain and exceptionally strong winds outside their shelter.

"Maybe if we talk about something . . ." she whispered.

"We could try." His lips were against her ear. "You first."

Trying to ignore their close proximity, Stacey took a deep breath and told Ed all about life in 1975. About airplanes and rockets and movies and televison and anything else that came into her head. For a while it seemed as if it was going to work, but as time wore on, their bodies just didn't want to forget.

The sensual feel of Stacey's body was intoxicating. Ed could feel her thighs pressing against his, the length of her body unconsciously teasing him. Maybe, he thought, if he moved a little he could get into a position that wasn't quite so disturbing. Trying to raise his body, he moved his hand in the cramped quarters and it accidentally brushed over her breast. He felt the nipple hard beneath the thin material, and a tingling shock shot through him.

"Stacey, I'm sorry," he said huskily.

He moved again, hoping to rectify what he'd done, but it only made matters worse. His hand landed right on top of the soft mound of flesh.

"My God!" he gasped. He closed his eyes as his hand instinctively began to caress her.

Stacey wanted to protest, but the attack on her senses was too

strong. All she could do was lie in his arms and moan. She
wanted to scream, but nothing came out. Suddenly his lips
pressed close against her ear.

"Stacey! Stacey! I can't help it, honey," Ed murmured helplessly, and with a deep groan he began kissing her neck. Chills
shot through her and she felt his huge body tremble.

His mouth found hers in the darkness and he kissed her
deeply, sensuously. His lips were soft and inviting, and tears
sprang to Stacey's eyes. Not because she didn't want it, but
because she did and yet she knew it was wrong.

As his kiss devoured her, Stacey found herself thinking, not of
Ed, but of Ben, and she was suddenly kissing him back.

He finally drew his mouth away and she gasped, half-sobbing.
"Oh, Ed," she whispered. "We can't, I mustn't. I can't do this
to Ben or to myself!"

"I know," he answered, his voice breaking. "But how do I
stop now? How do I tell my body it has no right to feel like
this?"

"I don't know," she said breathlessly. "But I just can't. As
much as I need it, I can't . . ."

He kissed her again, but harder this time, as if he wanted to
crawl inside her. His tongue touched her lips, not violating them,
but caressing them affectionately, then he reluctantly pulled his
mouth from hers and buried his face in her hair, his lips close to
her ear again.

"Don't move," he murmured agonizingly. "The way I feel
right now, I might explode, and it could be embarrassing."

"Oh, Ed!"

"Shhh, just lay still!"

She held her breath and suddenly realized what he meant.
While they had been kissing, the hard bulge in his pants had
found its way to her throbbing groin, and although clothes
separated them, the effect was devastating. She felt the pulsating
throb of him as he lay against her, fighting a battle with himself.

It was still raining and the wind was still blowing, but not quite
as hard. He knew he couldn't go on like this without giving in.
Yet he also knew he couldn't force her, and she'd never surrender willingly to anyone except Ben.

He kissed her one last time, reveling in the wonder her lips
brought him, and then backed off her as quickly as he could. He
rolled out into the rain and lay flat on his back, letting the cold
rain still his ardor.

"Ed!" she cried as the cold air penetrated her damp clothes,
making her shiver.

He rolled back onto his stomach and stuck his head under the overhang. Reaching in, he grabbed her hand. "I had to, honey," he said desperately. "I just couldn't take it anymore."

"I'm sorry."

"It's all right. It isn't your fault. It's my own damn fault for being in love with another man's wife," he said. "Of course, the same thing might have happened with any other beautiful woman stretched out beneath me, I don't know. But I know I'm not any saint, Stacey. I just couldn't stay like that anymore without doing something about it."

"Thanks, Ed," she whispered. "I love you for that."

"Like a friend?"

"I wish it could be more, but it can't." She looked beyond his head and saw the rain pelting down on the rest of his body. "You're getting soaked."

"I know," he said pleasantly. "And you know, it feels good. At least I can think rationally now."

"You'll catch pneumonia."

He laughed, his voice deep and husky. "That's better than catching hell from your husband."

This time she laughed, but the laugh was lost to him as he stuck his head outside again and realized that the rain had let up. It was slowing down to a misty drizzle and he saw the first faint streaks of dawn starting to break through the trees.

"My God, we've been gone all night," he said, dismayed. Stacey moved to the edge of the overhang and looked out. "Do you mind getting a little wet again?" he asked.

She scooted out from under the overhang, and he pulled her to her feet. They stood in the drizzling rain staring at each other, and Ed's smile broadened.

"I sure envy Ben, Stacey," he said. "You're one hell of a woman!"

Her face was streaked with dirt and her wet hair was plastered against her head, but to Ed she looked lovelier than he had ever seen her.

"Do you think you can make it back to camp?" he asked after a few minutes.

She nodded.

Ed glanced up at the sky, which was growing a lighter mixture of gray and blue by the minute. He knew that in a short time the rain would stop completely, the sun would come out and the earth would begin to warm up again.

As the light slowly filtered into the heavens, he glanced over to what was left of the woods. It made his skin crawl. Stacey followed his gaze, and she felt the gooseflesh rise on her arms. Some trees were standing, but others were torn up by the roots. Branches hung broken on some trees, yet others had been snapped off as if they were twigs rather than huge limbs. Some trees were split in half, and others looked as if they hadn't even been touched. It was an awesome sight. The log they had been hiding behind earlier had been shattered into a mass of pulp.

Ed didn't say a word, but took her hand and moved downriver a few feet from the overhang, then climbed up onto the littered grass that covered the floor of the woods. He stopped suddenly, and Stacey watched as he plucked a daisy from its stem.

"Amazing, isn't it," he said, "that a wind strong enough to lift a tree from the ground should leave a daisy intact, every petal in place."

Stacey looked up into his face, suddenly remembering. "The wagon train!"

"I know. I thought about it earlier but didn't want to worry you. There was nothing we could do."

"What do you think we'll find?"

"I don't know. It could have missed them completely. Then again . . . It's a long trek back."

"Do you think the Sioux will be back?"

"I doubt it, but just in case, I intend to watch the trail closer than I did last night." He sighed. "Are you ready?"

She nodded, and they began picking their way back toward the trail that led up out of Ash Hollow, over Windlass Hill and toward the field over two miles away where the camp had been last night. The closer they came to the campsite, the more apprehensive Ed got. Stacey knew he was worried. All signs of their passionate ordeal were gone from his eyes, which were now filled only with worry. The minute they left the hills, Ed knew the train had been hit.

Pieces of furniture were scattered haphazardly about, as were clothes, bits of canvas, pieces of the wagons, and what was left of the food supplies. It looked as if someone had ground everything together between two giant hands, flung it all toward the sky, and let the whole mess land at random.

Ed swore as they passed each remnant, and both he and Stacey were running by the time they reached the main body of what was left. Bass spotted them and broke into a sprint. "Where the hell have you been, Ed?" he asked anxiously when he had reached them.

"Stacey and I were jumped last night by some Sioux," Ed

explained hurriedly. "We've been holed up in Ash Hollow, trying to keep out of the twister."

"We didn't lose too many wagons," Bass exclaimed. "We've got twenty-seven left out of thirty-nine. There's ten dead, anywhere from thirty to fifty injured. I haven't been able to take count yet, and they've been hollerin' their heads off askin' where the hell you are. I didn't know what to tell them. All I knew was that last night you said you were headin' toward the Tanner wagon to see Stacey."

"Who's dead?" Ed asked calmly.

Bass gave him a list of names, which included old Mr. Bascomb and J.D. Tanner.

"J.D.?" exclaimed Stacey.

"They didn't pay any attention to the warnings. He and Bascomb climbed into the Bascombs' wagon to weather it out. Didn't find them until daylight. The wagon came down over in the woods beyond where the cattle were. Both of them were dead."

They turned and walked hurriedly toward what was left of the camp.

"How about the cattle?" asked Ed, squinting in the sunlight.

"Surprisingly, the twister whipped over their heads. Scared the hell out of them, and they tried to break, but we had them tied down too tight. Lost only a couple cows and three oxen. But with the wagons we lost, there won't be any problem."

They were closer now, and Ed's stomach churned as he saw what was left of the train. As with the trees, some wagons looked as if nothing had touched them and others weren't even there. All that was left of the circle was a haphazard group of wagons, two and three in a row, and large gaps in between. Litter was scattered from one end of the area to the other, and people were milling about as if in a daze.

It took two days to clean up what was left, bury the dead, and get things ready to roll again. During the first day, Stacey and Ed were together constantly, helping tend to those who were hurt. But the repercussions of their walk that night were still obvious. Stacey knew gossip was bandied about that they had been gone on purpose, that Stacey had lured Ed away from camp so they could be alone. Stacey was certain the rumors originated with Paula, but that didn't matter. Everyone had seen them come back together the next morning.

"I'm going to send a letter to the land office back in Omaha the first chance I get," Paula screamed at Stacey a few minutes after her father's body had been laid to rest beside the other nine victims of the storm. Her eyes were red and puffy from crying. "It was Ed Larkin's responsibility to take care of the train," she cried. "Not spend the night in the woods making love to you."

Stacey's jaw clenched furiously. "I've told you a hundred times since Ed and I got back this morning, Paula. Ed and I were captured by Sioux Indians. They were planning to run off with the horses before they were scared off by the tornado." She gazed at her disgustedly. "But then, I guess you'll believe whatever you want. I don't know why I'm even trying to explain it to you."

Stacey walked away from the graves and was surprised when Wade joined her. It was late afternoon and she hadn't seen him all day.

"Will you come take a look at Ginger, Stacey?" he asked as he studied her disheveled appearance. She hadn't bothered to change her dress or clean up. There was too much to do.

"What's the trouble?" she asked.

"It's her leg. Word's around that you seem to know what you're doing. I think it might be broken."

They headed toward Wade's wagons. He had been lucky. Both his wagons had been untouched. Ginger had only been hurt because she had been helping quiet some children in another wagon. She had gone inside one of the wagons to pull out one of the youngsters when the twister had hit. Both she and the unfortunate child had been hurled some fifty feet before hitting the bed of another wagon that had turned over. The little girl had been killed and Ginger was knocked unconscious. Now that she had come to, she was complaining that both her leg and her head hurt.

Wade said little on the way to his wagon, but his eyes told Stacey that he had heard the gossip.

Stacey cringed every time she crossed the campsite, watching everyone trying to put things back together again. In a way, she felt guilty, because while they had been going through all sorts of hell, she had been lying in Ed's arms, snug and safe. Her only battle had been with her conscience and the passions Ed's nearness had aroused. Maybe that's why it was so hard to face these people without flushing. She was embarrassed and more than a little remorseful.

Ginger was on the ground with a pillow beneath her head and a blanket over her. Everyone was gathered around, trying to make her more comfortable, while Rundy bathed a bruise on her forehead with warm water, hoping to loosen some splinters that had embedded themselves there when she'd hit the wagon.

"Maybe the next time you're in a twister you'll do like you're told and stay on the ground," Rundy was saying as he shook his head. "The fool kid you went after's dead anyway, so what good did it do you to get all banged up?"

"Shut up, Rundy," Ginger said, pouting. "What if I had saved her? Then you'd all be calling me a heroine. Just because she died, I was dumb for going after her. Well, at least I tried." She finished her tirade and glanced up at Stacey. "Hi, Stacey," she said, trying to smile through the pain. "I see Wade kept his promise for a change. Rumor is you've been helping all day with all the hurts. I've got a bad one."

Stacey knelt down, pulled back the covers, and inched up Ginger's skirt to bare her leg. One look told her what was wrong. Just to be certain, she ran her hands along both sides. There was no mistake. It felt like a clean break.

She turned to Wade. "You or the girls wouldn't happen to have any laudanum around, would you?"

"I don't think so, but what's it for?"

"Well, there doesn't happen to be a doctor on this train, and her leg has to be set. If you don't have anything to put her to sleep with, how about filling her with a bottle of your brandy." She looked down at Ginger. "Think you can get drunk enough not to feel it?"

Ginger smiled wanly, her big brown eyes meeting Stacey's question bravely. "I can get as drunk as a skunk if that's what you want."

Stacey nodded. "Good." She turned to Wade. "Have you ever helped set a broken leg?"

"Nope."

"Then send Rundy for Ed. And tell Ed to bring something for splints. We can tear up a sheet for bandages." She turned to Lil. "Do you have a clean sheet, Lil?"

Lil's blue eyes studied Stacey thoroughly; then, without saying a word, she climbed into the wagon and came back with a sheet.

"Where'd you learn how to set a leg?" Lil asked. Suddenly Stacey felt everyone's eyes on her.

"Does it matter?" she answered.

Lil shrugged. "I suppose not, but I bet it'd be interesting to find out."

Stacey watched a half-smile cross Lil's lips, revealing her gold eyetooth. The animosity in the woman's eyes was frightening. Stacey tried to ignore it.

It had been a long time since she had helped set a broken leg, and she had never done it alone. But there was no one capable, except perhaps Ed. Most of the injuries in the camp were super-ficial cuts, bruises, and bumps. Ginger was the only one with broken bones, except for a man Stacey suspected of having a couple of cracked ribs. Since there was no X ray, she had treated it as such and bound his rib cage to get the pressure off.

Wade watched, fascinated, as Ed and Stacey worked. Ed pulled the leg and Stacey eased it into place, bandaged it, and put on the splints. Ginger half-sang and half-cried through the ordeal, calling Ed "honey" a few times between curses and mumbling something about being nicer to him the next time. Stacey glanced at him surreptitiously while they worked and noted a flush on his face that surely wasn't caused by what he was doing.

Afterward, Ed and Stacey headed across camp to see what more had to be done. Ed glanced at Stacey, his face crimson. "I saw you listening to what Ginger was saying," he said reluctant-ly. "It doesn't mean a thing, Stacey. I admit I've had some dealings with her, but I want you to know it wasn't anything like what happened last night. What happened between us last night was special, even though it was wrong and won't ever happen again." He looked directly at her, his eyes intense. "I wish to hell you were married to someone besides Ben, so I wouldn't feel so damn guilty. But I want you to know that no matter what, my feelings for you won't ever change. And if you ever need me, if things ever go sour between you and Ben, I'm here."

She watched the longing in his eyes and felt terrible. She hadn't meant for Ed to love her. She had known he cared a little, but she had thought it was more friendship than passion. Well, it wasn't. Thank God he was like John, and loved her enough to understand. But, unlike John, he had probably been in and out of love a dozen times over the years. He'd bounce back. Ed, for all his gruffness, was like a big warm pussycat. She guessed it wasn't hard for him to love once he found the right person. She was certain he'd fall in and out of love again another half-dozen times before his life was over and yet still die a bachelor. She liked Ed, but he just wasn't marriage material.

She gazed up at him now, and smiled briefly. "Thank you, Ed," she said, blushing. "You know what I mean . . . I couldn't live with myself if things hadn't turned out the way they did."

"It wasn't anything, honey," he said, his voice warm. "Be-sides, I don't think we had enough room in those cramped quarters for what we had in mind. Now, did we?" Stacey saw the amused twinkle in his eyes and knew it would be all right.

She didn't see Wade again that first day. But the next evening, after spending the day helping people sort out their belongings, Wade came over to help her gather firewood.

"How is Ginger doing?" she asked as they piled sticks in the middle of the old bedspread.

"Complaining," he answered. "She hates having to stay put and says it'll kill her to stay in the wagon on the trail. I promised to prop her up near the back so she can at least see where she's been." He stopped and stared at her, his gray eyes troubled. "Stacey, are you aware of all the talk about you and Ed that's been going around?"

She held a piece of wood tightly and stared back at him. "How could I not hear it, especially since so much of it comes from Paula?"

"I haven't said anything to anyone else," he said quietly as he watched her. "But I saw you and Ed leaving the campsite the other night. I was on my way over myself, but Ed beat me to it."

"Then you saw us walk ahead on the trail. Didn't you see the Indians jump out from behind the bushes?"

"I didn't watch that long," he said. "I was peeved because you were willing to go walking alone with him. The only place you'll trust me alone is gathering wood where everyone from camp can see us."

"So?"

"So it means you still don't trust me."

Her eyes flickered warily. "Tell me, Wade, if you had to spend the night alone with me crammed into a space so small there was barely room to breathe, would you take advantage of the fact that it had been a long time since I'd felt what it was like to be in a man's arms? Would you make love to me?"

His eyes blazed. "Did he?"

"I'm asking you, Wade. Don't worry about what Ed did or didn't do. I'm asking you."

He studied her. She had cleaned up and washed her hair last evening, and the setting sun crowned her auburn curls with golden flames. Her figure was made for stroking and caressing. His eyes glistened. "I'd probably do the same thing Ed did," he said, his eyes devouring her. "He made love to you, didn't he?"

"No. And that's the difference between you and Ed, Wade."

"Are you trying to tell me he didn't even kiss you?"

She stared at him, unable to answer.

"He did kiss you!"

She started to shake her head, denying it.

"Don't lie, it's written all over your face," he said, sneering. "And you said he didn't make love to you!"

"He didn't!"

"I see. He did everything but, is that it, Stacey? He probably tore your feelings apart, didn't he?"

Her face turned crimson. "What Ed did or didn't do is my business, Wade. I didn't say he didn't want to make love to me. I said he didn't. It takes a strong man to turn away from something he wants."

"And a clever man to get as much as he can."

"Don't be absurd."

"Absurd? Who's being absurd? I'm only being logical. He gets to kiss and touch you all he wants, then, just because he stops at the vital moment, he's suddenly a saint."

"I didn't say that!"

"You didn't have to." Wade pulled the stick from her hand, threw it aside, then grabbed her, pulling her into his arms. He pulled her close, pinning down her arms, his slate-gray eyes stormy with passion as they challenged her.

"Let go of me, Wade," she said through clenched teeth.

"No!"

"Please!"

He didn't answer. Instead, his eyes bored into hers and he kept her body pressed firmly to his. For a long time they defied each other, their eyes locked, then slowly Stacey felt a piercing warmth begin to surge through her. His eyes were mesmerizing, their sensuous pull awakening the familiar and unwanted stirrings in her loins. She tried to squirm away, but the erratic movement of her body made her even more conscious of him.

Panicking, she closed her eyes in self-defense, but that too was a mistake. With her eyes closed the sensation of being held so close against him was even more distracting. She could feel the tingling sensations at the tips of her breasts, where they were pressed against his chest, and the hard muscle of his thighs melding smoothly against her. She could also feel the familiar hardness that told her he too was aroused. She wanted to open her eyes, but she was afraid to look back into his intense stare.

Suddenly, without warning, she felt his breath on her neck, followed quickly by his warm lips on her flesh. She clenched her teeth tightly, tensing.

"What's the matter, Red?" he whispered silkily against her ear. "I know you like it, so why pretend you don't?"

She managed to find her voice, but her words were strained.

"Wade, please . . . for God's sake, don't," she begged, misery and anger mixing together as she fought him.

"Don't worry, I won't force you," he said huskily. "But I'm going to show you that I can be a saint too—if that's what you want!"

His mouth suddenly came down on hers in a long, drawn-out kiss that was warm and passionate. His mouth sipped at hers hungrily, leaving her breathless. How could she ignore something that was conquering her so methodically? His lips left hers and ran over her eyes, her cheek, and the corners of her mouth, before returning again to nibble and sip seductively at her trembling lips.

"Damn you, Wade!" she muttered, half-sobbing against his mouth. He drew back his head and gazed into her face, which was flushed with a desire she didn't want to feel.

He saw the tears in the corners of her eyes. He was sure they were tears of surrender, and he stared at her hard. He didn't want her to surrender. Not yet, not within sight of the camp. There was time yet for what he planned to do. But he had proved to them both that in spite of her protestations of undying love for her husband he could get what he wanted from her.

Stacey felt the tears sting her cheeks. She was frightened, not only of Wade but also of her fickle body. It was so willing to betray her, first with Ed and now with Wade. She cried with tears of anger. Anger at Wade for doing this to her, and anger at herself for almost losing the fight, but he'd get nothing else from her. No surrender, she vowed, never.

Her eyes locked with his, but this time she saw only amusement in his face. He almost looked sorry for what he'd done. But he wasn't. The wicked smile that replaced his momentary expression of concern attested to how he really felt.

"I can have you anytime I want, Red, and don't you forget it," he bragged unmercifully. "I imagine Ed got just as much as I did. I just didn't want to feel cheated."

He released her, and for a second she thought her legs were going to give out.

"Are you all right?" he asked, frowning.

"Keep your hands off me!" she snapped as he moved to help her stand. She took a step back, her blue eyes suddenly flooded with tears. "You had no right to do that."

"I have just as much right as Ed Larkin."

"I hate you, Wade Savagge," she said furiously.

"No you don't, not really." He laughed. "You may hate the way I make you feel, because of your guilt. But if you really hated me, Red, your lips could never have given me what I just took.''

She wanted to slap that self-satisfied grin off his face, but she knew he was right. She didn't hate him, but she didn't love him either, no more than she had loved John or Ed. Yet, they had all managed to tear into her emotions. Oh, God, wasn't she ever going to reach the safety of Ben's arms? She watched Wade nonchalantly pick up a stick and set it on the bundle, and her anger at herself, him, and the whole rotten mess exploded inside her.

''Go ahead. You want to gather wood, just go ahead,'' she cried viciously. He stopped, surprised at the bitter onslaught of her words. ''Gather it all by yourself and take it back to Paula. Maybe she'll even reward you if you treat her right. She should be able to cool your ardor. But I'm not going to help you. Either I gather wood alone, or you gather it, but after what you just did, Wade, not only will I not be caught alone with you, I don't even want to see you.''

He sneered. ''So that's it, huh? It's all right for Ed, but not for me. Well, I'll tell you, dear lady, I made up my mind a long time ago that someday I was going to take what you denied me that night in the Paradise. That's a right I've earned the hard way. But I'm not going to take it by force. I'll never take it by force, Red. You'll see, someday you're going to be all too eager to give me what I want, and it sure as hell isn't friendship.''

She felt her stomach tighten, wary of the look in his eyes and the determined edge to his voice.

''But for now,'' he said, trying to sound easy and relaxed, ''I don't intend to do this by myself, so quit acting like I raped you and let's get the wood collected before someone gets to thinking the Sioux came back and captured us too.''

Anger was still smoldering deep inside her and she didn't know what to do.

''Well, come on,'' he said, acting as if nothing had happened. ''Get a move on. If we don't hurry, it'll be dark before we get back to camp.''

Stacey stared at him incredulously as he moved about picking up sticks again. Then, reluctantly, she joined him. But her mind wasn't on what she was doing. Her thoughts were in a turmoil as his warning sank in. Should she tell Ed, or should she just keep a closer watch on Wade and make sure it couldn't happen again?

By the time they returned to the wagon, she was so upset that she excused herself quickly, claiming that she had to check on a child who had been injured. In reality, she searched out a quiet place where no one could see her and cried softly until there were no tears left.

She left Wade with Paula. They watched Stacey head across the camp and then Paula turned to Wade.

"I saw you," she said flippantly.

He smiled. "Did you, now."

"Tell me, Mr. Savagge," she said, studying his handsome profile. "Are you in love with her?"

"Maybe."

"At least you want her, is that it?"

"You might say that."

"How nice," Paula said. Wade turned to her, eyes puzzled. "Don't look so surprised," she went on. "As you probably know, Stacey's husband is my former brother-in-law, but he's also very dear to me. Now, I know Ben, and if he ever discovered his precious Stacey had been unfaithful, he'd have nothing more to do with her. That's where you come in. If you can guarantee me that before this trip is over you'll bed Stacey Clayton—not rape her, mind you, she has to go willingly—I'll make it worth your while."

"How worth my while?"

This time Paula smiled, her green eyes glowing with anticipation. "I heard you're headed for Virginia City, Nevada. My father had friends out there in high places, men I know myself, who owed him a few favors. It's not unusual for a man to start out in a gaming house and end up on the top of the heap. It happens all the time. A few words in the right places, a little money changing hands. Why, who knows where it might lead. After all, politics and gambling aren't that different, you know. It's all a matter of luck, and occasionally a little larceny. What do you think?"

He studied her closely, remembering the whispered rumors about J.D. Tanner's dubious connections.

"No time limit?" he asked.

"Anytime you please, but before you leave the train."

He thought for a few minutes, weighing the prospects. As far as making love to Stacey went, he intended to accomplish that regardless. He wanted her for himself. To hell with her husband. But an offer like Paula's made the prospect even sweeter. It might be just what he needed to make life more interesting.

"All right," he said. "You're on. One unfaithful wife for a few words in the right places. Shall we seal the bargain, Miss Tanner?" he asked, holding out his hand.

After shaking hands, Wade returned to his own wagon. Paula

watched him, pleased with her bargain. But neither of them was aware that another member of the wagon train was also trying to think of a way to get rid of Stacey Clayton.

Pearl had been perched on the seat of Wade's wagon for the past hour. Watching him return now, tears rimmed her eyes as she remembered the sight of Wade and Stacey near the edge of the woods locked in each other's arms. She too was trying to think of the best way to get Stacey out of her hair. She had hated Stacey ever since the day she'd discovered her wearing the turquoise dress, and she knew there'd be no satisfaction for her until Stacey was out of her life, one way or another. She'd think of a way; she had to, because Wade was hers, and he was going to stay hers. She'd think of a way. . . .

CHAPTER 18

They had left Salt Lake City for Fort Bridger early that morning. The stage had carried a full load of nine passengers from Boise to Salt Lake City, but now there were only four besides Ben and Caroline. It was already the middle of July, and the stage was, as usual, running way behind schedule.

They had lost time just outside of Portland, when a storm had turned the Barlow Road into a quagmire and swollen to overflowing every stream and river they crossed. By the time they reached Boise, they were already days behind schedule. It was a feat that would be frowned on by the owners of the stage line, who bragged about the efficiency of stage travel.

Ben had avoided contact with Caroline as much as possible, but under the circumstances it wasn't easy. Especially when she refused to be ignored.

She was taking the trip well, although there were times he was sure she regretted her decision to come. For instance, she had been less than happy between Boise and Salt Lake City, when the stage was full of men from the goldfields heading for the gaming tables in Nevada. Much to his chagrin, Ben had been forced to pretend she was with him to keep the men from getting nasty with her. He hadn't wanted to say anything, but he just wasn't the type who could sit back and see a woman in trouble without helping.

But, at the first relay station out of Boise, he had let Caroline know firmly but truthfully that she wasn't to construe his gentlemanly behavior as anything but a gesture of courtesy for a fellow passenger.

"I would have done it for anyone," he said as they waited for the fresh team to be harnessed. "I don't want you thinking there was anything more to it."

She smiled, her pale blue eyes steady on his face. "I understand perfectly, Ben," she said sweetly. "I'm just glad you've finally got over your mad."

"I'm not over what you call, my 'mad,'" he explained

271

quickly. "I just thought those men were getting out of hand. I still think what you've done was uncalled-for."

"There's an old saying, Ben—all's fair in love and war. My bargain's an open offer, you know. You can seal it anytime you want."

His eyes darkened as he stared at her. The small black hat she was wearing with its ribbons and lace had lost some of its stiffness and her black silk traveling suit had a powdery fine dust clinging along the folds. He wondered if she was planning to wear it for the whole trip, just as he wondered what was running through that conniving head of hers. She said she was going back East, but how far?

"You heard my answer the last time you offered," he said sternly, and once more he became quiet and reserved.

She studied his handsome face, feeling the stirring that always made her feel warm and weak. "There you go again," she said, watching him close himself off. "Why do you do that? So you're traveling with a woman you know would give anything to make love with you, but we don't have to be enemies, do we, Ben? Good heavens, we've got hundreds of miles to go yet. Besides, if you stay angry with me, those miners are going to know and your pretense at being my escort will fall flat on its face. Since we're forced to be together, why don't you just relax? Surely you wouldn't feel guilty just talking. It's rather silly to think anything could happen here on a stage full of people."

His eyes narrowed. "I don't trust you, Caroline."

"I don't blame you, I wouldn't trust me either, Ben. Not alone, anyway. But we're not alone, so don't you think you're being a little foolish?" She held out her gloved hand. "Truce?"

He didn't want to accept a truce, but he realized he was being a little foolish. After all, it was a long way to Fort Laramie. Maybe by the time they got there he could get her to change her mind and retract her offer. He shook her hand reluctantly. "All right, truce," he said slowly. "But don't think for one minute you've won anything, Caroline. Because I still think you're being nasty about the whole thing, and I won't change my mind."

She didn't answer. She only smiled and changed the subject, talking about the trip so far and the delays they'd had.

For the rest of the trip to Salt Lake City things went better. Caroline lapsed into her easygoing friendliness with him, talking about her years in Oregon and a number of other things unrelated to her immediate feelings. Ben relaxed more, suddenly glad for her company.

They had another delay in Salt Lake City, where they had to wait two days for a seat. Ben made sure he and Caroline were not put up at the same hotel and he avoided her deliberately during their stay. Caroline was put out by his behavior, but she bounced back easily once they were on their way again. She had had her suit cleaned and she looked fresh once more on the morning they had left. Now Ben glanced over at her and watched her eyes scan the scenery.

She was sitting opposite him, and occasionally he'd feel her eyes on him. Knowing she was staring, he'd become self-conscious.

There was one other woman, named Sara, on the stage, traveling with her husband. As the miles were left behind, she began to talk to Caroline. She and her husband were on their way back to St. Louis, where Sara's family lived, so she could stay with her mother until her baby was born.

"You know how mothers are," the young woman said, embarrassed. "I guess she still thinks of me as her little girl."

"And Sara's already twenty," said her young husband. "She's plenty old enough to take care of herself. But her mother insists."

Ben glanced over at the young couple holding hands, then shifted his feet into a better position, tilted his hat down over his eyes, and leaned his head back against the cushioned seat of the stage to relax while he listened to their conversation.

The two men beside him weren't related. One was a salesman on his way to Fort Laramie with a new line of drugs and medical instruments. The other man was an army sergeant on his way back to Fort Bridger after a month's leave. Neither man was exceptionally talkative. The salesman was thin and wiry, and wore glasses and a light brown suit. He parted his hair in the middle and covered it with a black derby. The sergeant was a rather pleasant-looking stocky man, with blond hair and sharp blue eyes that were on Caroline more often than not.

Ben listened, dozing off at times when the road wasn't too rough. Occasionally he shifted his position to glance out the window and then settled back again.

After leaving the Wasatch Mountain Range, whose breathtaking curves had elicited much conversation, they changed horses and reached Echo Canyon before nightfall. A good driver tried to make fifty miles a day, and some averaged sixty on a good run. This time their driver was making good time.

They made a quick stop again at a relay station to change

horses and eat the last meal of the day, which was a meat-filled stew served with homemade bread, raisin pie, and generous amounts of coffee. Ben didn't mind paying the two dollars for the meal this time, because for once it was worth it. Up until now, the meals had cost the same amount, but had hardly been edible.

For the first time on the trip, he was in a rather good mood when he settled into the coach once more and listened to the driver rouse the newly harnessed team. The pace would be fast until dark, when it would slow because it was harder to see the road.

They were a little over forty miles from Fort Bridger, moving along at a comfortable speed, when Ben was jolted out of his restless sleep by gunshots and the sudden jerk as the stage lurched forward.

"My God! What's happening?" yelled Caroline.

Sara, sitting next to her, began screaming hysterically, and Sergeant Meade, sitting at the other window, peeked out to see if he could catch sight of anything.

It was that weird time of morning when the sun hadn't begun to come up yet and the stars were fading in the sky. Pale gray was merging with the horizon, and dark shadows still clung to the land. The sergeant squinted to see in the awakening dawn. Suddenly he shouted, "Indians!"

"Oh, no!" Sara grabbed her husband and hung on to him as they were thrown about inside the coach that was now careening down the road at breakneck speed.

Ben straightened in his seat and leaned out the window, trying to catch sight of the Indians.

Three Arapaho were coming in from the side of the road. Two had rifles and the other was using a bow. They were bearing down on the stage with determination, and their war cries filled the air.

Ben slipped one of the Colts from his gunbelt and lifted it to the window as a hard thud hit the side of the coach and he saw feathers from an arrow close to the window. Without waiting for another, he leveled his gun at the Indian and began firing. But the coach was bouncing so erratically there was no way he could even take aim. His shots scattered the Indians a little, but they still came on.

On the other side of the stage, the sergeant was also firing out the window. He was hanging on to the side of the stage to steady himself, but he wasn't very successful either.

Overhead, the driver was shouting to the team, giving them their heads. He had lost his shotgun guard when the first round of shots hit, but there was no time for him to grab his own carbine as he whipped the big sorrels, trying to outdistance the attacking Indians. His mouth was working feverishly, clenching stubbornly one minute and yelling to the team the next. His hat was pulled down tight so it wouldn't fly off, but beneath the brim, his startled eyes suddenly caught sight of the rutted road up ahead.

Close to fifteen, maybe more, Arapaho were blocking it. He had to make a split-second decison. Knowing he couldn't plow through them to reach the relay station some five miles ahead, he veered the horses to the right and headed off the main road across the bumpy sand and sage.

The ground was dry and the horses kicked up dirt and stones as the driver maneuvered the big Concord stage between the shrubs and trees. All of the Indians were in pursuit now. The land was uneven and rocky, and he prayed the horses wouldn't hit a prairie-dog hole or anything else to slow them down.

He forced the stage on, whipping the horses at full gallop for some five or six miles, hoping to either outdistance or tire out the Indians, but it wasn't working. Suddenly reining to the left, he careened around a boulder and straightened out again, wishing he could head back toward the road. There was no way. Yet he couldn't keep on like this. Up ahead, the ground sloped, heading toward some cliffs. He was swerving the horses quickly to the left when he suddenly felt a hot, searing pain in his chest. The last thing he saw were his hands clenching the reins in panic, and then he pitched forward. He rolled off the seat, bounced off the front boot, and fell between the horses. Then he was lost behind the stage, a crumpled, broken heap on the ground.

The stage was running free now, with no driver, but inside, the passengers remained unaware that they were running blindly, while Ben and the sergeant still fired at the attacking Indians.

The women were huddled on the floor with the other two men, who were trying as best they could to shield the ladies. Ben glanced down for a second into Caroline's wide, frightened eyes, and then suddenly he felt a sickening thud on his chest. He stared out the window in surprise and saw smoke curl up from the end of the rifle in the hand of an Indian who was trying to get close enough to board the coach.

Ben tried to ignore the pain that was spreading into his right shoulder. He raised the gun again, but it was no use. The pain seared deep, radiating into his arm and neck. He gave a sharp groan as he felt another bullet hit his thigh with the force of a mule's kick. He looked down quickly. Blood was gushing from his left leg a few inches above the knee, and he stared at it in disbelief.

Caroline was off the floor in seconds. Still crouching, she reached out as Ben's body began to sag. She caught him against her and moved back onto the seat, cradling his long muscular body in her arms. He had passed out.

Above them, the Arapaho who had shot Ben shoved his carbine into a scabbard on his horse, leaned over as far as he could with his horse in full gallop, grasped the bar at the driver's seat, and pulled himself onto the coach. His well-trained horse kept pace alongside while the Indian, coal-black hair flying, face painted with red streaks, and dressed in only a breechclout, made his way to the front boot below the driver's seat. He poised himself, then dropped down onto the doubletree and held on to the tongue while he stooped to unfasten the harness attached to the whiffletrees. When the last toggle was released, the horses broke away and the Arapaho jumped clear, hitting the ground hard and rolling with the fall. He leaped quickly to his feet and was back on his horse again.

The sorrels veered to the left and the Arapaho followed, pulling them over, but the coach had built up momentum and it careened on alone, the tongue breaking on rocks before hitting the edge of a hill and starting down it, gathering speed as it rolled.

Inside, Caroline realized what had happened as the sergeant started yelling for everyone to brace themselves. She felt the downward pull of the runaway coach and held her breath, holding Ben close against her body to cushion him from whatever lay ahead.

The stage pitched one way and then another, lurching recklessly down the steep hill. It crashed through a clump of bushes and skidded sideways before taking to the air momentarily, where it twisted and turned and then came down with a crash. As it rolled end over end, the screams from inside mingled with the sickening crunch of wood and steel. Then suddenly it hit bottom and thudded to a stop, landing on its side, and everything went still.

At the top of the hill, the Arapaho watched only a few minutes longer before deciding what to do. They had the horses they were after. Why bother with scalps now?

They drove the horses to where more Indians were waiting with other horses they had stolen when they had burned down the relay station, and then all of them headed off toward the northeast, away from the road that led to Fort Bridger.

The only noise in the deep ravine was the sound of a coach wheel still turning slowly. When it too stopped, there was only silence. After a few minutes, a low moan came from inside the coach. It was barely audible above the gentle sighing of the wind and the songs of the morning birds. A small orange-breasted bluebird landed on the side of the fancy-painted coach and hopped around briefly before perching on one of the wheels, then it sang its greeting to the morning sun before spreading its colorful wings again and flying off.

Inside the stagecoach, Caroline stirred, hearing the lilting song of the little bird. For a brief moment she had no idea where she was, but then remembered and opened her eyes, looking into Ben's still face only inches from hers. His features were slack. Was he dead? God, no! He couldn't be.

She tried to move, and groaned, every muscle of her bruised and battered body sore. She felt like she had been beaten with a bullwhip. Taking a deep breath, she turned slightly as she heard a noise near her right side.

Sergeant Meade was staring at her, his eyes glazed with pain. "The other three are dead," he said, glancing at the broken bodies crushed against the other side of the coach. The body of the young expectant mother was jammed against the other seat, and her neck was obviously broken. It was hard to say what injuries had killed her husband and the salesman, but neither was breathing and blood was trickling from their mouths. "How about him?" he asked, motioning with his head toward Ben.

"I . . . I don't know yet," she gasped helplessly. "I . . ."

Her handbag was still hanging about her wrist and she took it off and set it on the floor beside her. Then she reached out easily and touched Ben's chest, trying not to get blood all over her hand from his wound. "It feels like he's breathing." She touched the pulse in the side of his neck. "He's still alive."

"Good." The sergeant gritted his teeth, then tried to move. He couldn't, and he glanced down at his useless leg, which was hanging at a strange angle just below the knee. "I was afraid of that. It's broken."

She frowned. "What are we going to do?"

"Well, since you're the only one who can move about, I suggest you climb out and see what's going on."

"Out there?"

"It'd be nice to know whether we're going to be scalped or not," he explained.

"You mean they might still be around?"

"I doubt it, or we'd have heard them by now. But it's best to be sure."

She was reluctant to leave Ben's side, but she knew they had to find out. Gingerly she scooted back away from Ben and rested his unconscious body against the side of the overturned stage-coach. Her knees were shaking as she stood up and grabbed the sides of the window above her, then pulled her body up and peeked her head out. There was no one in sight. Not a soul, and it was quiet except for the sounds of a world awakening to a sunshiny morning.

She pulled her head back into the coach. "I don't see anyone out there," she said. "Not even at the top of the hill."

The sergeant nodded as she lowered herself beside Ben and checked again to make sure he was still breathing.

"How bad's he bleeding?" asked the sergeant.

Caroline let her eyes move to where blood was seeping from a hole in Ben's jacket. She lifted the edge of the jacket and checked beneath it. "It's slow," she answered. "But he's got a hole in his thigh too." Her hand moved to his left leg, where blood was oozing from a hole in his buckskin pants.

The sergeant reached into his gunbelt and took out a knife from a sheath near where his gun hung. He held it out to Caroline. "Here," he said. "Tear the pants open and see how bad it is."

She clenched a hand against her breast in dismay. "Me?"

"You."

"But I've never . . ." She swallowed hard. "I can't!"

"You will if you want him to live," he said quickly. "And do the same with his shirt, so you can see what's underneath there." He shoved the knife forward again. "Here, now get with it."

She bit her lips and took the knife from his hand. Reaching down, she reluctantly tucked the knife into the edge of the hole and made long cuts, opening the leather to expose the wound. It was a neat wound, the flesh around it red with blood, but she could see bits of leather caught in the surrounding flesh. She grimaced.

The sergeant tried as hard as he could and managed to pull himself close enough to see. His face was contorted with pain as he gazed down at Ben's thigh. "It's got to be cleaned out," he said, his light blue eyes concerned. "Or it'll get infected. Is it all the way through."

She hadn't thought of that. She reached around slowly, fingered the material, and shook her head.

"Then the bullet has to come out too. . . ." He glanced at Ben's face. It looked like the face of a corpse, white and slack. "How he ever lived through that fall with a couple bullets in him, I'll never know," he said, then looked up once more into Caroline's hesitant blue eyes. "Check the other one," he ordered.

She lifted the edge of Ben's jacket and slit the shirt. Blood was still seeping, and pink cotton threads were mixed in with the flesh.

"Can you lift him?" the sergeant asked.

"I don't know."

"Try. We've got to see if that bullet went through. I doubt it, but we have to know."

Caroline rolled Ben partway over and checked his back where the bullet would have come through. For the first time, she realized he was wearing a money belt. But then, it stood to reason he'd need enough money to tide him over. She passed over it lightly as she examined him.

"It's still in him," she said.

"Damn!" The sergeant exhaled disgustedly as he glanced down at his leg. "Two of them to get out. Well, the first thing we gotta do is get out of here."

"How?"

He looked around carefully. She'd be able to make it out the overhead door, but there was no way she was going to get him or the guy with the bullets in him out that way. He rubbed the slight stubble of beard covering his chin as he tried to think of something. His leg hurt like hell and there was no question as to what had to be done. The only question was, should he try to get out first, or would he get out easier once it was finished? The latter seemed the better answer. He turned once more to Caroline. "I think you said your name's Caroline?" he asked.

"That's right."

"All right, Caroline," he said. "Since you're the only one who can move, I want you to push the door open, climb out, and get inside the back boot. That salesman said he had a sample case back there. Bring it. And I also want a couple spokes from one of the wheels, if you can get them." He frowned. "Do you have any baggage?"

"A small bag."

"Any petticoats?"

"Petticoats?"

"For bandages."

She nodded. "They're in the back."

"Good. Bring them."

She eyed him skeptically, glancing quickly at his broken leg. "I certainly hope you don't expect me to set your leg. I'd die!"

"You won't die, but you will help," he said quickly. "We don't have time to argue. Every minute the bullets are in your friend lessens his chances of surviving. Now, do what you're told, and hurry."

Tears welled up in her eyes. Fighting them back, she pushed the door overhead open, crawled out, and slid across the body of the coach. The coach was highly varnished and it was easy for her to slide down. She hit the ground, almost losing her balance, and then looked around.

It was already getting hot. The early-morning sun was arching slowly into the sky, bringing hot air up from the valley floor. Caroline lost little time. After a quick look around, she headed for the back boot. One end of the boot was hanging half-open and the remaining straps gave easily. She dragged things out one at a time until she found the sample case and her own carpet bag. She took out her petticoats and headed back toward the door of the stage. She set the things on the ground, then remembered the wheel spokes. One of the wheels sticking up in the air was broken and she grabbed two spokes from the ground where they had fallen. This done, she went to the stage door, grabbed hold of the bars on top of the stage roof, and pulled herself up so she could look in the door.

"I'll have to drop the stuff in," she called down to the sergeant. "I can't carry it and climb in too."

"You can't drop it in either," he yelled back. "You're liable to hit one of us."

"Nonsense." She went back, grabbed the spokes, and dropped them in on the far side, away from Ben and the sergeant. They clattered down, followed a minute later by the sample case, which she lowered down by tying it to one of her petticoats. She tossed the rest of the petticoats in after the case and climbed in herself.

Hurriedly she knelt to check on Ben. His eyes were open now, glazed and bewildered.

"He's delirious," she muttered, touching his forehead.

"Stacey?" Ben gazed up, his vision cloudy. All he could see was red hair and blue eyes. "Stacey?"

Caroline didn't answer. She squeezed his hand, then watched as he passed out again.

"Leave him and come over here," said the sergeant. "I need your help."

She moved over to the sergeant. "What do you want me to do?"

"First cut away my pants leg."

Using his knife, she cut the uniform material, slitting it from the bottom to high above the knee.

"Do you think you can pull the leg hard enough for me to ease it into place?" he asked.

She stared at him wide-eyed. "You mean you intend to do it yourself?"

"I did it fifteen years ago with the other leg when I was out scouting alone and my horse spooked and threw me. Only that time I had to tie it to a sapling and pull."

"I don't know if I can do it," she said hesitantly. "What if I do it wrong?"

"Look, just hang on tight," he said, gritting his teeth. "I'll do the rest."

She stared at him, eyes narrowing. "What if you pass out?"

"I won't."

She took a deep breath. "All right, let's get at it." She moved onto her knees before him, shoving her black silk skirt aside.

"You're going to have to tear strips from your petticoat first," he said. "They have to be ready to tie the leg in place once we set it."

She leaned back on her heels and began ripping one of the petticoats with a knife.

Half an hour later, she tied the last knot on the bandage that held the spoke splints in place.

The ordeal had taken its toll on the sergeant, and although he hadn't passed out, his face was ashen and he was licking blood from his lip where he had bitten it.

"You did a good job," he said unsteadily. He studied her, realizing she was still wearing her tiny black hat with ribbons and lace on it. It was loose and falling askew, but still attached, and looked rather incongruous flopping atop her head.

"Now for your friend," said the sergeant. He scooted across the floor, which was really the wall, since the coach was lying on its side. Ignoring the dead passengers, he grabbed the sample case, and after searching through its contents, pulled out a pair of long probing forceps. He checked through the rest of the things in the case and picked out a bottle wrapped in velvet. He smiled, amused. Evidently he had found part of the salesman's private stock of whiskey. "This should do," he said firmly.

He had Caroline turn Ben to a more accessible position. It was hard, because Ben was a deadweight, but she managed. He removed Ben's money belt for the time being, and with Caroline's help, cut the shirt off Ben's chest wound. He cleaned the outer edges of the wound with the whiskey, poured more on the forceps, and began probing.

Ben stirred a few times, mumbling incoherently, but he mercifully passed out again as the forceps moved deeper into the sinew and muscle.

Sergeant Meade was sweating profusely. His own leg was killing him, but he knew if he didn't get the bullets out right away they could lose the man before nightfall. His mouth twisted as he worked with the forceps, while Caroline alternated between wiping the sweat from his forehead and sopping up the blood with a whiskey-dampened piece of her petticoat.

When the sergeant finally managed to pull the bullet out, he closed his eyes and sighed heavily before moving to the leg. Cleaning the forceps with whiskey again, he started his probe. It took less time for the leg. When both bullets were safely in his hand, he instructed Caroline to pour more whiskey in both wounds and bandage them.

The sergeant himself leaned back and rolled a cigarette with shaky hands. "Been a long time since I've done anything like that," he said, rolling the cigarette back and forth between his fingers. "It sort of takes the starch out of a man."

Caroline eyed him curiously as he stuck the cigarette in his mouth and began hunting for a match. "I'm glad you were along," she said thoughtfully. "I couldn't have done what you did."

His eyes watched her closely. "It had to be done. What is he to you, anyway?"

She flushed. "A friend."

He lit the cigarette and took a long drag, his eyes on her face. "But you'd like him to be more?"

"Maybe."

"Your eyes say yes. You traveling together?"

"Not exactly." She pulled Ben's jacket and shirt down off his shoulder and tightly wrapped strips of cloth over the thick pad she had laid on the wound. His skin was cool beneath her fingers, and after tightening the last knot, she let her hand trail across the soft curly hairs on his chest. "He's on his way to Fort Laramie to find his wife."

"And you?"

"I'm on my way back East. My husband died a few months back and I couldn't see any reason for staying on in Portland."

"You're from Oregon?"

"My brother-in-law and Ben are partners in a lumber company there. Ben bought into the business after my husband's demise." She moved to Ben's leg, poured whiskey on the wound, and began bandaging while the sergeant smoked and watched her. "He thought his wife was dead," she went on. 'That she'd been killed by Indians on his way out here last year. But he got word she's still alive and he was hoping to catch up with the wagon train she's on at Fort Laramie."

"And you're hoping she won't be there."

"I guess you might say that." She tied off the bandage. "I think he's on a wild-goose chase. And even if she is alive, it's been almost a year. People can change in that time."

"And if things turn out all right for him?"

"Then I guess maybe I'll just keep going East," she answered. "But right now that's the least of my worries." She stared down at Ben, whose breathing was shallow. "Right now my only concern is keeping him alive. I'm grateful to you."

Sergeant Meade smiled. "You can be glad that salesman was along too, or we'd have had one hell of a time probing for those bullets with a knife."

She had momentarily forgotten about the three dead passengers in the corner. Now she glanced over at them, and her stomach churned at the sight. "What do we do with them?" she asked.

The sergeant had seen death before a hundred times, but the sight of the young woman who had seemed so happy at the prospect of becoming a mother made him wince.

"I was thinking," he said slowly. "At first I thought we ought to stay here in the coach and take them out, but on second thought . . . if we had landed upside down or right-side-up, it'd be all right. But we're on our side. It stands to reason we aren't going to get out of this ravine for a few days. If it rains, with the door and window directly overhead, we can't call this much of a shelter. I suggest we get ourselves out, then we'll worry about them. Maybe after we get some kind of shelter set up, we can decide."

"Now, let me get this straight," she said apprehensively. 'You expect me to lift you two out that door?"

He chuckled a bit. "We're in luck again," he said amiably. 'In fact, I never saw anybody have so much damn luck. My month's leave was spent prospecting in Nevada, and there's a small miner's pick and shovel and a tent in the back boot. If you can heft the pick and swing it, I think you can split the top of the stagecoach open and we can get out of here that way."

She stared at him in dismay, then looked at the roof of the coach with its sturdy planks. "You think I can chop through that?"

"I think you can do almost anything you decide to do. Especially if you think it'll help your friend here."

Caroline saw Ben's eyes flutter and she brushed a stray strand of hair from his forehead.

Ben's mind was in a whirl. He felt like he was floating up out of a dark black pit and the world was spinning around him. He tried to open his eyes, but they fell shut again. His forehead crinkled as he tried once more, and this time, with effort, his eyes stayed open. He stared into Caroline's worried face.

He tried to talk, but when he took a deep breath, it hurt so badly he coughed instead.

"Don't talk," she said quickly. "Just lie still."

He licked his lips and slowly raised his good arm to wipe his hand across his mouth. It felt dry, like cotton, and he felt the start of stubble at the ends of his mustache. This time he found his voice. "What happened?" he asked weakly. "I mean, besides the Indians."

Sergeant Meade answered. "They broke the horses loose and we ended up at the bottom of a ravine. The others are dead. There's just you, me, and her. Luck's with us, though. They could have decided to come down and scalp us. And we're lucky that dead salesman sold medical instruments, and we're lucky this little gal didn't get hurt, and we're lucky I got a pick and tent in with my things, and dammit, fella, you're about the luckiest fella I ever saw, because if I hadn't been on this stage, those bullets would probably still be in you."

"Then I guess I owe you my life, Sergeant. Thanks," he said hesitantly. "As for luck . . ." He thought of Stacey waiting for him. It wasn't luck that brought her back, it was something more. "I don't believe in luck, Sergeant. I think it's more than that."

"Maybe you're right, maybe not," the sergeant answered. "But whatever, it just seems too good to be true."

"We're not out of this mess yet," Caroline reminded him. "I'm stuck with two men who can't walk and three dead people. I wouldn't say we're so lucky."

"It all depends on how you look at it," Sergeant Meade said. "You'd be in a hell of a worse mess if we were both dead and you were the one with the broken leg, now, wouldn't you?"

"Touché," she said irritably. "But you don't have to worry

All you have to do is lie there and give orders while I do the work.''

''Then why don't you get to it,'' he said. ''It's gonna get stinkin' hot in here as the day goes on, and I wouldn't appreciate getting cooked to death.''

Caroline bristled as she stared at him, then glanced over at Ben. ''Are you comfortable enough?''

''I'll manage.''

She inhaled. ''All right, then, I'll get started.'' She gave the sergeant a disgruntled look and crawled back out the door.

There were dozens of things in the back boot, but she found the sergeant's belongings easily. The handles of the pick and shovel were sticking out the end of the bundle. They were wrapped up with his other things in an army tent. His pack wasn't the usual soldier's fare while on duty, but some of the items could be found in an army haversack, such as the eating utensils, the coffee beans, the matches inside a cartridge case to keep them dry, a small sewing kit, some cartridges, a razor, and some hardtack. There was also an extra pack of tobacco, a small saucepan, and dirty clothes.

She carried the pick over to where the top of the stagecoach lay exposed and set to work. The pick was heavy, but she managed to whack away at the roof, and before long the wood began to splinter.

An hour later, she finally had a hole near the ground big enough to get them through. She stooped over and looked inside. ''What now?''

''Now get us out of here,'' said the sergeant. He told her to cut the leather covering off the back boot and lay it over the wood, then she helped him scoot through the hole, dragging his helpless leg. Once he was out, he stayed near the opening and helped her as best he could with Ben. The fact that Ben was conscious helped, but it was still hard for her to maneuver his long muscular frame through the hole. When he was finally out, Sergeant Meade made him stay on the edge of the leather.

He had Caroline use the leather as one would a blanket, to slide him across the ground, and she headed toward a nearby tree. When she had settled Ben beneath it, she went back after the sergeant. After depositing him beside Ben, she sat down on the ground herself, completely exhausted from the ordeal.

Her clothes were dusty and dirty, there was a rip in her skirt, and she had finally lost the floppy little hat. She glanced toward the smashed stagecoach and saw her hat lying crumpled in the dirt. It didn't even resemble a hat anymore. She glanced over at

Ben, and knowing he was in pain, she wished there was something more she could do. Then she remembered the matches and saucepan.

Without a word to either of the men, who looked beyond caring, she stood up and glanced around. Water! Everyone in the stagecoach carried canteens. She was heading back toward the stagecoach when the sergeant lazily opened his eyes.

"Where are you going?" he asked.

"Since I'm the only one who can move around, I guess it's up to me to see we all get fed and watered," she answered abruptly. "So if you don't mind, I'm going to confiscate anything we can use from what's left of the coach." Turning, she continued on her way back to the wrecked stage.

Her handbag was still on the floor, and she rummaged through it and found her canteen, then tucked the handbag on her arm. She felt like a pack rat as she went through the rest of the things. Besides the sergeant's meager rations, she found enough water left in the canteens to fill the saucepan. She also remembered Sara's husband saying he had bought an extra loaf of bread at the last stop to help his wife with her bouts of nausea. There was over half a loaf left. It was wrapped in a piece of cloth that looked none too appetizing from the outside, but it was clean inside. It wasn't much, but along with the sergeant's hardtack and the coffee beans, it would be better than nothing.

She deposited everything near the tree where the men were sitting, then quickly gathered bits and scraps of wood to get a small fire going. While the coffee was brewing, she took a short walk to see if there was any way out of the ravine besides the steep incline they had fallen over. There wasn't. At least not in sight. But she did find a small stream with clear water that might come in handy. It flowed down the ravine from somewhere between the hills and in the distance, it looked like the land where the stream originated leveled off.

Ben lay against the rough tree with his eyes half-open, watching Caroline. He frowned when she wandered farther away from the stagecoach than he thought safe. She didn't stay long, however. When she returned, she delved into the back boot again and brought the rest of the sergeant's belongings back with her.

"How do you put up this tent?" she asked.

The sergeant squinted at her in the hot morning sun. He told her how to pitch the tent, then watched her progress, correcting her here and there when she got things tangled. By the time the coffee beans had brewed to color the water, Caroline had managed to get the tent up. It wasn't too sturdy; but it was some cover if they needed it. After inspecting her handiwork, she brought the saucepan of coffee to the two wounded men.

"Sorry there's no cream or sugar, gentlemen," she quipped amiably as she set it down between them. "But it's the best I can do on such short notice. Oh, yes, and I hope you're not averse to drinking out of the same saucepan. Unfortunately, I don't know what the sergeant's done with his cup."

"I lost my tin cup down a rock slide," Sergeant Meade said, smiling for the first time as he looked over at Ben. "Coffee's coffee. Let her give you some first. You look a little pale around the gills."

Ben's dark eyes thanked the sergeant as Caroline held the saucepan up and spooned a little into Ben's mouth. He felt so damned helpless. For a brief moment he almost felt guilty about his harsh treatment of Caroline earlier on the trip. But something in her eyes brought back the memory of her bargain and the guilt vanished, replaced by anger at having to depend on her for everything. She finished giving him coffee and handed the saucepan to the sergeant, using part of a petticoat to hold the hot pan.

Sergeant Meade sipped at the dark liquid as he watched Caroline break bits of bread and put them in Ben's mouth. She seemed to be enjoying his helplessness. He studied her, watching the satisfied look in her eyes each time she did something for Ben.

"You'd better eat some too," Ben said. Caroline broke off a chunk and handed it to the sergeant.

Finally she took some for herself with a sip of coffee. When the bread was finally gone, she sat back on her heels, facing them. "Now what do we do?" she asked.

Sergeant Meade took over again. He kept Caroline busy the rest of the morning. First he had her use his pick and knife to cut two stout poles from some nearby saplings. The pick chewed up the end of the poles a bit, but they would have to do. The poles had a Y fork at the top, and after padding the Y with more of her petticoat leftovers and part of one of her heavy linen skirts, the sergeant had makeshift crutches to hobble around on. They weren't elaborate, but they did hold him up.

His next thoughts were for the dead passengers. At first he thought it best to get them out of the stagecoach and bury them, but on second thought he was certain Caroline could never dig a hole deep enough in the hard sun-baked ground. So instead, he had Caroline crawl into the coach and cover the bodies with the leather from the boot. Then he made her haul in enough rocks to cover the whole mess, so that animals couldn't get at the corpses. It wasn't much of a burial, but it was the best they could do.

While Caroline carried the rocks, Ben slept, but the sergeant had other things in mind. He made sure his army Colt was loaded, moved a short distance away from their camp, and sat quietly on a rock, scanning the terrain.

At first Caroline was furious because she had to do everything. But every time she glanced at Ben or heard him call out, the work didn't seem so bad. At least she was alive, and except for the bumps and bruises, she wasn't hurt. Most important, she had Ben to herself. But they were in serious trouble, and she knew it. It might be days before anyone found them, and Ben's wounds could easily become infected. Whiskey wasn't all that good as a disinfectant. She was a little more optimistic, however, when Sergeant Meade returned with two rabbits. At least they'd have food for a while.

Ben was awake again when the sergeant handed the rabbits to Caroline, who was poking up the fire. Ben tried to smile. "You're a pretty good shot," he said, watching the sergeant limp toward him on crutches. "Seems to me I only heard two shots fired."

"Comes from having to fend for myself too many times," he answered. Leaning his crutches against the tree, he sat down beside Ben. "I've been thinking," he said as he watched Caroline looking over the rabbits with disgust. He had cleaned them for her, but evidently she wasn't used to cooking and he wondered if she even knew how to cut them up. He went on, watching her out of the corner of his eye. "I don't think we should stay here. At least not any longer than we have to. While I was sitting on that rock, I spotted some caves a good distance to the north, near where the land levels off. In the first place, those dead bodies, even though they're heaped with stones, are going to attract scavengers. We're also too exposed to the wind and weather here. Let's face it, it's going to be a while before either of us can move any distance. I thought maybe we could hole up in the cave until we're both able to walk or until somebody happens to find us. What do you think?"

Ben too was watching Caroline, who was still staring perplexed at the skinned rabbits. "You've got the crutches, but how do I get there?" he asked.

The sergeant motioned with his head toward the tent. "We'll make a travois out of the tent, and Caroline can pull you. I'm sure if the Indian women can do it, she can."

Ben frowned at the thought of Caroline struggling over the uneven ground with him stretched out on a travois behind her. "Is that the only way?"

"Can you think of any other?"

"Are you sure it's necessary to move? What if someone comes looking for us?"

"And what if they don't?" The sergeant pulled out his pouch of tobacco and began to roll a cigarette. "They won't be expecting us at Fort Bridger until sometime tonight, and they'll probably think it's just a delay. Usually they don't start worrying for a day or two. Stages are always late, contrary to popular belief, and nobody's going to report anything from the relay station. They're probably all dead. I saw smoke off in that direction while we were running from the Arapaho. No, if anyone does come, it probably won't be for two or three days at the most. By that time, we could be dead of exposure. Especially you." He eyed Ben knowingly. "The lady says you're on your way to meet your wife. If you intend to see her, we're going to have to get you someplace where it won't matter what the weather does. At least until you can travel on your own."

Ben wasn't about to argue. For one thing, he didn't have the strength, and for another, Sergeant Meade was doing a hell of a good job playing boss. Caroline wasn't the easiest female to order around, but Meade seemed to be getting away with it. Maybe it was his gruff manner. He clearly didn't appreciate anyone bucking him, and Caroline carried out his orders with only a minimal resistance.

After washing the rabbits in the stream and stewing them in the saucepan a few pieces at a time, Caroline wrapped them in a clean petticoat and filled some of the canteens with water. She then helped the sergeant fasten the canvas tent onto the poles she had cut for the travois.

By the time the travois was ready, it was too late to start toward the caves, so they each had a piece of rabbit, some coffee, and settled down for the night. Caroline had spread out the clothes from the various carpet bags to make beds. She eased Ben onto one and then gathered more wood for a large fire to keep any animals away during the night.

Finally she sat down beside Ben and gazed at his head resting on a rolled-up suit jacket. "Are you all right?" she asked.

He smiled. "I'm fine."

She looked over at the sergeant, who was sitting up watching the fire. "And you? Comfortable enough?"

His blue eyes studied her. She looked exhausted. "Why don't you lie down yourself? You've had a rough day. I'm going to sit up for a while."

Caroline sighed. A rough day? My God! It was hell. Her back

was sore, her muscles tired, her feet hurting. She had even broken the heels off her shoes to be able to walk easier on the rough ground. A rough day! That was a laugh. She closed her eyes and started to stretch, but didn't have the strength and yawned instead.

"You'll be all right?" she asked the sergeant.

"I'm fine. Now, get some sleep."

She gazed down at Ben, wishing she could crawl beside him and cuddle close. But she was uncertain of what would happen if she tried, and she wasn't about to be embarrassed in front of the sergeant. There would be time enough for that later. She covered Ben with a blanket she had found in the baggage, bunched a skirt up for a pillow, and lay down close, but not too close, to Ben, where she could keep an eye on him through the night. In no time, she was sound asleep.

Morning came with a red glow out of the east. It filtered into the ravine like a flood of pink gold, and with it came the birds again, peering at the three sleepers curiously before flying off to greet the day.

Caroline groaned as her sore muscles moved, and gasped with pain when she tried to sit up. My God, it hurt! She was stiff all over, and it took a good ten minutes of moving, stretching, and bending to get the kinks out.

The sergeant was also awake and waiting for his morning coffee. It was the first thing she did, after hiding behind the stagecoach to relieve herself.

As she headed back toward the fire, she wondered what she'd do if Ben had to relieve himself. She decided she'd let the sergeant handle it, since he seemed to like being boss.

Ben woke while she was counting out coffee beans. She imagined that the sergeant had helped Ben with any private matters while she was off getting water from the stream for the coffee, because when she got back the two were talking quite amiably and Ben's face was flushed.

She had no idea at that time that anything was wrong. After a breakfast of rabbit meat and weak coffee, they confiscated everything else they could from the stagecoach. The most important thing they found was candles. There was one good candle in the side lamp and some others under the driver's seat. It would be enough for light when they reached the cave. They hung Ben's money belt over his good shoulder, maneuvered him onto the travois, covered him with the extra clothes and blankets they were taking, and began their long trek upstream toward the caves. Caroline pulled the travois, her handbag swinging incongruously from her arm as she trudged along.

It was rough going. Although the sergeant was tough and muscular, the crutches were crude and wore sore patches under his arms unless they rested every so often. It was during one of these rests that Caroline noticed the flush on Ben's face had deepened and that he was no longer breathing easily. She pulled off the hat shading his face to get a better look. His eyes were feverish and cloudy.

"Something's wrong," she exclaimed hurriedly.

"It's the wounds," said Sergeant Meade. "That rotgut whiskey must not have been strong enough." He looked on ahead. The cave was about a quarter-mile off, but there were dark clouds billowing on the horizon. He noted the change in the smell of the air. "It's gonna rain."

"Oh, no." She looked up at him. "What do we do?"

"We put the hat back over his face and get the hell out of here," he said. "If we don't make that cave before the rain hits, we're all in trouble."

He picked up his crutches while she hoisted up the travois, and they moved on once more through the rock-strewn valley toward the rolling green hill that held the caves. The last few yards were uphill, and Caroline was breathing heavily when she finally stepped into the shelter of the cave.

Its mouth was wide and it was deep. It was more like a deep overhang than a regular cave, but it was out of the weather, which was already beginning to blow up now, the clouds emitting low rumbles off in the distance.

In no time at all, Caroline had Ben settled and had picked a spot for a fire where the smoke would escape instead of filling the cave. She quickly gathered firewood, trying to beat the rain, while the sergeant rested his leg.

He was wearier than he had let on, but Caroline had guessed as much. She said little as he lit the candle lamp from the stage. By the time she had the fire built, lightning was streaking the sky and the first few drops of rain were splattering down. A short while later, a wall of water sealed them into the cave.

The rain lasted all night and on through the next morning. By the time the sun came out late the next afternoon, they both knew Ben was in deep trouble. In spite of Caroline's gentle care, he was getting worse. The wounds were festering and his fever was out of hand. She plied him with hot broth and coffee and bathed him with cold rainwater, trying to bring down the fever. Nothing helped.

Sergeant Meade sat for a long time staring at the man. He dreaded what he was going to have to do, but there was no way out. He had shoved some instruments from the salesman's sample case in his pocket, and now he pulled out a searing iron used to cauterize wounds.

Ben had been incoherent most of the day, and the sergeant knew he couldn't wait much longer. He scooted across the floor of the cave to where Caroline knelt beside Ben. Her hands were gently wiping his forehead, but her soft words of endearment were lost on the man, who lay mumbling on the floor with his head cushioned by a rolled-up blanket.

"How is he?" he asked, concerned.

"Worse. His head's burning up." She looked over at the sergeant. "What should I do?"

He handed the searing iron to her. "Heat this," he said calmly. "Get it red-hot. I'm going to cauterize the wounds."

"That'll kill him!"

"It'll kill him if I don't."

She shuddered as her hands fingered the long, ugly instrument that looked like a poker with a weight on the end. "Will it work, do you think?" she asked.

"It won't unless you get going," he said quickly. "I'd like to get it done before our candle burns out. That was the last one."

Once more Sergeant Meade worked on Ben, searing the wound deep, burning into the proud flesh. Caroline couldn't take it. She stood at the entrance to the cave and stared out toward the lowering afternoon sun, praying that the cauterizing hadn't come too late.

The next evening the fever broke, and Sergeant Meade breathed a sigh of relief. He had begun to like this tall, good-looking man who seemed to occupy Caroline's thoughts so completely. He sat next to him now, gazing out the door of the cave at the setting sun.

"How long do you think we'll be here?" Ben asked, still weak from his bout with the fever.

"Well, unless we die of starvation first, about four or five weeks. Maybe more. Why?"

"That's impossible," Ben said. "I've got to meet Stacey. I can't be stuck here in no-man's-land."

The sergeant laughed, a low chuckle. "How you gonna get anyplace? I'm the only one who could possibly get us back to the fort without getting lost, and I won't be able to travel until this leg is healed." He shrugged. "I'm sorry, Ben. I wish I could give you better news, but, between those wounds of yours and my bum leg, it looks like we're stuck here for a good long spell." He glanced toward the cave entrance, where Caroline stood. She had washed her hair in the stream down below, and the late-afternoon sun made it gleam like fire.

She was still wearing her black skirt, but she had discarded the suit jacket and her camisole, still damp from her bath, revealed the soft, delicate lines of her body.

Ben followed the sergeant's eyes and felt a disturbing anger well up in him as Caroline stared at him openly with inviting eyes. She was at it already. He might have know. She was going to fight him all the way. Well, he wouldn't let her win. And yet, he was stuck with her in this lonely place. It was probably just what she wanted. But he would not end up beholden to her, no matter how nice she was. He wouldn't let her interfere. No, Caroline wasn't going to seal her bargain, of that he was certain. He closed his eyes, shutting out the sight of her, and thanked God that they weren't completely alone. At least with the sergeant here, it wouldn't be as hard to fight her.

CHAPTER 19

The wagon train had pulled wearily into Fort Bridger the day before. It was weeks since they had left Ash Hollow and moved on to new challenges along the trail. The familiar places—Chimney Rock, Scott's Bluff, Fort Laramie, Independence Rock, the Sweetwater River, and South Pass—were all behind them now, as were a bout with smallpox and another skirmish with Indians, which had been staved off with the help of troops from Fort Laramie. Unlike the summer before, Bass had arrived in time with the soldiers.

Now they were relatively safe again. Although the Arapaho had been harassing the settlers and soldiers, the wagon train had managed to reach Fort Bridger without any serious trouble.

It was almost the end of August and they had made better time the past three hundred miles than they had expected. They had lost five more wagons in the aborted Indian attack, and now twenty-two wagons were corralled outside the gates of Fort Bridger. Stacey enjoyed the scenery in this part of the country which was new to her. In spite of the tension between herself and Paula, just the thought that she was getting closer to Oregon and Ben kept her spirits up.

She had remained angry with Wade for a long time, but like so many scoundrels, Wade was too likable to stay mad at indefinitely. By the time they reached Fort Laramie, she had already softened toward him. She had to check on Ginger's injured leg occasionally, and unfortunately, Wade always seemed to be around when she did. But she still didn't trust him. She kept her distance and made sure she was never alone with him. However, by the time they had reached Independence Rock, his past indiscretions had lost their impact, and once more he was joining Stacey in the evenings to gather wood.

Stacey had never told Ed about Wade's improper advances, but he had sensed that Wade was giving her trouble. When his anger finally cooled, Ed was curious and kept his eyes on her protectively.

294

It had been hard for Ed, but he had never been one to moon over a woman he couldn't have. He'd been in love before and had learned years ago that his heart was rather fickle. As much as he told himself Stacey was the most wonderful woman he'd ever met, in a way he was glad she was married to Ben, because he knew marriage to her would be disaster. She was the kind of woman who needed her man with her, and his feet were too itchy to stay in one place for long. So he convinced himself that if he couldn't have Stacey, he'd rather Ben Clayton had her than anyone else.

They had arrived at Fort Bridger late in the afternoon and were planning to spend two days there, replenishing supplies, greasing wagons, and making certain everything was in good shape for the rest of the trip.

The evening of the second day at the fort, there was a dance in the mess hall and Ed asked Stacey if she'd let him escort her.

She agreed, and when Ed came to call for her, he was surprised to see her wearing the turquoise dress from the Paradise. She had repaired the burned spot and it looked as lovely as ever.

"Wade refused to take it back," she told him guiltily. "So I thought as long as everyone else will be wearing their Sunday best, and since I don't have any Sunday best . . ."

"You look lovely," Ed said, and she complimented him on his own appearance.

Ed was wearing a coat of soft, light tan doeskin with a white shirt sporting a dark brown cravat and brown leather pants tucked into his heeled boots. The familiar gunbelt was still resting on his hips, but he had replaced his everyday hat with a new one he'd picked up at a trading post near the Big Sandy.

"Where's your Simon Legree?" Ed asked, not seeing Paula anywhere.

More than one person had given Paula that nickname after watching her treatment of Stacey. "She went on ahead with some other women."

"How's she been treating you lately?"

"Surprisingly, quite well. In fact, she told me to forget about pressing the clothes today if I thought it would make me too tired to go out this evening."

"You're joking."

"Not at all." Stacey pulled her white shawl around her shoulders. "I ironed anyway because I don't trust her. I can't figure out what she has in mind. It certainly wasn't compatible with her usual behavior. She's even being nice to Wade when he comes by."

"Strange," Ed reflected. He glanced off toward Wade Savagge's wagon, where Wade was waiting to escort Pearl, Aunt Lil, and the other ladies to the dance. Ginger's leg had healed nicely, but she was still limping slightly. Ginger glanced momentarily toward the Tanner wagon, and Ed flushed as he held his arm out for Stacey. "Shall we?" he asked.

Stacey smiled, accepting his arm, and they headed toward the fort.

When Ed and Stacey arrived, the orchestra, which consisted of two fiddles and a guitar, was just starting the first number. Even though all the windows were open, the place was hot and stuffy. But it had been so long since they'd had a chance to let their hair down, nobody seemed to mind the heat.

Everyone was laughing and carefree, and Stacey smiled as she watched her neighbors from the train dancing by, eyes gleaming and feet kicking up to the sprightly music. It wasn't long before she set aside her shawl, Ed tossed his hat on a chair, and they joined them.

But before long, Stacey realized people were staring at her rather curiously. She had piled her hair atop her head and was wearing the sparkling imitation diamond earrings that went so beautifully with the dress. It was the first time many of them had seen her dressed up. She looked as if she had stepped out of a fancy ballroom, and unlike Wade's ladies, who were all ostentatious and overdressed, Stacey looked every bit as respectable as a lady of fashion. Only her work-worn hands gave her away, and there were moments when she wished she could hide them in a pair of white gloves.

At first she felt a little self-conscious because of the stares. It reminded her too much of the country club back home, and the mess her life had been. But after awhile she tried not to let it bother her, and as the evening wore on, she danced with one partner after another until her feet hurt. Had she been aware that rumors were already circulating that she had once entertained in a saloon, she might have paid a little more attention. But she was completely surprised when, near the end of the evening, someone in the crowd requested her to sing.

Embarrassed, she faltered at first, but after some coaxing from the crowd, and a special request from the fort commander, she could no longer beg off. So for almost three-quarters of an hour, while the musicians rested, she sat before the crowd playing the guitar and singing.

Much to her surprise, the women enjoyed her performance as much as the men, who cheered after every song.

"I don't think I've heard anything quite so beautiful," said the commander's wife, Margaret, after Stacey finished singing.

Stacey was standing next to the woman's husband. General Mark Highland, the fort commander, was a balding but rather nice-looking man in his late forties. His brown eyes studied her seriously as he congratulated her and Stacey was thanking him when a young captain suddenly appeared. "Sorry to interrupt, General Highland," he said, saluting, "but I thought it best to report now rather than wait until morning."

"What is it, Captain?"

"My patrol just got in," he answered anxiously. "It's the relay station. The Arapaho hit it again, got every horse and burned the new building down. We brought in a couple survivors."

The general frowned. "That's the second time in two months."

"Yes, sir," the captain said. "Another thing, sir. That stage that never made it from Salt Lake City some four or five weeks ago, the one with the sergeant on it, we finally found it today, sir. Evidently that storm the night we searched kept us from spotting it. It had gone over into a steep ravine about five or six miles from the main road. We found it at the bottom this afternoon."

"Anyone around?"

"What was left of three bodies in the coach, sir. Someone had buried them under a pile of rocks, but there wasn't a soul around. Looks like there may have been a campfire near the stage at one time, and the stage is on its side with a big hole cut in its top. Nothing else, except all the clothes and things are scattered around the area."

"Do you remember how many people were supposed to be on that stage?" the general asked.

The man shook his head. "I'm not sure, I think maybe five or six."

"You think the Indians got the rest?"

"Probably. Only it seems strange . . . the candle lamp's missing off the side of the stagecoach. Why would the Indians want that?"

"Who knows, but then again, it could have broken off. No other signs of life around there, you say? No sign of the sergeant?"

"None. If he did walk away . . ."

"You're sure one of the bodies wasn't his?"

"Yes, sir. We brought in two men and a woman. It wasn't the pleasantest thing to do, sir, but I checked. The sergeant wasn't one of them."

"Hmmm . . ." The general didn't like the sound of it.

Sergeant Meade was one of the best trackers he had, and an old friend. He'd been in the army since he was a lad of seventeen and had served exclusively in the Wyoming Territory. He knew the land around here almost as well as the Indians. The general rubbed his chin. "I don't remember the names of all the passengers, but we'll check the list on that telegram from Salt Lake City in the morning, Captain. And tomorrow you can head out with a detail and scout around. Maybe you can come up with something. Besides, there's another stage due in sometime tomorrow. You can keep an eye out for them. I wouldn't want the same thing to happen to them." He straightened, inhaling. "But for tonight, let's not spoil things. I'm sure I saw your wife here somewhere. She's probably been waiting for a dance with you."

"Thank you, sir," the captain said, saluting.

"Excuse me, General," Ed said as the captain walked away. "But don't tell me our old friend Meade's gotten himself killed?"

Ed had been through this territory enough to know men like Meade. Everyone at Fort Bridger knew and respected Sergeant Morgan Meade.

"I certainly hope not," the general replied. "He was on a month's leave, said he was going to strike it rich out in Nevada and come back and buy up the whole territory from the government. You know how he was. He was due back on the stage in July, but the stage never made it. The Arapaho were after the horses, I guess. Burned all the relay stations within fifty miles and drove off every bit of stock. We figured Meade was dead by now. Three bodies, the captain said." His eyes studied Ed thoughtfully. "I think we could lay bets on the sergeant, Mr. Larkin. What do you think? And I bet they'll find him alive."

"I hope so," Ed said, then turned to Stacey as the music started up again. "Now, if Stacey will just honor me with this dance . . ."

"Go ahead, have fun," said the general, trying to put his worry over an old friend behind him. "I know I'm going to enjoy myself. It isn't every day we get to relax with such pleasant company. And thank you again, Stacey, ma'am, for singing. It was lovely." He turned to his wife and escorted her onto the dance floor. But even with the lilting music of the violins, the general had a hard time keeping the worry from his eyes.

The next morning at seven, tired but happy from the evening of dancing, Stacey pulled her mules into line as Ed hollered, "Catch up!" and once more they moved down the trail. She was in her old pants and shirt again. Her shoes had worn out weeks before and she had bought a pair of boots from a cobbler in Fort Laramie. They were comfortably worn and scuffed by now and she braced them against the boards at her feet as she whipped the reins to get the animals into line. Once out on the trail, she settled back and gazed around, prepared to enjoy the scenery.

Paula was in the back of the wagon on her cushioned perch, glorying in the sweet remembrance of her bargain with Wade Savagge. Soon, she told herself, very soon, and she smiled to herself as the wagon rolled along.

The days went on. They forded Muddy Creek and Little Muddy Creek, and moved northwest up into the valley of the Bear River, which they followed to Soda Springs. Soda Springs fascinated Stacey. Its name came from the waters that poured from the springs. There was even one spring that Wade wanted to take with him.

"Tastes like beer," he said, licking his lips. Stacey sympathized with him, since he was planning to open another saloon in Nevada.

She and Wade were still on good terms, although occasionally the looks he gave her made her remember his threat. He once more seemed to be a perfect gentleman, but she didn't like some of the responses her body surprised her with when he was near. He never blatantly flirted with her, but he did little things, like picking a leaf from her hair and allowing his fingers to touch the flesh of her neck where he knew she was sensitive. His eyes would rake over her, but seconds later his expression would change, belying her accusations. She was forced to shove her doubts to the back of her mind and hope she was mistaken.

Two weeks later they rolled into Fort Hall on the Snake River. Again the wagons were greased and the supplies replenished in preparation for the long stretch of trail along the Snake River toward Fort Boise. At Fort Hall they picked up the remnants of an earlier train. The newcomers planned to break away fifty miles south of Fort Hall and head toward the Humboldt and on south. Wade Savagge's wagons would go with this new group. They were to be bossed by a man named Ezra Goshon, who had led a number of wagons over the route before. When they finally pulled out of Fort Hall, Stacey was pleased that she had only a few more days to put up with the uncertainty of traveling with Wade.

Their second night out from the fort, they corralled the wagons, set up camp beside the Snake River, and fell into the same routine they had followed every night since starting their long journey.

Stacey was in the middle of fixing a rabbit stew. The men had done some hunting during their two-day stay at Fort Hall, and Ed had, as usual, shared his game with Stacey and Paula, who had no man to hunt for them. Occasionally Stacey joined the men, her accuracy at skeet shooting from her former life coming in handy, but Paula had demanded her help with too many things during their stay at Fort Hall for her to accept Ed's invitation to go on the hunt.

She dropped some dried carrots into the stew and watched Paula heading away from their wagon, wondering where Paula was going. She had been acting strangely all day. Stacey watched the quick movements of her walk and noticed that she kept glancing back furtively to see if she was being watched. Oh, well, Stacey thought, maybe she was upset because, after tomorrow, she wouldn't be able to throw Wade Savagge's unwanted attentions up to her. She watched Paula disappear along the circle of wagons and shrugged, turning back to the stew.

Paula's eyes darted back again and again as she walked farther away from the wagon. She greeted people along the way, trying to be pleasant in spite of her anger. Wade's wagon had moved into line with the new group, and Paula was glad, because she certainly didn't want Stacey to know she was looking for him.

Aunt Lil, Ginger, and Hazel were at the fire working on supper when Paula arrived, but Wade wasn't about. Although they were surprised to see Paula, they readily told her where she could find Wade.

"He and Pearl went with Rundy and Ox to take the mules over," Lil explained.

Paula bit her lip. Well, maybe that was for the best. After all, Stacey had already taken their mules from the harness, so there would be no chance of running into her while they talked.

Paula found Wade easily enough, but he had difficulty getting rid of Pearl. "Look, love," he said when he saw Paula approaching. "Why don't you go freshen up now that we have the mules settled, and after dinner I'll help you gather wood."

Pearl looked at him skeptically. "You promised the same thing last night, then ended up helping Stacey again and sending Ox over to help me. I don't like it, Wade. You spend too much time with her. You say you don't care, that you're only helping her out of a sense of obligation because she's a friend. Well, I think you're a liar!"

"Have I ever turned from you, Pearl?" he asked quickly. "Have I ever once made you feel as if I didn't want you?"

Her eyes were cloudy with anger. "Oh, I know you want me," she said simply. "After all, you have to sleep with someone when you can't have what you really want. Yes, you've made me feel unwanted. You do it every time you set eyes on that woman, and I don't like it."

"Well, you don't have much choice," he said hurriedly, trying to get the words out before Paula got close enough to hear. "Because I intend to make friends with whomever I want, whenever I want. You don't have any claims on me, honey, remember. So let loose. I told you a long time ago that no woman was going to put a brand on me, and I meant it. Either you take me as is, or you don't take me at all. Which is it, love? As is, or nothing?"

"I'll make you pay someday, Wade," she said through clenched teeth. "Go ahead, talk to Paula Tanner about your precious Stacey Clayton. But mind you, someday you'll pay for the way you've treated me, and she'll pay too."

Paula watched Pearl flounce off and turned to Wade. "What's bothering her?" she asked.

"Jealousy," he said simply.

"That's what I came to talk to you about," Paula retorted. "I gave you every chance to do what you had to do the night of the dance back at Fort Bridger, and you let her slip through your hands. And you've had more than a dozen chances since then and you've done nothing. Are you aware, Wade, that you have just tonight left to fulfill your obligation?"

"I'm aware of it."

"You mean you aren't going to admit you've failed?"

"Nope."

"You have, you know. You said you were going to make love to her before you left the train. Well, tomorrow's the day, and I haven't seen guilt written all over her face yet."

"Look. Let me do it my way, all right? I know what I'm doing. I'm not going to take her by force, so it has to be done just right. But I'll guarantee, Miss Tanner, that if you give Stacey the whole evening off, by tomorrow morning she will have forgotten about going to Oregon. She'll be heading for the Humboldt with me."

"You're crazy. She'll never do that, even if you do succeed."

"Won't she? Ah, how naive you are, Miss Tanner. The lady in question would never feel worthy of going back to the husband she loves after giving herself willingly to another man, believe me. The thought that he might possibly reject her would be more than she could bear, and it's better to have another love than no love at all.''

''Stacey isn't that honest. She won't give him up that easily. She'd wait to hear Ben's reaction, if nothing else.''

''I don't think so. Look, just let me handle it. Our agreement still goes. One unfaithful wife for a letter of recommendation, which I expect you to have ready in the morning. You keep your part of the bargain, I'll keep mine.''

''Tonight, then?''

''Tonight.''

She stared at his handsome face. Wade was so sure of himself. Well, maybe he was right. Maybe he knew Stacey better than she did. After all, a man could sense things in a woman that another woman couldn't even suspect. She had to take the chance. She had to get Stacey out of Ben's life, and if this was the only way it could be done, she'd wish Wade luck. She agreed to give Stacey the evening off.

Pearl had other ideas. Immediately after leaving Paula and Wade, she decided to have a showdown with Stacey once and for all, and headed toward the Tanner wagon, anger and jealousy driving her. There was no way she was going to let Stacey Clayton come between her and Wade. No way!

She reached the Tanner wagon quickly and looked around. The pot of stew was bubbling over the fire, but Stacey was nowhere in sight. She was trying to decide whether to stay or come back later when she heard a faint noise coming from inside the wagon. She was just about to throw back the flap over the wagon's door, when she stopped stock-still, then gently she lifted only a corner of it, and without making a sound, peeked in.

Stacey stood in the middle of the wagon washing off the dirt and grime of the day, wearing nothing but her bra and a ragged pair of nylon briefs. She had been wearing the underpants under her slacks when she'd come back through time. She had been trying to make them last until the end of the trip, because bloomers were too bulky to wear under the men's pants. The briefs were almost worn out from washing them in the lye soap, but as long as the elastic around the middle held them up, she'd keep them on.

She was scrubbing the dirt from her arms, humming as she drew the washcloth over them. Oblivious of the fact that Pearl was watching her from the back of the wagon, Stacey was happily contemplating Wade's departure the next day. It was like a burden being lifted, because no matter how nice he was, she still didn't trust him.

Puzzled, Pearl watched every movement Stacey made. Stacey was wearing some sort of funny-looking garment on top. It seemed to be holding her breasts, with straps going over her shoulders. Pearl had never seen anything like it before in her life. She studied it for a long time; then her eyes fell to Stacey's drawers, if that's what one could call them. They weren't bloomers. There was hardly enough room in them for Stacey to move, yet she seemed comfortable enough. Pearl's eyes wandered over Stacey's figure, shadowed inside the canvas wagon. Even in the dim light, it was easy to see that she had a figure worthy of Wade's admiration. The thought sickened her.

Deftly Pearl lowered the corner of the flap and looked around again. There were people going by a short distance away, but no one was paying any attention to her.

She stood for a few minutes remembering all the nights she had sat by herself waiting for Wade to come back from the Tanner wagon. She knew that when Wade made love to her, he was only using her to take the place of the woman he really wanted.

At first she thought he was just trying to get even with Stacey for the Paradise. No matter how much he denied it, she knew the fire had somehow been Stacey's fault, and the look on his face that night had been filled with revenge. But as the days and weeks went by, Pearl began to realize it was far more than the fire. And ever since the night she saw Wade kissing Stacey, she knew her suspicions were right.

Tears welled up in her eyes, and they narrowed shrewdly as she remembered the sight of Stacey standing in the wagon just now, half-naked. The thought that Wade would someday see her like that was too much to bear. Slowly, without fully realizing what she was doing, she lifted the canvas flap again.

Stacey was washing her face when Pearl quietly climbed into the back of the wagon. She began to rinse herself off, and then suddenly froze, a sixth sense telling her she wasn't alone.

The hair on her neck prickled, and she pressed the washcloth close to the base of her throat as she whirled around. She let out a startled gasp as she saw someone standing in the other end of the wagon.

"Paula?" she asked hesitantly.

No one answered.

"Come on, Paula, quit trying to frighten me."

Pearl took a step toward Stacey, and she recognized her in the dim light.

"Pearl?"

"Yes, it's Pearl!" Her voice was low, husky.

"What are you doing here? What do you want?" The terrible anxiety that had held Stacey in its grip only moments before was replaced now by a new fear, a gnawing fear based on the hateful look on Pearl's partially shadowed face.

In the dim light Pearl's eyes looked dazed, irrational, and strangely troubled. It was an unnatural look, one Stacey had seen before when she'd been nursing. The kind of look that has no basis in reality.

"Pearl? Are you all right?" she asked as the woman stood quietly staring at her.

"All right? Yes, I'm all right," Pearl said. Her voice sounded weird. "But you won't be if you don't stay away from Wade!"

Stacey's heart sank. "Wha . . . what do you mean?"

"You know what I mean," she said quickly. Suddenly the dazed look was gone from her eyes, and they grew cold. "I warned you a long time ago, Stacey Clayton. I warned you the first time I saw you wearing my turquoise dress."

Stacey's eyes shrewdly appraised Pearl. She wasn't crazy, not in the sense that she didn't know what she was doing. She knew very well what she was doing. Stacey's eyes searched her face, then traveled to her clenched fist. As Pearl raised it, Stacey flinched.

"I told you to stay away from him!" Pearl warned, waving her fist in Stacey's face. "Why didn't you leave him alone?"

"I didn't do a thing!"

"You did!" Pearl's eyes narrowed. "You made him fall in love with you. You could have stopped him. He's mine, Stacey. Mine! You have no right to him!"

"I don't want him!"

"Don't lie!" Pearl shook with anger. "I've seen the way you look at him."

"Don't be ridiculous." Stacey tried to reason with her. "In the first place, I don't give a damn about Wade Savagge. You can have him. And in the second place, you're all leaving the train tomorrow, so I don't know why you're getting so upset."

"Because I don't trust you, and I don't trust Wade. He has something planned, I know. You're going with us, aren't you?"

"No!"

"I'll teach you to mess with my man!" she shrieked. Before Stacey had a chance to reply, Pearl grabbed her hair.

Stacey inhaled sharply with the pain, dropping the washcloth so her hands were free to defend herself. With all her might she lunged toward Pearl, hoping to throw her off balance so she could free her head.

They fell toward the back of the wagon, bumping against boxes and trunks. Stacey pushed against Pearl's chin with one hand while beating against her arm with her right elbow, trying to get Pearl to break her hold. But Pearl only tightened her grip.

Stacey didn't want to hurt Pearl, but she wasn't about to let her yank her hair out by the roots. With Pearl's chin pushed up, Stacey shoved her elbow into Pearl's Adam's apple as hard as she could.

Pearl gasped, choking, and grabbed with one hand for Stacey's throat.

Stacey turned her body and plowed into Pearl's midriff with her fist. Then she reached up and pried the fingers of Pearl's other hand from her hair.

Tears streamed down Pearl's face, but she wasn't about to let Stacey get away. Still gasping and gurgling for air, she grabbed Stacey's arm, trying to keep Stacey's hand from prying her fingers loose. But Stacey managed to succeed, yanking her head away from Pearl's grasp.

Her head free, Stacey swung her left arm wide and caught Pearl on the side of the face. Blood spurted from the corner of Pearl's mouth. With one quick jerk Stacey freed her right arm and backed away toward the front of the wagon.

But nothing she did to Pearl fazed her. Suddenly Stacey was scared. Pearl was like a madwoman. She once more moved toward Stacey, oblivious of the blood on her mouth or the pain in her throat that made it hard to breathe. She had only one thought in mind.

Stacey continued to back up until her hands touched the side of the washbasin. She picked it up quickly, and as Pearl came at her again, she doused her right in the face.

Pearl sputtered and stopped, cursing. She wiped her eyes as Stacey stood plastered against the front of the wagon, hoping Pearl would give up. She wasn't about to. Pearl's only thought was to hurt Stacey. Her eyes fell on another box where Stacey's knife lay. Pearl's eyes narrowed, and she scooped up the knife. Hefting it deftly, she pointed the blade toward Stacey. Her hazel eyes grew wild, her nostrils flared and before Stacey had time to realize what was happening, she leaped forward, cutting the air as Stacey stared in disbelief.

There was only one thing to do. Stacey leaned back over the

box, lifted her feet, and drew in her knees. As Pearl reached her, Stacey flung out her feet, catching Pearl in the chest.

Pearl flew back onto her knees, but she held on to the knife. She gained her feet and steadied herself again, then came at Stacey once more, even more determined.

"For God's sake, Pearl, stop it!" screamed Stacey, but Pearl didn't seem to hear. They were fighting in only a few feet of space, and Stacey had no clothes for protection. She couldn't let Pearl reach her with the knife. She looked around quickly, grabbed her dress from the bed, and held it in front of her as a shield.

Again Pearl came at her. Stacey was ready. She flung the dress, tangling it around Pearl's hand. With the knife useless, Pearl, now sobbing uncontrollably, began flailing at Stacey with her other hand, fingers clawing the air. Stacey caught her wrist, but Pearl managed to wrench free, and once more her sharp nails came at Stacey's face. This time Stacey had no time to grab Pearl's wrist. Instead, she ducked, and Pearl took advantage of the opening. She lunged at Stacey again, and although the knife was still tangled in the dress, she pointed it at Stacey as she rushed forward.

Stacey saw her quick movement. She grabbed the ends of the material, hoping to deflect the knife, but instead, she bent Pearl's arm. When she hit Stacey, Pearl's elbow rammed into Stacey's ribs and her hand twisted inside the tangled dress. As a result, instead of slipping into Stacey, the knife blade slid quickly between Pearl's own ribs and she let out a startled shriek.

Pearl stared down at her midsection as if in shock. The knife was still in her hand and she pulled it out of her flesh, staring transfixed at the blood filtering onto her dress. Her knees went weak, her head began to spin, and she thought she was going to throw up. Pearl sank to the floor of the wagon, crumpled up against one of the trunks.

Hands shaking as she stared at Pearl, Stacey took a deep breath. My God! What was she going to do?

Stacey's first thought wasn't that Pearl had tried to kill her. Her first thought was to stop the bleeding.

Quickly she grabbed the material around the wound and ripped it away. But Pearl was wearing a boned corset, and the material was too strong for Stacey to tear.

She didn't want to touch the knife, so she took out the scissors from her sewing box and cut the corset away. The wound wasn't very deep. Thank God the knife had been a small one. It looked like it had only gone in a few inches.

She worked quickly. Using some of J.D.'s good brandy, she cleaned and disinfected the wound and then bandaged it.

Pearl was coming to. She lay on her back, eyes closed. Her side hurt like hell. Then she remembered. Quickly she opened her eyes and started to move, but Stacey pushed her back to the floor.

"Lie still," Stacey said irritably. "Unless you want it to start bleeding again."

Pearl stared up at her, eyes wary. "Stacey?"

"Who else."

Her voice was weak. "What are you doing?"

"I stopped the bleeding and bandaged the wound," she answered. "Although I certainly don't know why I should, after what you tried to pull."

Pearl swallowed painfully and tears sprang to her eyes. "I only wish I'd succeeded."

"Well, you didn't." Stacey stood up quickly, realizing she was still wearing only her pants and bra. She grabbed her petticoats and yellow calico dress and slipped them on. Her blue calico was still twisted around the knife, and she picked it up. The knife clattered to the floor of the wagon and Stacey set it aside, then looked down at Pearl.

Pearl's hazel eyes were still sparking with anger and jealousy. Her dark hair, the color of thick black coffee, was disheveled. With her cut dress and corset, she looked even worse.

Stacey was wondering whom to go see first, Ed or Wade, when Paula came climbing into the wagon. She stopped halfway in and froze, staring at Pearl.

"What happened?" she asked.

Pearl closed her eyes. She didn't want to see anyone, certainly not Paula.

"A little accident," Stacey said. "If you'll stay with her, I'll go after Ed."

"But how . . . what . . . ?"

"She tried to kill me," Stacey said simply. "But it didn't work. Now, will you watch her while I go get someone?"

Paula nodded, amazed at Stacey's coolness. She had no idea that Stacey was still trembling inside.

Stacey slipped on her shoes and climbed out of the wagon, but she didn't have to go far. Ed was on his way to see her, and she almost bumped into him as she turned from the wagon.

"Am I glad to see you," she said, relieved.

"What's the matter?"

"Pearl went off half-cocked . . . I'm sorry . . ." She laughed uneasily. "Pearl went a little crazy and tried to knife me, Ed," she said slowly. "Instead, she got hurt. She'll be all right. She's in the wagon with about a two- or three-inch-deep slit in her side. I've bandaged it, but somebody has to tell Wade and get her back to her own wagon."

"Who's with her now?"

"Paula." Suddenly Stacey looked around. People were standing two and three abreast staring at her, and she wished she could sink into the ground and disappear.

Ed saw the look of dismay on her face. "They heard the noise and knew something was wrong. Someone sent for me. I'm afraid we aren't going to be able to keep it a secret."

"Oh, bully." She took a deep breath. "This is just what I don't need."

He squeezed her arm. "Brace up. Come on, let's go back in the wagon and see just how badly she's hurt."

Ed told the people standing around to go back to their wagons, and then joined Stacey at Pearl's side.

"I hope you'll get her out of here, Ed," Paula said quickly.

Pearl's eyes were hostile. She was anything but remorseful about what had happened. In a way, she was glad she hadn't actually killed Stacey, because she could have been hung for murder, but she was sorry Stacey had gotten off so easily. Damn her anyway! Wade was up to something, and Stacey had been lying. She just knew it. Otherwise, why had she overheard Wade tell Rundy that after tomorrow he'd have everything he'd ever wanted? Pearl stared up at Ed, her mouth set in a grim line.

"I'll take you back to your wagon," he said.

She inhaled angrily. "And I suppose you'll tell Wade?"

"What do you think?"

"Damn you! Damn all of you!" she blurted out.

Ed grabbed a blanket from one of the makeshift beds in the wagon. "I'm going to have to use this," he said.

Paula nodded. "Go ahead."

He spread the blanket over Pearl, picked her up, and awkwardly made his way out the back of the wagon.

"I think you should come with me, Stacey," he said quickly.

She agreed, hoping she could help explain things to Wade. But Wade took it better than they expected. He was upset. Not because Pearl was hurt, but because she had pulled such a ridiculous stunt.

As he studied Pearl, who was cradled uneasily in Ed's arms, Wade's eyes, although distressed, were angry, and Stacey felt sorry for Pearl. She really loved Wade, and it was pitiful to see the hurt look on her face.

"This is terrible," Wade said after Ed took Pearl into the wagon. "I'm sorry, Red. I never thought she'd do something this crazy."

"Maybe she thinks she has a reason."

"Maybe she does have one."

"Wade, for God's sake," Stacey said irritably. "I think it's time you faced the fact that there's nothing between us."

"For you maybe, but not for me. It's not so easy to tell your heart to stop loving, Stacey." She started to protest, but he stopped her. "I know, I know, I'm not supposed to say these things. But we're leaving tomorrow, and I can't leave without saying them."

"That's another thing," she cut in angrily. "Who gave Pearl the idea that I'm going with you?"

"She said that?"

"She implied it! What are you up to, Wade?"

He laughed, trying to cover his guilt with his easygoing charm. "Do I look like I'm up to something? Come on, Stacey, we both know how Pearl gets carried away. Don't make it into something it's not."

At that moment, Ed climbed out of the wagon and stood beside Stacey. "She'll be all right," he said. "But I suggest you have a long talk with her, Wade. She could have killed Stacey."

"You think I don't know that."

Ed turned to Stacey. "Ready to go back to your wagon now?" he asked.

She nodded, then glanced up at Wade. "I might as well say good-bye now, Wade," she said solemnly.

He panicked. "Now? We don't leave until tomorrow."

"I know."

"But . . . Stacey, I know things haven't gone all that well for us, but . . . I was hoping we could part friends."

"We are."

"You call this parting friends? I was hoping to have a few minutes alone, so we could really say good-bye."

"You know I can't do that, Wade. Good-byes can get sticky. I'll just say thanks for your friendship and wish you all the luck in the world with your new venture in Nevada."

He stared at her hard, determined this wasn't going to be their last good-bye. In fact, there wasn't going to be a good-bye, not between him and Stacey. There couldn't be.

"Wade?" she said softly. "Good-bye?"

"Good-bye," he said frowning.

She gazed into his eyes, but unable to read what was behind them, she took Ed's arm and they walked away.

Wade watched them disappear along the circle of wagons. Good-bye! His jaw clenched tightly. The evening wasn't over yet. He wasn't about to give up his plans. With a determined sigh, he turned to his own wagon and Pearl.

Some hours later, Stacey sat alone in front of the fire, her thoughts miles away. Paula had told her she didn't have to bother with anything after supper this evening. She said Stacey should just rest, since she had been through such a trying experience. It wasn't at all like Paula, and Stacey wondered what she was up to.

After supper, Stacey had gathered the wood anyway, but then she decided to take Paula up on her offer and relax for a while. Now, as she watched the flames, she remembered her fight with Pearl. It reminded her of the day Beth had burst into the operating room, confronting her with the same ferocity and foul accusations that Pearl had thrown at her. Both women had had that same savage look in their eyes. Two women, both accusing her of making their men fall in love with her. Was she to blame? The thought was frightening.

She shut her eyes, remembering John's kindness when everything in her life was so topsy-turvy. No, she had done nothing to encourage him, except be his friend. It wasn't her fault John had fallen in love with her, any more than it was her fault that Wade believed there was more between them than just friendship. And Ed, too, but at least he didn't have any wife or girlfriend ready to tear her hair out, although there were times Ginger gave her rather strange looks.

She opened her eyes. All of it was ridiculous anyway. No matter how many men came into her life, no one could compare to Ben. He was the only man she loved. The only man who could still the yearning ache inside her that made her weak with longing. There were still so many miles to go. If only he could be here with her now. She shivered expectantly.

"You're not cold?" asked Wade from behind her left shoulder.

She whirled around. He was standing only a few feet away. The firelight cast shadows on his face that brought out his classic features, and she realized once again how good-looking he was in rather a rascally, devil-may-care way.

"I thought we said good-bye," she said, her eyes hardening.

"We did. I didn't come to say good-bye. I was wondering if

you could take another look at Pearl. She feels a little feverish, and I think something's wrong.''

"Can't Lil take care of it?''

"She doesn't know anything about knife wounds. Please?''

She eyed him skeptically. "You're sure that's all it is?''

"Promise.'' He held out his hand to help her to her feet.

She accepted his assistance and they headed toward Wade's wagons.

"We've moved her to the other wagon,'' he explained as they approached his camp. "She's in the one with the piano now, where it's a little quieter. Come on, I'll help you in.''

Stacey should have suspected something right away, because no one else was around, but she was daydreaming, wondering what might have caused the fever. She let Wade help her into the wagon, and it was only then, as his hands spanned her waist, that she became suspicious.

"Wade?'' She squinted in the faint light to see into the wagon's interior. It was deserted. "Where's Pearl?'' she asked as her feet hit the floor.

"I'm sorry, Stacey,'' he said huskily. "But I couldn't say good-bye the way you wanted to. Not like that.''

His hands were still on her waist and she tried to back away, but he held her firmly.

"Please, don't be mad at me,'' he pleaded. "Please, Red.''

"What do you want from me, Wade?'' she asked.

"Don't you know?''

"You'll never get it.''

"Won't I?'' His eyes softened seductively. "You know you need me, Red. Why don't you just admit it?''

He pulled her close against him. She felt a sudden twinge run through her, and throbbing ripples attacked her body, weakening her knees.

"No!'' she exclaimed breathlessly, trying unsuccessfully to pull away. "No, Wade, don't, please!''

"Why not?'' He bent down and pressed his lips to her ear. "I love you, Red,'' he whispered softly. "I wanted to hurt you for what happened to the Paradise, but I couldn't. All I want now is to make love to you. Let me love you, honey. Don't push me out of your life so cruelly without even any memories.''

"Don't worry, you'll have memories,'' said a gruff voice from the back of the wagon. Wade and Stacey both whirled around as two figures emerged from the shadows beyond the piano.

Jed Cato's broad features were shadowed in the lamplight, but they recognized him right away. Both he and another of Ed's hired hands, Will Harris, held guns in their hands.

"Lookee here," said Will to Jed. "Looks like the gamblin' man's makin' headway with the little lady after all."

"What do you want?" asked Wade, pulling Stacey closer to shield her from their guns. For once she didn't protest.

"Want? We want the money that's in that there safe," Jed answered quickly. "We was gonna take it without botherin' you none, but the damn thing's too heavy to take on a horse, and it'd make too much noise to blow it open here. So we've been waitin' for you to open it for us."

Wade gritted his teeth. Dammit! And he had told Ox and Rundy to make themselves scarce so he'd be alone with Stacey. "What if I don't open it?" he asked.

"Then maybe the little lady here doesn't mind how her face is put together."

Wade sucked his breath in, trying to hold back his anger. He couldn't lose the money. Yet, he couldn't let them touch Stacey either.

"Well, fella, what'll it be?" asked Cato. "You gonna open the safe, or do we start in on your lady friend?"

"You so much as touch her and I'll kill you," Wade snarled.

Cato grabbed Stacey's arm. Wade tried to fend him off, but Harris pointed his gun at Stacey's head.

"Hold it, Savagge," said Harris. "Let go of the little lady, unless you want me to blow a hole right through her."

Wade froze, then slowly released Stacey.

"Now, open the safe!" Harris demanded.

Wade had no choice. Reluctantly he moved to the small safe and dropped down onto one knee. He glanced up at the two men and saw Stacey's worried face. He couldn't let anything happen to her. His hands began to fumble nervously at the combination.

Between the dim light and his angry frustration, it took Wade a good five minutes to open the safe. Once he was finished, he stood up and turned to the men. "How far do you think you'll get, gentlemen?" he said. "The minute you ride away, we'll come after you."

Harris gazed at him cagily. "I'm glad you thought of that. We'll take them with us, Cato," he said abruptly. "He's right. If we leave them here, what's to stop them from coming after us? We take them with us, and we got hostages to bargain with."

Stacey's heart was pounding as she tried to break out of Cato's grip. "You wouldn't dare!" she cried.

"Listen to the lady," Cato said flippantly. "Who the hell does she think she is, anyway?" Suddenly he grinned. "You know, taking them ain't gonna be such a bad idea. Ed Larkin ain't gonna risk anything happenin' to her. She's the best insurance we got against bein' caught."

"Right," confirmed Harris. "Now, keep the two of them quiet while I fill the saddlebags."

Wade watched with mixed emotions as Will Harris shoved all the money that stood between him and poverty into the saddlebags. He wanted to stop him. Damn, how he'd like to smash into him and grind his face into the floor. But he couldn't take the chance. Jed Cato still had the upper hand. He was holding Stacey's arm in a viselike grip, his gun against her head. Wade's eyes blazed as he watched Harris take the last few dollars, then straighten and turn his gun on Wade.

"All right, fella, let's step out," he said quickly.

Wade stood his ground.

"Move!" ordered Harris viciously.

Wade glanced quickly at Stacey, then headed for the back of the wagon.

"Follow them," Cato said, shoving Stacey after Wade and Harris.

Harris and Cato had picked a perfect time of evening to carry out their plan. Everyone was either asleep or out visiting, and the camp was fairly quiet. Before they started toward where the livestock was bedded down for the night, Stacey heard the women laughing and talking in Wade's other wagon. Damn him, she thought. If he hadn't tried to pull another fast one on her, they wouldn't be in this mess.

It was a long walk to the horses, and Wade and Stacey shuffled reluctantly the whole way. Harris' patience was running thin. He and Cato had so far managed to keep the drop on them, but now they had to steal horses for their captives and saddle them. Their own horses were ready to go.

Harris had Cato hold his gun on Stacey while he forced Wade to saddle two other horses.

"Where are the guards?" Wade asked as he fastened the cinch on the last horse.

Harris laughed. "Cato and I drew guard duty tonight."

"That figures."

"You finished?" asked Harris.

He nodded.

"Good."

Much to Wade's surprise, they let him help Stacey into her

saddle. The men eyed her limbs appreciatively as she tucked her skirt and petticoats in to keep them from flying up.

After they had all mounted, Harris and Cato wrapped ropes around the saddle horns on both horses and tied their captives' hands down, then they grabbed the reins and secured the saddle-bags to their own saddle horns.

"Ready?" asked Harris.

"Ready!" echoed Cato, and as they headed away from the line of horses, spurring their mounts toward the hills in the distance, they were unaware that a lone figure was standing a few yards away, in the deep shadows, watching them melt into the darkness.

CHAPTER 20

Ben took a long drink from his canteen and leaned back against the tree trunk. He stared off across the valley to the small peck in the distance that was supposed to be Fort Bridger. For a while he had thought they would never make it. Especially a few days before, when they had almost run into an Arapaho raiding party.

They had spent almost six weeks in that damn cave, waiting for his wounds and Sergeant Meade's leg to heal. When they finally left it behind, they moved out of the ravine and headed toward the main road again. But they had had to change plans and move farther north into the hills to keep out of the Indians' lands. The sergeant knew what he was talking about when he said they raided the area regularly.

But now the fort was only a few hours away. At last! He'd lost so much time. He patted the money belt around his waist, had he hadn't lost it. He glanced back to where Caroline was struggling across the rock-strewn ground in her heelless shoes, still tightly clutching her battered handbag.

"Need some help?" he asked.

She looked disgusted. "Don't put yourself out."

He studied her thoughtfully. She was still mad. Well, so was e. She had been trying her best ever since they'd been thrown together in this miserable situation to get him to forget his convictions and make love to her. Her ploys were subtle, he had to admit. The warm eye contact, a gentle touch here and there. The intimate way she had of talking to him, trying to make him aware of her body. A day hadn't gone by without her trying to wear him down one way or another. This morning had been the limit.

He enjoyed watching her trying to seduce him by combing her hair, thrusting out her breasts when she knew he couldn't help but notice. She had no way of knowing that just having her near, with her red hair and blue eyes, kept his thoughts on Stacey. Without realizing it, she had been defeating her own purpose.

315

But he had to admit that there were times it was hard to kee
his hands off. She was tempting as hell, but all he had to do wa
remember the agony he had felt that night by the river, and th
itch to satisfy the ache in his loins faded. He knew he woul
satisfy his yearning when he was with Stacey again.

This morning, however, had been different. They had bee
walking cross-country for days. Sergeant Meade had kept the
alive during their stay in the cave by his prowess at shootin
rabbits and by instructing Caroline on which wild plants an
berries were edible. The man was a regular storehouse of info
mation, and knew the land like a man born to it.

Ben was thankful they had him along. For more reasons tha
one. This morning had been no exception. They had camped la
night in a comfortable spot beneath some trees, where the gra
was soft and the warm breezes reached them. He had fall
asleep quickly and dreamed all night long of Stacey and the da
when he'd finally reach her.

He was still dreaming of her when the first hint of dawn cre
into the dark shadows around him. In fact, he wasn't just drean
ing of her. He was dreaming he was making love to her, ar
slowly, as his body began to wake to reality, he felt soft sk
beneath his hands and warm lips on his mouth.

He dredged his thoughts out of the dream and his eyes fle
open. He pushed Caroline away, turning from her face, whi
was flushed from the warmth of the kiss.

He dropped his hands from where they had been caressing h
back, but his lips were still burning with passion. His ey
suddenly went cold, their dark depths sparking furiously. "Wh
the hell do you think you're doing?" he asked unsteadily.

Caroline wasn't prepared for the antagonism in his eye
"You were kissing me," she said softly.

"The hell I was!"

"All right, then, I was kissing you," she retorted. "But yo
were kissing me back."

"I told you before, Caroline," he said. "Your bargain stink
and if you think your little tricks are going to entice me, you'
sadly mistaken."

She was smarting, and he knew it. He hadn't meant to hu
her. She had nursed him back to health and he owed her for tha

His hand brushed away a stray curl from her cheek. "Look,
he said huskily, feeling like a heel. "If Stacey hadn't con
back, it might have worked for us, I don't know. But I'm n
going to take a chance on losing the one person in the world wh
means more to me than life itself by accepting your bargai

:an't you understand that? When I made love to you back in
'ortland, I had no idea Stacey was alive. There was a difference.
f I made love to you now, knowing she is alive, I'd never be
ble to face her again.''

"But she wouldn't have to know. Please, Ben," she pleaded
assionately. "I need you. It isn't fair."

"It's the way it has to be!"

"Why? Don't I deserve something? Why does she have to
ave it all? I nursed you, helped keep you alive for her. Doesn't
iat count for anything? Just once, Ben," she whispered, forget-
ng her pride. Her hand was caressing his chest and Ben felt his
ɔins throbbing. Her hand moved lower and her voice dropped
ɛductively. "It'd be so good, Ben," she murmured, the warm
voman scent of her reaching him. "It's still dark enough, we
ould slip away by ourselves. I love you, Ben, don't do this to
ne, please."

He had stared up at her, his body warring with what he knew
vas right. Then suddenly her lips were once more touching his.
'or a few brief moments he reveled in the feel of them. The kiss
vas heady, like wine, and he was reminded of Stacey. Stacey!
.gain he pushed Caroline away.

"Ben . . . ?"

"No!" he cried breathlessly. "Goddammit, Caroline, I don't
vant any part of it!"

"But . . ."

"I'm not going to Stacey with another woman's scent on me,
nd I mean it." He stood up, straightened his clothes, and glanced
ver to where Sergeant Meade was sleeping about ten feet away.
hen he looked down at Caroline, whose mouth was open in
rotest.

"Don't say it," he said quickly. "It won't do any good.
othing will. I know you think I owe you something, and maybe
do, but not what you're asking."

Her eyes darkened. "All right, Ben. Go to your damned wife,
ee if I care. Only remember, it was your idea not to accept my
argain. You've had a choice."

"Some choice!"

"It's the only one you'll get," she said angrily. She turned
om him as Sergeant Meade began to stir.

That was this morning. Now Ben stood leaning against the
ee as Caroline called to the sergeant, who was still walking
ɔme hundred feet ahead of them. "Morgan Meade, how can we
ɛep up with you when you move at that pace!"

The sergeant stopped and looked back. He was still limping a little, but the leg had healed well under the circumstances. He smiled congenially, his stocky frame easily visible against the green landscape. They were on top of a rolling hill overlooking a plain that stretched out before them for several miles. The hills, although green, were strewn with rock formations and the earth was gravelly at times. Meade watched Caroline head toward him. She was stumbling over the rocky ground, her ragged dress held up as if it were a ball gown.

She was quite a sight. He had watched her over the weeks trying to keep herself pretty for Ben Clayton's sake. Sometimes it was amusing to see the lengths she'd go to trying to get his attention. He felt sorry for her because her ploys didn't work, yet he couldn't for the life of him figure out why. It was obvious Ben knew what she was doing. The strange part was that he was able to resist. Hell, any other man would have surrendered weeks ago. The man was either a saint or of that rare breed that took marriage vows seriously. One thing for sure, the encounter he saw between them this morning seemed to be the last straw.

They thought he had been asleep, but he had seen the whole thing. As his eyes shifted now to Ben, he marveled that the man had come away unscathed.

Caroline reached Meade and stopped, wiping stray hairs away from her damp forehead. It was a hot morning and she was perspiring heavily.

"How long before we reach the fort?" she asked.

"Another couple hours, if Ben quits dawdling," he answered. "Come on, Clayton, let's go!"

Ben fastened his canteen on the belt of his buckskin pants and started down the short incline after Caroline.

When they were all together again, they struck out once more toward the fort.

It was almost noon when Sergeant Meade let out a whoop, swung his arm in an arc, and hailed the fort. They quickened their paces, and half an hour later they were being ushered into the commander's office.

"Morgan, my God, am I glad to see you," the general said as he shook hands with his old friend. "I thought the Arapaho had your hair for sure by now."

Sergeant Meade saluted, then grinned. He shook the general's hand as he rubbed the top of his dusty blond head with his other hand. "Now, what would they want this for, General?" he said. "By the time it dried out, there wouldn't be enough left to hang on a coup belt."

The general let his eyes sift over Sergeant Meade. "You've st weight."

He nodded, then glanced at Ben and Caroline. "We all have. his is Ben Clayton and Mrs. Caroline Jaquette. Ben, Caroline, y superior officer and longtime friend, General Mark Highland."

Caroline nodded, murmuring a quick greeting. She was tired, d not up to her usual banter. But who would be, standing in ont of a stranger in a ripped and dirty dress, heelless shoes, and raggling hair. She felt miserable.

General Highland knew they were tired, but he had to have swers to a few questions right away. He shook Ben's hand and alked behind his desk.

"All right, exactly what happened, Sergeant?" he asked lemnly.

Sergeant Meade quickly related the unusual events of the past w weeks.

Occasionally Ben or Caroline interrupted with some incident e sergeant either forgot or purposely passed over, trying not to orify his role in their ordeal. When he was finished, General ighland glanced at Ben. "Seems to me I should know you, r," he said.

"I was through here last year, late in the season, on my way Oregon. I believe we met then. Ed Larkin introduced us."

"Oh, yes, I vaguely remember now. You're returning to Fort aramie, Mr. Clayton?"

"I was," he answered. "Only now I'm not sure I'll have to that far. I was hoping to reach Ed Larkin's wagon train. It as due at Fort Laramie weeks ago, so it should be close to here y now."

"Close?" The general's frown deepened. "Ed Larkin's train ent through here about a week ago."

"You mean I've missed it?"

"I'm afraid so." Mark Highland saw the anxiety on Ben's ce. "They made exceptionally good time coming down from e Big Sandy. By now they should be nearing Fort Hall. Did Ed ow you were coming, Mr. Clayton?"

"No. You see, I'm looking for my wife. Maybe you remem- r seeing her. She's supposed to be on Ed's train. She's quite autiful, deep red hair, blue eyes. I don't know what wagon she ight have been on."

General Highland thought for a minute. "The only one I can ink of who fits your description was Ed Larkin's lady friend. me to think of it," he said, embarrassed, "she could be your ife. I remember that her name was Stacey. But I'm afraid I

didn't catch her last name, even when she was introduced t
sing.''

"Sing? Ed's lady friend? What the hell are you talking about?"
Ben asked.

General Highland straightened abruptly. Evidently he'd bun
gled himself into a rather delicate situation. Well, there was n
way he could retract his statement. "I guess I have a bit c
explaining to do. You see, Ed Larkin's wagons were here fo
two days. Their last night here we had a dance. The men get
little restless at times, and the trains going through give them
chance to let off a little steam. It helps moral. Mr. Larki
escorted the woman I referred to. I had no idea who she was
only that she was headed west. I assumed, since they wer
rather . . .''—he cleared his throat—''rather friendly, that she wa
someone special. My mistake.''

Ben's eyes hardened. "And the singing?''

"It seems someone in the crowd heard her sing when she wa
working at a saloon back in Omaha, before she joined the train
She has a lovely voice, Mr. Clayton,'' he added quickly. "I wa
surprised myself at the contrast.''

"Contrast?''

Again General Highland's face reddened. "Why, certainly
sir. The first time I saw her, when she was wearing those dirt
old men's clothes and driving that wagon, I never dreamed tha
she'd show up at the dance looking like such a lady. She wa
dressed in the latest fashion, and made quite an impression o
everyone. Ed claims she was a real big help to him on the wa
out. He didn't have any doctor along and he said she know
almost as much about medicine as any physician. Wasn't eve
afraid to wade right in and help when they had an outbreak c
smallpox. And she also helped patch up a dozen or more peopl
after a twister hit. You should be proud of her.''

Ben's eyes were steady on the general, and Highland suddenl
became very uncomfortable. He had explained as best he coulc
but for some reason he had a feeling his explanation had falle
short.

Ben didn't know what to think. The general's words had h
him right between the eyes. Stacey singing in a saloon? Wearin
men's clothes? He understood the doctoring, but the rest?

"Did you meet my wife personally, General?'' Ben aske
curtly.

"Yes, sir,'' the general nodded.

"And she said nothing about heading west to meet me?''

"There really was no need, Mr. Clayton. After all, it was ju

short introduction in a crowded room. I seldom hear about the
rivate lives of the people who go through here, as you'll
emember from your own stay the last time you were here."

He had a point, and Ben had to concede.

General Highland glanced over at Sergeant Meade. "You
now, it never even dawned on me. The night of the dance, the
atrols found the stagecoach you'd abandoned at the bottom of
he ravine. If I had only paid more attention to your wife's last
ame, I might have realized the next morning when I checked the
elegram from the stage company listing the passengers that were
iissing that the names were the same. As I say, though, every-
ne was simply calling her Stacey, and the last name didn't seem
hat important."

"Did she have her own wagon, General Highland?" Ben
sked.

"I have no idea, Mr. Clayton. The only reason I happen to
emember she was driving a wagon was because I was outside
he fort talking to Ed when she drove by, and I remembered
hinking she was a man at first. That's when Ed told me not to
e deceived by looks, and told me about her helping on the
rip."

"I see." Ben inhaled sharply, feeling Caroline's eyes on him.

"You seem rather surprised, Mr. Clayton," the general said
esitantly. "Didn't you know your wife had been singing in a
aloon?"

"I thought my wife was dead until a couple months ago,
ieneral," Ben answered. "I had no idea what she had been
oing in Omaha. All I knew was that she had been there in April
nd then had joined Ed Larkin's wagon train and was heading
oward Oregon. I was hoping to meet her along the way."

"Then you'll be heading for Fort Hall?"

"If it's at all possible."

"There aren't any stages between here and Fort Hall, Ben,"
aid Sergeant Meade. "You'll have to go back to Salt Lake City
nd head up to Boise again and meet her there."

"The hell I will," said Ben roughly. "It'd be just my luck to
iiss her in Boise." He addressed the general. "Is there anyone
t the fort I could hire to take me cross-country?"

The general nodded. "I might be able to find someone." He
lanced at Caroline, who had been more than a little interested in
is conversation with Ben. "What about you, Mrs. Jaquette?
ou're heading east?"

She glanced quickly at Ben, her eyes mischievously alive. In
pite of her bedraggled appearance, she was once more delight-

fully charming and candid. "I was, General," she said sweetly
"But now, since so much has happened . . . I don't think
really like the idea of having to cross all those terrible miles an
perhaps go through another horrible experience with Indians
No, I believe I've changed my mind. I've decided to accompan
Ben to Fort Hall and go back to Oregon." She heard Ben's quic
intake of breath and turned to him. "That is, if Ben doesn'
mind. After all, he and my brother-in-law are in business to
gether and everyone did think it was foolish of me to decide t
go back East after my husband's death. Now I'm beginning t
agree with them. You don't mind if I come along, do you
Ben?"

How could he say no without causing a scene? Damn he
anyway! "It's your life, Caroline," he said irritably. "Besides,
have a feeling you'd come whether I liked it or not."

"Good heavens, Ben, are you still upset with me?" Sh
turned to General Highland. "We had a little misunderstanding
this morning, General," she continued coyly. "And I'm afrai
Ben's still a little irritated, but he'll get over it. Won't you
darling? But you know, General, I am terribly tired and hun
gry," she exclaimed. "We've been talking ever so long. Is it a
all possible for us to clean up, have a bite to eat, and fee
presentable again?"

Once more General Highland's face turned crimson and h
apologized for being so thoughtless. He instructed one of hi
orderlies to take the two civilians to the mess hall and have th
cook fix them something to eat.

"Then take Mrs. Jaquette to my wife and see if she can fin
her something to wear. Mr. Clayton can clean up in the bar
racks." He turned to the sergeant. "You I'd like to have a few
more words with."

Sergeant Meade nodded, and watched Ben and Caroline leav
the office.

"What is it with those two, Morgan?" General Highlan
asked his friend when the door had closed.

"Hell, Mark, it's the same old thing," he retorted as Genera
Highland poured out two glasses of whiskey. "She's in lov
with him, he's in love with his wife. She nursed him back t
health and figures he owes her something. From some of thei
conversation, I get the impression there was more to their friend
ship than just hand holding until he discovered his wife was stil
alive."

"You think she should go with him?"

"I don't think you could stop her."

General Highland sipped at his whiskey and eyed his friend curiously. "How would you like to go along?"

"Me?"

"I know, you just got back. But I need a courier for Fort Hall. You're the best I've got, Morgan. I figure you can kill two birds with one stone. I've got some papers . . . contracts, maps. They have to go to Fort Hall. I was waiting for McGaffey to come down from Wind River since you weren't here. Now that you're back . . . Rest up tonight, get some supplies. Since you already know the two people you have to guide, it'll be easier."

Morgan's eyes narrowed cagily. "Tell me, what's his wife like, Mark?"

"I really messed that one up, didn't I?" he said, then emptied his glass. "I honestly thought she was Larkin's lady, although there were a number of men who tried to claim her attention during the evening. One man in particular seemed to succeed. A gambler named Savagge. She used to work for him, from what I gathered. Word got back to me that some of the men were even betting on which gentleman would walk her back to her wagon."

"You still haven't told me what she was like."

"Let's put it this way, Morgan. Margaret said she was glad the lady was just passing through."

"She's that pretty?"

"Not just pretty. There's something about her. Even in men's clothes she . . ." He shook his head. "Believe me, I'm glad she was passing through, too. She's the kind of woman that could stir up a lot of trouble without even trying."

"Phew!" Meade downed the rest of his whiskey and handed his glass back to the general. "What do you think of Caroline Jaquette?"

"Even with the red hair and blue eyes, she's a poor substitute. She's attractive enough, but as I said, Clayton's wife has a way about her . . ." He frowned. "You don't mind going, do you?" he asked. "I mean, I could get someone else to take them, and let you go on by yourself."

"Not on your life." The sergeant chuckled. "I wouldn't miss the end of this charade for anything. If you hadn't asked, I'd have volunteered."

"Not beginning to like the little widow yourself, are you, Morgan?"

Sergeant Meade shook his head. "Hell, no, Mark. I'll leave the marrying to you."

"By the way," said the general, "how'd you do in the goldfields?"

"Let's put it this way, sir," said the sergeant. "My enlistment's up the end of next month, but I'll still be saluting you for a long time to come."

General Highland smiled. He was glad. Morgan was one of the best men he had, and everyone liked him. Besides, he was sure the man would never be happy anywhere else, just as he was certain Meade would end his days as a bachelor.

A short time later, Meade found Ben at one end of the barracks in an empty room, his six-foot-four frame immersed in a tub of hot water.

"You can thank the general for the tub," Sergeant Meade said amiably as he poked his head into the room. "We usually shower out back in a stall with cold water."

"I'll do that," said Ben.

"Did you get enough to eat?" he asked thoughtfully.

"More than enough." Ben sighed, luxuriating in the warm water. He glanced down at the scarred wound on his leg, then touched the indentation in his right shoulder. It was going to scar too. Oh, well, at least he was alive. "I didn't eat too much, though," he called back as Morgan Meade's head disappeared again from the doorway. "I was afraid too much food might make me sick. But it sure tasted a hell of a lot better than that rabbit diet we've been on the past few weeks."

"It kept you alive, didn't it?"

"I'll concede that. Only, my ribs are sticking out. Unless I put on a little weight before we reach Fort Hall, Stacey won't even recognize me."

Morgan peeled off his dirty uniform, and joined Ben in the other room, where another tub of hot water was set up. He grabbed a washcloth and soap, stepped out of his underwear, and got into the other tub. "Christ, this feels good," he said as he sank into the hot water.

"My sentiments exactly," Ben agreed.

Both men had managed to keep themselves shaved and washed, but there had been no streams deep enough for real bathing. Besides, the soap they had in their pockets had lasted just so long.

Morgan soaped his stocky body, taking time to enjoy the hot water. As he lathered himself, he glanced surreptitiously at Ben. "How would you and the lovely widow like some company to Fort Hall?" he asked.

"What did you do, volunteer?"

"Nope, I was asked. The general figures as long as we got along so well the past few weeks, it'd be foolish to have you hire a guide. Besides, he has to send a courier to Fort Hall. The two of you might as well ride along with me.'' He began to rinse off some of the suds, watching Ben out of the corner of his eye. ''Think the lady'll really go with us?''

Ben's eyes snapped. ''What do you think?''

''I think you've got a problem, Ben. One that's not going to be easy to solve. I just hope your wife understands.''

Ben stared at the barrack wall. Would she understand? But then, there were some things Stacey was going to have to help him understand, too. Like, what the hell was she doing singing in a saloon, and why was she dressing like a man? And why was General Highland under the impression that she was Ed Larkin's woman?

''You were awake this morning, weren't you, Meade?'' Ben asked after a few minutes.

Morgan flushed. ''Afraid so. I couldn't help but see what went on. . . . How long do you think you can hold out?''

Ben rested his head against the edge of the tub. ''You've never seen my wife, Morgan,'' he said dreamily. ''Stacy's not only the most beautiful woman I've ever known, she's the most exciting. There's just something about her . . . Being married to her was like being in heaven. When I thought I'd never see her again, I felt like I was dead too.''

''Where does Caroline come in?''

''Blue eyes, red hair . . . unfortunately, a man has to go on living. The first time I saw her, she reminded me of Stacey. I guess I wasn't beyond pretending.''

''Nobody can blame you for that.''

''I blame myself. I don't like hurting Caroline, but anything I felt for her was all wrapped up in my feelings for Stacey. I even warned her that I hadn't been able to let go yet. She said she was willing to take the chance. Now she doesn't want to let go.''

''I heard her mention something about a bargain . . . ?''

Ben's eyes snapped. ''One I'll never accept! And one I'd rather not talk about, if you don't mind.''

Morgan shrugged. ''I didn't mean to pry.''

''You didn't. It's just that for all Caroline's good points, she's not exactly a saint. There are times when I wish to hell I'd never laid eyes on her.''

Morgan Meade glanced over at Ben. There was fury in the man's eyes, and he wondered just what Caroline's bargain was. He was glad he was going along, if only because he had to see who was going to win out in the end. And he was anxious to meet this woman Ben called his wife. The whole affair was intriguing.

When they were through with their baths, Sergeant Meade decked himself out in a clean uniform. Ben had to put his old clothes back on, but he did replace his pink cotton shirt with a dark blue army one. But beneath the shirt, he was wearing the same bloodstained money belt he had hung on to throughout their long ordeal. His other clothes were washed and mended, although there was a neat hole in his jacket where the bullet had found its target.

He stood now beside Sergeant Meade outside the barracks and watched the activity in the fort. The sun was sinking on the horizon and the sky was swept with shades of pale pink. There were a few civilians running about, but on the whole, Ben saw only soldiers. He watched closely as a weary detail came in from a two-day patrol.

"You like this kind of life, don't you, Morgan?" he said to the sergeant.

Morgan nodded, "I guess I just sort of grew up to it. My folks were killed when I was just a kid, and the army's the only parents I've known. I joined when I was seventeen. That's too many years ago to count." His eye suddenly caught a glimpse of red near one of the buildings, and they settled appreciatively on the woman walking toward them. "Well, didn't she clean up nice and pretty," he said matter of factly.

Ben saw her too. She was wearing a pale green dress that clashed with her blue eyes and emphasized the sunburn on her face. It was one of Margaret Highland's everyday dresses. Luckily Margaret was thin and the dress fit Caroline perfectly.

"Well, hello, gentlemen," she said, stopping directly in front of them. "I must say you both look decidedly different. It's marvelous what a little soap and water will do." Her eyes studied Ben for a long minute. "Did you shave, Ben?" she asked curiously. "It seems to me I see whiskers blending into your mustache."

"Do you, now?" Ben said, amused. He rubbed his chin. "You know, I think you're right."

"You're not growing a beard?"

"Why not?"

She exhaled, disgusted. "Because you wouldn't look good in a beard."

This time Ben's smile was broad enough to show the deep dimples in both his cheeks. "Well, how about that," he said curtly. "Did you know that, Sergeant?"

Sergeant Meade could barely contain himself. Now he understood why Ben hadn't shaved earlier. Morgan frowned studiously. "Well, now, I hadn't thought much about it, Ben. But now you mention it . . . Seems to me a bushy chin just might hamper your looks a bit. But then, I'm not a lady, so I don't much mind." He addressed Caroline. "By the way, ma'am, I don't know as anyone's told you yet, but I'm to take you folks to Fort Hall."

"You?" She was surprised. "You mean I have to put up with you ordering me around again?"

"You don't have to go," Ben countered.

She gave him a disgusted look. "Don't be ridiculous. You know I can't stay here." She glanced once more at the sergeant. "What did you do, volunteer?"

"Nope. Orders."

"In other words, we have no choice."

"That's about it. Well, if you two will excuse me, I've got some things to get ready."

"When do we leave?" she asked as he started to walk away.

"Tomorrow morning at dawn," he said, continuing on his way.

She stared after him, dumbfounded. "Tomorrow morning?" She turned to Ben. "Why so soon?"

"You don't have to go."

"Come on, Ben, stop it," she demanded heatedly. "You know very well I won't change my mind. It's just that I thought we'd get a chance to rest for a day or two."

"And let the wagon train get that much farther ahead of us? Besides, General Highland's papers have to reach Fort Hall as soon as possible. That means we'll be riding fast and resting little." He eyed her curiously. "By the way, I hope you don't expect me to buy you a horse. I may do some stupid things, but I'm not that gullible."

"I wouldn't dream of it," she said testily. "I have my own money, and I've already made arrangements about a horse."

"Ah, yes," he answered, amused. "The little handbag."

"You have your money belt, I have my handbag."

"How about clothes?"

"I've taken care of that, too."

"You're really determined to go, aren't you?"

Her eyes bored into his. "I have to, Ben. I know you say it's over, but I can't accept that, not until I see for myself how things are between you and this resurrected wife of yours."

"Suit yourself."

"I intend to. Now, if you'll excuse me, I have a few things to attend to."

As he watched her walk away, anger smoldered inside him. She was going to keep at it. His hand moved to his chin. Maybe it'd work, and maybe it wouldn't; he'd just have to wait and see. But whatever happened, he promised himself firmly that he wasn't going to let her get to him.

That evening they both ate dinner with General Highland and his wife, Margaret. The meal went well, although Ben could have done without Caroline's light banter. She was still wearing the green dress, and in the candlelight it made the pale blue of her eyes take on a green cast. They looked like the eyes of a cat, and for a brief moment he was reminded of Paula. What a comparison. But it really wasn't a fair one. Caroline was never as vicious or spoiled as Paula. For a long time he let the dinner conversation go on around him while he thought over the past.

His life with Ann had been a constant struggle to avoid Paula's sly flirtations. She had made no pretense over the years of still wanting Ben, and she became even more blatant after Ann's death. Unlike Caroline, Paula wasn't fun to be around. Her sense of fairness was warped and her disposition was nasty. For all her blond beauty, she was hard to admire. She was spoiled and insensitive to others' feelings.

He watched Caroline as she told the general and his wife about the horrors of being stuck in a cave. No, her eyes held none of the self-centered pride that frightened men away from Paula. Instead, Caroline's eyes were mischievously alive. More often than not, laughter dwelt in them, although it was usually mixed with a generous portion of worldly sophistication and unbridled passion. Innocence was lost to her, yet one could never call her anything but a lady.

He was jolted suddenly from his daydreaming by the general's wife. "Is something wrong, Mr. Clayton?" she asked guilelessly. "You've been so quiet."

"No, ma'am, everything's fine," he said quickly, his deep voice echoing in the dining room. "I was just thinking about the trip ahead of us and seeing my wife again."

"Oh, yes. Your wife sings so beautifully, and she's such a lovely person. Tell me, how long has it been since you've seen her?"

"Almost a year."

"And to think you thought she was dead all this time. Mark told me about your dilemma. I do hope everything turns out all right for you. As I said, we met her briefly while she was here, and she made quite an impression."

Ben flushed as he felt Caroline's eyes on him. He quickly changed the subject, avoiding talk about his wife as much as possible for the remainder of the evening.

That night Ben slept in the barracks with Morgan Meade, and the next morning, after a hurried breakfast, he helped Morgan finish getting things ready. They were to take two packhorses with supplies. Ben managed to buy a roan gelding with a blaze on its face from a civilian horse trader who lived at the fort. The saddle and bridle he bought at the trading post.

Now, as he tightened the cinch on the saddle, he wondered how Caroline had fared. Last night she had said she had everything arranged. Probably the result of having befriended General Highland's wife, although nothing had been said about her traveling arrangements last evening during dinner.

He turned abruptly as Morgan let loose an exclamation, and then froze as he followed the gaze of Sergeant Meade's twinkling blue eyes.

Caroline was wearing a pair of men's gray pants that were so tight she was going to have to be careful sitting down. Tucked into the waist was an old blue flannel army shirt like the one Ben wore. Like Ben's, it was dangerously open in front, making it obvious that she wore nothing beneath it. Somewhere she had found a pair of leather boots. In her hand she was carrying a floppy wide-brimmed army hat and over her arm hung a buckskin jacket. With her other hand she was leading a white-stockinged brown mare, saddled and ready to ride.

She stopped a few feet from the two men, and her blue eyes crinkled good-humoredly. "Well, now, do I or don't I pass inspection?" she asked with a musically seductive voice.

Ben turned back to his horse.

She stared at his back for a minute. Before he had turned away, his eyes had revealed only too well what he thought of her outfit. "What's wrong with it?" she asked.

He didn't answer, and Morgan went back to fastening some bundles on the back of one of the packhorses.

"Ben, I asked you, what's wrong with it?"

"Not a thing," he said. He was purposely ignoring her, something he know went against her grain. There was only one reason she'd wear an outfit so tight it left little to the imagination, and he wasn't about to give her the satisfaction of knowing it had the slightest effect on him. "Are you about ready, Morgan?" he asked quickly.

Meade nodded as General Highland came toward them from his house across the parade ground. He was still adjusting his hat and tugging on the tails of his uniform jacket. "Well, I see you're all ready to leave," he said briskly. His eyes avoided the lovely young widow, who seemed a little piqued. But then, he had warned her that his eldest son's suit pants might be a shade too tight. "You have the dispatches, Sergeant?" he asked Morgan.

"Yes, sir."

"Good. Then I'll wish you luck and see you in about two or three weeks. I'll telegraph ahead to tell them you're on your way as soon as the lines are fixed again." He turned to Ben. "I'm sorry we weren't able to get through to Fort Hall and leave a message for your wife, Mr. Clayton. But as you probably know, it takes a while sometimes when the Indians cut the lines. As soon as the lines are spliced again, I'll see that word's sent."

Ben thanked him, and they all said good-bye. Ben let Sergeant Meade help Caroline into the saddle, and she tried to act like she didn't mind, but her eyes betrayed her. However, by the time they rode out of the fort, she was more relaxed and the three of them fell into an easy canter side by side for the first mile or so, then they swung out single file as they left the wagon trail, heading for the short-cut that Morgan said would lop off about ten miles.

They had been riding hard for the past five days, making forty to fifty miles a day. Tonight, when they stopped to make camp, Morgan announced that they should reach Fort Hall sometime the next afternoon.

Ben was restless as all hell. Morgan said they had covered the two hundred and sixty-some miles in less than half of the time it had taken the wagons, and there was a good chance the wagon train would still be at Fort Hall.

They had finished eating a half-hour earlier. Ben sat by the fire, going over what lay ahead and hashing out the days that were behind them. He glanced across the open flames of the fire to where Caroline sat talking to Morgan. Morgan was telling her something about the goldfields in Nevada, but Ben wasn't paying much attention to what they were saying.

He stared at Caroline, watching the way the firelight animated her face. She had taken the trip better than he had expected, but it wasn't the first time Caroline had surprised him. For a lady used to luxuries, she had taken their hardships amazingly well.

Sometimes Ben wished his feelings for her were less admirable. It would make it much easier to ignore her. He stared at her, feeling a deep stirring in his loins and remembering yesterday's events.

They had camped the night before near a spot along the river where the water was especially deep. After eating early, the sergeant had decided to see if he could bring down some game for the next day. At least that's what he had told Ben and Caroline. In reality, he had caught a glimpse of something behind them on the trail earlier and he wanted to make a quick check of the area.

Ben watched apprehensively as Morgan left camp on foot. That was strange. Usually the sergeant hunted from the back of his horse. Ben watched him disappear into the heavy underbrush along the river, as Caroline walked up behind him.

"Since when has he taken to hunting this late in the day?" she asked.

"Maybe he's getting tired of rabbit and figures he might get a raccoon or two."

"You're joking!"

"Not at all. Don't tell me you've never heard of eating raccoons?"

"Only if I absolutely have to." She shuddered. "The thought's disgusting."

Caroline glanced up into Ben's face. It was the first time they had been alone in the past five days. He was so sure his five-day growth of beard would discourage her romantic notions. If he only knew, there was nothing he could do to stop her heart from skipping beats whenever she looked at him. Now, this is crazy, Caroline, she told herself. A grown woman, especially one with any common sense, would be back in Oregon letting some rich, doddering old man make a fool of himself over her. Or at least she'd be on her way East, where there were dozens of men willing to lavish their money and attentions on her. But no, Caroline Jaquette is somewhere in a forest, sweat dripping between her breasts, gazing expectantly into the eyes of a man she knows damn well she has no right to.

"I don't know why you don't shave," she said softly. "If you think hiding behind that brush you call a beard is going to scare me off, you're sadly mistaken."

"For Christ's sake, Caroline," he defended himself. "Will you quit pushing. Dammit, you've been at me ever since we started."

"Been at you? All I did was point out how strange it was for General Highland to mistake your wife for the wagon master's mistress."

"He didn't mistake her for his mistress!"

"Oh, yes, I'm sorry, 'his special lady.' Come on, Ben, what's the difference?"

"A lot."

"To you maybe. To other people there isn't much difference. And if you'd been paying attention to the conversation at the general's dinner the other night, you would have heard Margaret Highland drop that tidy piece of gossip about the gambler your wife worked for in Omaha. Is it my fault I had to explain to you that people couldn't tell if she'd be leaving the dance with the wagon master or the gambler? You wouldn't even have known the gambler was with the wagon train if I hadn't told you. Maybe I should tell you the rest, too. I talked to Margaret Highland at some length after you left that night. She said the man's name was Savagge and that he spent a great deal of time with your wife at the dance. They had everyone talking."

"You're lying."

"I wish I were. Ben, don't you see? I know you think she's special, but what if she's changed? After all, you said you had known her less than four months when you married her. What do you know about her? Where is she from, what kind of a person is she? You've purposely shut me out, and yet there's no guarantee you'll pick up your life with her again."

"You don't know what you're talking about," he said angrily. "You have no idea who Stacey is or what we had together. And as far as the gossip goes, that's all it is—gossip. I've lived with it before . . . I know how it can distort the best of intentions, so don't tell me anything more about Stacey, Caroline. I won't listen."

"Fine, hide your head in the sand, then. But I think you've got a surprise coming, Ben," she said stubbornly. "I just hate to see you hurt, that's all."

"I can handle it," he said arrogantly, and started to walk away.

"Ben, I'm sorry. Please . . . I've been a nasty bitch lately, I know. But I guess it's been a matter of self-preservation. It's hard to be with a person every day, remembering how it was, telling yourself it'll never happen again, yet praying with all your heart it will."

"Caroline . . . ?" He looked into her eyes and saw that, for the first time in days, they were devoid of the usual malicious, self-satisfied look that accompanied her barbs about Stacey. She had been trying to put doubts into his head for the past five days. Was it any wonder he had kept his distance? But now he hesitated. The setting sun was turning her hair to flame, and her eyes were shadowed just enough for their color to be deepened. Something about the way she was looking at him, the open admiration perhaps, softened the contours of her face, and a slow, spreading desire began to fill him. It had been so long. So terribly long.

He touched her hair and sifted his fingers through it leisurely.

Caroline held her breath. Ben's eyes were still on hers, and she couldn't move.

His hand dropped to the flesh of her neck, and her skin was hot beneath his touch. His eyes slid down to the dampness glistening between her breasts, and he began to wonder what it would be like to feel the softness of a woman's breast beneath his lips again.

Without realizing it, his body swayed toward Caroline's until the sudden contact sent throbbing shocks clear through him. He didn't want to feel like this. He fought every savage pulsation, but his body was so starved that it was responding. He tried to stop it, but he wanted Caroline. Really wanted her.

For the first time since they met, he wanted her, but it had nothing to do with love. He knew that as surely as he knew the sun would rise again. He wanted her for the same reason men had wanted women for centuries, to still the ache that had been gnawing away at him for weeks.

His mouth touched hers lightly, and then she was in his arms and he was kissing her long and hard. The wall between them was crumbling explosively. Then it happened again. As he became lost in the rapture of the moment, he wasn't kissing Caroline anymore. He was kissing Stacey, and her name escaped his lips. It slipped out softly, and Caroline's lips fumbled erotically against his as she whispered back.

"No, Ben, no, darling, it's Caroline, love, Caroline," she murmured, her body pressing close to his. "Love me, Ben, oh, yes, love me . . ."

But instead of igniting him further, Caroline's words made him shudder. His lips left hers reluctantly and he stared down into her flushed face. "Caroline . . . ?"

"Yes?" she whispered softly. She gazed up into his bewildered face and suddenly her eyes widened in terror as she felt him pull away. He was breathing deeply, as if he'd been drowning and was now gasping for air.

"No!" he said abruptly. "Don't talk, don't say a word, and for God's sake"—his voice was breathless—"don't make more out of it than what it is!"

"What is it, Ben?" she asked helplessly. "What's the matter?"

"Nothing."

"Damn you!" she blurted softly. For the first time, he saw tears in her eyes. "And damn her for doing this to you!"

He stared at her for a long time before abruptly walking away toward the river to cool off. The moment was past, but not forgotten. Now, as he sat watching Caroline and Morgan across the fire from him, he realized how close he had come last night to letting his body betray him. Once more he had almost let his body dictate to his heart, and he didn't like it. He had to reach Stacey soon, because, quite apparently, the longer he was away from her, the more tempting Caroline became.

He shifted his position in front of the fire as Caroline moved toward him.

"Why so nervous?" she asked as she dropped down beside him.

"Who's nervous?"

"Oh, Lord! You're like a little boy who's been out too late and doesn't know what's waiting for him when he gets home," she said. "Honestly, Ben, for a grown man you're a wreck." She frowned. "What kind of a woman is she, anyway? She's turned a perfectly good man like you into a quivering mess."

"Don't be ridiculous." His voice was strong, husky.

"Well, maybe I am exaggerating," she said, eyes snapping impishly. "But I certainly will be glad when the mystery is over and I get to meet this woman who has you so completely under her spell." She cocked her head as she pulled her legs up, hugging her knees. "I enjoyed last night," she said softly. "Even if it didn't last long."

"Forget it."

"Like I forgot that night down by the river? Never, love. At least not until I know for sure there's no hope left. Maybe not even then. It depends."

"On what?"

"On you and me. I've come a long way, Ben, and I don't give up easily, as you know. If I have the slightest doubt that things aren't going to turn out the way you want, I'm going to make your life miserable until you have to admit I'm right."

"You're crazy," he said, suddenly amused. It was so like Caroline. At least with her he knew what to expect. "Don't you have any pride left, Caroline?"

"Pride? What's pride?" she asked, laughing delightedly from deep inside. "Oh, yes, pride . . . that's what makes spinsters out of nice young ladies and grouchy old hags out of lovely old ladies. No, Ben, I guess I don't have any pride, not where you're concerned anyway. I can't afford to."

"I'm sorry." And he really was.

"I know," she said. "I like you too." They were interrupted as Morgan asked if they wanted more coffee before he cleaned up the pot.

The next morning Ben shaved his beard off, all but his mustache, in the hope that Stacey would be waiting at Fort Hall. But when they reached the fort, close to sundown that afternoon, they discovered that the wagon train had pulled out early the day before. The telegram Ben had asked General Highland to send hadn't arrived yet.

"The line's still down," one of the captains said. "Seems some Indians are staked out on a hill overlooking the poles, so the men can't do the repairs. I'm heading out there now with a detail to see if we can scare them off. The wires should be working again in no time."

Ben was pleased for the army, but it didn't help him much. Stacey still had no idea he was on his way.

"If we leave first thing in the morning, we should reach them before they get to the California cutoff," Morgan said as they led their horses toward the corral.

"You're going with us the rest of the way?" Caroline asked.

"Yup, general's orders. When I know you're finally safe and sound with Ed Larkin, I'll head back toward Fort Bridger."

Caroline glanced over at Ben, but he didn't seem to notice. His eyes were on the horizon and his thoughts were miles away. She had been hoping they'd be alone the rest of the way. Well, at least they were still together. When they rode out the next morning toward the Snake River, Caroline knew that, one way or another, by nightfall she'd finally know what this whole madcap race across the country was about. She'd find out once and for all whether her big gamble was going to pay off.

CHAPTER 21

Bass straightened from behind the tree where he had been hiding. Squinting into the darkness, he watched the four horses carry their burdens toward the hills. He was having a hard time believing his eyes, but he knew there couldn't be any mistake. However, he wasn't about to stick around and try to figure it out. He broke into a run and headed back toward camp.

"What the hell's the matter?" asked Ed as Bass rushed up to him and slid to a quick stop.

"Cato and Harris just kidnapped Stacey and Wade," he said hurriedly.

"The hell they did! Why?"

"How should I know?"

"Let's check Wade's wagon," Ed said, and hurried toward the other end of camp, with Bass at his heels. One wagon was quiet, but the other was full of women, their voices carrying to the two approaching men.

"Which wagon you going to look in?" asked Bass.

Ed headed toward the quiet wagon with long, sure strides. Inside, they found two glasses and a bottle of champagne set out beside Wade's makeshift bed that was fancied up with some satin pillows. Nothing else was out of place, but the safe was open and empty.

"Where are Rundy and Ox?" he asked Bass. "Have you seen either one?"

"Nope."

Ed headed for Wade's other wagon and knocked on the weather-beaten side. "Lil! Come out here, Lil!"

The babble of female voices inside hushed and Lil stuck her head out. "What on earth are you yelling about out here?" she complained irritably. "We just got Pearl settled down."

"With all that noise in there?"

She looked disgruntled. "What do you want?"

"Where are Rundy and Ox?"

"Well, now, how should I know? Why don't you ask Wade?"

"Because Wade's been robbed and kidnapped."

"He what!"

"Bass saw them ride off," Ed explained. "He said it's a couple of men I hired back in Omaha. Evidently they had Wade open the safe and took him and Stacey with them."

"Stacey? What was she doing with Wade?"

"That's what I'm trying to find out."

Lil let Ed help her out of the wagon, smoothed the skirt of her lavender dress, and walked over to Wade's other wagon to check it for herself.

"Damn, that's all the money Wade had," she said anxiously. "And the rest of us too."

"Well, wherever it is, he's with it," Ed said. "I was hoping Rundy and Ox would know something."

The firelight emphasized the age lines in Lil's face as she pointed down the circle of wagons to where some men were sitting around a makeshift table playing cards. "You'll probably find them in the poker game," she said, frowning. "What are you going to do?"

"We're going after them, naturally. But it's going to take time. A trail's hard to follow after dark."

"You're leaving now?"

"As soon as I can get enough men together, but first I want either Rundy or Ox to tell me why Stacey was with Wade."

"In the meantime, you're letting the robbers get away."

"They won't get far. Bass can track anything with four feet, or two for that matter."

He was right. Bass was one of the best scouts in the business. After learning that Wade had told Ox and Rundy to make themselves scarce because he was planning to entertain Stacey that evening, Ed rounded up eight of his best hands. He left Pete Hatcher, the cook, in charge with just enough men to guard the livestock.

Bass made a torch and led the men off toward the hills. He picked up the trail quickly, despite the dark, but with only a torch to light the way, the going was slow.

Two miles up ahead, the four horsemen were quickly putting distance between themselves and anyone who might discover what they'd done. Cato and Harris knew these hills and they soon had the peaks of the Bannock mountain range in sight. The moon was just coming up as they left an old creek bed and moved up a draw toward the range of small peaks in the distance.

Stacey was hanging on to the saddle horn as hard as she could, trying to stay on the horse. With her hands tied and the horse stumbling in the dark, it was hard to stay seated. Jed Cato was leading her horse and Will Harris had Wade's reins, and neither man was being any too gentle. Wade protested loudly a couple of times, but it did little good. "Dammit!" he hollered at Harris as they moved across a scrub-covered clearing. "If you don't quit going so fast, I'm going to end up with a lame horse. Can't you slow down?"

"Nope!" growled Harris. He spurred his horse into a new burst of speed, and Wade bent low to try to soothe the harried animal.

It was well past midnight when Harris finally brought Wade's horse to a halt. Cato reined up Stacey's horse alongside his own.

"What now?" asked Cato breathlessly.

"We rest," said Harris. He dismounted, still holding the reins on Wade's horse.

"What about us?" Wade asked.

"What about you?"

"Don't we get a chance to stretch our legs?"

"Not yet," said Harris, tethering Wade's horse to a small tree. "You'll get your chance."

"When?"

"When I say so."

Wade glanced over at Stacey. The moonlight was turning her hair to a deep mahogany, and the sight brought a lump to his throat. He had had such marvelous plans for tonight. Soft cushions on his bed, a bottle of champagne served in long-stemmed glasses, and the rest . . . Just the thought made him tremble. Damn these insufferable bastards! All the money he had was in those saddlebags. He was losing his money and his woman. It wasn't fair. If he could just get his hands loose. . . .

Stacey glared at Wade. She was furious. This was all his fault. Damn him! It was a hot night and her clothes were sticking to her. She couldn't even brush the stray hair from her eyes. She threw her head back and blew at the hairs, but they didn't budge. She leaned down and rubbed her face across her tied hands, and the strands finally dislodged. Meanwhile, Cato fastened her reins to a tree about ten feet from Wade.

"I don't suppose you have any water," she said.

"Yeah, we got water," said Harris. "But not for you."

"That's what I thought." She licked her lips. They were dry and her mouth felt gritty.

They rested for a quarter of an hour; then the outlaws took turns moving off into the darkness to relieve themselves. They gave no thought to the fact that their captives might have to do the same. Stacey gritted her teeth as the horses once more bolted off into the night.

Far behind them, Bass was slowly but doggedly following the trail. It was a little past midnight when Ed called a halt and dismounted to confer with Bass.

"I think it'd be a good idea if we quit for tonight, Bass," he said. "You look tired. We can bed down here and start out fresh at dawn. You know yourself we can move faster in the daylight."

Ed was right. Bass's eyes were tired, and more than once the tracks had blurred before his eyes. It might not have been so bad if he hadn't been out all last night scouting ahead. He had figured on getting a few hours' sleep tonight, but instead, he was still on his feet, fighting to keep awake.

"A couple hours' sleep should do it, Ed," he said, hating to have to give up. "Besides, the men could probably use it, too."

They tethered their horses and spread out their bedrolls to grab a couple hours' sleep.

Ben spurred his horse into an easy canter. Ordinarily they stopped at nightfall, but since they were so close, Morgan insisted they keep moving. He couldn't stand to see Ben so restless, and Caroline was bitchier than usual.

Squinting his eyes in the darkness, Ben suddenly felt a strange thrill run through him. Campfires! The wagon train was dead ahead. He wanted to shout, yell, ride in swinging his hat in the air, but instead he stayed behind Sergeant Meade and rode in slowly.

It was close to eleven o'clock, and Morgan looked around curiously. People were wandering all over the place, and by the time they dismounted, a small crowd had gathered. Unusual for a wagon train. Usually everyone went to bed by eight or nine. At this hour, the camp should be deserted.

Pete had watched the strangers riding up, but it wasn't until they reached his wagon that he recognized Sergeant Morgan Meade from Fort Bridger.

"Well, I'll be damned. Meade!" he exclaimed. "What the hell are you doin' here? I thought the Indians got your scalp."

"Brought you a friend," Morgan said congenially. He motioned toward Ben.

Pete squinted, not quite certain of what he saw. Then his face went white. "Oh, my God! Ben Clayton?"

Ben looked down at the feisty cook. He shook Pete's hand as he glanced around. "What's going on, Pete?" he asked curiously.

"Oh, Lord," Pete said helplessly. "What am I goin' to tell you?"

"What are you talking about? Where's Stacey, Pete?"

"That's just it," said Pete, rattled. "She ain't here."

Ben's face fell. "She . . . ? What do you mean she isn't here? She was with the train at Fort Hall."

Suddenly a voice cut through the murmuring crowd. "Ben? Good heavens, Ben, is that you?"

Ben jerked around and stared in disbelief as Paula Tanner pushed her way through the crowd. She looked as shocked as Ben felt.

Her green eyes stared at him. It was Ben. He was wearing a mustache again, like he had when he first came back from the war. But it was Ben. She let out a sharp cry and started toward him with her arms outstretched.

Ben stared transfixed as Paula bolted toward him, then at the last moment, he forced himself to accept the fact that he wasn't seeing things and grabbed her to stop her from throwing herself into his arms.

"What the devil are you doing here?" he asked, frowning.

Feeling his hands holding her back, Paula flushed. "I wrote to you . . . sent you a telegram. You knew we were coming."

He glanced at the crowd. "Where's J.D.?"

Her voice broke. "He's dead . . . Oh, Ben, what's the matter . . . what's wrong? Aren't you glad to see me?"

He inhaled reluctantly, just as Caroline stepped up beside him.

Caroline stared at the blond woman and her blue eyes flickered irritably. "Well, another of your conquests, Ben?" she asked quietly.

This time Ben's face flushed crimson. "Caroline, this is my first wife Ann's sister, Paula Tanner. Paula, Caroline Jaquette, Mrs. Caroline Jaquette."

"Mrs.? And where is Mr. Jaquette?" Paula asked curtly.

"He passed away some months ago," Caroline offered.

Ben felt a little too uncomfortable as the air between the two women bristled. He turned to Paula. "You said J.D.'s dead?"

"There was a tornado back along the Platte River, near a place they call Ash Hollow. Of course, he might not have died if our wagon master hadn't been neglecting his duties with your wife."

Ben's eyes darkened. "What are you talking about?"

"She ain't talkin' about nothin'," said Pete quickly. "There wasn't nothin' anybody could do."

"Wasn't there?" asked Paula angrily. "If he'd been in camp he could have stopped my father and Mr. Bascomb from going into that wagon. But no, he had to spend the night in the woods making love to another man's wife."

"That ain't true!"

"Isn't it? You saw them come back the next morning. We all did.".

"They'd been captured by Indians."

"Now, wait a minute," Ben said quickly. "What the hell is this all about?"

Paula gazed at him with misty eyes, but it was hard to tell if the tears were real or meant to stir up sympathy. "I'll tell you what it's about. While everyone on the wagon train was fighting for their lives in the tornado that killed my father, Ed Larkin and your wife spent the night in the woods somewhere alone."

Ben's eyes narrowed as he turned from Paula to Pete. "Where's Ed?" he asked, his voice deepening.

"He ain't here, Ben," Pete answered.

"Where's my wife?"

Pete shifted his feet uncomfortably. "Stacey and a man named Wade Savagge were kidnapped earlier this evening. Ed's gone after them with Bass and some of the men."

Ben stared at Pete in disbelief. "What happened?"

"We don't rightly know. All we know is that Wade Savagge had a safe in his wagon. The safe is empty and Bass saw two of our hired hands headin' out of camp with Stacey and Wade tied to horses. He and Ed took eight men and went after them. They've been gone about an hour already. I'm supposed to take care of things until they get back."

Ben's thoughts were in a quandary. This wasn't the way it was supposed to be. Stacey was supposed to be here to meet him, and everything was supposed to be all right. He had waited so long.

Paula's voice cut into his thoughts and kindled his anger. "And the question, Ben, is what was your wife doing alone with Wade Savagge in his wagon? His aunt said the bed was made up nicely and there was a bottle of champagne set out. If you ask me, Stacey was having a cozy little *tête-à-tête* with Mr. Savagge."

"Nobody asked you!" Ben said through clenched teeth. He looked at Pete. "I want the answers from beginning to end, Pete," he said quickly.

Pete shrugged. "I'll try."

"You're damned right you'll try." He turned to Caroline and Sergeant Meade. "Take care of my horse, Morgan," he said. Caroline winced at the anger she saw in his eyes. "I'll be back." He turned to Pete. "Alone, Pete."

Reluctantly Pete pushed his way through the crowd. He stopped in front of a campfire and Ben stood beside him. But the crowd had followed them.

"Come on," Pete said briskly. "These yahoos ain't gonna let us be," and he led Ben out of the circle of wagons toward the livestock corral. He found a quiet spot away from prying ears and turned to Ben. "All right, I guess this is good enough."

"What's going on, Pete?" Ben asked, his voice heavy with emotion. "I got a telegram in Portland telling me Stacey was in Omaha. When I tried to reach her there, I learned she had joined Ed's train, but ever since I decided to come meet her, nothing's gone right. Now I'm not even sure I have a wife to take back to Oregon with me."

"What have you heard besides what Paula Tanner just said?" Pete asked curiously.

Ben told him about the gossip he had heard at Fort Bridger. "I heard she was singing in the gambler's saloon in Omaha."

"That she was," said Pete. "I heard her myself. In fact, that's where we ran into her. Ed, Bass, and myself had just arrived that mornin' and we was quenchin' our thirst at the new saloon, and there she was up on the stage singin' like a nightingale."

Ben frowned as Pete went on, telling him about the fire and how Stacey earned her passage by working for the Tanners.

"And that shrew gave her one hell of a time, too," Pete added.

"Why didn't Stacey work for somebody else?"

"There wasn't no one else needed anybody." Pete's eyes squinted knowingly. "All Stacey wanted, all she ever talked about, was when she was gonna see you again."

"If that's so, then why all the gossip?"

"You know how gossip is, Ben. You remember how it was the last time. There wasn't no truth to nothin' those folks were sayin', but that didn't keep them from sayin' it."

Ben stared off toward the camp. "Then you're telling me there's nothing to any of it? That it's all nothing but gossip?"

Pete hesitated just enough to make Ben suspicious.

"Pete, I want the truth. Is Ed messing around with my wife?"

"He ain't messin' around with her, Ben," he said. "No, sir. But they're friends. Real good friends."

"Like how good?"

Pete hated being put on the spot. Any fool could tell by the way Ed fawned all over Stacey that he was crazy about her. "I guess you could say he thinks a lot of her, Ben. But he always did, you know that. He's been sort of keepin' an eye on her for you, makin' sure that Savagge fella don't get out of hand. Now, if you're gonna start worryin', he's the one who's causin' her all the trouble. She's been havin' one hell of a time keepin' him in his place. Ed's only been tryin' to help. He wouldn't do nothin' to hurt her, or you."

"But they were alone all night during the storm?"

"Yep. They went for a walk and some Sioux jumped 'em. Sure they was gone all night, but that don't mean nothin' happened. That woman's so danged much in love with you she's been goin' through hell just to be with you, and now you got the nerve to go accusin' her—"

Ben's eyes hardened. "I didn't accuse her . . . it seems to be common knowledge."

"Well, it ain't common knowledge to me."

"You say this Savagge gent's been after Stacey?"

"He's been tryin' every way he can to get to her, but it ain't done him no good."

"Until tonight?"

"Just because Paula Tanner listens to gossip don't mean it has any meanin'. Sure, maybe he did think he was gonna entertain Stacey, but that don't mean she was goin' along with it."

"I wish that I could believe you, Pete," Ben said angrily. "But it isn't just what Paula said. It's everything."

"Don't make a mistake, Ben," Pete said. "Wait until you talk to Stacey, then judge for yourself what's what."

Ben frowned. "You say Ed's been gone about an hour?"

"About that." Pete glanced off toward the camp. "By the way," he said suspiciously. "Who's the lady rode in with you and Sergeant Meade, this Caroline what's-her-name?"

"Jaquette? She's my business partner's sister-in-law," Ben answered dryly. His stomach doubled into a big knot. Caroline! For a few minutes he had forgotten about Caroline. "Do you think maybe you can find her a place to stay tonight, Pete? We've been on the road since early morning, and I imagine she's tired by now."

Pete eyed him curiously. Ben's face was flushed and he was nervous. "How come she's with you?" Pete asked after a few minutes of silence.

"That, Pete, is my business," Ben replied curtly.

"Thought as much," Pete said candidly. "And you're accusin' Stacey? You better do some purgin' yourself, Ben Clayton. Because Stacey's gonna take one look at that woman and then you're gonna be answerin' the questions."

Ben's jaw tightened. Pete was right. Much as he hated to admit it, he had been no saint himself. But that was different. He had never expected to see Stacey again. "Thanks, Pete," he said quickly. "Now, let's get back to camp. I could do with some strong coffee."

It was just breaking dawn when Cato and Harris once more reined their horses to a halt and climbed from the saddle. This time, much to Wade and Stacey's surprise, they started untying their hands.

"You mean you're actually going to let us get off these damn horses?" asked Wade.

"Hey, look, we don't have to," Harris said roughly. "But we figured you and your lady friend might fare better with a little stretch."

Wade watched him closely, noting the relaxed way he carried himself. Will Harris was overconfident and that was bad, for Harris. Wade straightened in the saddle as his hands were freed. He rubbed them thoroughly to get the circulation going again, and glanced over at Stacey, who was doing the same thing.

"Come on, get down," ordered Harris.

Wade did as he was told. "Mind if I help the lady down?" he asked as his feet hit the ground.

Harris shrugged. "Go ahead."

Wade walked over and lifted his arms. Stacey practically fell into them. Every bone in her body ached, and she was certain she had blisters on her rear end from the unscheduled ride, and her bladder felt like it was about to burst.

For the first time since she met him, Wade's arms felt safe and secure. She buried her face in his chest. "I'm scared, Wade," she murmured, and his arms tightened about her.

"Shhhh . . . don't worry. They won't hurt us," he whispered. He glanced over at Harris and Cato, who were watching them, amused. "What now?" Wade asked huskily.

"Now we go take a leak, one at a time," Harris said, grinning. "Starting with me, then Cato, then you and the little lady." With that, he nodded to Cato, who pointed his gun directly at Stacey.

When they were all finished, they settled down to eat. Surprisingly, Harris gave both captives a sip of water and some jerky to chew on.

"How far do you think you can get before they discover what you've done?" Wade asked as he bit into the jerky.

Harris smiled. "Far enough." He motioned with his head toward a break in the mountains. "Beyond that's a trail down to Salt Lake City and a dozen places we can get lost in."

"And us?" asked Stacey.

Harris' eyes narrowed shrewdly. "Why, you're goin' with us. At least partway. With you two along, nobody would dare get too close. That's why we figured we'd better keep you alive for a while."

Wade stared at the man, once more noting how relaxed he was. Neither he nor Cato seemed too worried about their captives' abilities to do anything about their predicament. For the first time in hours, Wade felt a slim thread of hope. If they would just stay nonchalant and off guard . . . Both men's guns were lying across their laps, and although they kept watch on Stacey and Wade, there were moments when both men became lax.

Wade glanced toward the horizon, watching the early-morning sky turn red. Evening gray, morning red, sets the rain down on his head, he thought knowingly. But so far, no clouds were in sight.

He bit off a piece of jerky, pressing his arm against his black frock coat to feel the bulge in the inside pocket where he kept his small pistol. He wondered if Stacey had felt it when he helped her dismount. Cato and Harris had mistakenly figured that because Wade wasn't wearing his gunbelt, he was unarmed. They hadn't bothered to search him, but until now there had been no chance to use the small weapon.

Watching the two men across from him, Wade began to wonder. He was fast with the pistol and it wasn't a derringer with just one shot. It was a small pepperbox with five shots in it. He only had to slip it into his hand when they were off guard. As he continued to chew on his jerky, his eyes strayed to their two captors, who at the moment were arguing over who was going to take the next swig from their bottle of whiskey.

Wade's heart began to pound and his muscles tensed. Neither man was paying much attention to him and Stacey. Should he take the chance? Once he was back on the horse, he'd never be able to reach the small pistol. But what if he missed? His eyes narrowed slightly. He had to make a choice. And as he studied the two men, he knew he had to take the chance. After all, he had been up against worse odds before on the streets of New York and come out on top.

Gingerly he moved into a better position and lifted his hand, pretending to hang on to the jerky to bite off another piece. Instead, his other hand slipped into his frock coat and his fingers deftly clenched the butt of the small weapon. Inch by inch he pulled it from its hiding place, using the sleeve of his left arm to hide it as best he could, and with one quick movement, before Harris and Cato even realized what was happening, he had placed all five bullets into them. Both men, stunned, crumpled into a bloody heap, the bottle of whiskey spilling over them as they took a last strangled breath of air and then were still.

Wade leaped to his feet, ready to fight with his hands if either man was faking, but one look told him they were dead.

He turned at the sound of a strangled sob from behind him.

"Stacey?" He hurried to her. She was staring up at him, her mouth hanging open. He touched her chin and shut her mouth, then knelt on one knee before her. "Honey? It's all right, Red. We're all right now, they're dead."

She swallowed hard and found her voice. "Both of them?"

"Both of them."

She sighed. "Oh, my God! I didn't know what was happening."

"It was the first chance I had. I had to wait until they weren't watching us too closely."

"I thought I'd felt a gun earlier," she said. "But I thought it was a derringer and I knew a derringer would be useless against them."

"I learned a long time ago that when you gamble for a living, it doesn't do to use a derringer. Not when there are up to five men in a poker game," he explained. "I had this little job specially made," he said, hefting the small pistol with its wide, multiple barrel. It was still smoking and Stacey stared at it with distaste.

"It was the only way, honey," Wade said, seeing her shocked face.

Stacey had seen blood and death a hundred times over in the course of her work at the hospital, but this was something far different. She was a part of this, and her eyes misted over as she stared at Wade. "What do we do now?" she asked softly.

He pulled her to her feet. "We try to find our way back to camp." A low rumble filled the air, and he looked up at the sky, where a mass of dark clouds was forming on the horizon. He was right. Dawn was bringing rain, and the golden-red sunrise was quickly being replaced by swirling clouds. Streaks of lightning were tearing the sky apart, lighting up everything around them.

"We'd better get out of here," Wade said. "I can try to follow our tracks back, but if it rains hard enough, we'll lose them. We'll ride their horses." He helped Stacey mount. Her seat was still sore, and she hit the saddle reluctantly.

He was gentle with her and squeezed her arm affectionately as he handed her the reins, then as soon as she was settled on the horse, he walked over to the dead men. He took Cato's gunbelt and put it on, then shoved Harris' gun in his pants. Finally he mounted his horse.

"We're just leaving them here like that?" she asked.

He nodded, handing her the reins for one of the extra horses. "It's what they deserve," he said roughly. "I don't have a shovel to bury them, and it would take forever to find enough rocks to cover them. Besides, you don't think they were planning on letting us live, do you? Once they were in the clear, we'd have been crow bait instead of them."

"I know." She shuddered, looking at him hopefully. "Let's just get out of here."

He winked at her and dug his horse in the ribs, motioning for her to follow, and he began back tracking, following what he was sure was the way they had come earlier.

But Wade wasn't much of a woodsman. For the first half-hour or so he managed to follow their own fresh tracks, but then it began to rain. Before long the rain was coming down in heavy sheets, the wind whipping at them as they made their way between the mountains, following trails Wade was just guessing at now. There wasn't even anyplace to find shelter.

Some hours later, when the rain finally let up, Wade reined up, glanced about, and frowned.

Stacey pulled up behind him and wiped the wet hair from her tired eyes. "We're lost, aren't we?" she asked.

He hated to admit it. "I guess I took a wrong turn back somewhere."

"It's no wonder." She glanced up at the sky, watching the last dark clouds moving off toward the east, and shivered in her wet clothes. "I wish we could have found someplace to hole up while it rained."

He looked at her apologetically. "I know, you're tired and cold. Maybe I can spot someplace now that it's quit raining. I realize we're already wet, but we can at least catch a little sleep."

"That's all right. All I want to do is get back to camp as soon as possible."

Wade took a look at the landscape again, thoroughly confused. "Got any ideas which way we should go?" he asked.

Stacey was as much at a loss as he was. "All I know is we seemed to be heading southeast when we left camp. If we head northwest, we should reach either the camp, or the Snake River, or Fort Hall."

He smiled, his gray eyes twinkling at her. "Don't worry, we'll make it. But I insist we rest for a while, if we can find a place, so keep your eyes open."

For the next few hours they rode at a slow, even pace. Both they and the horses were tired, but every time Wade wanted to stop, Stacey insisted they go on.

Finally, as the sun began to sink below the horizon, Wade reined up near an overhang.

Stacey watched him dismount and walk toward her. Her eyes were heavy and she felt numb as he pulled her from the saddle and cradled her in his arms.

"Wade, we can't stop," she mumbled.

"Hush. You're ready to collapse."

He set her down on the soft grass beneath the overhang, and tied the horses to a nearby tree.

It was cool in the shade of the overhang, and although the hot sun had dried Stacey's clothes, she began to chill. Wade saw her tremble and put his frock coat on her, pulling it tightly around her faded yellow calico dress.

"Warmer?" he asked.

She nodded.

He gathered sticks and twigs and lit a fire, using some matches that had been in one of the saddlebags. Every muscle in his body ached and his stomach was so empty it was beginning to hurt. They had found some food in the saddlebags, but they had to dole it out sparingly since they had no idea how soon they'd reach help. And Wade wasn't much of a hunter. It was easy to hit a target as big as a man, but a little rabbit running through the underbrush was different.

As soon as the fire had caught, he slowly dropped to the ground next to Stacey. He stared at the small fire and leaned against the wall of earth behind him. "I'm sorry, Red," he said softly. "I never expected things to end up like this."

The heat from the fire was warming her and turning her numbness to a drowsy lethargy. She didn't even have the energy to answer him.

"Stacey?" he questioned.

"Mmmhmmmm . . . ?"

"Are you all right?"

"Mmmhmm . . ."

He watched her eyes close, and a flood of warmth enveloped him. He had to hold her, keep her safe. Slowly, gently, he pulled her into his arms.

Stacey felt Wade's arms enfold her and tried to protest, but she had no strength left. She was tired, so tired, and Wade's arms felt soft and warm. She curled up against him and let sleep claim her.

Wade held Stacey close, listening to her soft, steady breathing. He knew she was oblivious of where she was and whom she was with. But he knew. God, yes, he knew. His arms tightened around her and he rested his lips against her forehead. She was his. For a few hours, no one could take her from his arms, and as darkness surrounded them, his eyes closed too, and he slept the sleep of the dead.

Up in the hills to the southeast of them some five or six miles, Bass, Ed, and the rest of the men had come onto a grisly scene. They had lost the trail during the storm, but had kept moving southeast anyway. It wasn't until after the sun came back out and they saw vultures that they knew they were on the right track. Afraid of what he might find, his heart in his mouth, Ed rode toward the vultures.

What they did discover was a total shock. Stacey and Wade were nowhere in sight. Instead, the bodies of the two hired hands were covered with flies and bugs, and the vultures had already begun to claim their portion.

Ed studied the dead men for a long time before giving orders to have the bodies covered with rocks, then he and Bass walked to the other side of the clearing and gazed toward the lowering sun.

"Evidently Wade's a better man with a gun than I thought," Ed said thoughtfully.

"Where do you think they went?" Bass asked.

"Lost, I imagine. Neither Wade nor Stacey knows their way around in the wilderness."

"You think they got enough brains to head northwest?"

"Maybe . . . maybe not." He glanced at the sun. "We got about two hours before dark, and I sure as hell don't intend to go back until we find them," he said. "So we better get started now."

After covering the bodies with rocks, Ed and his men mounted up. One of the men suggested they take the bodies back, but since Ed was the law out on the trail, he couldn't see any reason for it. After all, it was obvious what must have happened. His only concern now was that two greenhorns were lost in the mountains, and one of them was a woman he cared for deeply.

Bass took the lead once more, beginning to backtrack down the slope. Ed hoped to God Bass could pick up their trail before dark, but it didn't work out that way.

They had only covered three miles when night caught them and they were forced to camp beside a small stream. They built a fire to keep away the animals and shared the little food they had brought with them.

Bass set the horses to graze near the edge of the stream, then turned to Ed, who was sitting next to the fire rolling a cigarette. Ed was trying not to show how upset he was, but Bass had been with him long enough to know that he was really worried. They had no idea how much food Stacey and Wade had with them, and these hills were hard enough for experienced men to challenge.

"Don't worry, Ed, we'll find them," Bass assured him.

Ed took a deep drag off his cigarette. "I hope so, Bass. And I'm glad Stacey's not out here in these mountains alone, but, dammit, does she have to be with that man!"

Bass gave Ed a startled look. "You don't think he'll try anything, do you?"

Ed threw his cigarette into the fire. "Well, I'll tell you, Bass, if he so much as lays a hand on her, he's going to be the sorriest gambler this side of the Mississippi. Now, let's get some sleep." But sleep was hard to come by. All Ed could think of was Stacey somewhere out there in the darkness with Wade Savagge.

It was still dark out, but the edges of dawn were creeping up on the horizon. The fire had burned low and only a few glowing embers remained.

Wade stirred restlessly, his arms still around Stacey. He opened his eyes groggily, and for a minute he thought he was still dreaming. The ground was hard, and he felt stiff. Something was poking him between the shoulder blades. He shifted his position, trying not to wake Stacey. But when he moved, she stirred and snuggled close again. His breathing quickened.

It felt so good to hold her in his arms like this without her protesting, and the warmth of her body against his was slowly bringing him back to life.

Stacey was warm and cozy as she awakened from what seemed like a drugged sleep. She savored the heat from Wade's body, not realizing at first where she was or what was happening. All she knew was that for the first time in months, the emptiness inside her was gone. A warm glow began to spread within her, and without thinking, she reveled in it, then she gradually opened her eyes and stared into Wade's warm face. "Wade . . . ?"

His hand caressed her face, the fingers teasing, and her heart skipped a beat.

"Please . . . Wade!" She was still groggy, but she knew she shouldn't be here. Only, her protests didn't seem to be doing much good, because he didn't stop.

His hand moved to her neck and shoulders and he slowly unbuttoned the front of her calico dress. When she tried to stop him, his mouth suddenly covered hers. He sipped at her lips tenderly, teasing them with each touch as he murmured her name over and over again.

Her breast was warm beneath his hand as he slipped it under her bra, feeling the nipple harden in his fingers, and Stacey's head was reeling, her body responding wantonly to what he was doing. She didn't want this, and yet she did. Her heart screamed for Ben, but her body cared little who was serving it, tantalizing it with memories of other loves. As his arms eased from about her and he laid her on the ground, she wanted to die. She felt his warm, electric hand covering her torso beneath the bodice of her dress, and she tried to fight the feelings he was arousing with every ounce of her strength. Nothing worked. Her body was betraying her, throbbing with want and need. Tears came to her eyes.

His hand moved beneath the folds of her skirt and stroked her thighs with passionate caresses as his mouth continued to take the lifeblood from her lips, his tongue penetrating the deep, sweet fullness of her mouth.

Stacey was lost. She hadn't felt like this since the last time Drew had made love to her, and suddenly she couldn't take it anymore. All the fight, all the strength, was suddenly drained from her and she moaned helplessly.

Wade reached down and unfastened his pants, making room for his swollen manhood. Then deftly he pulled her nylon briefs down, and with one quick movement his body covered hers, his lips nuzzling her neck. He started to lower himself, ready to plunge into her; then suddenly he stopped, his body poised, yet tense.

She was crying. Not just little whimperings or murmurings that would have had little, if any, effect on him. She was sobbing pitifully, as if her heart were breaking, as if she were in terrible pain.

Wade lifted his head from her neck and stared down into her face as the faint light of dawn crept into the sky.

As Wade watched the tears streaming down her face and heard the sobs wrenched from deep within her, something inside him rebelled, and without warning, he felt himself soften, and there was nothing he could do.

"Stacey, honey, what is it?" he gasped breathlessly. But she was beyond answering, beyond feeling. Her body was limp, the fight gone from it.

For the first time in her life Stacey had given up. She had no strength to fight the world anymore. She was crying not only because of the moment, but also because of all the anger, hurt, and frustration she had suffered through the past months. For Drew's betrayal and losing her daughters. For Paula's viciousness and Pearl's anger. And now for Wade's invasion of her body. But most of all she was crying because she wanted the man above her to be Ben. It would be so easy to close her eyes and pretend he was here with her, yet deep in her heart she knew he wasn't.

"Red, honey, I can't do anything when you're crying like this," Wade whispered fervently. "God, honey, don't cry. Please don't cry." But Stacey was unable to stop the sobbing, and because of it Wade's body had suddenly become a useless tool.

There wasn't a woman on the face of the earth he couldn't make love to as long as she was willing, but it only took tears to reduce him to nothing. Ever since that night years ago when he had made love to a girl and discovered it was her first time only when she began screaming at the top of her lungs, he had been like this. Tears were a sign of pain, and he couldn't hurt any woman in this way. His body was to be enjoyed, not dreaded.

He stared down at Stacey, whose pain hurt as deeply as any physical pain could, and he shuddered and slipped from her. Shoving his softened member back inside his clothes, he wrapped his arms about her and tried to soothe her. Damn, he never thought she'd carry on like this.

Stacey felt the withdrawal of Wade's body, and the sobs that were racking her body became murmuring protests. "Oh, Wade, I want Ben, I need Ben, I can't go on like this, so torn inside."

Wade kissed her lightly on the mouth and sat up, his back to her.

She had defeated him, and he had been so sure he would win. Had she known what tears would do to him? He glanced back into her blue eyes. They were looking up at him now in wonder, and her body was trembling with the violence of everything that had happened.

"You win," he said finally, his eyes snapping aggressively. "You know that, don't you? You win, Red." He stared at the dying ashes of the fire as a gentle breeze reached them and dawn filtered in among the mountains and trees.

It was over. His only chance at making love to her, and it had turned into a sham. He stared hard at the fire, sensing her movement behind him. He heard her sniff, gulping back a sob.

"Wade . . . ?" Her voice was unsteady. "I'm sorry, I didn't know . . . I couldn't . . . Not like that . . . I'd rather have you rape me than do what you were doing."

He turned to her, his eyes still passionately alive. "I couldn't rape you if I wanted to, Stacey. It takes a cruel man to force a woman. I've never forced one in my life."

"You still have Pearl."

"Pearl?" He laughed bitterly. "Even with your nose all sunburned and your face all dirty, you're more than she can compare with, Red," he said softly. He turned to her quickly, moving onto his knees and pulling her up by the shoulders. He had to try, just one more time. "Come with me, Red," he whispered softly, his eyes searching her face. "When we get back to camp, leave that nasty bitch you work for and come to Virginia City with me. Please, Red. I'll give you the sun and moon, the stars if you want them. You don't even have to deal faro if you don't want to. All you have to do is be around for me to love."

Stacey felt his urgent longing, and her heart sank. "I don't love you, Wade. I never could."

"I don't care. My love can be enough for both of us. Please, Red. The first time I laid eyes on you, I knew I'd found someone special." His face grew solemn, and she trembled. "I'm going to ask you once more, Red, and only once more."

"And if I still say no?"

"Then I'll never ask again." His lips spoke for him as he kissed her long and sensuously, until she was breathless. Then he drew his mouth from hers. "Please, Red," he whispered in anticipation.

"No, Wade, I can't. I'm going to Ben. He's my life, my love, and I'll not settle for less."

His hands fell from her shoulders and he sat back on his heels, staring at her. He had promised to abide by her decision, but it hurt. Quickly he avoided her eyes and stood up, staring out into the warm sunshine that was evaporating the steam from the damp morning mists.

"At least it looks like we have a nice day for traveling," he said. He tried to make his voice sound normal, but Stacey was all too aware of the strain in it.

She stood up, wincing as she put all her muscles into play again, and realized she still had his black frock coat wrapped around her. She watched him get some food from the saddlebags and bring it back for her.

"Here, madam. Your morning biscuit," he said, forcing a hint of playfulness into his voice.

She ate the biscuit while she watched him, feeling a twinge of regret. Wade wasn't that bad, not really. At times there was a violent streak that forced its way into the open, but deep down, he was like a little boy. He only fought and struck out at things because he felt the world had handed him a raw deal. No, Wade wasn't all bad, but there was a little too much larceny in his heart for Stacey to be able to love him. Even now she didn't really trust him.

When they were through with the biscuits, they left the overhang and headed northwest. With their extra horses in tow, they searched the landscape for a familiar landmark that would tell them they were heading in the right direction.

They had been riding for about an hour when Wade reined up and cocked his head, his eyes on the hills above them. As Stacey reined in, she too heard the voice. It was coming from somewhere in the mountains above. Wade glanced at Stacey with hard eyes, trying to mask the disappointment he felt.

It wasn't just losing the bargain with Paula. It was much more than that. He had been so sure. He had known Stacey had been attracted to him right from the start, and he'd been so certain he could make her forget her husband. A man she hadn't seen for almost a year. But he had failed and now he cursed himself. He hadn't even kept his vow to make her pay for the Paradise. He was a fool, a stupid lovesick fool. Turning from her as she searched for the source of the voice, he knew it was over.

He shaded his eyes from the morning sun and squinted, searching the landscape. Finally he pointed, and Stacey followed the direction of his finger.

Far above them, descending the side of the green mountain, she saw a group of horsemen. It was hard to recognize anyone at first, but as they drew nearer Stacey breathed a sigh of relief.

Ed and Bass rode the lead horses, followed by a number of hands from the wagon train. She watched them descend, waving to them and thanked God that she wasn't going to have to spend another night alone in these hills with Wade Savagge.

CHAPTER 22

Ben was wearing out the grass in front of the campfire at Ed's wagon. Pete had let Caroline bunk inside, and Ben had slept under the wagon with Pete.

Ben had spent the day before pacing restlessly, wishing Sergeant Meade would give in and head into the hills with him. But later, when dark clouds had rolled out of the northwest, bringing heavy rains, Ben had been glad Meade had had sense enough to stay with the wagon train.

Now Ben was pacing again. He stopped momentarily and glanced at Caroline, who was talking to an older woman about Oregon. Ben turned toward Wade's wagon. He wished he knew what the hell was going on. Pete had assured him that Stacey had been faithful and that the rumors were only rumors, but there was more to it than that. There had to be. Why else would that woman named Pearl, the one everyone referred to as Wade's woman, have tried to knife Stacey? Pete hadn't even mentioned the incident. Ben wouldn't have known about it at all if Caroline hadn't brought it up while they were huddled in the wagon yesterday, sitting out the storm.

He watched Caroline from a distance. Watched the sun gleaming on her red hair, watched the animated way she had of talking. Her wit brought a glow to her pale blue eyes, and he remembered the first time he had seen her, when he had been reminded of Stacey. But she was nothing like Stacey. No woman was. He closed his eyes and conjured up a mental picture of Stacey as he had last seen her. He was so torn and mixed up inside. Caroline had to be wrong; everyone had to be wrong. Stacey wasn't the sort of woman they were making her out to be. There had to be some other explanation for the rumors and gossip. There just had to be!

As he stood with his eyes closed, the late-afternoon sun hot on his face, he suddenly heard excited voices. His eyes flew open as Pete called to him. ''They're back, Ben!'' he yelled as he ran

cross the encampment, motioning for Ben to follow. "Come
n. They're comin' down out of the hills."

Minutes later Ben stood beside Pete on the outer edge of the
ncampment, where a crowd had gathered to watch as a group of
iders, barely the size of ants at first, wound their way down
rom the surrounding hills.

Pete stood on one side of Ben, Caroline on the other, but Ben
vas oblivious of both of them as he counted the horses inching
heir way down from the mountains. Ed had taken Bass and eight
ther men, but now there were a dozen riders in view. He held
is breath. Was one of the other two Stacey? Or was he too late?
he thought that something might have happened to her had
ickened him more than once during the long wait. To lose her
gain would be too hard to take.

Suddenly he saw a telltale flash of red beneath the hat of one
f the riders. His heart did a flip that weakened his knees, and
is six-foot-four frame trembled.

She was all right! She was astride, riding on her own. He
vaited anxiously, his heart in his eyes as the riders reached the
pen field only a short distance away, then prodded their horses
ito a canter and rode in.

Stacey was tired and weary. The sun hurt her eyes, and she'd
ave given almost anything for a pair of sunglasses. But Bass's
at was all she had, and every bone in her body ached, not
ounting what she was certain were blisters on her rear end. Her
gs, still bare, were full of scratches and bug bites. She was
ertain she was the sorriest sight anyone could see. She was still
rapped in Wade's frock coat, to help keep her arms from
unburning, and was riding beside Ed, with Wade on her right.

"Looks like we got a welcoming committee," said Ed as he
aw the people lined up waiting.

She glanced over at him. From the moment they had been
escued, she had felt the tension between Ed and Wade. She had
ssured Ed that Wade had behaved like a gentleman, but she
new he didn't believe her. Well, that was their problem. All she
anted now was to go to her wagon, get some food in her
omach, and get off this damned horse.

As they neared the camp, Stacey's eyes searched the waiting
rowd. Suddenly they stopped on the man standing next to Pete.
e was tall, so tall he towered over everyone else, and there was
omething about his stance, the broad shoulders, the familiar
ay he tilted his head. She reined in her horse and Ed slowed
eside her.

"Ed?" she asked, her voice breaking. "Didn't you say the last time you saw Ben he was wearing a mustache?"

Ed nodded and squinted at the figure of the man. The sun was silhouetting the crowd, and Stacey couldn't see the man's face as clearly as she wanted, but she was so sure. She licked her lip nervously, dug her horse in the ribs, and broke into a quick canter again. She didn't take her eyes off the man, but moved forward anxiously, her heart pounding.

It was Ben! It was! She let out a strangled cry, spurring her horse on into a full gallop, with only one thought in mind as she left the others behind. Suddenly she reached him, yanked up on the reins, and stared incredulously into his face as tears streamed down her cheeks.

"Ben! Oh, my God, it *is* you!" she cried fervently. Their eyes met, a brief moment of startled recognition passing vibrantly between them; then she fell toward him.

His arms wound around her, holding her close, and he felt the heat of her passion and the warmth and love that glowed between them, and his heart swelled. It was as if the months of separation had never been, as if they had always been together, and he was filled with a wonder that brought a throbbing to his loins. Her hands touched the sides of his face and she held his head between them, reveling in the feel of his flesh beneath her palms. This was Ben, her beloved Ben!

They didn't even realize it, but all eyes were on them now, including Caroline's, and for the first time since she had been introduced to Ben Clayton, Caroline began to understand what this woman meant to him, and it hurt.

There was nothing hidden that wasn't revealed in the look that passed between the two of them, and as Stacey stared into Ben's dark eyes, his mouth caught hers in a feverent kiss.

Ed and Wade dismounted slowly, watching the amorous reunion. Moments later, when Ben finally drew his mouth from Stacey's, he suddenly became aware of the people around him and let his arms ease from about her, setting her down so her feet touched the ground.

Glancing down at Stacey, he slowly began to regard her in a critical light. She was a complete mess. Her hair was curling riotously, her face was dirty, her dress torn and dirty, and she was wearing a man's black frock coat. He glanced up toward the men who had dismounted, his eyes falling quickly on the only man among them who could own the coat.

The man had dark curly hair and gray eyes. His mouth was somewhat cynical above the fancy ruffles of his white shirt. He wore a gray satin vest and gray pants that fit all too well over his muscular frame. This, then, had to be Wade Savagge. Ben felt a jealous twinge settling in his breastbone like a lead weight.

He straightened to his full height and gazed back down at Stacey.

She clutched her hat tightly and looked up at Ben, still hardly believing he was standing next to her, and tears welled up in her eyes again. She smiled uneasily. "I look terrible," she said self-consciously. She saw Ben's eyes sift over her. She touched the front of her dress and the lapels of Wade's coat and frowned. She had forgotten she still had it on. Slipping her arms from it, she turned and gave it to Wade. As he took it, his eyes caught hers, and Stacey's jaw tightened. "Wade, I'd like you to meet my husband, Ben Clayton. Ben, this is Wade Savagge. If it hadn't been for Wade," she added quickly. "we might still be out there with those two horrible men."

Ben's eyes darkened. "And if I'm not mistaken, Mr. Savagge," Ben said roughly as he looked at Wade, refusing to shake hands, "if it hadn't been for you, my wife wouldn't have been out there in the first place. Am I right?"

Wade flushed. Damn! The man certainly didn't mince words. His eyes narrowed shrewdly. Maybe things weren't so cozy after all. He flung the coat over his arm. "And if the lady's willing?" he asked flippantly.

"Wade!" Stacey was mortified.

Ignoring Ben, he smiled at her; and his eyes sparkled mischievously. "At least it was fun while it lasted, Red," he said casually.

He was brought up short by Ben's harsh voice. "Apologize to my wife, sir!" he said curtly.

Wade hesitated. "What for?"

Ben's eyes danced menacingly. "For giving these people the impression there's been more between you and Stacey than simple friendship."

Wade's eyes gleamed. "And I, sir, think you should have a long talk with the wife you haven't seen for almost a year." His jaw tensed stubbornly, and he grabbed the two saddlebags that contained his money. "Now, if you don't mind, Mr. Clayton, I have things to do," and he walked away, strolling determinedly toward Aunt Lil and the others who were waiting for him anxiously.

Ben took a step, as if to go after Wade, but Ed intervened.

"Drop it, Ben," he said. "Don't you know he's just goading you? You're doing just what he wants you to do." Ed glanced around at the crowd and waved his arms for them to disperse "All right, everybody, back to your own wagons. It's all over The two men who robbed Mr. Savagge are dead, he's got hi money back, and both he and Stacey Clayton are still alive, s there's no reason for anymore concern. Come on, let's let Mr and Mrs. Clayton have a little breathing room.''

The crowd reluctantly began to break up. As they did, Stacey noticed one woman in particular whom she'd never seen before Instead of moving away, the woman held her ground next t Ben. Meanwhile, Ed had turned back to Ben.

"Ben, glad to see you,'' Ed said as he shook his hand. "It's hell of a shock, but your timing's fine. Stacey can use a goo shoulder to cry on.''

Ben took Ed's hand reluctantly. "I hear she's been usin yours until now,'' he said abruptly.

Ed quickly let go of Ben's hand. "Well, God damn, Ben,'' h said heatedly. "What can you expect? She's been through hel and back. What happened to her is enough of a burden to bea without having to face it alone. Don't begrudge me having th chance to help a friend, please.''

Ben stared at him hard. "You know what's happened to her?' he asked, not certain whether Ed knew the truth.

"She'll tell you all about it,'' Ed said, displeased at th jealousy apparent in Ben's attitude toward him. But he coul understand. To love a woman like Stacey wasn't the easiest thin in the world. He turned his head as a sultry voice suddenly spok from beside Ben.

"Well, so this is your precious wife,'' Caroline said, lookin Stacey over carefully.

Ben flushed crimson. He'd forgotten Caroline even existed She was still wearing her men's clothes, and her pale blue eye looked Stacey over carefully, challenging her.

"Who are you?'' asked Stacey.

Caroline smiled. Stacey's face was dirty, her hands callused her nails chipped, and she was anything but presentable after he ordeal. Even so, it was obvious that it would take little to brin out the best in her.

Ben straightened uncomfortably as he looked at Stacey. "Stacey this is Caroline Jaquette. Caroline, my wife, Stacey Clayton.''

Stacey nodded, staring hard at the other woman. "And jus who is Caroline Jaquette?'' she asked curiously.

Ben's flush deepened. "I've bought into a lumber company i Portland,'' he explained hurriedly, feeling the tension that wa

uilding between the two women. "Mrs. Jaquette's a widow,
ny partner's sister-in-law."

Stacey inhaled sharply. "I see you've had a shoulder to cry on
oo," she said bluntly, and Ben regarded her with guilty eyes.

"I think the two of you better do like Wade suggested, and
ave a long talk," said Ed uncomfortably.

Ben stared into Stacey's blue eyes. They were suddenly alive
ith hostility.

"Maybe we'd better," he said apprehensively. He took Stacey's
rm and headed toward Ed's wagon.

"If you don't mind, I'd like to clean up a little," Stacey said,
hanging her direction. "My clothes are in the Tanner wagon. I
ssume by now you know Paula's on the train too."

"I've talked to her."

"I can see that. From the remarks you've been throwing
round, I assume she was quite a bundle of information. But of
ourse, Paula's always willing to enhance what I do with her
wn little imaginings."

"She didn't imagine the bottle of champagne they found in
Vade Savagge's wagon," he protested angrily. "And she didn't
ake up the story he told those weird characters who work for
m, about not bothering him so he could entertain you without
eing disturbed. And I'm sure as hell she couldn't order that
asanova to say what he said back there either."

"Good heavens, Ben!" she cried furiously. "Certainly he
inks he's in love with me. I don't deny that, but as Ed said, he
as just trying to get a rise out of you back there, that's all."

"And that's another thing," snapped Ben. "I didn't just get
y information from Paula Tanner. Everyone on this train seems
 think there's some sort of special bond between you and Ed
arkin. What's the matter, Stacey, couldn't you even wait for
e?" he asked bitterly.

She stopped. They were at the Tanner wagon, and she sud-
enly felt cold, all alone, and empty inside. She gazed up into
en's angry eyes, her own filled with tears. "I thought you
anted to talk," she said helplessly.

"I do."

"No, you don't. You want to argue and accuse. Well, I don't
ink this is the time," she burst out furiously. "I'm tired, upset,
nd at this point I don't even feel human, and I'm liable to do or
y something I'll regret for the rest of my life. So if you don't
ind, I'm going to go in the wagon, clean up, and try to calm
yself down. Then maybe we can talk."

"Stacey . . . ?"

"No, Ben," she insisted stubbornly, tears rolling down her cheeks. "I've given everything up to come back to you because love you, and I thought you loved me. So I didn't do thing right, so I made mistakes, but I did wait for you, Ben. No matter what you hear, what anyone says, I did wait for you." She let out a hard sob, gulping back. "Now, let me go. We'll talk later when I can think straight."

She turned from him abruptly and hurried into the wagon. She dropped onto the floor in a heap, and sobs almost strangled her as they burst forth.

Ben watched her go, his heart in a turmoil. His head was reeling from the hurt he had seen in her eyes, yet he couldn't completely dismiss everything he had heard. Nor could he forget the arrogant look on Wade Savagge's face when he had flaunted his intimacy with Stacey in front of everyone.

He straightened stubbornly, tears filling the corners of his own eyes, and turned quickly on his heel. He headed toward Wade wagon. There were a few things he was going to get settled once and for all.

By the time he reached Wade's wagon, his tears had been replaced by a cold reserve that had masked his feelings more than once over the years.

Wade had returned the money to the safe and was standing by the fire drinking a cup of hot coffee and telling the girls about what had happened, when Ben walked up.

"Mr. Savagge?" Ben said sternly. "I'd like to talk to you, if may."

Wade studied him closely. Ben's dark eyes were smoldering and his jaw was tense, but his fists weren't clenched and his fingers weren't itching near his gun butt, so Wade nodded. "Anytime," he said cautiously.

Ben glanced around at Aunt Lil and the girls. "Alone, if you don't mind."

Wade took a sip of coffee and wandered off toward the wagon where Pearl was still bedded down.

When they were out of earshot, Wade glanced once more Ben. "Care for some coffee?" he asked.

"No, thanks. This isn't a social visit."

Wade shrugged. "What's on your mind?"

"You know damn well what's on my mind," exclaimed Ben "I want to know exactly how close your friendship is with Stacey."

"I suppose if I tell you, you'll challenge me and we'll have prove who's the better man," Wade said casually. "But I'd better warn you, sir, I know how to use a gun."

"So do I," Ben assured him. "But I didn't come here to kill you. All I want is the truth."

"The truth?" Wade's mind was working furiously. If he could convince Stacey's husband that he had made love to her, there was every chance Paula was right and he would turn her out. Maybe then she'd accept his offer to go to Virginia City. He had to try just one more time. He couldn't give in without fighting for her, even if he had to fight dirty. "The truth is, Mr. Clayton," he began confidently, "that your wife found my charms quite adequate as a substitute for your own. We spent the night alone out there in the hills, sir, and she gave herself to me willingly. When it was over, I asked her to give up this stupid notion of hers to chase you all the way to Oregon. She declined. Loyalty, duty, I don't know what she has in mind, but believe me, sir," he lied unabashedly, "I'm certain, given the chance, and free of you, she'd gladly go to Virginia City with me."

Ben stared at him, dumbfounded. An empty, hollow feeling seeped into him, the pain of loss so strong it hurt. Then he frowned, remembering the look in Stacey's eyes when she had insisted she had remained faithful. "You're lying!" he snarled viciously.

Wade sneered. "Am I? How do you know for sure. Think it over. You've been separated for a long time and she's a passionate woman. How long did you think she could live without a man to give her the love she needs?"

Ben stared at Wade furiously, then without saying another word, he walked away, only to run into Ed a few wagons down the line. Ed was making rounds, telling everyone they would be leaving first thing in the morning.

Ed saw the troubled look on Ben's face and noted that he was coming from Wade's wagons. He cursed softly to himself, wondering what Wade might have told Ben.

"Where's Stacey?" Ed asked anxiously as he joined Ben.

"She's getting cleaned up."

"How did the talk go?"

"Not too well the first time around, I'm afraid."

"What's the matter with you, Ben?" Ed asked heatedly. "What the hell do you want from Stacey anyway?"

"I want the truth."

"Such as?"

"If she's still in love with me, Ed, why did she let Wade Savagge make love to her?" he said bitterly.

"Who says he did?"

"He does."

"The man's a liar."

"Is he? How do you know? Were you there?"

"In a way, yes." Ed's eyes were intent on Ben's face. "Since you haven't heard the whole story yet, I'll tell you, Ben. Stacey told me Wade tricked her into going to his wagon by telling her Pearl needed her. That's why she happened to be with him when he was robbed. The kidnapping was an afterthought. The two men who did the job figured Stacey and Wade would make good hostages. Fortunately they hadn't searched Wade, and he had a small gun hidden in his coat. He got the drop on them while they were arguing over a bottle of whiskey. True, they were alone in those hills before we found them, and it's true I wasn't with them then, but when I asked Stacey if Wade had forced himself on her, I believed her when she said no."

"He says he didn't have to force her. That she was willing."

"Hogwash!" Ed exclaimed. "Ben, Stacey told me where she's from originally. Now, come with me and I'll tell you something I think you ought to know." He looked directly into Ben's eyes, hoping that what he was about to tell him would ease some of his heartache. He took Ben back to his wagon, then proceeded to tell him Stacey's story. He explained about how she had ended up back in the same swimming pool in the future and the events that followed when she tried to pick up her old life again. Ed even told Ben about her husband's betrayal and her sudden journey back again into the past.

"She told me about that diary, too, Ben. The way you wrote in it every day after she was gone, and how it kept her going when she thought she was at the end of her rope."

"It seems she confided in you a great deal," Ben said belligerently.

Ed still sensed Ben's hostility. "She had to have someone, Ben. Do you realize how hard it's been for her? She had to put up with Paula's outrageous demands, and folks don't really understand her, Ben. You know that. She talks different than they do, says things they don't understand. It's the same thing she went through before all over again. She's not like other women, Ben. We both know it, and other people sense it."

"She claims she waited for me."

"She did."

Ben eyed Ed suspiciously. "Wade isn't the only man whose name has been linked with Stacey's Ed," he finally said. "And I think you know what I mean."

"You've been talking to Paula."

"And a few others."

"Nothing happened, Ben," Ed said convincingly. "Not that it wouldn't have been nice if it had. I think the world of Stacey, you know that."

"You're in love with her!"

"All right, in my own way, yes," he confessed. "I guess maybe I am, but I've loved a lot of women over the years. I'll get over it. The important thing is that she doesn't love me. She's your wife. Who are you going to believe, Ben, a man whose scruples are less than honorable? A woman whose sense of decency doesn't even extend to her own sister's husband? I heard the way Paula Tanner chased you, even while her sister was alive. Or are you going to believe a woman who's given up everything for you? Her husband, children, the life she was born to. Why do you think God sent her back here? To betray you? So help me, Ben, even if her body were starved for love, she'd never willingly let any other man touch her. I know."

Ben saw the truth in Ed's eyes, and something more. "You tried to make love to her, didn't you?" he asked hesitantly.

"Yes, dammit, I tried," Ed half-whispered. "If you could even call it that. It didn't start out that way, Ben, honestly it didn't," he explained. "But when the tornado hit, I found an overhang on the riverbank, that was just big enough to hold the two of us if I covered her and sheltered her from the storm. So help me, Ben, I didn't want to feel what I did, nor did she, but we're only human. I wanted her, yes. I don't know if it was me she wanted, or just to feel a man's arms again, but we were both so . . . It would have been so easy . . . That's why I say Wade Savagge is a liar. Stacey no more gave herself to him in those hills than she gave herself to me on that riverbank. You're the only man she'll ever give herself to willingly, Ben. The only one."

Ben stared long and hard at Ed, startled by his confession, and accepting it with mixed emotions. He was furious because Stacey had let another man touch her, yet relieved because it had gone no further. Had Wade lied? After all, the episode on the riverbank had been months ago, and Ed didn't possess the same suave charm that exuded from Wade Savagge. He didn't know whom to believe.

"I'll have to think it over," he said bitterly, then turned away. He walked off toward the livestock corral, where he could watch the sun go down and try to decide what to do. There was no doubt that he loved Stacey, but was he going to be able to forgive her if Wade was telling the truth?

Meanwhile Stacey had picked herself up from the floor of the wagon, dried her eyes, and let the numbness set in. She was like a lost soul as she took off the yellow calico dress, poured water into the washbasin, and began to wash up. Now and then tears rimmed her eyes and she would sniff them back, determined to keep them from overpowering her. She clenched her teeth angrily. All this, and for what? How could Ben say he loved her and not believe her? Had he changed? Or maybe she had changed. What was the matter, anyway?

Suddenly anger replaced her self-pity and she tightened her jaw stubbornly. Who the heck did he think he was, anyway? She had come all this way to be with him, and he turned on her like this. Damn his stubborn pride, anyway.

She finished washing, slipped on fresh petticoats, and looked around for something to wear. She had three clean outfits left: the turquoise dress, her russet blouse and the old skirt Amos had given her, and the navy-blue dress she had bought in Cleveland. She had been saving it to wear when she arrived in Oregon, so Ben could see her at her best. But she was just ornery enough, now, after his unfair criticism, to strike back. Making a quick decision, she reached for the turquoise dress.

Caroline had watched the angry exchange between Ben and Stacey, seen Stacey's tearful departure into the Tanner wagon, and observed Ben's visit to Wade's wagon. She knew all wasn't well. When Ben finally met up with Ed, she knew by the look on his face that with each new accusation, his precious wife was losing esteem in his eyes. She still wanted Ben in spite of the strong feelings she knew he had for Stacey. So while Ben was with Ed, Caroline decided it was time she had a little talk with his wife. As Stacey tried to fasten her dress up the back, a soft, sultry voice from the other side of the wagon offered to do it for her.

"Here, let me help," said Caroline congenially. Stacey's fingers froze on the hooks. She had completely forgotten about the redhead who faced her now.

"If you'd like," Stacey said curiously.

Caroline fastened the dress while Stacey watched her in the mirror hanging over the washbasin. Caroline Jaquette was pretty. Her blue eyes were pale, more like the sky than the sapphires in Stacey's eyes. Was she traveling with Ben? She had to be. How did he introduce her? As a widow? His partner's sister-in-law?

For the moment Stacey's tears were replaced by suspicion as she closely examined this lovely woman who was wearing a tight pair of men's pants that emphasized every curve.

"Thank you," Stacey said hesitantly as Caroline finished fastening the dress. Her lips forced a half-smile. "You're traveling with my husband?"

Caroline smiled back. "You mean it finally dawned on you?"

Stacey's eyes narrowed slightly. "What do you mean?"

This time Caroline laughed, low and husky. "Ah, Mrs. Clayton . . . or should I call you Stacey?" She looked too self-satisfied. "Didn't it ever occur to you, my dear, that your husband might have found someone to take your place during the past year? After all, as far as he was concerned, you were dead."

Stacey stared at her in disbelief. "You're lying!"

"Am I, now? Strange you should think that. Why else do you think I'm here?"

"I don't know."

"Exactly." Caroline's eyes traveled over Stacey. She had combed her hair and fastened it with a clasp on each side, and in the turquoise dress it took on a deep mahogany glow. With the brilliance of her eyes, and in spite of the sunburn on her nose, she was gorgeous. But Caroline refused to be intimidated by her. She wanted Ben badly enough to lie. "I'm here, Stacey, because Ben didn't have the courage to tell you on his own. Oh, he put on a good show out there. He's hoping he can pick up the pieces and everything will be all right between the two of you again. But you see, I don't want to give him up, my dear. I can't. I love Ben, and I'm sure he loves me. It's just this obsession he's got about coming after you. He thinks he's still in love with you. How foolish some men are. Just the other night, when he was making love to me, he tried to tell me it was the last time, that when we reached you it would have to end between us. Only I don't think it will."

"The other night?" Stacey asked in disbelief.

Caroline looked surprised. "Why, certainly. We've been traveling together for weeks now. You see, we left Portland in June on the stage, shortly after Ben received your telegram. Before we reached Fort Bridger, the stagecoach was attacked by Indians. It was dreadful. Ben was shot, the stage crashed, and we were isolated in the wilderness for almost six weeks. I took care of Ben all that time. Then it was another week making our way to Fort Bridger and on to Fort Hall. Now, surely you can't possibly think I slept alone all that time, can you?"

Stacey couldn't believe her ears, yet the woman seemed so sure of herself. "But Ben knew I was alive!"

"So?"

"And . . . and he still made love to you?"

"My dear, I think you'd better wake up from your dream world," Caroline said lightly. "He may have loved you once, but a year's a long time."

Stacey stared at Caroline long and hard, and her eyes narrowed. She was mad. The nerve of him! Accusing her, when all the time he was sleeping with this . . . this . . .

"Excuse me, Mrs. Jaquette," she said heatedly. "But Ben and I have some talking to do," and without saying another word, she left the wagon hurriedly, climbing out as best she could with the fancy dress on.

Caroline watched Stacey stalk off; then Paula Tanner came around the corner of the wagon, and she quickly left.

Paula watched both women leave and tensed, wondering what had been going on. Ben was so upset he wouldn't even talk to her, and she had to know if Wade had succeeded. She fingered the letter in her pocket and headed toward Wade's wagon.

She found him standing alone, gloating over his victory with Ben.

"Well, you look pleased," she said crisply.

"Score a royal flush for Wade Savagge," he offered candidly.

She stared, startled. "You mean you succeeded? Stacey let you make love to her?"

He remembered the letter Paula had promised and smiled. He had already lied to Ben, so what was the difference? "Didn't I say she would? The lady is signed, sealed, and delivered. Now, where's your end of the bargain?"

Paula eyed him skeptically. "How do I know you're telling the truth?"

"Look, I already told her husband. What more do you want?"

But Paula still wasn't sure. Stacey hadn't acted like a woman who had just betrayed the man she loved. "I want the truth, Wade," she insisted. "I don't believe you. You'd lie to your own mother if you thought you could get away with it."

He smiled. "You drive a hard bargain. All right, so I didn't actually break her down. But the results are the same, aren't they? Her husband thinks I made love to her, and there's no way he can prove I didn't, so the bargain's been kept as far as I'm concerned."

Paula's green eyes darkened. He was right, really. As long as

Ben thought Stacey had made love with Wade willingly . . . she pulled out the letter and handed it to Wade. "It isn't exactly what I bargained for, but I guess it'll do. The name of the man to give the letter to is on the letterhead," she said calmly. "He'll see that you're taken care of when you get to Virginia City."

Wade unfolded the paper and whistled as he saw the name. "A big man indeed," he said enthusiastically. "Thanks."

"Not at all. Reward for services rendered. Thank you, Mr. Savagge," she said, and walked briskly away.

A lot of good that's going to do you, honey, Wade mused softly to himself. Or maybe you didn't take a good long look at the company Mr. Ben Clayton was traveling with. Wade smiled, pleased with himself as he shoved the letter into his pocket. He turned around quickly, but not quickly enough to see Ginger duck back behind the corner of his wagon.

Ginger had heard the whole conversation between Wade and Paula. As she left her hiding place, she clenched her fists angrily. Of all the nerve. Wade had gotten away with an awful lot over the years, but he wasn't going to get away with this one. Not if she could help it. She turned quickly and hurried away.

Stacey found Ed at his wagon talking with Pete and a soldier Stacey had never seen before. "Where's Ben?" she asked Ed angrily after he had introduced her to Sergeant Meade.

"What's the matter with you?" Ed asked, puzzled.

"I'll tell you what's the matter with me," she answered bitterly. "Caroline Jaquette's what's the matter with me! He's accusing me!" she yelled. "When all the time, all across the country, he's been sleeping with that . . . that redhead! Well, we'll just see who's guilty of what. Now, where's Ben?"

Ed nodded toward a grove of trees close to the river. "He went in that direction. Said he had to think things over."

"I'll let him think things over," she said furiously. She set out across the field, oblivious of the growing darkness.

"Now, there's one mad lady," said Morgan Meade.

Ed glanced at him surreptitiously. "Any truth to it?" he asked.

"Hell, no. But I don't think she's in any mood to be convinced of that." He chuckled. "You know, I was wondering what kind of a woman Stacey Clayton was, what kind of a woman it took to hold a man like Ben, and damn if she wasn't worth coming to see. Christ, I'd go to hell and back if I thought I could come up with one just like her."

Ed frowned, wondering if it had been wise to tell Stacey where Ben was without first trying to calm her down.

     *   *   *

Stacey was across the field from the woods when she saw a vague figure moving leisurely among the trees. Ben was walking slowly, his hands in his pockets and his eyes cast down to the uneven ground. It was getting darker by the minute as she entered the woods and called out to him.

He turned at the sound of her voice and waited for her.

"Well, I hope you haven't been waiting too long," she said as she reached him. There was no sign of tears in her eyes anymore. There was only a hard, cold anger that took fire as she stared at him. "There was someone I had to talk with before we finished our conversation," she said quickly.

He nodded. "The same here."

"Oh?"

"I went to see Wade."

"And?"

His eyes bored into hers, their dark orbs accusing. "He said you let him make love to you."

"He lied!"

"Oh, did he? How do I know that?"

"Because I say so," she answered. "He may have kissed me, and he may have done everything he could think of to make me surrender, I'll admit that. I was tired and weak, and half-asleep, and so starved for you I could hardly fight anymore, but, by God, he didn't make love to me. And what he did do, he didn't do with my permission, and that's more than I can say for you!"

"Me? What are you talking about?"

"I'm talking about Caroline Jaquette, that's what I'm talking about!" she yelled. "I know all about your traveling companion."

Ben's face fell. "She told you?"

"That's right, she told me. And you had the nerve to accuse me of not waiting for you!"

He stared at her, confused. "My God, how can you compare it, Stacey? You knew I was alive. You knew I was in Oregon. I thought I'd never see you again. What was I supposed to do, spend the rest of my life making love to a diary?"

"You knew I was alive, Ben," she insisted.

"But I didn't think I'd ever see you again."

"What do you mean, you didn't think you'd ever see me again? You were on your way to meet me! You made love to her all the way out here. She told me so!"

"I made love to her back in Oregon the night before your telegram reached me," he answered truthfully. "And I haven't made love to her since."

"So you say!"

"That's right, so I say!"

They stared at each other, and suddenly the air vibrated between them. They held their breaths as the truth began to dawn on both of them.

"You . . . you mean you didn't make love to her on the way out here?" Stacey asked hesitantly.

"No. I admit she tried," he answered huskily, his voice breaking. "And I admit there were times she reminded me of you and it was hard not to respond. A couple of times I almost did. But no, I didn't make love to her."

They continued to stare at each other, and Ben saw the fire in Stacey's eyes warm to a soft glow.

"And you didn't let Wade make love to you either, did you?" he whispered incredulously.

"No, I didn't, I couldn't, darling. I just couldn't," she said softly. "Don't you see what's happened? Wade lied to you."

"And Caroline lied to you!"

"Oh, Ben, how could I have believed her?"

"And how can you forgive me?"

He reached out and touched her face, his fingers caressing her cheek.

Chills ran through her, and she stared at him, tears rimming her eyes.

"What is it?" he asked.

"I thought you didn't love me," she cried.

"Oh, God!"

"I wanted to die!"

His fingers moved to her neck, and he cupped her head and went down. "I do love you, sweetheart. I never stopped loving you," he whispered softly. "Can you forgive me?" His lips touched hers, sipping at them lovingly, sending exquisite shocks through every nerve in her body.

When he finally drew his mouth away, their lips were trembling and he was breathless. "You still do it to me, don't you?" he whispered huskily. Both hands were in her hair now, and his eyes were devouring her. "Just to look at you, touch you . . . Oh, God, darling, I've missed you so." He drew her head to his lips and gave her a kiss of surrender that tore them both apart.

Stacey shuddered, and he drew his mouth from hers reluctantly. "What is it?" he asked breathlessly.

She sighed. "Oh, Ben, I want you . . . I need you now," she cried.

He inhaled, pleased, and his body shook. "I need you too," he whispered softly.

His hands pulled her close against him, molding her body to his, and as he kissed her again, he began to undress her gently, lovingly. He dropped her clothes aside, then took off his own and threw them beside hers. When they were both standing naked in the dim light of dusk, he gazed at her for a long moment, admiring the sensuous curves he remembered so well. Suddenly she shivered.

He saw the tremor and snatched his shirt from the pile of clothes. "You're cold. Here," he said quickly, wrapping his big woolen army shirt about her.

"I wasn't cold," she whispered, staring into his dark eyes. "I was remembering."

He inhaled. "So was I."

He drew her into the circle of his arms and they sank to the ground. With the shirt beneath her, he eased her onto her back in the soft grass, his own body stretched out against her, protecting her from the cool night air. It was a chilly night, but he didn't even feel it because of the heat that flooded his long, lean body.

He gazed down into her eyes, then reached out, touching the side of her face with his fingers, hardly daring to believe that she was really with him. "How do I tell you how much I love you?" he murmured passionately. "Words are so inadequate."

"Just tell me," she whispered. "With words, with your heart it doesn't matter. Just so I know."

His lips brushed her lightly, like a butterfly's wings, as he kissed her, first on one side of her mouth and then on the other. She trembled again.

"I thought you said you weren't cold?"

"I'm not," she sighed, her eyes warm with desire.

He smiled, kissing her cheeks and eyelids. He covered her face with light feathery kisses and she purred her acceptance. His lips teased and caressed her face and throat, and then he looked down into her radiant eyes as his hand eagerly shoved aside the shirt, freeing her full breasts.

His fingers circled a soft mound of flesh longingly, raising the rosy tip, then he bent lower, his tongue tracing its hardened edge, outlining the velvety soft skin that surrounded it. She moaned softly with delight.

Burying her hands in his hair, she clung to him as waves of love washed over her like the surf on a beach, building to a crescendo that made her heart pound unmercifully.

His hand left her breast and traveled down her body, kneading her bare skin, then his face dropped to the valley between her breasts, and the sweet musky scent of her filled him with a desire so strong he wanted to cry out. Instead, he breathed deeply and raised his head to meet her eyes.

"Let me look at you, darling," he said, his voice breaking. "Let me see in your eyes what I know is in your heart." Slowly, reverently, he moved over her, his eyes locking with hers, then as he lowered himself very carefully, entering her hesitantly, a little at a time, he savored the moment as if it were their last moment on earth. Her eyelids drooped, her lips parted, and she gasped, arching upward to receive him with a hunger that brought tears to her eyes.

He thrust deep, then saw the tears. "You're crying?"

"For joy, my love, for joy," she gasped breathlessly. "I thought I'd never feel your love again. Never have you to hold me or love me." Her eyes were smoldering, desire mixing with the tears. "Oh, don't stop now, Ben. Please, darling, don't ever stop," she cried, and as her words caressed him, filling him with delight, he began to move in and out slowly, methodically, until they both climaxed in a shattering peak of pleasure.

Ben lay above her for some time, still in her, his face buried against her neck, letting the wonder of his release carry him to heights of rapture he thought had been lost to him. His breathing was shallow and his body was still trembling as his lips caressed her ear.

"Stacey! Stacey!" As her name escaped his lips, she felt a flood of heat course through her. It spread inside her like wine, heady and intoxicating, and she wanted to crawl inside him, become a part of him.

He kissed the throbbing pulse beneath her ear, then lifted his head and looked deep into her eyes, still glazed with passion, then once more he began to move, gently, sweetly, and she felt the intimate thrill of his flesh meeting hers. She cherished every moment, every thrust, as each new sensation coursed through her, from her head down her back, and into her hips and swelling loins. His hands played on her body, stroking and touching, while his lips burned against her mouth, drawing the strength from her until once more she clung to him, climaxing with waves of love that ebbed and flowed again and again as if they'd never end.

Feeling her body surrender to him, Ben groaned, plunging deep, and let out a strangled cry that was muffled against her mouth, and as he kissed her, climaxing with all the savage fury of a starving man, his tongue slipped out to mingle with hers, and they both reached an ecstasy that left them spent.

Stacey lay motionless beneath him, her heart barely beating and her body satiated. He rested his head against hers with his lips lightly touching her ear.

"I remembered well," he said breathlessly. She sighed, for she too remembered. Ben had always made her feel like this. He had never left her wanting as Drew had. This was truly love, not just an act to relieve an instinctive urge. This was from the heart, a giving of everything, a holding back of nothing. Slowly she sank her fingers into his hair as she reveled in the feel of his body against hers, and she knew he was still feeling too. As they lay together in the cool grass, Ben pulled his shirt up around them and lay close to her, stroking and petting her. His lips told her with loving words and tender kisses just how much he really cared.

It was pitch dark when Stacey finally spoke in a soft and unsteady voice. "I suppose we should go back. They'll wonder where we are."

He sighed. "Mmmhmm."

"Ben, did you hear?"

He stirred. "I suppose. We have to tell them all sometime, I guess." Reluctantly he slipped from her and their bodies untwined. As he helped her back into her clothes, he kissed her again and again, continuing to love her with a gentle warmth that told her this was only the beginning.

Once dressed, they stood beneath the trees looking at each other, the wonder of love still making their bodies throb. They kissed again until they were both breathless; then he led her slowly through the woods.

They moved into the open and sauntered along, holding hands. Neither of them spoke. There was no need for words. Their bodies had said it all. Finally Ben stopped and turned Stacey to face him.

She gazed up into his face, remembering, and her heart pounded with the memory.

Again his hands moved into her hair, and he smiled. "Forgive a fool?" he asked softly.

She smiled as if in a dream. "For what?"

"For doubting you."

"You're forgiven," she whispered.

He was just about to kiss her again when they were interrupted by Ginger and Sergeant Meade, hailing them from the direction of the camp. It was hard to see, and at first Stacey and Ben didn't recognize the intruders.

"We have company," Ben said reluctantly.

"Tell them to go away."

He laughed warmly and deeply. "I'd love to, my darling. But what would they think of us, especially since we've already been missing for a couple of hours?" He let his hands drop from her hair and turned to meet the approaching couple.

"I'm sorry, Ben," Morgan said. He quickly took stock of the situation and flushed. "We've been looking all over for you two. But I have a feeling maybe we aren't needed here after all."

"I don't care if we are or not," Ginger said from beside him. "I think they should know."

"Know what?" asked Ben. He was holding Stacey's hand and he squeezed it affectionately.

Ginger's face reddened as she looked at the two of them. "I wanted you to know Wade lied," she said hurriedly. "I know he told you that Stacey slept with him, but it's not true."

"How do you know?" Ben asked.

"Because I heard him and Paula Tanner talking. She gave him a letter of introduction to somebody in Virginia City who can help him in exchange for Wade's telling you that Stacey let him make love to her. He even gloated over it."

"Does he know you know?"

"Nope. But Stacey's been a friend to me." Ginger blushed self-consciously. "I haven't had many friends over the years, but she fixed my leg when it was broke . . . and don't go believing all that stuff about her and Ed, either," she admonished Ben. "Ed likes her, yeah, but that's as far as it goes. I know."

Ben smiled. "You and Ed?"

She nodded proudly. "I like him. He's a great guy. And he'd never do anything to hurt you, Mr. Clayton. So don't go believing all you hear, understand!"

Ben's smile broadened. "Thank you. Ginger, isn't it?"

"Uh-huh."

"Thank you, Ginger," he said. "But I knew he lied."

"You did? How?"

"Stacey told me."

"You believed her?"

He frowned, amused. "Shouldn't I have?"

"Well, yes," she said, a little startled. "But the way you . . I thought you were mad."

"I was at first. Until I realized Stacey was telling the truth."

"When did you realize that?" asked the sergeant curiously.

Ben pulled Stacey against him, relishing the feel of her body against his own. "When I learned that Caroline told Stacey I'd been sleeping with her on the way out here, and I knew it wasn't true."

"Believe me," Morgan told Stacey. "As an eyewitness, I'll testify to that. Not that she didn't want him to, mind you. You never saw a lady quite so determined. But believe me, your husband was more determined. You can take my word for it, Mrs. Clayton, the lady lied."

Stacey nodded. "I know, Ben told me."

"Then I guess we came for nothing," said Ginger, disappointed.

"Not at all," Stacey said graciously. "It's good to have it all confirmed."

"Yes, thank you both," said Ben and looked down at Stacey, smiling, then turned back to the sergeant. "By the way, Morgan?" he asked. "What's the best way for us to get back to Portland without having to stay with the wagon train?"

"You really ask for the hard ones, don't you, Ben?" Morgan said, rubbing his chin. "Well, now. It's a good day's ride back to Fort Hall, and today's Thursday. If I'm not mistaken, a stage comes down from the Yellowstone every Saturday, then heads to Boise, where it meets the stages to Salt Lake City and parts west. We can leave for Fort Hall in the morning. If we ride straight through, you should get there in time to get the stage out Saturday morning, with a little time to spare. As you know, Ben, the stages make close to sixty miles a day if the weather's good. With luck you can be in Portland in ten days to two weeks."

"That's better than two more months on a wagon train." Ben glanced down at Stacey. "What do you think?"

She smiled. "I'm with you."

"You'd better be."

"Then it's settled?" Morgan asked.

"That's right."

"What about Caroline, Ben?" Morgan asked thoughtfully.

Stacey felt Ben stiffen. "I forgot about her. Maybe she can stay with the train. Or better yet, why don't you take her back east with you?"

"With me? Hell, I don't want her." The sergeant grinned. "Women are trouble enough, redheads especially. Look what you've had to go through for this one," he said, laughing. "Besides, I don't think she's going to give up that easily."

"Maybe you'd better talk to her, Ben," Stacey said. "The sergeant's probably right. If she'd stoop to lying, there's no telling what she might do when she finds out it didn't work."

"Then I want you with me," he said quickly. "Because I'm tired of trying to convince her all by myself."

Stacey agreed, and they all headed back toward the wagons.

CHAPTER 23

After spending the night in each other's arms beneath Ed's wagon, Stacey and Ben woke early. By the time dawn was creeping into the sky, bringing with it the promise of a warm day, Stacey was sitting astride a horse, wearing her old pants and shirt. She watched as Ben made a last-minute check of everything on his horse, then mounted. He reined up beside her and they joined Sergeant Meade outside the circle of wagons.

Stacey gazed about, watching the wagon train preparing to leave. For the first time since Ben had appeared, she realized that she was no longer a part of it. The hustle and bustle of breaking camp, the anticipation of the day on the trail—she felt none of it anymore, and she was glad.

As she studied the wagons, letting a touch of nostalgia creep into her thoughts, she also let her mind wander back to last evening. At first, Caroline had been furious when she learned her little scheme hadn't worked. Then her fury had turned to hurt and resentment. But Caroline, fortunately, wasn't used to getting her own way in life. She had learned to adapt to disappointment. Although there were tears in her eyes when she faced Stacey and Ben, her quick wit came readily to her rescue.

"So I lied," she said flippantly. "But you can't really blame a lady for trying, now, can you? After all, look at him," she went on, gesturing toward Ben, who was holding Stacey's hand. "I'd have been out of my mind to let something like that get away too easily. Especially after a generous taste of his wares. He did tell you about Oregon, my dear, didn't he?" she asked Stacey.

"Yes, he told me, but that was before he knew I was alive."

"Well, anyway, I guess I have only myself to blame for this whole mess. He warned me before he made love to me that he was still in love with you, and that's when he thought you were dead. I should have heeded the warning and realized that if you were strong enough to hold him from the grave, I'd never have a chance competing with you in the flesh. Ah, well, *c'est la vie!''*

Paula hadn't taken the news as well. Her surface beauty faded quickly as her sharp tongue cursed Stacey for taking Ben from her, even though Ben assured her that he had never been hers in the first place. She ranted, cried, pleaded, attacked, and, in the end, she turned her back on them. She refused even to speak to them the rest of the evening, especially after Ben confessed that they knew all about her little deal with Wade Savagge. As Stacey sat on her horse now, watching everyone bustle around, she wondered what Paula was going to do. One thing was certain: Paula not only took defeat ungraciously, she was also not the pleasantest woman to be around. Stacey glanced off toward the Tanner wagon.

Paula sat on the seat of her wagon, the reins in her hands and angry tears in her eyes. She had had to beg for help to harness the mules because the collars were too heavy for her to lift by herself. Her breakfast had also been miserable, because she had forgotten what she had learned back in Omaha about baking biscuits, and ended up with biscuits that were burned on the outside and soft and doughy on the inside. Even the coffee she had made was too weak.

Now, as she sat stoically, wearing a red silk dress Stacey had laundered for her, she stared down at the reins in her hands, and the enormity of her situation overwhelmed her. The tears in her eyes overflowed and ran down her cheeks. Her hands! Her soft, beautiful hands were going to get all blistered and her nails would get chipped and broken from driving the mules. She didn't even have a pair of gloves to start out with, as Stacey had had. She sniffed. Her lovely delicate hands! She lifted her blond head pathetically and bit her lip to keep back more tears. She was going to have to do everything: the laundry, the cooking, the driving. All the things Stacey had been doing, she was going to have to do all by herself. And on top of it all, she didn't even have anyplace to go anymore.

Stacey frowned as she saw the pitiful look on Paula's face. Would she show up in Oregon? Oh, God, she hoped not. Her thoughts were suddenly interrupted as Caroline peeked out from behind the back of Ed's wagon and called to her. Stacey slowly reined her horse toward her. Suddenly Caroline stepped out into the open, and Stacey's eyes widened.

Last night when she had packed her clothes, Stacey had taken off the fancy dress Wade had given her and left it in Paula's wagon. Sort of a gesture to Ben, to let him know she didn't want any part of the man.

Now Caroline stood before her, her gray pants and old shirt replaced by the turquoise dress. Her hair was pulled back in a fancy upswept hairdo that made her look very lovely.

"How do you like it, Stacey?" Caroline asked glibly. "Paula was throwing it out, and I couldn't see it go to waste." Her hands slid down the satin and she smiled. "You know, I actually feel like a lady again."

"And you look like one too," said a familiar masculine voice.

Stacey turned quickly in the saddle to see Wade Savagge approaching, his eyes on Caroline.

Wade had taken defeat in the same way Caroline had. A little more cynically perhaps, but he had bounced back well. Stacey convinced him there was nothing he could do that would make Ben ever stop loving her. Naturally, he had blamed her for letting him fall in love with her in the first place, and he vowed he'd never be able to look at another woman again. But later, Ben had assured her that men like Wade Savagge would never be without someone to love. Now, as Stacey watched him appraising Caroline's figure, she knew Ben had been right.

Caroline looked up into Wade's gray eyes and suddenly realized something she had noticed yesterday but had tried to ignore. The man was downright sensuous. He had dark curly hair, warm gray eyes, and a graceful way of walking that emphasized the muscles beneath his well-tailored clothes. And his smile was terribly disarming. Not quite as appealing as Ben's dimpled smile, perhaps, but there was a magnetism about him. The same kind of magnetic charm and vitality that had first attracted her to Ben. She smiled as he put his hands on his hips and surveyed her closely. He took Caroline's hand and turned her around to get the full effect.

"Charming," he said as his eyes pored over her appreciatively. He glanced over to where Stacey sat on her horse wearing her old clothes. Caroline reminded him a great deal of Stacey. Of course, she wasn't Stacey, but she was pretty in her own right. Then, there was the red hair and blue eyes . . . "What do you think, Red?" he asked Stacey congenially. "Do you think she could do it?"

Stacey smiled as she saw Caroline flirtatiously eyeing Wade. "Why don't you ask her."

He laughed, his eyes gripping hers briefly before he turned back to Caroline. "Tell me, you wouldn't happen to know how to deal faro, would you, Mrs. Jaquette?'' he asked smoothly. ''Or perhaps you know how to sing?''

Caroline stared into his warm gray eyes, and a shiver went through her, raising gooseflesh on her arms. Was he asking her . . . ? He was! He certainly was! She took a deep breath and her heart started pounding unmercifully. ''Why, Mr. Savagge, do call me Caroline, please,'' she said softly. ''I've never dealt faro, no, but I have played. I imagine it wouldn't be too hard to learn, and I've always loved to sing. Do you have something in mind?''

He smiled wickedly. ''Do I have something in mind? My dear lady,'' he said, taking Caroline's arm and leading her away, ''I'm going to be opening a casino in Virginia City, Nevada, and I seem to have lost my faro dealer.''

He stopped suddenly and turned back to face Stacey as Ben moved his horse up beside her. Wade stared at Stacey briefly and there was a sadness in his eyes. He had wanted her so badly. Ah, well, if he couldn't have her, Caroline just might work. He smiled, an ache in his heart. ''Oh, yes. Good-bye, you two,'' Wade called back jovially. ''And if you're ever down Virginia City way, drop in. I think I've found myself a new faro dealer. Good luck to you both.'' He saluted casually and then cut short Caroline's own good-bye, claiming all her attention again and they headed back toward Wade's wagons, talking amiably.

''Do you think she'll go with him'' Ben asked curiously.

Stacey smiled. ''What do you think?'' She shook her head. ''And poor Pearl. She's going to spend the rest of her life sleeping in Wade's bed when he can't find someone else, and dying inside every time he does. Why do so many women fall in love when they know it will only hurt them?''

''Who knows? But I wouldn't bet a dime either way on who's going to come out on top in that friendship. Putting Wade and Caroline together is like inviting the spider to live with the fly.'' He laughed, relieved that he didn't have to worry about Caroline anymore.

At that moment, Morgan Meade rode up and told them it was time to pull out. They said a friendly good-bye to Ed, after making him promise to stop by if he ever got to Portland, and Ben thanked him rather sheepishly for helping Stacey along the way. Then, as Ed hollered ''Catch up!'' and the wagon train began to roll, they grabbed the ropes on their packhorses, waved good-bye, and headed down the road in the opposite direction, back toward Fort Hall.

*   *   *

It took a little longer to get back to the fort than they had anticipated. Stacey's seat was still smarting from her long ride with the outlaws. Although she had ridden occasionally with Ed and some of the men, she hadn't been prepared to spend so many hours in the saddle, riding hard and being unable to control the way she sat on the horse. So they had to move at a slower pace. And then her horse threw a shoe, which also slowed them down. Consequently, instead of arriving late in the evening, they arrived shortly before dawn on Saturday, which left them only enough time to catch the stage. Stacey wasn't about to ride all the way to Portland wearing her old pants and shirt, so while Ben bought their tickets, Sergeant Meade found a place for her to change, and she put on the navy-blue grosgrain dress she had bought in Cleveland. She perched the little straw bonnet on her head and tied the navy-blue ribbons under her chin, and in less than an hour after arriving at the fort, they said good-bye to Sergeant Meade and boarded the Concord stage for Oregon and home.

Almost two weeks and six hundred miles later, Stacey and Ben stepped off the stage in Portland. He got off first, then helped her down and they both looked at each other for a long, hard minute before turning to face the family they knew would be waiting.

Ben had sent a telegram the day before, asking for someone to meet them, and as the stage pulled in, Frieda, Ethan, Becky, and Charlotte were lined up at the side of the road, nervously waiting.

Stacey stared at them, and a feeling of apprehension swept over her, until her eyes fell on Becky. Becky looked all grown-up in an emerald-green taffeta dress, her coppery hair partly hidden beneath a dark green velvet bonnet with ribbons fluttering from the sides. But the grown-up clothes couldn't hide her impish face, and her nose scrunched up excitedly as she smiled.

Charlotte stood beside her, wearing a dress of deep burgundy velvet trimmed with black velvet and lace. Her hair was caught up in a mass of dark curls with a black velvet bonnet tied beneath her chin. She looked like such a lady as she held her head high and studied Stacey intently. And she looked so much like her father.

Beside her, Ethan was dressed in his Sunday best, his black hat clenched in his hand and Frieda was at his left in her blue poplin dress. Her eyes held a spark of relief as she stared at Stacey and Ben.

"Well, are you all going to just stand there staring?" asked Ben. He took a step toward them, and Becky couldn't wait any longer. She let out a squeal, forgetting she was supposed to act like a lady, and jumped into his arms, knocking her bonnet off, and he kissed her, then she turned to Stacey and stared at her ardently, the joy on her face all too apparent.

"I knew he'd bring you home to us," she said eagerly. "Frieda said not to get our hopes up, but I knew . . . I just knew."

She didn't wait for Stacey to make the first move, but grabbed her, hugging her exuberantly, and tears filled Stacey's eyes as she hugged her back. Finally Stacey released her and held her at arm's length.

"My heavens, you've grown so!" exclaimed Stacey in surprise. "You're almost as tall as I am."

"I'm going to be tall like Daddy," she said happily. "And probably taller than Char."

Charlotte had hurried to her father too, only with a little less spirit. Her feminine graces held her in check, but it was plain to see that she was relieved to have him home. As Ben hugged Charlotte, he shook Ethan's hand, then let go of Charlotte and gave Frieda a squeeze.

Charlotte stepped back while her father hugged Frieda and she glanced at Stacey. Stacey held her breath, waiting for Charlotte to give her the cold shoulder. Ben had cautioned Stacey that Charlotte had had a tantrum before he left. But instead of greeting Stacey coldly, Charlotte smiled rather stiffly. "I'm glad he found you, Stacey," she said solemnly. "He missed you terribly."

Stacey stared at her dumbfounded. This from Charlotte? It wasn't exactly a friendly greeting, but it was civil, and that was amazing. She tried to mask her surprise, but Frieda could see she had expected a totally different welcome from the girl. Frieda whispered a few friendly words of encouragement to Stacey as she gave her a big hug. Then Stacey thanked Charlotte for the greeting and shook hands with Ethan.

Finally they retrieved their bags and walked to the two-seated carriage. Ben let Charlotte and Becky sit up front with Ethan, who was driving, while he and Stacey sat in the back with Frieda. On the way home, he told them about the trip while Stacey stared at the scenery in awe. When they finally pulled in the drive, the sight of the house brought tears to her eyes.

Although painted white and set majestically beneath large trees, it had a rustic look, with a number of stone chimneys easing above the sloping roof. Her eyes lifted to the balcony over the front porch and she stared in wonder.

Ethan stopped the buggy and helped the girls out. Ben's arm was around Stacey, and he looked down at her face apprehensively. "Well, you're home, Mrs. Clayton," he whispered softly in her ear. "Do you like it?"

She inhaled ecstatically. "Is this really, finally, going to be my home, Ben?" she asked. "Or will I be torn from you again?"

"Never, darling. Never again," he cried harshly. "Because I'll never let you out of my sight." He tightened his arm on her shoulder. "Come on, I'll show you around."

Later that evening, the flickering light of the kerosene lamps brought a rosy glow to all the rooms. The excitement of their arrival was beginning to fade and the household was slowly getting back to normal. Stacey loved the house. It was so different from the modern split-level Drew had built for her in Gates Mills. She knew she would miss all the conveniences of that other house, but her new home was rustic and cozy. It had a solid warmth about it, and it also had the one most important ingredient of all in it. Ben was here. It was still thrilling and new for her to be with him again, and more than once during the evening Stacey had found herself staring at him intently, almost afraid that if she took her eyes away he'd disappear.

She stood in their bedroom now, wearing the thin blue nightgown and wrapper she had bought in Cleveland. They were faded and tattletale gray from being washed so many times in creeks along the trail, and she knew she looked anything but attractive. She hoped Ben wouldn't mind, because it was all she had. She stood in front of the dresser and gazed at herself in the mirror. The soft glow from the lamp and flickering flames from the fireplace made her auburn hair catch fire and turned her brilliant blue eyes a deep purple. But shadows danced in the hollows of her cheeks, and she realized for the first time that she had lost weight. It couldn't be too much, however, because her breasts were still high and firm and her hips were slightly padded.

She glanced down at the faded nightgown and noticed a tiny rip in the lace between her breasts. The nightgown and wrapper were thin and it was cool in the bedroom, since it was the middle of September. She shivered and turned toward the fireplace for warmth then sat on the vanity bench, picked up a hairbrush, and stroked her long hair until it shone. It was still damp from her bath and it curled riotously. That's where Ben was now, taking a bath. While she had bathed, he had been in the library talking to Charlotte.

After a few minutes, Stacey primped her hair into place, then set the brush down and stared into the mirror again. The sunburn had started to fade, and her hands! She looked at them, pleased. The nails weren't long, but they weren't chipped and broken either. Becky had brought her a small pair of scissors, and although she still had calluses, her nails were all even. She only wished she had some cologne or perfume. Charlotte had brought her some scented soap to use in her bath. It smelled nice, and would have to do, but it wasn't what Stacey would have preferred.

She frowned, remembering some other small things Charlotte had done for her. It puzzled her. Charlotte hadn't been overly loving or affectionate, and there was still a hint of repression in her attitude, but something had happened to change her. Was that why she had asked to speak to Ben alone in the library? At first Stacey thought Charlotte was afraid Ben might join her in her bath, but now she began to wonder.

She was gazing into the mirror thoughtfully when the door clicked behind her. She turned quickly and saw Ben come in. He shut the door behind him and leaned back against it, sighing.

He was wearing a long red quilted robe, and apparently nothing else. "At last," he cried softly, and came toward her. "Stacey Clayton, if I'd had to spend one more day on that stage without being able to touch you, I'd have screamed."

She looked up into his dark eyes, her own alive with longing. "You mean we're really finally alone?"

He pulled her to her feet and his hands slipped under her wrapper. He kissed her neck, his lips slowly caressing her ear and sending chills down her spine.

"You feel good," he whispered huskily. She moaned softly. He drew his head back and looked deep into her eyes.

"Oh, Ben," she murmured softly. "Am I really here? Is it really you, or am I dreaming?"

He pulled her hard against him and she felt the strength of his muscular frame through the robe. "Do I feel like a dream?" he asked.

"You feel like heaven." She reached up and touched his mustache, her fingers caressing it softly. "And I love the mustache. You look so sexy."

He kissed her fingers. "You don't think it tickles?"

"Who told you that?"

"No one."

"Fiend!"

He laughed playfully, then picked her up and set her gently on the bed. "Do you realize, Mrs. Clayton," he whispered passionately, "that in all the while we've known each other, I've only made love to you in a bed once?"

She stared at him, a warm flush sweeping through her. "Do you remember what it was like?"

He nodded. "Shall we try it again?"

"Let's do."

His eyes traveled down to the thin material of her wrapper that covered her breasts. He could see the dark outlines of her hardened nipples and the firm mounds of warm flesh they rested on. His eyes paused briefly, then continued down her body, which was covered lightly by the faded blue material. Reaching out, he touched her ankle and his hand traveled up her leg. She trembled as his fingers slowly pushed up the material until it reached her waist, then his hand brushed lightly across her stomach and dipped down into the patch of dark red hair beneath it.

"Unfasten my robe, love," he whispered. Stacey pulled the sash, and as the robe fell open, her hand touched his chest. His skin felt warm and sensuous, the hairs curling between her fingers, and her lips parted.

"Love me, Ben," she pleaded breathlessly. "Please, love me." He stretched out beside her and moved his body against hers as his lips covered hers hungrily.

As he moved over her, his robe fell around them, cloaking their bodies in a cocoon, and he felt her flesh against his, hot, inviting. As he kissed her deeply, his tongue parted her lips and felt the moist, warm sweetness of her mouth. His body was burning with a wild, savage elation. Every nerve was tense, and shocks of delight were pulsating through him. He felt her beneath him, soft and warm, and he kissed her breathlessly. Her neck, her lips, his hands caressing her, pulling her hips up to meet him, and as he entered, he drew back his head and searched her eyes, watching the rapture flood them as he plunged deep.

She moaned and called his name, arching to meet him and once more she was transported to a world of wonder where she floated on clouds and her body throbbed with ecstasy.

He moved slowly at first, letting her feel every thrust and magnifying his own pleasure until his loins throbbed. Then, as he quickened his pace to reach deep inside her, he heard her give out a wild cry of abandon, followed by a wave of ecstatic groans that told him she had come. And with her release, his came too. The moment was theirs and theirs alone.

Stacey clung to him, her arms inside his robe. She was in heaven. His eyes locked with hers, and he kissed her full on the mouth as he once more began to move in her, and he didn't draw out again until he knew that there was no more want in her eyes, that she was filled with all the love he could give her.

This was what she needed, what she craved, what Drew could never seem to give her. This was love like no other.

When he knew she was ready, he drew out and held her in his arms, looking into her face with an expression of sheer wonder. "Well, which do you like better, love, the woods or the bed?" he asked contentedly.

"Oh, the bed, definitely," she whispered. "But it has nothing to do with your performance. It's only that here I don't have to contend with the twigs and the ants."

He laughed, and kissed her hard on the mouth. But he grew serious as he brushed a stray hair from her face. "How many times I've wanted to have you here to hold like this," he said. "Every night before bed, I'd write in the diary, then I'd lie here, close my eyes, and pretend I could see you reading it a hundred and ten years from now. I wanted to die because you weren't here beside me. Now I don't have to pretend."

She reached out and touched his face. "The diary . . . I'd almost forgotten about the diary. You still have it, don't you?" she asked.

"That's something else I have to tell you," he said abruptly. "It's about my talk with Charlotte."

"Yes."

"I found out why she decided to let you be a part of the family."

She stared at him curiously. "Why?"

"Do you really want to know?"

"Yes."

"You won't be upset with her?"

"I hope not."

He inhaled. "She read your diary. She said she was so angry after I left that she wanted to find out once and for all what there was about you that made me willing to give up my life for you. So she decided the answer was in the diary."

Stacey's face reddened. "There were private things in that diary, Ben."

"I know. Some I put there myself. She apologized for having read it, but she said if she hadn't, she wouldn't have understood what we feel for each other. And she knows where you're from now too. She said at first it was such a shock she didn't want to believe it, but the more she read, the more she knew it had to be true. She hasn't told the others, not even Ethan. She said she won't unless you want her to. But she's trying to understand."

"That must be why she's been staring at me so strangely," Stacey said.

"I suppose." His eyes looked troubled. "She said she'll never really accept you as a mother, and she still resents the fact that I seem to love you more than I loved Ann, but she's willing to try. I didn't know what to say to her, Stacey. What could I say under the circumstances?"

"That you love her."

"I did."

"Then that should be enough." She raised up and looked down into his face. Her hand touched the scar on his right shoulder. "You went through so much to be with me," she said softly.

"You're worth even more. And look what you did to be with me. I couldn't ask for a better love."

She sighed contentedly and laid her head on his bare chest, letting the curly hairs tickle her cheek. "Ben, there's something I have to do."

His hand curved about her neck. "What?"

She looked into his dark eyes. How often she had tried to tell their color. But they were so dark, she couldn't distinguish the pupils from the irises.

"Where's the diary?" she asked.

"In the top drawer of the desk. Why?"

"May I see it?"

His frown deepened. "If you want."

He started to get up, but she pushed him back. "No, stay here. Climb under the covers and wait for me. What I have to do won't take long, and I have to do it all by myself."

She kissed him, then stood up, straightened her night clothes, and walked to the desk, while he bunched the pillow under his head so he could watch her.

She hesitated before opening the drawer, but she knew she had to. Slowly she took out the ledger and stared at it. The last time she had seen it, it was old and musty, the cover crumbling with age. Now it still looked fairly new. A little worn on the corners from being carried around in Ben's suitcase, but still in good shape.

She picked it up and all the memories she had tried so hard to forget came flooding back to her. She clutched it to her breast for a minute, tears suddenly filling her eyes as she thought of Chris and Renee. It had been her one regret in coming back to Ben, to have to give them up. And Drew. The pain of Drew's betrayal still hurt. Not as much as at first, but it was still there

With her back to Ben, she closed her eyes to make the final
break. The pain was here again, but thank God it was only a
passing memory.

She laid the diary on the desk and slowly turned the pages
until she came to one that was blank. She sat down at the desk
and turned to Ben. "Where's the ink?" she asked.

He stared at her curiously. "In the second drawer on the right.
There's a pen in there with it. What are you going to do?"

She was close to tears. "I have to make one more entry," she
answered hesitantly. She dipped the pen in the ink and began to
write:

September 14, 1866.

She paused briefly, choosing her words carefully, and then
went on.

Dear Drew,
   I don't know exactly where to start, but I know
sometime in the future you will read this, and I hope
you'll understand. By now, you know that I'm never
coming back, and I don't want to. When I disappeared
on April 18, 1976, I went back once more in time. It
has taken me a while, and much has happened, but I'm
with Ben again and I'm very happy. My one regret has
been having to leave Chris and Renee behind. I love
them and miss them terribly.

Her eyes filled with tears, but she went on.

   Tell them I love them and think about them often,
and ask them to forgive me for all the hurt, pain, and
humiliation I've caused them. I didn't mean to hurt
anyone, but I guess you didn't mean to hurt me either.
It's just the way things happen. But that's over now.
Tell Shelley good-bye and that I love her and miss her.
Tell John thanks for being such a dear, but it wouldn't
have worked. He'll understand. And most of all, Drew,
I want to say good-bye to you. I know you tried, we
both did, and I thank you for that, because in spite of
what you think, I did love you. But I guess it wasn't
enough. Leslie proved that. I only hope you'll make her
happy.
   By the time you read this, I will be dead and buried,

and over a hundred years will have gone by. But don't grieve for me, any of you, please, because right now I'm more alive than I have ever been before, and I intend to live a long full life with the man who is dearer to my heart than anyone else has ever been. Forgive me, I have found my love. Now I must say good-bye.

Stacey

She wiped her eyes and lifted the pen reluctantly, hoping she had said everything without being too maudlin. She read it over and then put the diary away. She stood up, then saw her handbag beside the diary. She reached down, picked it up and took out the digital watch, then rummaged around until she found the small beaded pouch with the money in it. She stared at it all for a few minutes, then put it back in the handbag and put the handbag back in the drawer beside the diary. Before closing the drawer she stared down at the diary, wondering how long it would be before Drew found her message. Finally she walked to the dresser, blew out the lamp, and turned toward the bed. It was over, all over, that other life. This was where she belonged, and Ben was waiting, waiting to love her.

The wrapper slipped from her shoulders as she walked across the floor, and she tossed it and her nightgown on the bed. Ben lifted the covers and she slid in beside him. The only light in the room came from the flickering flames in the fireplace.

He pulled her close and tucked the down-filled quilt about her shoulders looking into her eyes with love. "What did you do?" he asked curiously.

"I said good-bye to Drew."

"Is it over?"

"All over," she answered softly, and as she melted into his arms, his lips claiming hers in a love that transcended even time and space, she knew that someday, somewhere in the future, Drew and the girls would read the diary, and she hoped they'd understand.

About the Author

The granddaughter of an old-time vaudevillian, Mrs. Shiplett was born and raised in Ohio. She is married and lives in the city of Mentor-on-the-Lake. She has four daughters and several grandchildren and enjoys living an active outdoor life.

Fabulous Fiction From SIGNET

More Bestsellers From SIGNET

Buy them at your local
bookstore or use coupon
on next page for ordering.

Exciting Fiction from SIGNET